FORTUNE'S FOOL

FORTUNE'S FOOL

RAFAEL SABATINI

COSIMO CLASSICS
NEW YORK

Fortune's Fool

© 2005 Cosimo, Inc.

All rights reserved. No part of this book may be used or reproduced in
any manner whatsoever without prior written permission except in the
case of brief quotations embodied in critical articles or reviews.
For information, address:

Cosimo, P.O. Box 416
Old Chelsea Station
New York, NY 10113-0416

or visit our website at:
www.cosimobooks.com

Fortune's Fool originally published by the Houghton Mifflin Company
in 1922.

Library of Congress Cataloging-in-Publication Data
A catalog record for this book is available from the Library of Congress

Cover design by www.wiselephant.com

ISBN: 1-59605-609-6

CONTENTS

FORTUNE'S FOOL

FORTUNE'S FOOL

CHAPTER I

THE HOSTESS OF THE PAUL'S HEAD

THE times were full of trouble; but Martha Quinn was unperturbed. Hers was a mind that confined itself to the essentials of life: its sustenance and reproduction. Not for her to plague herself with the complexities of existence, with considerations of the Hereafter or disputations upon the various creeds by which its happiness may be ensured — a matter upon which men have always been ready to send one another upon exploring voyages thither — or yet with the political opinions by which a nation is fiercely divided. Not even the preparations for war with Holland, which were agitating men so violently, or the plague-scare based upon reports of several cases in the outskirts of the City, could disturb the serenity of her direct existence. The vices of the Court, which afforded such delectable scandal for the Town, touched her more nearly, as did the circumstance that yellow bird's-eye hoods were now all the rage with ladies of fashion, and the fact that London was lost in worship of the beauty and talent of Sylvia Farquharson, who was appearing with Mr. Betterton at the Duke's House in the part of Katherine in Lord Orrery's "Henry the Fifth."

Even so, to Martha Quinn, who very competently kept the Paul's Head, in Paul's Yard, these things were but the unimportant trifles that garnish the dish of life. It was upon life's main concerns that she concentrated her attention. In all that regarded meat and drink her learning — as became the hostess of so prosperous a house — was probably unrivalled. It was not merely that she understood the mysteries of bringing to a proper succulence a goose, a turkey, or a pheasant; but a chine of beef roasted in her oven was like no chine of beef at any other ordinary; she could perform miracles with marrow-bones; and she could so dissemble the umbles of venison in a pasty as to render it a dish fit for a prince's table. Upon these talents was her solid prosperity erected. She possessed, further — as became the mother of six sturdy children of assorted paternity — a discerning eye for a fine figure of a man. I am prepared to believe that in this matter her judgment was no whit inferior to that which enabled her, as she boasted, to determine at a glance the weight and age of a capon.

It was to this fact — although he was very far from suspecting it — that Colonel Holles owed the good fortune of having lodged in luxury for the past month without ever a reckoning asked or so much as a question on the subject of his means. The circumstance may have exercised him. I do not know. But I know that it should have done so. For his exterior — his fine figure apart — was not of the kind that commands credit.

Mrs. Quinn had assigned to his exclusive use a cosy little parlour behind the common room. On the window-seat of this little parlour he now lounged, whilst Mrs. Quinn herself — and the day was long past in which it had been her need or habit with her own plump hands to perform so menial an office — removed from the table the remains of his very solid breakfast.

The lattice, of round, leaded panes of greenish, wrinkled glass, stood open to the sunlit garden and the glory of cherry trees that were belatedly in blossom. From one of these a thrush was pouring forth a *Magnificat* to the spring. The

thrush, like Mrs. Quinn, concentrated his attention upon
life's essentials, and was glad to live. Not so Colonel Holles.
He was a man caught and held fast in the web of life's complexities. It was to be seen in his listless attitude; in the
upright deep line of care that graved itself between his
brows, in the dreamy wistfulness of his grey eyes, as he
lounged there, shabbily clad, one leg along the leather-
cushioned window-seat, pulling vacantly at his long clay
pipe.

Observing him furtively, with a furtiveness, indeed, that
was almost habitual to her, Mrs. Quinn pursued her task,
moving between table and sideboard, and hesitated to
break in upon his abstraction. She was a woman on the short
side of middle height, well hipped and deep of bosom, but
not excessively. The phrase "plump as a partridge" might
have been invented to describe her. In age she cannot have
been much short of forty, and whilst not without a certain
homely comeliness, in no judgment but her own could she
have been accounted beautiful. Very blue of eye and very
ruddy of cheek, she looked the embodiment of health; and
this rendered her not unpleasing. But the discerning would
have perceived greed in the full mouth with its long upper
lip, and sly cunning — Nature's compensation to low in-
telligences — in her vivid eyes.

It remains, however, that she was endowed with charms
enough of person and of fortune to attract Coleman, the
bookseller from the corner of Paul's Yard, and Appleby, the
mercer from Paternoster Row. She might marry either of
them when she pleased. But she did not please. Her regard
for essentials rendered the knock-knees of Appleby as repul-
sive to her as the bow-legs of Coleman. Moreover, certain
adventitious associations with the great world — to which
her assorted offspring bore witness — had begotten in her a
fastidiousness of taste that was not to be defiled by the

touch of mercers and booksellers. Of late, it is true, the
thought of marriage had been engaging her. She realized
that the age of adventure touched its end for her, and that
the time had come to take a life companion and settle
soberly. Yet not on that account would Martha Quinn
accept the first comer. She was in a position to choose.
Fifteen years of good management, prosperity, and thrift
at the Paul's Head had made her wealthy. When she pleased
she could leave Paul's Yard, acquire a modest demesne in
the country, and become one of the ladies of the land, a
position for which she felt herself eminently qualified. That
which her birth might lack, that in which her birth might
have done poor justice to her nature, a husband could supply.
Often of late had her cunning blue eyes been narrowed in
mental review of this situation. What she required for her
purposes was a gentleman born and bred whom fortune
had reduced in circumstances and who would, therefore, be
modest in the matter of matrimonial ambitions. He must
also be a proper man.

Such a man she had found at last in Colonel Holles. From
the moment when a month ago he strode into her inn followed by an urchin shouldering his valise and packages, and
delivered himself upon his immediate needs, she had recognized him for the husband she sought, and marked him for
her own. At a glance she had appraised him; the tall, soldierly figure, broad to the waist, thence spare to the ground;
the handsome face, shaven like a Puritan's, yet set between
clusters of gold-brown hair thick as a cavalier's periwig, the
long pear-shaped ruby — a relic, no doubt, of more prosperous days — dangling from his right ear; the long sword
upon whose pummel his left hand rested with the easy grace
of long habit; the assured poise, the air of command, the
pleasant yet authoritative voice. All this she observed with
those vivid, narrowing eyes of hers. And she observed, too,

the gentleman's discreditable shabbiness: the frayed condition of his long boots, the drooping, faded feather in his Flemish beaver, the well-rubbed leather jerkin, worn, no doubt, to conceal the threadbare state of the doublet underneath. These very signs which might have prompted another hostess to give our gentleman a guarded welcome urged Mrs. Quinn at once to throw wide her arms to him, metaphorically at present that she might do so literally anon.

At a glance she knew him, then, for the man of her dreams, guided to her door by that Providence to whose beneficence she already owed so much.

He had business in town, he announced — at Court, he added. It might detain him there some little while. He required lodgings perhaps for a week, perhaps for longer. Could she provide them?

She could, indeed, for a week, and at need for longer. Mentally she registered the resolve that it should be for longer; that, if she knew her man and herself at all, it should be for life.

And so at this handsome, down-at-heel gentleman's disposal she had placed not only the best bedroom abovestairs, but also the little parlour hung in grey linsey-woolsey and gilded leather, which overlooked the garden and which normally she reserved for her own private use; and the Paul's Head had awakened to such activity at his coming as might have honoured the advent of a peer of the realm. Hostess and drawer and chambermaid had bestirred themselves to anticipate his every wish. The cook had been flung into the street for overgrilling the luscious marrow-bones that had provided his first breakfast, and the chambermaid's ears had been soundly boxed for omission to pass the warming-pan through the Colonel's bed to ensure of its being aired. And although it was now a full month since his arrival, and in all that time our gentleman had been lavishly entertained upon the best meat and drink the Paul's Head could offer, yet in all that time there had been — I repeat — neither mention of a reckoning, nor question of his means to satisfy it.

At first he had protested against the extravagance of the entertainment. But his protests had been laughed aside with good-humoured scorn. His hostess knew a gentleman when she saw one, he was assured, and knew how a gentleman should be entertained. Unsuspicious of the designs upon him, he never dreamed that the heavy debt he was incurring was one of the coils employed by this cunning huntress in which to bind him.

Her housewifely operations being ended at last — after a prolongation which could be carried to no further lengths — she overcame her hesitation to break in upon his thoughts, which must be gloomy, indeed, if his countenance were a proper index. Nothing could have been more tactful than her method, based upon experience of the Colonel's phenomenal thirst, which, at all times unquenchable, must this morning have been further sharpened by the grilled herrings which had formed a part of his breakfast.

As she addressed him now, she held in her hand the long pewter vessel from which he had taken his morning draught.

"Is there aught ye lack for your comfort, Colonel?"

He stirred, turned his head, to face her, and took the pipestem from between his lips.

"Nothing, I thank you," he answered, with a gravity that had been growing upon him in the last fortnight, to overcloud the earlier good-humour of his bearing.

"What — nothing?" The buxom siren's ruddy face was creased in an alluring smile. Aloft now she held the tankard, tilting her still golden head. "Not another draught of October before you go forth?" she coaxed him.

As he looked at her now, he smiled. And it has been left on record by one who knew him well that his smile was irresistible, a smile that could always win him the man or woman upon whom he bestowed it. It had a trick of breaking suddenly upon a face that in repose was wistful, like sunshine breaking suddenly from a grey sky.

"I vow you spoil me," said he.

She beamed upon him. "Isn't that the duty of a proper hostess?"

She set the tankard on the laden tray and bore it out with her. When she brought it back replenished, and placed it on a coffin-stool beside him, he had changed his attitude, but not his mood of thoughtfulness. He roused himself to thank her.

She hovered near until he had taken a pull of the brown October.

"Do you go forth this morning?"

"Aye," he answered, but wearily, as if reduced to hopelessness. "They told me I should find his grace returned to-day. But they have told me the same so often already, that . . . " He sighed, and broke off, leaving his doubts implied. "I sometimes wonder if they but make game of me."

"Make game of you!" Horror stressed her voice. "When the Duke is your friend!"

"Ah! But that was long ago. And men change . . . amazingly sometimes." Then he cast off the oppression of his pessimism. "But if there's to be war, surely there will be commands in which to employ a practised soldier — especially one who has experience of the enemy, experience gained in the enemy's own service." It was as if he uttered aloud his thoughts.

She frowned at this. Little by little in the past month she had drawn from him some essential part of his story, and although he had been far from full in his confidences, yet she had gleaned enough to persuade herself that a reason existed why he should never reach this duke upon whom he depended for military employment. And in that she had taken comfort; for, as you surmise, it was no part of her intention that he should go forth to the wars again, and so be lost to her.

"I marvel now," said she, "that you will be vexing yourself with such matters."

He looked at her. "A man must live," he explained.

"But that's no reason why he should go to the wars and likely die. Hasn't there been enough o' that in your life already? At your age a man's mind should be on other things."

"At my age?" He laughed a little. "I am but thirty-five."

She betrayed her surprise. "You look more."

"Perhaps I have lived more. I have been very busy."

"Trying to get yourself killed. Don't it occur to you that the time has come to be thinking o' something else?"

He gave her a mildly puzzled glance, frowning a little.

"You mean?"

"That it's time ye thought o' settling, taking a wife and making a home and a family."

The tone she adopted was one of commonplace, good-humoured kindliness. But her breathing had quickened a little, and her face had lost some of its high colour in the excitement of thus abruptly coming to grips with her subject.

He stared a moment blankly, then shrugged and laughed.

"Excellent advice," said he, still laughing on a note of derision that obviously was aimed at himself. "Find me a lady who is well endowed and yet so little fastidious in her tastes that she could make shift with such a husband as I should afford her, and the thing is done."

"Now there I vow you do yourself injustice."

"Faith, it's a trick I've learnt from others."

"You are, when all is said, a very proper man."

"Aye! But proper for what?"

She pursued her theme without pausing to answer his frivolous question. "And there's many a woman of substance who needs a man to care for her and guard her — such a man as yourself, Colonel; one who knows his world and commands a worthy place in it."

"I command that, do I? On my soul you give me news of myself."

"If ye don't command it, it is that ye lack the means, perhaps. But the place is yours by right."

"By what right, good hostess?"

"By the right of your birth and breeding and military rank, which is plain upon you. Sir, why will you be undervaluing yourself? The means that would enable you to take your proper place would be provided by the wife who would be glad to share it with you."

He shook his head, and laughed again.

"Do you know of such a lady?"

She paused before replying, pursing her full lips, pretending to consider, that thus she might dissemble her hesitation.

There was more in that hesitation than either of them could have come near imagining. Indeed, his whole destiny was in it. Upon such light things do human fates depend that had she now taken the plunge, and offered herself as she intended — instead of some ten days later, as eventually happened — although his answer would have varied nothing from what it ultimately was, yet the whole stream of his life would have been diverted into other channels, and his story might never have been worth telling.

Because her courage failed her at this moment, Destiny pursued the forging of that curious chain of circumstance which it is my task to reveal to you link by link.

"I think," she said slowly at last, "that I should not be sorely put to it to find her. I . . . I should not have far to seek."

"It is a flattering conviction. Alas, ma'am, I do not share it." He was sardonic. He made it clear that he refused to take the matter seriously, that with him it never could be more than a peg for jests. He rose, smiling a little crookedly. "Therefore I'll still pin my hopes to his grace of Albemarle. They may be desperate; but, faith, they're none so desperate as hopes of wedlock." He took up his sword as he spoke, passing the baldric over his head and settling it on his shoulder. Then he reached for his hat, Mrs. Quinn regarding him the while in mingling wistfulness and hesitation.

At last she roused herself, and sighed.

"We shall see; we shall see. Maybe we'll talk of it again."

"Not if you love me, delectable matchmaker," he protested, turning to depart.

Solicitude for his immediate comfort conquered all other considerations in her.

"You'll not go forth without another draught to . . . to fortify you."

She had possessed herself again of the empty tankard. He paused and smiled. "I may need fortifying," he confessed, thinking of all the disappointment that had waited upon his every previous attempt to see the Duke. "You think of everything," he praised her. "You are not Mrs. Quinn of the Paul's Head, you are benign Fortune pouring gifts from an inexhaustible cornucopia."

"La, sir!" she laughed, as she bustled out. It would be wrong to say that she did not understand him; for she perfectly understood that he paid her some high and flowery compliment, which was what she most desired of him as an earnest of better things to follow.

CHAPTER II

ALBEMARLE'S ANTECHAMBER

THROUGH the noisy bustle of Paul's Yard the Colonel took his way, his ears deafened by the "What d'ye lack?" of the bawling prentices standing before The Flower of Luce, The White Greyhound, The Green Dragon, The Crown, The Red Bull, and all the other signs that distinguished the shops in that long array, among which the booksellers were predominant. He moved with a certain arrogant, swaggering assurance, despite his shabby finery. His Flemish beaver worn at a damn-me cock, his long sword thrust up behind by the hand that rested upon the pummel, his useless spurs — which a pot-boy at the Paul's Head had scoured to a silvery brightness — providing martial music to his progress. A certain grimness that invested him made the wayfarers careful not to jostle him. In that throng of busy, peaceful citizens he was like a wolf loping across a field of sheep; and those whom he met made haste to give him the wall, though it should entail thrusting themselves or their fellows into the filth of the kennel.

Below Ludgate, in that evil valley watered by the Fleet Ditch, there were hackney-coaches in plenty, and, considering the distance which he must go and the desirability of coming to his destination cleanly shod, Colonel Holles was momentarily tempted. He resisted, however; and this was an achievement in one who had never sufficiently studied that most essential of the arts of living. He bethought him — and sighed wearily over the reflection — of the alarming lightness of his purse and the alarming heaviness of his score at the Paul's Head, where he had so culpably lacked the strength of mind to deny himself any of those luxuries with

which in the past month he had been lavished, and for
which, should Albemarle fail him in the end, he knew not
how to pay. This reflection contained an exaggeration of
his penury. There was that ruby in his ear, a jewel that
being converted into gold should keep a man in ease for the
best part of a twelvemonth. For fifteen years and through
many a stress of fortune it had hung and glowed there amid
his clustering gold-brown hair. Often had hunger itself
urged him to sell the thing that he might fill his belly. Yet
ever had reluctance conquered him. He attached to that
bright gem a sentimental value that had become a superstition. There had grown up in his mind the absolute
conviction that this jewel, the gift of an unknown whose life
he had arrested on the black threshold of eternity, was a
talisman and something more — that, as it had played a
part in the fortunes of another, so should it yet play a part
in the fortunes of himself and of that other jointly. There
abode with him the unconquerable feeling that this ruby
was a bond between himself and that unknown, a lodestone
that should draw each to the other ultimately across a whole
world of obstacles and that the meeting should be mutually
fateful.

There were times when, reviewing the thing more soberly,
he laughed at his crazy belief. Yet, oddly enough, those were
never the times in which dire necessity drove him to contemplate its sale. So surely as he came to consider that, so
surely did the old superstition, begotten of and steadily
nourished by his fancy, seize upon him to bid him hold
his hand and suffer all but death before thus purchasing
redemption.

Therefore was it that, as he took his way now up Fleet
Hill, he left that jewel out of his calculations in his assess-
ment of his utterly inadequate means.

Westward through the mire of the Strand he moved, with

his swinging soldierly stride, and so, by Charing Cross, at last into Whitehall itself. Down this he passed towards the chequered embattled Cockpit Gate that linked one side of the palace with the other.

It was close upon noon, and that curial thoroughfare was more than ordinarily thronged, the war with Holland — now an accomplished fact — being responsible for the anxious, feverish bustle hereabouts. Adown its middle moved a succession of coaches to join the cluster gathered about the Palace Gate and almost blocking the street from one row of bourne posts to the other.

Opposite the Horse Guards the Colonel came to a momentary halt on the skirts of a knot of idlers, standing at gaze to observe the workmen on the palace roof who were engaged in erecting there a weather-vane. A gentleman whom he questioned informed him that this was for the convenience of the Lord High Admiral, the Duke of York, so that his grace might observe from his windows how the wind served the plaguey Dutch fleet which was expected now to leave the Texel at any hour. The Lord Admiral, it was clear, desired to waste no unnecessary time upon the quarter-deck.

Colonel Holles moved on, glancing across at the windows of the banqueting-house, whence, as a lad of twenty, a cornet of horse, some sixteen years ago, he had seen the late King step forth into the sunlight of a crisp January morning to suffer the loss of his head. And perhaps he remembered that his own father, long since dead — and so beyond the reach of any Stuart vengeance — had been one of the signatories of the warrant under which that deed was done.

He passed on, from the sunlight into the shadow of Holbein's noble gateway, and then, emerging beyond, he turned to his right, past the Duke of Monmouth's lodging into the courtyard of the Cockpit, where the Duke of Albemarle had his residence. Here his lingering doubt on the score of whether his grace were yet returned to Town was set at rest by the bustle in which he found himself. But there remained another doubt; which was whether his grace, being now returned, would condescend to receive him. Six times in the course of the past four weeks had he vainly sought admission. On three of those occasions he had been shortly answered that his grace was out of Town; on one of them — the last — more circumstantially that his grace was at Portsmouth about the business of the fleet. Twice it was admitted — and he had abundant evidences, as now — that the Duke was at home and receiving; but the Colonel's shabbiness had aroused the mistrust of the ushers, and they had barred his way to ask him superciliously was he commanded by the Duke. Upon his confession that he was not, they informed him that the Duke was over-busy to receive any but those whom he had commanded, and they bade him come again some other day. He had not imagined that George Monk would be so difficult of access, remembering his homely republican disregard of forms in other days. But being twice repulsed from his threshold in this fashion, he had taken the precaution of writing before presenting himself now, begging his grace to give orders that he should be admitted, unless he no longer held a place in his grace's memory.

The present visit, therefore, was fateful. A refusal now he must regard as final, in which case he would be left to curse the impulse that had brought him back to England, where it was very likely he would starve.

A doorkeeper with a halbert barred his progress on the threshold. "Your business, sir?"

"Is with His Grace of Albemarle." The Colonel's tone was sharp and confident. Thanks to this the next question was less challengingly delivered.

"You are commanded, sir?"

"I have reason to believe I am awaited. His grace is apprised of my coming."

The doorkeeper looked him over again, and then made way.

He was past the outer guard, and his hopes rose. But at the end of a long gallery a wooden-faced usher confronted him, and the questions recommenced. When Holles announced that he had written to beg an audience —

"Your name, sir?" the usher asked.

"Randal Holles." He spoke it softly with a certain inward dread, suddenly aware that such a name could be no password in Whitehall, for it had been his father's name before him — the name of a regicide, and something more.

There was an abundance of foolish, sensational, and mythical stories which the popular imagination had woven about the execution of King Charles I. The execution of a king was a portent, and there never yet was a portent that did not gather other portents to be its satellites. Of these was the groundless story that the official headsman was missing on the day of the execution because he dared not strike off the head of God's anointed, and that the headsman's mask had covered the face of one who at the last moment had offered himself to act as his deputy. The identity of this deputy had been fastened upon many more or less well-known men, but most persistently upon Randal Holles, for no better reason than because his stern and outspoken republicanism had been loosely interpreted by the populace as personal rancour towards King Charles. Therefore, and upon no better ground than that of this idle story, the name of Randal Holles bore, in those days of monarchy restored, the brand of a certain infamous notoriety.

It produced, however, no fearful effect upon the usher. Calmly, mechanically repeating it, the fellow consulted a

sheet of paper. Then, at last, his manner changed. It became invested by a certain obsequiousness. Clearly he had
found the name upon his list. He opened the studded door
of which he was the guardian.

"If you will be pleased to enter, sir . . ." he murmured.

Colonel Holles swaggered in, the usher following.

"If you will be pleased to wait, sir . . ." The usher left
him, and crossed the room, presumably to communicate his
name to yet another usher, a clerkly fellow with a wand, who
kept another farther docr.

The Colonel disposed himself to wait, sufficiently uplifted
to practise great lengths of patience. He found himself in a
lofty, sparsely furnished antechamber, one of a dozen or
more clients, all of them men of consequence if their dress
and carriage were to be taken at surface value.

Some turned to look askance at this down-at-heel in-
truder; but not for long. There was that in the grey eyes of
Colonel Holles when returning such looks as these which
could put down the haughtiest stare. He knew his world and
its inhabitants too well to be moved by them either to respect or fear. Those were the only two emotions none had
the power to arouse in him.

Having met their insolence by looking at them as they
might look at pot-boys, he strode across to an empty bench
that was ranged against the carved wainscoting, and sat himself down with a clatter.

The noise he made drew the attention of two gentlemen
who stood near the bench in conversation. One of these,
whose back was towards Holles, glanced round upon him.
He was tall, and elderly, with a genial, ruddy countenance.
The other, a man of about Holles's own age, was short and
sturdily built with a swarthy face set in a heavy black periwig, dressed with a certain foppish care, and of a manner
that blended amiability with a degree of self sufficiency. He

flashed upon Holles a pair of bright blue eyes that were, however, without hostility or disdain, and, although unknown to the Colonel, he slightly inclined his head to him in formal, dignified salutation, almost as if asking leave to resume his voluble conversation within this newcomer's hearing.

Scraps of that conversation floated presently to the Colonel's ears.

"... and I tell you, Sir George, that his grace is mightily off the hooks at all this delay. That is why he hurried away to Portsmouth, that by his own presence he might order things ..." The pleasant voice grew inaudible to rise again presently. "The need is all for officers, men trained in war ..."

The Colonel pricked up his ears at that. But the voice had dropped again, and he could not listen without making it obvious that he did so, until the speaker's tones soared once more.

"These ardent young gentlemen are well enough, and do themselves great credit by their eagerness, but in war ..."

Discreetly, to the Colonel's vexation, the gentleman again lowered his voice. He was inaudibly answered by his companion, and it was some time before Holles heard another word of what passed between them. By then the conversation had veered a point.

"... and there the talk was all of the Dutch ... that the fleet is out." The sturdy, swarthy gentleman was speaking. "That and these rumours of the plague growing upon us in the Town — from which may God preserve us! — are now almost the only topics."

"Almost. But not quite," the elder man broke in, laughing. "There's something else I'd not have expected you to forget; this Farquharson girl at the Duke's House."

"Sir George, I confess the need for your correction. I should not have forgotten. That she shares the public tongue with such topics as the war and the plague best shows the deep impression she has made."

"Deservedly?" Sir George asked the question as of one who was an authority in such matters.

"Oh, most deservedly, be assured. I was at the Duke's House two days since, and saw her play Katherine. And mightily pleased I was. I cannot call to mind having seen her equal in the part, or indeed upon the stage at all. And so thinks the Town. For though I came there by two o'clock, yet there was no room in the pit, and I was forced to pay four shillings to go into one of the upper boxes. The whole house was mightily pleased with her, too, and in particular His Grace of Buckingham. He spoke his praises from his box so that all might hear him, and vowed he would not rest until he had writ a play for her, himself."

"If to write a play for her be the only earnest his grace will afford her of his admiration, then is Miss Farquharson fortunate."

"Or else unfortunate," said the sturdy gentleman with a roguish look. "'Tis all a question of how the lady views these matters. But let us hope she is virtuous."

"I never knew you unfriendly to his grace before," replied Sir George, whereupon both laughed. And then the other, sinking his voice once more to an inaudible pitch, added matter at which Sir George's laughter grew until it shook him.

They were still laughing, when the door of Albemarle's room opened to give exit to a slight gentleman with flushed cheeks. Folding a parchment as he went, the gentleman crossed the antechamber, stepping quickly and bestowing nods in his passage, and was gone. As he vanished at one door, the usher with the wand made his appearance at the other.

"His grace will be pleased to receive Mr. Pepys."

The swarthy, sturdy gentleman cast off the remains of his laughter, and put on a countenance of gravity.

"I come," he said. "Sir George, you'll bear me company." His tone blended invitation and assertion. His tall companion bowed, and together they went off, and passed into the Duke's room.

Colonel Holles leaned back against the wainscoting, marvelling that with war upon them — to say nothing of the menace of the plague — the Town should be concerned with the affairs of a playhouse wanton; and that here, in the very temple of Bellona, Mr. Pepys of the Navy Office should submerge in such bawdy matters the grave question of the lack of officers and the general unpreparedness to combat either the Dutch or the pestilence.

He was still pondering that curious manifestation of the phenomenon of the human mind, and the odd methods of government which the restored Stuarts had brought back to England, when Mr. Pepys and his companion came forth again, and he heard the voice of the usher calling his own name.

"Mr. Holles!"

Partly because of his abstraction, partly because of the omission of his military title, it was not until the call had been repeated that the Colonel realized that it was addressed to himself and started up.

Those who had stared askance at him on his first coming, stared again now in resentment to see themselves passed over for this out-at-elbow ruffler. There were some sneering laughs and nudges, and one or two angry exclamations. But Holles paid no heed. Fortune at last had opened a door to him. Of this the hope that he had nourished was swollen to a certainty by one of the things he had overheard from the voluble Mr. Pepys. Officers were needed; men of experience in the trade of arms were scarce. Men of his own experience

were rare, and Albemarle, who had the dispensing of these
gifts, was well acquainted with his worth. That was the
reason why he was being given precedence of all these fine
gentlemen left in the antechamber to cool their heels a while
longer.

Eagerly he went forward.

CHAPTER III
HIS GRACE OF ALBEMARLE

At a vast writing-table placed in the middle of a lofty, sunny room, whose windows overlooked St. James's Park, sat George Monk, K.G., Baron Monk of Potheridge, Beauchamp, and Tees, Earl of Torrington and Duke of Albemarle, Master of the Horse, Commander-in-Chief, a member of His Majesty's Privy Council, and a Gentleman of the Bedchamber.

It was a great deal for a man to be, and yet George Monk — called a trimmer by his enemies and "honest George" by the majority of Englishmen — might conceivably have been more. Had he so willed it, he might have been King of England, whereby it is impossible that he could have served his country worse than by the restoration of the Stuart dynasty, which he preferred to effect.

He was a man of middle height, powerfully built, but inclining now, in his fifty-seventh year, to portliness. He was of a dark complexion, not unhandsome, the strength of his mouth tempered by the gentleness of his short-sighted eyes. His great head, covered by a heavy black periwig, reared itself upon too short a neck from his massive shoulders.

As Holles entered, he looked up, threw down his pen, and rose, but slowly, as if weighted by hesitation or surprise. Surprise was certainly the expression on his face as he stood there observing the other's swift, eager advance. No word was uttered until no more than the table stood between them, and then it was to the usher that Albemarle addressed himself, shortly, in dismissal.

He followed the man's withdrawal with his eyes, nor

shifted them again to his visitor until the door had closed. Then abruptly concern came to blend with the surprise still abiding in his face, and he held out a hand to the Colonel whom this reception had a little bewildered. Holles bethought him that circumspection had ever been George Monk's dominant characteristic.

"God save us, Randal! Is it really you?"

"Have ten years wrought such changes that you need to ask?"

"Ten years!" said the Duke slowly, a man bemused. "Ten years!" he said again, and his gentle almost sorrowing eyes scanned his visitor from foot to crown. His grip of the Colonel's hand tightened a moment. Then abruptly, as if at a loss, or perhaps to dissemble the extent to which he was affected by this meeting, "But sit, man, sit," he urged, waving him to the armchair set at the table so as to face the Duke's own.

Holles sat down, hitching his sword-hilt forward, and placing his hat upon the floor. The Duke resumed his seat with the same slowness with which he had lately risen from it, his eyes the while upon his visitor.

"How like your father you are grown!" he said at last.

"That will be something gained, where all else is but a tale of loss."

"Aye! You bear it writ plain upon you," the Duke sadly agreed, and again there broke from him that plaintive, "God save us!"

Randal Holles the elder had been Monk's dearest friend. Both natives of Potheridge in Devon, they had grown to manhood together. And though political opinions then divided them — for Monk was a King's man in those far-off days, whilst the older Holles had gone to Parliament a republican — yet their friendship had remained undiminished. When Monk at last in '46 accepted a command from Cromwell in the Irish service, it was the influence of Holles which had procured both the offer and its acceptance. Later, when Holles the younger decided for the trade of arms, it was under the ægis of Monk that he had taken service, and it was due as much to Monk's friendship as to his own abilities that he had found himself a Captain after Dunbar and a Colonel after Worcester. Had he but chosen to continue under the guidance of his father's friend, he might to-day have found himself in very different case.

The thought was so uppermost now in the Duke's mind that he could not repress its utterance.

Holles sighed. "Do I not know it? But . . ." He broke off. "The answer makes a weary story and a long one. By your leave, let us neglect it. Your grace has had my letter. That is plain, since I am here. Therefore you are acquainted with my situation."

"It grieved me, Randal, more deeply, I think, than anything I can remember. But why did you not write sooner? Why did you come vainly knocking at my door to be turned away by lackeys?"

"I had not realized how inaccessible you are grown."

The Duke's glance sharpened. "Do you say that bitterly?"

Holles almost bounded from his seat. "Nay — on my soul! I vow I am incapable of that, however low I may have come. What you have, you have earned. I rejoice in your greatness as must every man who loves you." With mock cynicism as if to cover up any excessive emotion he might have used, he added: "I must, since it is now my only hope. Shorn of it I might as well cast myself from London Bridge."

The Duke considered him in silence for a moment.

"We must talk," he said presently. "There is much to say." And, in his abrupt fashion, he added the question: "You'll stay to dine?"

"That is an invitation I'd not refuse even from an enemy."

His grace tinkled a little silver bell. The usher appeared.

"Who waits in the anteroom?"

Came from the usher a string of names and titles, all of them distinguished, some imposing.

"Say to them with my regrets that I can receive none before I dine. Bid those whose business presses to seek me again this afternoon."

As the usher removed himself, Holles lay back in his chair and laughed. The Duke frowned inquiry, almost anxiously.

"I am thinking of how they stared upon me, and how they'll stare next time we meet. Forgive me that I laugh at trifles. It is almost the only luxury I am still able to afford."

Albemarle nodded gloomily. If he possessed a sense of humour, he very rarely betrayed the fact, which is possibly why Mr. Pepys, who loved a laugh, has written him down a heavy man.

"Tell me now," he invited, "what is the reason of your coming home?"

"The war. Could I continue in Dutch service, even if the Dutch had made it possible, which they did not? For the last three months it has been impossible for an Englishman to show his face in the streets of The Hague without being subjected to insult. If he were so rash as to resent and punish it, he placed himself at the mercy of the authorities, which were never reluctant to make an example of him. That is one reason. The other is that England is in danger, that she needs the sword of her every son, and in such a pass should be ready to afford me employment. You need officers, I learn — experienced officers . . ."

"That's true enough, God knows!" Albemarle interrupted him, on a note of bitterness. "My anteroom is thronged

with young men of birth who come to me commended by the
Duke of This and the Earl of That, and sometimes by His
Majesty himself, for whom I am desired to provide com-
missions that will enable these graceful bawcocks to command their betters . . ." He broke off, perceiving, perhaps,
that his feelings were sweeping him beyond the bounds of
his usual circumspection. "But, as you say," he ended presently, "of experienced officers there is a sorry lack. Yet that
is not a circumstance upon which you are warranted to
build, my friend."

Holles stared blankly. "How . . . ?" he was beginning,
when Albemarle resumed, at once explaining his own words
and answering the unspoken question.

"If you think that even in this hour of need there is no
employment for such men as you in England's service," he
said gravely, in his slow, deep voice, "you can have no
knowledge of what has been happening here whilst you have
been abroad. In these past ten years, Randal, I have often
thought you might be dead. And I ask myself, all things
being as they are, whether as your friend I have cause, real
cause, to rejoice at seeing you alive. For life to be worth living must be lived worthily, by which I mean it must signify
the performance of the best that is in a man. And how shall
you perform your best here in this England?"

"How?" Holles was aghast. "Afford me but the occasion,
and I will show you. I have it in me still. I swear it. Test
me, and you shall not be disappointed. I'll do you no dis-
credit." He had risen in his excitement. He had even paled
a little, and he stood now before the Duke, tense, challeng-
ing, a faint quiver in the sensitive nostrils of his fine nose.

Albemarle's phlegm was undisturbed by the vehemence.
With a sallow fleshly hand, he waved the Colonel back to
his chair.

"I nothing doubt it. I ask no questions of how you have

spent the years. I can see for myself that they have been ill-spent, even without the hints of your letter. That does not weigh with me. I know your nature, and it is a nature I would trust. I know your talents, partly from the early promise that you showed, partly from the opinion held of you at one time in Holland. That surprises you, eh? Oh, but I keep myself informed of what is happening in the world. It was Opdam, I think, who reported you *'vir magna belli peritia.'*" He paused, and sighed. "God knows I need such men as you, need them urgently; and I would use you thankfully. But . . ."

"But what, sir? In God's name!"

The heavy, pursed lips parted again, the raised black eye-brows resumed their level. "I cannot do so without expos-ing you to the very worst of dangers."

"Dangers?" Holles laughed.

"I see that you do not understand. You do not realize that you bear a name inscribed on a certain roll of vengeance."

"You mean my father's?" The Colonel was incredulous.

"Your father's — aye. It is misfortunate he should have named you after him. But there it is," the deliberate, pon-derous voice continued. "The name of Randal Holles is on the warrant for the execution of the late King. It would have provided a warrant for your father's own death had he lived long enough. Yourself you have borne arms for the Parliament against our present sovereign. In England it is only by living in the completest obscurity that you'll be al-lowed to live at all. And you ask me to give you a command, to expose you prominently to the public gaze — to the royal eye and the royal memory, which in these matters is unfad-ing."

"But the act of indemnity?" cried Holles, aghast, seeing his high hopes crumbling into ashes.

"Pshaw!" Albemarle's lip curled a little. "Where have you lived at all that you do not know what has befallen those whom it covered?" He smiled grimly, shaking his great black head. "Never compel from a man a promise he is loath to give. Such promises are never kept, however fast you may bind them in legal bonds. I wrung the promise of that bill from His Majesty whilst he was still a throneless wanderer. Whilst he was at Breda I concerted with him and with Clarendon that there should be four exceptions only from that bill. Yet when, after His Majesty's restoration, it was prepared, it left to Parliament such exceptions as Parliament should deem proper. I saw the intention. I pleaded; I argued; I urged the royal promise. Finally it was agreed that the exceptions should be increased to seven. Reluctantly I yielded, having no longer the power effectively to oppose a king *de facto*. Yet when the bill came before the Commons — subservient to the royal promptings — they named twenty exceptions, and the Lords went further by increasing the exceptions to include all who had been concerned in the late king's trial and sundry others who had not. And that was a bill of indemnity! It was followed by the King's proclamation demanding the surrender within fourteen days of all those who had been concerned in his father's death. The matter was represented as a mere formality. Most were wise enough to mistrust it, and leave the country. But a score obeyed, conceiving that they would escape with some light punishment."

He paused a moment, sinking back into his chair. A little smile twisted the lips of this man who had no sense of humour.

"It was announced that those who had not surrendered were excluded from the Bill of Indemnity, whilst, as for those who having surrendered were to be supposed included in it, a loyal jury found a true bill against them. They were

tried, convicted, and sentenced to death. Major-General
Harrison was the first of them to suffer. He was disem-
bowelled over yonder at Charing Cross. Others followed,
until the people, nauseated by the spectacle provided daily,
began to murmur. Then a halt was called. There was a
pause, at the end of which the executioners began again.
Nor were those sentenced in that year the only ones. Others
were indicted subsequently. Lambert and Vane were not
brought to trial until '62. Nor were they the last. And it
may be that we have not reached the end even yet."

Again he paused, and again his tone changed, shedding its
faint note of bitterness.

"I do not say these things — which I say for your ears
alone here in private — to censure, or even criticize, the
actions of His Majesty. It is not for a subject to question
too narrowly the doings of his King, particularly when that
King is a son concerned to avenge what he considers, rightly
or wrongly, the murder of his father. I tell you all this solely
that you may understand how, despite my ardent wish to
help you, I dare not for your own sake help you in the way
you desire, lest, by bringing you, directly or indirectly, under
His Majesty's notice, I should expose you to that vengeance
which is not allowed to slumber. Your name is Randal
Holles, and . . ."

"I could change my name," the Colonel cried, on a sudden
inspiration, and waited breathlessly, whilst Albemarle considered.

"There might still be some who knew you in the old
days, who would be but too ready to expose the deception."

"I'll take the risk of that." Holles laughed in his eagerness, in his reaction from the hopelessness that had been
settling upon him during Albemarle's lengthy exposition.
"I've lived on risks."

The Duke eyed him gravely. "And I?" he asked.

"You?"

"I should be a party to that deception . . ."

"So much need not transpire. You can trust me not to allow it."

"But I should be a party none the less." Albemarle was graver than ever, his accents more deliberate.

Slowly the lines of Holles's face returned to their habitual grim wistfulness.

"You see?" said the Duke sadly.

But Holles did not wish to see. He shifted restlessly in his chair, swinging at last to lean across the table towards the Duke.

"But surely . . . at such a time . . . in the hour of England's need . . . with war impending, and experienced officers to seek . . . surely, there would be some justification for . . ."

Again Albemarle shook his head, his face grave and sad.

"There can never be justification for deceit — for falsehood."

For a long moment they faced each other thus, Holles striving the while to keep the despair from his face. Then slowly the Colonel sank back into his chair. A moment he brooded, his eyes upon the polished floor, then, with a little sigh, a little shrug, a little upward throw of the hands, he reached for the hat that lay on the floor beside him.

"In that case . . ." He paused to swallow something that threatened to mar the steadiness of his voice " . . . it but remains for me to take my leave . . ."

"No, no." The Duke leaned across and set a restraining hand upon his visitor's arm. "We part not thus, Randal."

Holles looked at him, still inwardly struggling to keep his self-control. He smiled a little, that sad irresistible smile of his. "You, sir, are a man overweighted with affairs; the burden of a state at war is on your shoulders, I . . ."

"None the less you shall stay to dine."

"To dine?" said Holles, wondering where and when he should dine next, for a disclosure of the state of his affairs must follow upon this failure to improve them, and the luxury of the Paul's Head could be his no longer.

"To dine, as you were bidden, and to renew acquaintance with her grace." Albemarle pushed back his chair, and rose. "She will be glad to see you, I know. Come, then. The dinner hour is overpast already."

Slowly, still hesitating, Holles rose. His main desire was to be out of this, away from Whitehall, alone with his misery. Yet in the end he yielded, nor had occasion thereafter to regret it. Indeed, at the outset her grace's welcome of him warmed him.

The massive, gaudy, untidy woman stared at him as he was led by Albemarle into her presence. Then, slapping her thighs to mark her amazement, up she bounced, and came rolling towards him.

"As God's my life, it's Randal Holles!" she exclaimed. And hoisting herself on tiptoe by a grip of his shoulders she resoundingly kissed his cheek before he guessed her purpose. "It's lucky for George he's brought you to excuse his lateness," she added grimly. "Dinner's been standing this ten minutes, and cooling do spoil good meat. Come on. You shall tell me at table what good fortune brings you."

She linked an arm through one of his, and led him away to their frugal board, which Mr. Pepys — who loved the good things of this world — has denounced as laden with dirty dishes and bad meat. It was certainly not ducal, either in appurtenances or service. But then neither was its hostess, nor could any human power have made her so. To the end she was Nan Clarges, the farrier's daughter and the farrier's widow, the sempstress who had been Monk's mistress when he was a prisoner in the Tower some twenty years ago, and whom — in an evil hour, as was generally believed — he had subsequently married, to legitimize their children. She counted few friends in the great world in which her husband had his being, whilst those she may have counted in her former station had long since passed beyond her ken. Therefore did she treasure the more dearly the few — the very few — whom she had honoured with that name. And of these was Randal Holles. Because of his deep regard for Monk, and because of the easy good-nature that was his own, he had in the early days of Monk's marriage shown a proper regard for Monk's wife, treating with the deference due to her married station an unfortunate woman who was smarting under the undisguised contempt of the majority of her husband's friends and associates. She had cherished that deference and courtesy of Holles's as only a woman in her situation could, and the memory of it was ineffaceably impressed upon her mind.

Clarendon, who detested her as did so many, has damned her in a phrase: "*Nihil muliebris præter corpus gerens.*" Clarendon did not credit her with a heart, under her gross, untidy female form, a woman's heart as quick to respond to hate as to affection. Holles could have enlightened him. But, then, they never knew each other.

The trivial, unconsidered good that we may do on our way through life is often a seed from which we may reap richly anon in the hour of our own need.

This Holles was now discovering. She plied him with questions all through her noisy feeding, until she had drawn from him, not only the condition of his fortunes, but the reason of his return to England, the hopes he had nourished, and her own husband's wrecking of those hopes. It put her in a rage.

"God's life!" she roared at her ducal lord and master. "You would ha' turned him like a beggar from the door? Him — Randal!"

His grace, the dauntless, honest George Monk, who all
his life had trodden so firmly the path of rectitude, who
feared no man, not even excepting the King whom he had
made, lowered his proud, grave eyes before this termagant's
angry glance. He was a great soldier, as you know. Single-
handed once he had faced a mutinous regiment in Whitehall,
and quelled its insubordination by the fearless dominance of
his personality. But he went in a dread of his boisterous
vulgar duchess that was possibly greater than the dread in
which any man had ever gone of him.

"You see, my love, according to my lights . . ." he was beginning uneasily.

"Your lights quotha!" she shrilled in scorn. "Mighty
dim lights they be, George, if you can't see to help a friend
by them."

"I might help him to the gallows," he expostulated.
"Have patience now, and let me explain."

"I'll need patience. God knows I shall! Well, man?"

He smiled, gently, as if to show that he used gentleness
from disinclination to assert his mastery. As best he could,
seeing that he was subjected the while to a running fire of
scornful interruptions, he made clear the situation as already
he had made it clear to Holles.

"Lord, George!" she said, when he had finished, and her
great red face was blank. "You are growing old. You are
not the man you was. You, a kingmaker! La!" She withered him with her scorn. "Where are the wits that helped
King Charles Stuart back to his own? You wasn't put off by
the first obstacle in they days. What would ye be without
me, I ask myself. It needs me to help ye see how ye can help
a friend without bringing him under notice of them as might
do him a hurt."

"If you can do that, my dear . . ."

"If I can? I'd ha' my brains fried for supper if I couldn't.

I would so — damme! For 'tis all they'd be good for. Is there no commands in your bestowing but commands here at home?"

His eyebrows flickered up, as if something in his mind responded to her suggestion.

"Are there no colonies to this realm of England? What of the Indies — East and West? There's a mort o' them Indies, I know, whither officers are forever being dispatched. Who'd trouble about Randal's name or story in one o' they?"

"Egad! 'Tis an idea!" The Duke looked at Holles, his glance brightening. "What should you say to it, Randal?"

"Is there a post for me out there?" quoth the Colonel eagerly.

"At this very moment, no. But vacancies occur. Men die in those outlandish parts, or weary of the life, or find the climate intolerable and return. There are risks, of course, and . . ."

Holles cut in briskly. "I have said that I have lived on risks. And they'll be less than those you represent as lying in wait for me here at home. Oh, I'll take the risks. Right gladly I'll take the risks. And I've little cause to be so wedded to the old world that I'd not exchange it for the new."

"Why, then, we'll see. A little patience, and it may be mine to offer you some place abroad."

"Patience!" said Holles, his jaw fallen again.

"Why, to be sure. After all, such posts do not grow like apples. Keep me informed of where you are lodged, and I will send you word when the occasion offers."

"And if he doesn't send word soon do you come and see me again, Randal," said her grace; "we'll quicken him. He's well enough; but he's growing old, and his wits is sluggish."

And the great man, whose eye had daunted armies, smiled benignly upon his termagant.

CHAPTER IV

CHERRY BLOSSOMS

COLONEL HOLLES knelt on the window-seat at the open casement of his parlour at the Paul's Head. Leaning on the sill, he seemed to contemplate the little sunlit garden with its two cherry trees on which some of those belated blossoms lingered still. Cherry blossoms he was contemplating, but not those before him. The two trees of this little oasis in the City of London had multiplied themselves into a cherry orchard set in Devon and in the years that were gone beyond reclaiming.

The phenomenon was not new to him. Cherry blossoms had ever possessed the power to move him thus. The contemplation of them never failed to bring him the vision that was now spread before his wistful eyes. Mrs. Quinn's few perches of garden had dissolved into an acre of sunlit flowering orchard. Above the trees in the background to the right a spire thrust up into the blue, surmounted by a weather-vane in the shape of a fish — which he vaguely knew to be an emblem of Christianity. Through a gap on the left he beheld a wall, ivy-clad, crumbling at its summit. Over this a lad was climbing stealthily — a long-limbed, graceful, fair-haired stripling, whose features were recognizable for his own if from the latter you removed the haggard lines that the years and hard living had imprinted. Softly and nimbly as a cat he dropped to earth on the wall's hither side, and stood there half crouching, a smile on his young lips and laughter in his grey eyes. He was watching a girl who — utterly unconscious of his presence — swept to and fro through the air on a swing that was formed of a single rope passed from one tree to another.

She was a child, no more; yet of a well-grown, lissom grace that deceived folk into giving her more than the bare fifteen years she counted to her age. Hers was no rose-and-lily complexion. She displayed the healthy tan that comes of a life lived in the open far away from cities. Yet one glance into the long-shaped, deeply blue eyes that were the glory of her lovely little face sufficed to warn you that though rustic she was not simple. Here was one who possessed a full share of that feminine guile which is the heritage from Mother Eve to her favoured daughters. If you were a man and wise, you would be most wary when she was most demure.

Swinging now, her loosened brown hair streamed behind her as she flew forward, and tossed itself into a cloud about her face as she went back. And she sang as nearly as possible in rhythm with her swinging:

> "Hey, young love! Ho, young love!
>   Where do you tarry?
> Whiles here I stay for you
>   Waiting to marry.
> Hey, young love! Ho, young . . . "

The song ended in a scream. Unheard, unsuspected, the stripling had crept forward through the trees. At the top of her backward swing he had caught her about the waist in his strong young arms. There was a momentary flutter of two black legs amid an agitated cloud of petticoat, then the rope swung forward, and the nymph was left in the arms of her young satyr. But only for a moment. Out of that grip she broke in a fury — real or pretended — and came to earth breathless, with flushed cheeks and flashing eye.

"You give yourself strange liberties, young Randal," said she, and boxed his ears. "Who bade you here?"

"I . . . I thought you called me," said he, grinning, no whit abashed by either blow or look. "Come, now, Nan. Confess it!"

"I called you? I?" She laughed indignantly. "'Tis very likely! Oh, very likely!"

"You'll deny it, of course, being a woman in the making. But I heard you." And he quoted for her, singing:

> "Hey, young love! Ho, young love!
> Where do you tarry?"

"I was hiding on the other side of the wall. I came at once. And all I get for my pains and the risk to a fairly new pair of breeches is a blow and a denial."

"You may get more if you remain."

"I hope so. I had not come else."

"But it'll be as little to your liking."

"That's as may be. Meanwhile there's this matter of a blow. Now a blow is a thing I take from nobody. For a man there is my sword . . ."

"Your sword!" She abandoned herself to laughter. "And you don't even own a penknife."

"Oh, yes I do. I own a sword. It was a gift from my father to-day — a birthday gift. I am nineteen to-day, Nan."

"How fast you grow! You'll be a man soon. And so your father has given you a sword?" She leaned against the bole of a tree, and surveyed him archly. "That was very rash of your father. You'll be cutting yourself, I know."

He smiled, but with a little less of his earlier assurance. But he made a fair recovery.

"You are straying from the point."

"The point of your sword, sweet sir?"

"The point of my discourse. It was concerning this matter of a blow. If you were a man I am afraid I should have to kill you. My honour would demand no less."

"With your sword?" she asked him innocently.

"With my sword, of course."

"Ugh. Jack the Giant-Killer in a cherry orchard! You

must see you are out of place here. Get you gone, boy. I don't think I ever liked you, Randal. Now I'm sure of it. You're a bloody-minded fellow for all your tender years. What you'll be when you're a man . . . I daren't think."

He swallowed the taunt.

"And what you'll be when you're a woman is the thing I delight in thinking. We'll return to that. Meanwhile, this blow . . ."

"Oh, you're tiresome."

"You delay me. That is why. What I would do to a man who struck me I have told you."

"But you can't think I believe you."

This time he was not to be turned aside.

"The real question is what to do to a woman." He approached her. "When I look at you, one punishment only seems possible."

He took her by the shoulders in a grip of a surprising firmness. There was sudden alarm in those eyes of hers that hitherto had been so mocking.

"Randal!" she cried out, guessing his purpose.

Undeterred he accomplished it. Having kissed her, he loosed his hold, and stood back for the explosion which from his knowledge of her he was led to expect. But no explosion came. She stood limply before him, all the raillery gone out of her, whilst slowly the colour faded from her cheeks. Then it came flowing back in an all-suffusing flood, and there was a pathetic quiver at the corners of her mouth, a suspicious brightness in her drooping eyes.

"Why, Nan!" he cried, alarmed by phenomena so unexpected and unusual.

"Oh, why did you do that?" she cried on a sob.

Here was meekness! Had she boxed his ears again, it would have surprised him not at all. Indeed, it is what he had

looked for. But that she should be stricken so spiritless,
that she should have no reproof for him beyond that plaintive question, left him agape with amazement. It occurred
to him that perhaps he had found the way to tame her; and
he regretted on every count that he should not have had
recourse before to a method so entirely satisfactory to himself. Meanwhile her question craved an answer.

"I've been wanting to do it this twelvemonth," said he
simply. "And I shall want to do it again. Nan, dear, don't
you know how much I love you? Don't you know without
my telling you? Don't you?"

The fervent question chased away her trouble and
summoned surprise to fill its place. A moment she stared at
him, and her glance hardened. She began to show signs of
recovery.

"The declaration should have preceded the . . . the . . .
affront."

"Affront!" he cried, in protest.

"What else? Isn't it an affront to kiss a maid without a
by-your-leave? If you were a man, I shouldn't forgive you.
I couldn't. But as you're just a boy" — her tone soared to
disdainful heights — "you shall be forgiven on a promise
that the offence is not to be repeated."

"But I love you, Nan! I've said so," he expostulated.

"You're too precocious, young Randal. It comes, I suppose, of being given a sword to play with. I shall have to
speak to your father about it. You need manners more than
a sword at present."

The minx was skilled in the art of punishing. But the lad
refused to be put out of countenance.

"Nan, dear, I am asking you to marry me."

She jumped at that. Her eyes dilated. "Lord!" she said,
"What condescension! But d'you think I want a child tied
to my apron-strings?"

"Won't you be serious, Nan?" he pleaded. "I am very serious."

"You must be, to be thinking of marriage."

"I am going away, Nan — to-morrow, very early. I came to say good-bye."

Her eyelids flickered, and in that moment a discerning glance would have detected a gleam of alarm from her blue eyes. But there was no hint of it in her voice.

"I thought you said it was to marry me you came."

"Why will you be teasing me? It means so much to me, Nan. I want you to say that you'll wait for me; that you'll marry me some day."

He was very close to her. She looked up at him a little breathlessly. Her feminine intuitions warned her that he was about to take a liberty; feminine perversity prompted her to frustrate the intention, although it was one that in her heart she knew would gladden her.

"Some day?" she mocked him. "When you're grown up, I suppose? Why, I'll be an old maid by then; and I don't think I want to be an old maid."

"Answer me, Nan. Don't rally me. Say that you'll wait."

He would have caught her by the shoulders again. But she eluded those eager hands of his.

"You haven't told me yet where you are going."

Gravely he flung the bombshell of his news, confident that it must lend him a new importance in her eyes, and thus, perhaps, bring her into something approaching subjection.

"I am going to London, to the army. My father has procured me a cornetcy of horse, and I am to serve under General Monk, who is his friend."

It made an impression, though she did not give him the satisfaction of seeing how great that impression was. To do her justice, the army meant no more to her just at that moment than champing horses, blaring trumpets, and waving banners. Of its grimmer side she took as yet no thought: else she might have given his news a graver greeting. As it was, the surprise of it left her silent, staring at him in a new wonder. He took advantage of it to approach her again. He committed the mistake of attempting to force the pace. He caught her to him, taking her unawares this time and seizing her suddenly, before she could elude him.

"Nan, my dear!"

She struggled in his arms. But he held her firmly. She struggled the harder, and, finding her struggles ineffective, her temper rose. Her hands against his breast she thrust him back.

"Release me at once! Release me, or I'll scream!"

At that and the anger in her voice, he let her go, and stood sheepishly, abashed, whilst she retreated a few paces from him, breathing quickly, her eyes aflash.

"My faith! You'll be a great success in London! They'll like your oafish ways up yonder. I think you had better go."

"Forgive me, Nan!" He was in a passion of penitence, fearing that this time he had gone too far and angered her in earnest. "Ah, don't be cruel. It is our last day together for Heaven knows how long."

"Well, that's a mercy."

"Ye don't mean that, Nan? Ye can't mean that ye care nothing about me. That you are glad I'm going."

"You should mend your manners," she reproved him by way of compromise.

"Why, so I will. It's only that I want you so; that I'm going away — far away; that after to-day I won't see you again maybe for years. If ye say that ye don't care for me at all, why, then I don't think that I'll come back to Potheridge ever. But if ye care — be it never so little, Nan — if you'll wait for me, it'll send me away with a good heart, it'll give me strength to become great. I'll conquer the world for you, my dear," he ended grandiloquently, as is the way of youth in its unbounded confidence. "I'll bring it back to toss it in your lap."

Her eyes were shining. His devotion and enthusiasm touched her. But her mischievous perversity must be dissembling it. She laughed on a rising inflection that was faintly mocking.

"I shouldn't know what to do with it," said she.

That and her laughter angered him. He had opened his heart. He had been boastful in his enthusiasm, he had magnified himself and felt himself shrinking again under the acid of her derision. He put on a sudden frosty dignity.

"You may laugh, but there'll come a day maybe when you won't laugh. You may be sorry when I come back."

"Bringing the world with you," she mocked him.

He looked at her almost savagely, white-faced. Then in silence he swung on his heel and went off through the trees. Six paces he had taken when he came face to face with an elderly, grave-faced gentleman in the clerkly attire of a churchman, who was pacing slowly reading in a book. The parson raised his eyes. They were long-shaped blue eyes like Nancy's, but kindlier in their glance.

"Why, Randal!" he hailed the boy who was almost hurtling into him, being half-blinded by his unshed tears.

The youth commanded himself.

"Give you good-morning, Mr. Sylvester. I . . . I but came to say good-bye . . ."

"Why, yes, my boy. Your father told me . . ."

Through the trees came the girl's teasing voice.

"You are detaining the gentleman, father, and he is in haste. He is off to conquer the world."

Mr. Sylvester raised his heavy grey eyebrows a little; the shadow of a smile hovered about the corners of his kindly mouth, his eyes looked a question, humorously.

Randal shrugged. "Nancy is gay at my departure, sir."

"Nay, nay."

"It affords her amusement, as you perceive, sir. She is pleased to laugh."

"Tush, tush!" The parson turned, took his arm affectionately, and moved along with him towards the house. "A mask on her concern," he murmured. "Women are like that. It takes a deal of learning to understand a woman; and I doubt, in the end, if the time is well spent. But I'll answer for it that she'll have a warm welcome for you on your return, whether you've conquered the world or not. So shall we all, my boy. You go to serve in a great cause. God bring you safely home again."

But Randal took no comfort, and parted from Mr. Sylvester vowing in his heart that he would return no more betide what might.

Yet before he quitted Potheridge he had proof that Mr. Sylvester was right. It was in vain that day that Nancy awaited his return. And that night there were tears on her pillow, some of vexation, but some of real grief at the going of Randal.

Very early next morning, before the village was astir, Randal rode forth upon the conquest of the world, fortified by a tolerably heavy purse, and that brand-new sword — the gifts which had accompanied his father's blessing. As he rode along by the wall above which the cherry blossoms flaunted, towards the grey rectory that fronted immediately upon the road, a lattice was pushed open overhead, and the head and shoulders of Nancy were protruded.

"Randal!" she softly called him, as he came abreast.

He reined in his horse and looked up. His rancour melted instantly. He was conscious of the quickening of his pulses.

"Nan!" His whole soul was in his utterance of the name.

"I . . . I am sorry I laughed, Randal, dear. I wasn't

really gay. I have cried since. I have stayed awake all night not to miss you now." This was hardly true, but it is very likely she believed it. "I wanted to say good-bye and God keep you, Randal, dear, and . . . and . . . come back to me soon again."

"Nan!" he cried again. It was all that he could say; but he said it with singular eloquence.

Something slapped softly down upon the withers of his horse. His hand shot out to clutch it ere it fell thence, and he found himself holding a little tasselled glove.

There was a little scream from above. "My glove!" she cried. "I've dropped it. Randal, please!" She was leaning far out, reaching down a beseeching hand. But she was still too far above him to render possible the glove's return. Besides, this time she did not deceive him with her comedy. He took off his hat, and passed the glove through the band.

"I'll wear it as a favour till I come to claim the hand it has covered," he told her in a sort of exaltation. He kissed the glove, bowed low, covered himself with a flourish, and touched the horse with his spurs.

As he rode away her voice floated after him, faintly mocking, yet with a choking quaver that betrayed her secret tears.

"Don't forget to bring the world back with you."

And that was the last of her voice that he had ever heard.

Five years passed before the day when next he came to Potheridge. Again the cherry trees were in blossom; again he saw them, tossed by the breeze, above the grey wall of the rectory orchard, as he rode forward with high-beating heart, a lackey trotting at his heels.

The elder Holles, who had removed himself permanently to London shortly after his son's going to Monk, had been dead these two years. If Randal had not accomplished his proud boast of conquering the world, at least he had won himself an important place in it, a fine position in the army, that should be a stepping-stone to greater things. He was the youngest colonel in the service, thanks to his own talents as well as to Monk's favour — for Monk could never so have favoured him had he not been worthy and so proved himself — a man of mark, of whom a deal was expected by all who knew him. All this he now bore written plainly upon him: his air of authority; his rich dress; the handsome furniture of his splendid horse; the servant following; all advertised the man of consequence. And he was proud of it all for the sake of her who had been his inspiration. From his heart he thanked God for these things, since he might offer them to her.

What would she look like, he wondered, as he rode amain, his face alight and eager. It was three years since last he had heard from her; but that was natural enough, for the constant movements demanded by his soldier's life made it impossible that letters should reach him often. To her he had written frequently. But one letter only had he received in all those years, and that was long ago, written to him after Dunbar in answer to his announcement that he had won himself a captaincy and so advanced a stage in his conquest of the world.

How would she greet him now? How would she look at him? What would be her first word? He thought that it would be his name. He hoped it might be; for in her utterance of it he would read all he sought to know.

They came to a clattering halt at the rectory door. He flung down from the saddle without waiting for his groom's assistance, and creaked and clanked across the cobbles to rattle on the oak with the butt of his riding-whip.

The door swung inwards. Before him, startled of glance, stood a lean old crone who in nothing resembled the corpulent Mathilda who had kept the rector's house of old. He stared at her, some of the glad eagerness perishing in his face.

"The ... the rector?" quoth he, faltering. "Is he at home?"

"Aye, he be in," she mumbled, mistrustfully eyeing his imposing figure. "Do ee bide a moment, whiles I calls him." She vanished into the gloom of the hall, whence her voice reached him, calling: "Master! Master! Here be stranger!"

A stranger! O God! Here all was not as it should be.

Came a quick, youthful step, and a moment later a young man advanced from the gloom. He was tall, comely, and golden-haired; he wore clerkly black and the Geneva bands of a cleric.

"You desired to see me, sir?" he inquired.

Randal Holles stood looking at him, speechless for a long moment, dumbfounded. He moistened his lips at last, and spoke.

"It was Mr. Sylvester whom I desired to see, sir," he answered. "Tell me" — and in his eagerness he was so unmannerly as to clutch the unknown parson's arm — "where is he? Is he no longer here?"

"No," was the gentle answer. "I have succeeded him." The young cleric paused. "Mr. Sylvester has been with God these three years."

Holles commanded himself. "This is bad news to me, sir. He was an old friend. And his daughter ... Miss Nancy? Where is she?"

"I cannot tell you, sir. She had departed from Potheridge before I came."

"But whither did she go? Whither?" In a sudden frenzy he shook the other's arm.

The cleric suffered it in silence, realizing the man's sudden distraction.

"That, sir, I do not know. I never heard. You see, sir, I had not the acquaintance of Miss Sylvester. Perhaps the squire . . ."

"Aye, aye! The squire!"

To the squire's he went, and burst in upon him at table in the hall. Squire Haynes, corpulent and elderly, heaved himself up at the intrusion of this splendid stranger.

"God in Heaven!" he cried in amazement. "It's young Randal Holles! Alive!"

It transpired that the report had run through Potheridge that Randal had been killed at Worcester. That would be at about the time Mr. Sylvester died, and his daughter had left the village shortly thereafter. At another season and in other circumstances Holles might have smiled at the vanity which had led him to suppose his name famous throughout the land. Here to his native Potheridge no echo of that fame had penetrated. He had been reported dead and no subsequent deed of his had come to deny that rumour in this village that was the one spot in all England where men should take an interest in his doings.

Later, indeed, he may have pondered it, and derived from it a salutary lesson in the bridling of conceit. But at the moment his only thought was of Nancy. Was it known whither she had gone?

The squire had heard tell at the time; but he had since forgotten; a parson's daughter was no great matter. In vain he made an effort of memory for Randal's sake and upon Randal's urging. Then he bethought him that perhaps his housekeeper could say. Women retained these trivial matters in their memories. Summoned, the woman was found to remember perfectly. Nancy had gone to Charmouth to the care of a married aunt, a sister of her father's, her only remaining relative. The aunt's name was Tenfil, an odd name.

To his dying day Randal would remember that instant ride to Charmouth, his mental anxiety numbing all sense of fatigue, followed by a lackey who at intervals dozed in his saddle, then woke to grumble and complain.

In the end half dead with weariness, yet quickened ever by suspense, they came to Charmouth, and they found the house of Tenfil, and the aunt; but they found no Nancy.

Mrs. Tenfil, an elderly, hard-faced, hard-hearted woman, all piety and no charity, one of those creatures who make of religion a vice for their own assured damnation, unbent a little from her natural sourness before the handsome, elegant young stranger. She was still a woman under the ashes of her years and of her bigotry. But at the mention of her niece's name the sourness and the hardness came back to her face with interest.

"A creature without godliness. My brother was ever a weak man, and he ruined her with kindness. It was a mercy he died before he came to know the impiety of his offspring — a wilful, headstrong, worldly minx."

"Madam, it is not her character I seek of you; but her whereabouts," said the exasperated Randal.

She considered him in a new light. In the elegance and good looks, which had at first commended him, she now beheld the devil's seal of worldliness. Such a man would seek her niece for no good purpose; yet he was just such a man as her niece, to her undoing, would make welcome. Her lips tightened with saintly, uncharitable purpose. She would make of herself a buckler between this malignant one and her niece. By great good fortune — by a heavenly Providence, in her eyes — her niece was absent at the time. And so in the cause of holiness she lied to him — although of this the poor fellow had no suspicion.

"In that case, young sir, you seek something I cannot give you."

She would have left it vaguely there, between truth and untruth. But he demanded more.

"You mean, you do not know . . . that . . . that she has left you?"

She braced herself to the righteous falsehood.

"That is what I mean."

Still he would not rest content. Haggard-faced he drove her into the last ditch of untruth.

"When did she leave you? Tell me that, at least."

"Two years ago. After she had been with me a year."

"And whither did she go? You must know that!"

"I do not. All that I know is that she went. Belike she is in London. That, at least, I know is where she would wish to be, being all worldliness and ungodliness."

He stared at her, a physical sickness oppressing him. His little Nan in London, alone and friendless, without means. What might not have happened to her in two years?

"Madam," he said in a voice that passion and sorrow made unsteady, "if you drove her hence, as your manner seems to tell me, be sure that God will punish you."

And he reeled out without waiting for her answer.

Inquiries in the village might have altered the whole course of his life. But, as if the unutterable gods of Mrs. Tenfil's devotions removed all chances of the frustration of her ends, Randal rode out of Charmouth without having spoken to another soul. To what end should he have done so, considering her tale? What reason could he have to disbelieve?

For six months after that he sought Nancy in all places likely and unlikely. And all that while in Charmouth Nancy patiently and trustfully awaited his coming, which should deliver her from the dreadful thraldom of Aunt Tenfil's godliness. Some day, she was persuaded, must happen that which she did not know had already happened; that he must seek her in Potheridge, learn whither she was gone, and follow. For she did not share Potheridge's belief that he was dead, though for a time she had mourned him grievously when first the rumour ran through her native village. Subsequently, however, soon after her migration to Charmouth, a letter from him had reached her there, written some months after Worcester fight, in which he announced himself not only safe and sound, but thriving, conquering the world apace, and counting upon returning laden with it soon, to claim her.

And meanwhile despair was settling upon young Randal. To have lived and striven with but one inspiration and one aim, and to find in the hour of triumph that the aim has been rendered unattainable, is to know one's self for Fortune's fool. To a loyal soul such as his the blow was crushing. It made life purposeless, robbed him of ambition and warped his whole nature. His steadfastness was transmuted into recklessness and restlessness. He required distraction from his brooding; the career of arms at home, in time of peace, could offer him none of this. He quitted the service of the Parliament, and went abroad — to Holland, that happy hunting-ground of all homeless adventurers. He entered Dutch service, and for a season prospered in it. But there was a difference, deplorable and grim. He was no longer concerned to build himself a position in the State. Such a thing was impossible in a foreign land, where he was a mercenary, a soldier of fortune, a man who made of arms a trade soulless and uninspired. With the mantle of the mercenary he put on a mercenary's habits. His easily earned gold he spent riotously, prodigally, as was ever the mercenary's way. He gamed and drank and squandered it on worthless women.

He grew notorious; a man of reckless courage, holding his life cheap, an able leader of men, but a dissolute, hard-drinking, quarrelsome Englander whom it was not safe to trust too far.

The reaction set in at last; but not until five years of this life had corroded his soul. It came to him one day when he realized that he was over thirty, that he had dissipated his youth, and that the path he trod must lead him ultimately to a contemptible old age. Some of the good that slumbered in the depths of his soul welled up to cry a halt. He would go back. Physically and morally he would retrace his steps. He would seize this life that was slipping from him, and remould it to the original intention. For that he would return to England.

He wrote to Monk, who then was the powerfullest man in the realm. But — Fortune's fool again — he wrote just too late. The restoration was accomplished. It was a few weeks old, no more. For one who had been a prominent Parliament man in the old days, and the son of a Parliament man still more prominent, there was no place by then in English service. Had he but made the application some months sooner, whilst the restoration was still in the balance, and had he then taken sides with Monk in bringing it about, he might by that very act have redeemed the past in Stuart eyes, setting up a credit to cancel the old debt.

The rest you guess. He sank thereafter deeper into his old habits, rendering himself ever more unfit for any great position, and so continued for five horrid years that seemed to him in retrospect an age. Then came the war, and England's unspoken summons to every son of hers who trailed a sword abroad. Dutch service could no longer hold him. This was his opportunity. At last he would shake off the filth of a mercenary's life, and go boldly home to find worthy employment for his sword.

Yet, but for the scheming credit accorded him by a tavern-keeper and the interest of a vulgar old woman who had cause to hold him in kindly memory, he might by now have been sent back, to tread once more the path to hell.

CHAPTER V

THE MERCENARY

COLONEL HOLLES took the air in Paul's Yard, drawn forth partly by the voice of a preacher on the steps of Paul's, who was attracting a crowd about him, partly by his own restlessness. It was now three days since his visit to the Cockpit, and although he could not reasonably have expected news from Albemarle within so short a time, yet the lack of it was fretting him.

He was moving along the skirts of the crowd that had collected before the preacher, with no intention of pausing, when suddenly a phrase arrested him.

"Repent, I say, while it is time! For behold the wrath of the Lord is upon you. The scourge of pestilence is raised to smite you down."

Holles looked over the heads of the assembled citizens, and beheld a black crow of a man, cadaverous of face, with sunken eyes that glowed uncannily from the depths of their sockets.

"Repent!" the voice croaked. "Awaken! Behold your peril, and by prayer and reparation set yourselves to avert it whiles yet it may be time. Within the Parish of St. Giles this week lie thirty dead of this dread pestilence, ten in St. Clement's, and as many in St. Andrew's, Holborn. These are but warnings. Slowly but surely the plague is creeping upon the city. As Sodom of old was destroyed, so shall this modern Sodom perish, unless you rouse yourselves, and cast out the evil that is amongst you."

The crowd was in the main irreverently disposed. There was some laughter, and one shrill, persistent voice that derided him. The preacher paused. He seemed to lengthen before them, as he raised his arms to Heaven.

"They laugh! Deriders, scoffers, will you not be warned? Oh, the great, the dreadful God! His vengeance is upon you, and you laugh. Thou hast defiled thy sanctuaries by the multitude of thine iniquities, by the iniquity of thy traffic. Therefore I will bring forth a fire from the midst of thee, and I will burn thee to ashes upon the earth in the sight of all them that behold thee."

Holles moved on. He had heard odd allusions to this pestilence which was said to be making victims in the outskirts and which it was alleged by some fools was a weapon of warfare wielded by the Dutch — at least, that it was the Dutch who had let it loose in England. But he had paid little heed to the matter, knowing that scaremongers are never lacking. Apparently the citizens of London were of his own way of thinking, if he might judge by the indifferent success attending the hoarse rantings of that preacher of doom.

As he moved on, a man of handsome presence and soldierly bearing, with the dress and air of a gentleman, considered him intently with eyes of startled wonder. As Holles came abreast of him, he suddenly stepped forward, detaching from the crowd, and caught the Colonel by the arm. Holles checked, and turned to find himself gravely regarded by this stranger.

"Either you are Randal Holles, or else the devil in his shape."

Then Holles knew him — a ghost out of his past, as he was, himself, a ghost out of the past of this other; an old friend, a brother-in-arms of the days of Worcester and Dunbar.

"Tucker!" he cried, "Ned Tucker!" And impulsively, his face alight, he held out his hand.

The other gripped it firmly.

"I must have known you anywhere, Randal, despite the change that time has wrought."

"It has wrought changes in yourself as well. But you

would seem to have prospered!" The Colonel's face was rejuvenated by a look of almost boyish pleasure.

"Oh, I am well enough," said Tucker. "And you?"

"As you see."

The other's grave dark eyes considered him. There fell a silence, an awkward pause between those two, each of whom desired to ask a hundred questions. At last:

"I last heard of you in Holland," said Tucker.

"I am but newly home."

The other's eyebrows went up, a manifestation of surprise.

"Whatever can have brought you?"

"The war, and the desire to find employment in which I may serve my country."

"And you've found it?" The smile on the dark face suggested a scornful doubt which almost made an answer unnecessary.

"Not yet."

"It would have moved my wonder if you had. It was a rashness to have returned at all." He lowered his voice, lest he should be overheard. "The climate of England isn't healthy at all to old soldiers of the Parliament."

"Yet you are here, Ned."

"I?" Again that slow, half-scornful smile lighted the grave, handsome face. He shrugged. He leaned towards Holles, and dropped his voice still further. "My father was not a regicide," he said quietly. "Therefore, I am comparatively obscure."

Holles looked at him, the eager pleasure which the meeting had brought him withering in his face. Would men ever keep green the memory of this thing and of the silly tie with which they had garnished it? Must it ever prove an insuperable obstacle to him in Stuart England?

"Nay, nay, never look so glum, man," Tucker laughed,

and he took the Colonel by the arm. "Let us go somewhere where we can talk. We should have a deal to tell each other."

Holles swung him round.

"Come to the Paul's Head," he bade him. "I am lodged there."

But the other hung back, hesitating a moment. "My own lodging is near at hand in Cheapside," he said, and they turned about again.

In silence they moved off together. At the corner of Paul's Yard, Tucker paused, and turned to look across at the doorway of Paul's and the fanatical preacher who stood there shrilling. His voice floated across to them.

"Oh, the great and the dreadful God!"

Tucker's face set into grimly sardonic lines. "An eloquent fellow, that," he said. "He should rouse these silly sheep from their apathy."

The Colonel stared at him, puzzled. There seemed to be an ulterior meaning to his words. But Tucker, without adding anything further, drew him away and on.

In a handsome room on the first floor of one of the most imposing houses in Cheapside, Tucker waved his guest to the best chair.

"An old friend, just met by chance," he explained to his housekeeper, who came to wait upon him. "So it will be a bottle of sack . . . of the best!"

When, having brought the wine, the woman had taken herself off and the two sat within closed doors, the Colonel gave his friend the account of himself which the latter craved.

Gravely Tucker heard him through, and grave his face remained when the tale was done. He sighed, and considered the Colonel a moment in silence with sombre eyes.

"So George Monk's your only hope?" he said, slowly, at last. Then he uttered a short, sharp laugh of infinite scorn.

"In your case I think I'd hang myself and have done. It's less tormenting."

"What do you mean?"

"You think that Monk will really help you? That he intends to help?"

"Assuredly. He has promised it, and he was my friend — and my father's friend."

"Friend!" said the other bitterly. "I never knew a trimmer to be any man's friend but his own. And if ever a trimmer lived, his name is George Monk — the very prince of trimmers, as his whole life shows. First a King's man; then something betwixt and between King and Parliament; then a Parliament man, selling his friends of the King's side. And lastly a King's man again, in opposition to his late trusting friends of the Parliament. Always choosing the side that is uppermost or that can outbid the other for his services. And look where he stands; Baron of this, Earl of that, Duke of Albemarle, Commander-in-Chief, Master of the Horse, Gentleman of the Bedchamber, and God knows what else. Oh, he has grown fat on trimming."

"You do him wrong, Ned." Holles was mildly indignant.

"That is impossible."

"But you do. You forget that a man may change sides from conviction."

"Especially when it is to his own profit," sneered Tucker.

"That is ungenerous, and it is untrue, of course." The Colonel showed signs of loyal heat. "You are wrong also in your other assumption. He would have given me all the help I needed, but that . . ."

"But that he counted the slight risk — nay; what am I saying? — the slight inconvenience to himself should any questions afterwards be asked. He could have averted in such a case all awkwardness by pleading ignorance to your past . . ."

"He is too honest to do that."

"Honest! Aye — 'honest George Monk'! Usually misfortune schools a man in worldly wisdom. But you . . ." Tucker smiled between contempt and sadness, leaving the phrase unfinished.

"I have told you that he will help me; that he has promised."

"And you build upon his promises? Promises! They cost nothing. They are the bribes with which a trimmer puts off the importunate. Monk saw your need, as I see it. You carry the marks of it plainly upon you, in every seam of your threadbare coat. Forgive the allusion, Randal!" He set a conciliatory hand upon his friend's arm, for the Colonel had reddened resentfully at the words. "I make it to justify myself of what I say." And he resumed: "Monk's revenues amount to thirty thousand pounds a year — such are the vails of trimmers. He was your friend, you say; he was your father's friend, and owed much to your father, as all know. Did he offer you his purse to tide you over present stress, until opportunity permits him to fulfil his promise? Did he?"

"I could not have taken advantage of it if he had."

"That is not what I ask you. Did he offer it? Of course he did not. Not he. Yet would not a friend have helped you at once and where he could?"

"He did not think of it."

"A friend would have thought of it. But Monk is no man's friend."

"I say again, you are unjust to him. You forget that, after all, he was under no necessity to promise anything."

"Oh, yes, he was. There was his Duchess, as you've told me. Dirty Bess can be importunate, and she commands him. He goes notoriously in terror of her. Yielding to her importunities he promised that which he will avoid fulfilling.

I know George Monk, and all his leprous kind, of which this
England is full to-day, battening upon her carcase with the
foul greed of vultures. I . . .''

He grew conscious that Colonel Holles was staring at him,
amazed by his sudden vehemence. He checked abruptly,
and laughed.

"I grow hot for nothing at all. Nay, not for nothing —
for you, old friend, and against those who put this deception
upon you. You should not have come back to England,
Randal. But since you're here, at least do not woo disappointment by nourishing your hopes on empty promises."
He raised his glass to the light, and looked at the Colonel
solemnly across the top of it. "I drink to your better fortune, Randal."

Mechanically, without answering a word, the Colonel
drank with him. His heart was turned to lead. The portrait Tucker had so swiftly painted of Monk's soul was
painted obviously with a hostile, bitter brush. Yet the facts
of Monk's life made it plausible. The likeness was undeni-
able, if distorted. And Holles — rendered pessimistic and
despondent by his very condition — saw the likeness and
not the distortion.

"If you are right," he said slowly, his eyes upon the table,
"I may as well take your advice, and hang myself."

"Almost the only thing left for a self-respecting man in
England," said Tucker.

"Or anywhere else, for that matter. But why so bitter
about England in particular?"

Tucker shrugged. "You know my sentiments, what they
always were. I am no trimmer. I sail a steady course."

Holles regarded him searchingly. He could not misunder-
stand the man's words, still less his tone.

"Is that not . . . Is it not a dangerous course?" he asked.

Tucker looked at him with wistful amusement.

"There are considerations an honest man should set above danger."

"Oh, agreed."

"There is no honesty save in steadfastness, Randal, and I am, I hope, an honest man."

"By which you mean that I am not," said Holles slowly.

Tucker did not contradict him by more than a shrug and a deprecatory smile that was of mere politeness. The Colonel rose, stirred to vehemence by his friend's manifest opinion of him.

"I am a beggar, Ned; and beggars may not choose. Besides, for ten years now I have been a mercenary, neither more nor less. My sword is for hire. That is the trade by which I live. I do not make governments; I do not plague myself with questions of their worth; I serve them, for gold."

But Tucker, smiling sadly, slowly shook his head.

"If that were true, you would not be in England now. You came, as you have said, because of the war. Your sword may be for hire; but you still have a country, and the first offer goes to her. Should she refuse it, the next will not go to an enemy of England's. So why belittle yourself thus? You still have a country, and you love it. There are many here who are ready to love you, though they may not be among those who govern England. You have come back to serve her. Serve her, then. But first ask yourself how best she may be served."

"What's that?"

"Sit down, man. Sit, and listen."

And now, having first sworn the Colonel to secrecy in the name of their old friendship — to which and to the Colonel's desperate condition, the other trusted in opening his heart — Tucker delivered himself of what was no less than treason.

He began by inviting the Colonel to consider the state to which misgovernment by a spendthrift, lecherous, vindic-

tive, dishonest king had reduced the country. Beginning
with the Bill of Indemnity and its dishonourable evasion, he
reviewed act by act the growing tyranny of the last five
years since the restoration of King Charles, presenting each
in the focus of his own vision, which, if bitterly hostile, was
yet accurate enough. He came in the end to deal with the
war to which the country was committed; he showed how it
had been provoked by recklessness, and how it had been
rendered possible by the gross, the criminal neglect of the
affairs of that navy which Cromwell had left so formidable.
And he dwelt upon the appalling license of the Court with
all the fury of the Puritan he was at heart.

"We touch the end at last," he concluded with fierce conviction. "Whitehall shall be swept clean of this Charles
Stuart and his trulls and pimps and minions. They shall be
flung on the foul dunghill where they belong, and a commonwealth shall be restored to rule this England in a sane and
cleanly fashion, so that honest men may be proud to serve
her once again."

"My God, Ned, you're surely mad!" Holles was aghast
as much at the confidence itself as at the manner of it.

"To risk myself, you mean?" Tucker smiled grimly.
"These vampires have torn the bowels out of better men in
the same cause, and if we fail, they may have mine and welcome. But we do not fail. Our plans are shrewdly laid and
already well advanced. There is one in Holland who directs
them — a name I dare not mention to you yet, but a name
that is dear to all honest men. Almost it is the hour. Our
agents are everywhere abroad, moulding the people's mind,
directing it into a sane channel. Heaven itself has come to
our help by sending us this pestilence to strike terror into
men's hearts and make them ask themselves how much the
vices by which the rulers defile this land may not have provoked this visitation. That preacher you heard upon the

steps of Paul's is one of our agents, doing the good work, casting the seed in fertile places. And very soon now will come the harvest — such a harvest!"

He paused, and considered his stricken friend with an eye in which glowed something of the light of fanaticism.

"Your sword is idle and you seek employment for it, Randal. Here is a service you may take with honour. It is the service of the old Commonwealth to which in the old days you were stanch, a service aiming at these enemies who would still deny such men as you a place in England. You strike not only for yourself, but for some thousands in like case. And your country will not forget. We need such swords as yours. I offer you at once a cause and a career. Albemarle puts you off with promises of appointments in which the preference over worth is daily granted to the pimpish friends of the loathly creatures about Charles Stuart's leprous Court. I have opened my heart to you freely and frankly, even at some risk. What have you to say to me?"

Holles rose, his decision taken, his face set. "What I said at first. I am a mercenary. I do not make governments. I serve them. There is no human cause in all the world to-day could move me to enthusiasm."

"Yet you came home that you might serve England in her need."

"Because I did not know where else to go."

"Very well. I accept you at your own valuation, Randal — not that I believe you; but not to confuse the argument. Being here, you find the doors by which you counted upon entering all closed against you, and locked. What are you going to do? You say you are a mercenary; that your concern is but to give a soulless service to the hand that hires you. I present you to a liberal taskmaster; one who will richly reward your service. Since to you all service is alike, let the mercenary answer me."

He, too, had risen, and held out a hand in appeal. The Colonel looked at him seriously awhile; then he smiled.

"What an advocate was lost in you, Ned!" said he. "You keep to the point — aye; but also you conveniently miss it. A mercenary serves governments *in esse;* the service of governments *in posse* is for enthusiasts; and I have had no enthusiasms these ten years and more. Establish your government, and my sword is for your hire, and gladly. But do not ask me to set my head upon the board in this gamble to establish it; for my head is my only remaining possession."

"If you will not strike a blow for love, will you not strike one for hate: against the Stuart, whose vindictiveness will not allow you to earn your bread?"

"You overstate the case. Though much that you have said of him may be true, I will not yet despair of the help of Albemarle."

"Why, you blind madman, I tell you — I swear to you — that in a very little while Albemarle will be beyond helping any man, beyond helping even himself."

Holles was about to speak, when Tucker threw up a hand to arrest him.

"Do not answer me now. Let what I have said sink home into your wits. Give it thought. We are not pressed for a few days. Ponder my words, and if as the days pass and no further news comes to you from Whitehall — no fulfilment of this airy promise — perhaps you will regard things differently, and come to see where your interest really lies. Remember, then, that we need skilled soldiers as leaders for our movement, and that an assured welcome awaits you. Remember, too — this for the mercenary you represent yourself — that the leaders now will be the leaders still when the task is accomplished, and that theirs will be the abiding rewards. Meanwhile, Randal, the bottle's not half done. So sit you down again, and let us talk of other matters."

Going home towards dusk, the thing that most intrigued the Colonel was the dangerous frankness that Tucker had used with him, trusting a man in his desperate case with a secret so weighty upon no more than his pledged word and what Tucker remembered of him in the creditable state from which he had long since fallen. Reflection, however, diminished his wonder. Tucker had divulged no facts whose betrayal could seriously impair the plotters. He had mentioned no names; he had no more than vaguely alluded to a directing mind in Holland, which the Colonel guessed to be Algernon Sidney's, who was beyond the reach of the Stuart arm. For the rest, what had he told him? That there was a serious movement afoot to overthrow the Stuart dynasty, and restore the Commonwealth. Let Holles carry that tale to the authorities, and what would happen? He could impeach by name no man but Tucker; and all he could say of Tucker was that Tucker had told him these things. Tucker's word would be as good as Holles's before a justice. On the score of credit, Holles's antecedents would be the subject of inquiry, and the revelation of them would result in danger to himself alone.

Tucker had not been as ingenuous and confiding as he had at first supposed. He laughed a little to himself at his own simplicity. Then laughed again as he reviewed the proposal Tucker had made him. He might be desperate, but not desperate enough for that — not yet. He caressed his neck affectionately. He had no mind to feel a rope tightening about it. Nor would he yet despair because of what Tucker, largely for the purposes of his own advocacy, had said of Albemarle. The more he considered it, away from Tucker now, the more persuaded was he of Albemarle's sincerity and good intentions.

CHAPTER VI

MR. ETHEREDGE PRESCRIBES

ON his return to the Paul's Head from that treasonable talk with Tucker, the Colonel found a considerable excitement presiding over that usually peaceful and well-conducted hostelry. The common room was thronged, which was not in itself odd, considering the time of day; what was odd was the noisy, vehement babble of the normally quiet, soberly spoken merchants who for the main part composed its custom. Mrs. Quinn was there listening to the unusually shrill voice of her bookseller-suitor Coleman, and her round red face, which the Colonel had never seen other than creased and puckered in smiles of false joviality, was solemn for once and had lost some of its normally high colour. Near at hand hovered the drawer, scraping imaginary crumbs from the table with his wooden knife, as a pretext for remaining to listen. And so engrossed was his mistress that she left his eavesdropping unreproved.

Yet, for all her agitation, she had a coy glance for the Colonel as he stalked through, with that lofty detachment and arrogant unconcern of his surroundings which she found so entirely admirable in him. It was not long before she followed him into the little parlour at the back, where she found him stretched at his ease on his favourite seat under the window, having cast aside sword and hat. He was in the act of loading a pipe from a leaden tobacco-jar.

"Lord, Colonel! Here be dreadful news," she told him.

He looked up, cocking an eyebrow.

"You'll have heard?" she added. "It is the talk of the Town."

He shook his head. "Nay, I heard nothing dreadful. I

met a friend, an old friend, over there by the Flower of
Luce, and I've been with him these three hours. I talked
to no one else. What is this news?"

But she was frowning as she looked at him scrutinizingly
with her round blue eyes. Her mind was shifted by his light
words to her own more immediate concerns. He had met a
friend — an old friend. Not much in that to arouse anxiety, perhaps. But Mrs. Quinn moved now in constant dread
of influences that might set the Colonel on a sound worldly
footing likely to emancipate him from his dependence upon
herself. She had skilfully drawn from him enough of the details of his interview with Albemarle to realize that the help
upon which he counted from that quarter had not been
forthcoming. He had been put off with vague promises, and
Mrs. Quinn knew enough of her world not to be greatly per-
turbed by that. None the less she would have set all doubts
at rest by leading the Colonel into the relationship in which
she desired to hold him, but that as yet the Colonel mani-
fested no clear disposition to be led. And she was too crafty
a huntress to scare her quarry by premature and too direct
an onslaught. The only anxiety, yielding to which she might
have committed that imprudence, was on the score of the unexpected. She knew that the unexpected will sometimes
happen, and this mention of a friend — an old friend, with
whom he had spent some hours in intimate talk — was
disquieting. She would have liked to question him on the
subject of that friend, and might have done so but for his
insistent repetition of the question:

"What is this news?"

Recalled to it thus, the gravity of the news itself thrust out
the other matter from her mind.

"That the plague has broken out in the City itself — in a
house in Bearbinder Lane. It was brought by a Frenchman
from Long Acre, where he lived, and which he left upon find-

ing the pestilence to be growing in his neighbourhood. Yet
it seems he was already taken with the disease, which now
the wretch has brought to our threshold, as it were, without
benefit to himself."

The Colonel thought of Tucker and his scaremongering
emissaries.

"Perhaps it is not true," said he.

"Aye, but it is. Beyond a doubt. It was put about by a
preacher rogue from the steps of Paul's to-day. At first folk
did not believe him. But they went to Bearbinder Lane, and
there found the house shut up, and guarded by command of
my Lord Mayor. And they do say that Sir John Lawrence is
gone to Whitehall to take order about this, to concert measures for staying the spread of the pestilence; they are to close
playhouses and all other places where people come together,
which will likely mean that they will be closing taverns and
eating-houses. And what should I do in that case?"

"Nay, nay," Holles comforted her. "It will hardly come
to that. Men must eat and drink or they starve, and that's
as bad as the pestilence."

"To be sure it is. But they'll never think of that in their
zeal and their sudden godliness — for they'll be in a muck-
sweat o' godliness now that they see what a visitation has
been brought upon us by the vices of the Court. And this to
happen at such a time, with the Dutch fleet, as they say,
about to attack the coast!"

She railed on. Disturbed out of her self-centred existence
into a consideration of the world's ills now that she found
herself menaced by them, she displayed a prodigious volu-
bility upon topics that hitherto she had completely ignored.

And the substance of her news was true enough. The Lord
Mayor was at that very moment at Whitehall urging immediate and drastic measures for combating the spread of the
pestilence, and one of these measures was the instant closing

of the playhouses. But since he did not at the same time
urge the closing of the churches, in which the congregating of
people was at least as dangerous as in the theatres, it was
assumed at Court that Sir John was the cat's-paw of the
Puritans who sought to make capital out of the pestilence.
Besides, the visitation was one that confined itself to the
poorer quarters and the lower orders. Heaven would never
be so undiscriminating as to permit this horrible disease to
beset persons of quality. And then, too, Whitehall's mind
at the moment was over-full of other matters: there were
these rumours that the Dutch fleet was out, and that was
quite sufficient to engage such time and attention as could
be spared from pleasure by the nation's elect, following in
the footsteps of their pleasure-loving King. Also a good
many of the nation's elect were exercised at the time by personal grievances in connection with the fleet and the war.
Of these perhaps the most disgruntled — as he was certainly
the most eminent — was His Grace of Buckingham, who
found the nation sadly negligent of the fact that he had come
all the way from York, and his lord-lieutenancy there, to
offer her his valuable services in her hour of need.

He had requested the command of a ship, a position to
which his rank and his talents fully entitled him, in his own
view. That such a request would be refused had never entered his calculations. But refused it was. There were two
factors working against him. The first was that the Duke of
York cordially disliked him and neglected no chance of
mortifying him; the second was that the Duke of York, being Lord Admiral of the Fleet, desired to take no risks. There
were many good positions from which capable naval men
could be excluded to make way for sprigs of the nobility.
But the command of a man-of-war was not one of these.
Buckingham was offered a gun-brig. Considering that the
offer came from the King's brother, he could not resent it in

the terms his hot blood prompted. But what he could do to mark his scorn, he did. He refused the gun-brig, and enlisted as a volunteer aboard a flag-ship. But here at once a fresh complication arose. As a Privy Councillor he claimed the right of seat and voice in all councils of war, in which capacity it is probable he might have done even more damage than in command of one of the great ships. Again the Duke of York's opposition foiled him, whereupon in a rage he posted from Portsmouth to Whitehall to lay his plaint before his crony the King. The Merry Monarch may have wavered; it may have vexed him not to be able to satisfy the handsome rake who understood so well the arts of loosening laughter; but between his own brother and Buckingham there can have been no choice. And so Charles could not help him.

Buckingham had remained, therefore, at Court, to nurse his chagrin, and to find his way circuitously into the strange history of Colonel Randal Holles. His grace possessed, as you know, a mercurial temperament which had not yet — although he was now approaching forty — lost any of its liveliness. Such natures are readily consoled, because they readily find distractions. It was not long before he had forgotten, in new and less creditable pursuits, not only the humbling of his dignity, but even the circumstance that his country was at war. Dryden has summed him up in a single line: He "was everything by starts, and nothing long." The phrase applies as much to Buckingham's moods as to his talents; it epitomizes the man's whole character.

His friend George Etheredge, that other gifted rake who had leapt into sudden fame a year ago with his comedy "The Comic Revenge," had been deafening his ears with praises of the beauty and talent of that widely admired and comparatively newly discovered actress Sylvia Farquharson. At first Buckingham had scoffed at his friend's enthusiasm.

"Such heat of rhetoric to describe a playhouse baggage!"
he had yawned. "For a man of your parts, George, I protest
you're nauseatingly callow."

"You flatter me in seeking to reprove," Etheredge laughed.
"To be callow despite the years is to bear the mark of greatness. Whom the gods love are callow always; for whom the
gods love die young, whatever be their age."

"You aim at paradox, I suppose. God help me!"

"No paradox at all. Whom the gods love never grow old,"
Etheredge explained himself. "They never come to suffer
as do you from jaded appetites."

"You may be right," his grace admitted gloomily. "Pre-
scribe me a tonic."

"That is what I was doing: Sylvia Farquharson, at the
Duke's House."

"Bah! A play actress! A painted doll on wires! Twenty
years ago your prescription might have served."

"You admit that you grow old. Superfluous admission!
But this, let me perish, is no painted doll. This is an incar-
nation of beauty and talent."

"So I've heard of others that had neither."

"And let me add that she is virtuous."

Buckingham stared at him, opening his lazy eyes. "What
may that be?" he asked.

"The chief drug in my prescription."

"But does it exist, or is your callowness deeper than I
thought?" quoth Buckingham.

"Come and see," Mr. Etheredge invited him.

"Virtue," Buckingham objected, "is not visible."

"Like beauty, it dwells in the beholder's eye. That's why
you've never seen it, Bucks."

To the Duke's playhouse in Lincoln's Inn Fields his disgruntled grace suffered himself, in the end, to be conducted.
He went to scoff. He remained to worship. You already

know — having overheard the garrulous Mr. Pepys — how from his box, addressing his companion in particular and the whole house in general, the ducal author loudly announced that he would give his muse no rest until he should have produced a play with a part worthy of the superb talents of Miss Farquharson.

His words were reported to her. They bore with them a certain flattery to which it was impossible that she should be impervious. She had not yet settled herself completely into this robe of fame that had been thrust upon her. She continued unspoiled, and she did not yet condescendingly accept such utterances from the great as no more than the proper tribute to her gifts. Such praise from one so exalted, himself a distinguished author and a boon companion of the King's, set a climax upon the triumphs that lately she had been garnering.

It prepared her for the ducal visit to the green room, which followed presently. She was presented by Mr. Etheredge with whom she was already acquainted, and she stood shyly before the tall, supremely elegant duke, under the gaze of his bold eyes.

In his golden periwig he looked at this date not a year more than thirty, despite the hard life he had lived from boyhood. As yet he had come to none of that grossness to be observed in the portrait which Sir Peter Lely painted some years later. He was still the handsomest man at Charles's Court, with his long-shaped, dark blue eyes under very level brows, his fine nose and chin, and his humorous, sensitive, sensual mouth. In shape and carriage he was of an extraordinary grace that drew all eyes upon him. Yet at sight, instinctively, Miss Farquharson disliked him. She apprehended under all that beauty of person something sinister. She shrank inwardly and coloured a little under the appraising glance of those bold, handsome eyes, which seemed to penetrate too far. Reason and ambition argued her out of that instinctive shrinking. Here was one whose approval carried weight and would set the seal upon her fame, one whose good graces could maintain her firmly on the eminence to which she had so laboriously climbed. He was a man whom, in spite of all instinctive warnings, she must use with consideration and a reasonable submission.

On his side, the Duke, already captivated by her grace and beauty upon the stage, found himself lost in admiration now that at close quarters he beheld her slim loveliness. For lovely she was, and the blush which his scrutiny had drawn to her cheeks, heightening that loveliness, almost disposed him to believe Etheredge's incredible assertion of her virtue. Shyness may be counterfeited and the simpers of unsophistication are easily assumed; but a genuine blush is not to be commanded.

His grace bowed, low, the curls of his wig swinging forward like the ears of a water-spaniel.

"Madam," he said, "I would congratulate you were I not more concerned to congratulate myself for having witnessed your performance, and still more Lord Orrery, your present author. Him I not only congratulate but envy — a hideous, cankering emotion, which I shall not conquer until I have written you a part at least as great as his Katherine. You smile?"

"It is for gratification at your grace's promise."

"I wonder now," said he, his eyes narrowing, his lips smiling a little. "I wonder is that the truth, or is it that you think I boasted? that such an achievement is not within my compass? I'll confess frankly that until I saw you it was not. But you have made it so, my dear."

"If I have done that, I shall, indeed, have deserved well of my audience," she answered, but lightly, laughing a little, as if to discount the high-flown compliment.

"As well, I trust, as I shall have deserved of you," said he. "The author must always deserve the best of his puppets."

"Deserve, aye. But how rarely does he get his deserts!"

"Surely you, Bucks, have little reason to complain," gibed Etheredge. "In my case, now, it is entirely different."

"It is, George — entirely," his grace agreed, resenting the interruption. "You are the rarity. You have always found better than you deserved. I have never found it until this moment." And his eyes upon Miss Farquharson gave point to his meaning.

When at length they left her, her sense of exaltation was all gone. She could not have told you why, but the Duke of Buckingham's approval uplifted her no longer. Almost did she wish that she might have gone without it. And when Betterton came smiling good-naturedly, to offer her his congratulations upon this conquest, he found her bemused and troubled.

Bemused, too, did Etheredge find the Duke as they drove back together to Wallingford House.

"Almost, I think," said he, smiling, "that already you find my despised prescription to your taste. Persevered with it may even restore you your lost youth."

"What I ask myself," said Buckingham, "is why you should have prescribed her for me instead of for yourself."

"I am like that," said Etheredge, — "the embodiment of self-sacrifice. Besides, she will have none of me — though I am ten years younger than you are, fully as handsome and almost as unscrupulous. The girl's a prude, and I never learnt the way to handle prudes. Faith, it's an education in itself."

"Is it?" said Buckingham. "I must undertake it, then."

And undertake it he did with all the zest of one who loved learning and the study of unusual subjects.

Daily now he was to be seen in a box at the theatre in Lincoln's Inn Fields, and daily he sent her, in token of his respectful homage, gifts of flowers and comfits. He would have added jewels, but that the wiser Etheredge restrained him.

"Ne brusquez pas l'affaire," was the younger man's advice. "You'll scare her by precipitancy, and so spoil all. Such a conquest as this requires infinite patience."

His grace suffered himself to be advised, and set a restraint upon his ardour, using the greatest circumspection in the visits which he paid her almost daily after the performance. He confined the expressions of admiration to her histrionic art, and, if he touched upon her personal beauty and grace, it was ever in association with her playing, so that its consideration seemed justified by the part that he told her he was conceiving for her.

Thus subtly did he seek to lull her caution and intoxicate her senses with the sweet poison of flattery, whilst discussing with her the play he was to write — which, in his own phrase, was to immortalize himself and her, thereby eternally uniting them. There was in this more than a suggestion of a spiritual bond, a marriage of their respective arts to give life to his dramatic conception, so aloof from material and personal considerations that she was deceived into swallowing at least half the bait. Nor was it vague. His grace did not neglect to furnish it with a certain form. His theme, he told her, was the immortal story of Laura and her Petrarch set in the warm glitter of an old Italian frame. Nor was that all he told her. He whipped his wits to some purpose, and sketched for her the outline of a first act of tenderness and power.

At the end of a week he announced to her that this first act was already written.

"I have laboured day and night," he told her; "driven relentlessly by the inspiration you have furnished me. So great is this that I must regard the thing as more yours than mine, or I shall do it when you have set upon it the seal of your approval." Abruptly he asked her, as if it were a condition predetermined: "When will you hear me read it?"

"Were it not better that your grace should first complete the work?" she asked him.

He was taken aback, almost horror-stricken, to judge by his expression.

"Complete it!" he cried; "without knowing whether it takes the shape that you desire?"

"But it is not what I desire, your grace . . ."

"What else, then? Is it not something that I am doing specially for you, moved to it by yourself? And shall I complete it tormented the while by doubts as to whether you will consider it worthy of your talents when it is done? Would you let a dressmaker complete your gown without ever a fitting to see how it becomes you? And is a play, then, less important than a garment? Is not a part, indeed, a sort of garment for the soul? Nay, now, if I am to continue I must have your assistance as I say. I must know how this first act appears to you, how far my Laura does justice to your powers; and I must discuss with you the lines which the remainder of the play shall follow. Therefore again I ask you — and in the sacred cause of art I defy you to deny me — when will you hear what I have written?"

"Why, since your grace does me so much honour, when you will."

It was intoxicating, this homage to her talent from one of his gifts and station, the intimate of princes, the close associate of kings, and it stifled, temporarily at least, the last qualm of her intuitions which had warned her against this radiant gentleman. They had become so friendly and intimate in this week, and yet his conduct had been so respectful and circumspect throughout, that clearly her instincts had misled her at that first meeting.

"When I will," said he. "That is to honour me, indeed. Shall it be to-morrow, then?"

"If your grace pleases, and you will bring the act . . ."

"Bring it?" He raised his eyebrows. His lip curled a little as he looked round the dingy green room. "You do not propose, child, that I should read it here?" He laughed in dismissal of the notion.

"But where else, then?" she asked, a little bewildered.

"Where else but in my own house? What other place were proper?"

"Oh!" She was dismayed a little. An uneasiness, entirely instinctive, beset her once again. It urged her to draw back, to excuse herself. Yet reason combated instinct. It were a folly to offend him by a refusal? Such a thing would be affronting by its implication of mistrust; and she was very far from wishing to affront him.

He observed the trouble in her blue eyes as she now regarded him, but affected not to observe it, and waited for her to express herself. She did so after a moment's pause, faltering a little.

"But . . . at your house . . . Why, what would be said of me, your grace? To come there alone . . ."

"Child! Child!" he interrupted her, his tone laden with gentle reproach. "Can you think that I should so lightly expose you to the lewd tongues of the Town? Alone? Give your mind peace. I shall have some friends to keep you in countenance and to join you as audience to hear what I have written. There shall be one or two ladies from the King's House; perhaps Miss Seymour from the Duke's here will join us; there is a small part for her in the play; and there shall be some friends of my own; maybe even His Majesty will honour us. We shall make a merry party at supper, and after supper you shall pronounce upon my Laura whom you are to incarnate. Is your hesitancy conquered?"

It was, indeed. Her mind was in a whirl. A supper party at Wallingford House, at which in a sense she was to be the guest of honour, and which the King himself would attend! She would have been mad to hesitate. It was to enter the great world at a stride. Other actresses had done it — Moll Davis and little Nelly from the King's House; but they had done it upon passports other than those of histrionic talent. She would have preferred that Miss Seymour should not have been included. She had no great opinion of Miss Seymour's conduct. But there was a small part for her, and that was perhaps a sufficient justification.

And so she cast aside her hesitation, and gladdened his grace by consenting to be present.

CHAPTER VII

THE PRUDE

On the evening of the day that had seen the meeting between Holles and Tucker, at about the same hour that Sir John Lawrence was vainly representing at Whitehall the expediency of closing the theatres and other places of congregation in view of the outbreak of plague within the City itself, His Grace of Buckingham was sitting down to supper with a merry company in the great dining-room of Wallingford House.

Eleven sat down to a table that was laid for twelve. The chair on the Duke's right stood empty. The guest of honour, Miss Farquharson, had not yet arrived. At the last moment she had sent a message that she was unavoidably detained for some little time at home, and that, if on this account it should happen that she must deny herself the honour of sitting down to supper at his grace's table, at least she would reach Wallingford House in time for the reading with which his grace was to delight the company.

It was in part a fiction. There was nothing to detain Miss Farquharson beyond a revival of her uneasy intuitions, which warned her against the increase of intimacy that would attend her inclusion in the Duke's supper-party. The play, however, was another affair. Therefore she would so time her arrival that she would find supper at an end and the reading about to begin. To be entirely on the safe side, she would present herself at Wallingford House two hours after the time for which she had been bidden.

His grace found her message vexatious, and he would have postponed supper until her arrival but that his guests did not permit him to have his own way in the matter. As the truth was that there was no first act in existence, for the Duke had not yet written a line of it and probably never would, and that supper was to provide the whole entertainment, it follows that this would be protracted, and that however late she came she was likely still to find the party at table. Therefore her late arrival could be no grave matter in the end. Meanwhile, the empty chair on the Duke's right awaited her.

They were a very merry company, and as time passed they grew merrier. There was Etheredge, of course, the real promoter of the whole affair, and this elegant, talented libertine who was ultimately — and at a still early age — to kill himself with drinking was doing the fullest justice to the reputation which the winecup had already earned him. There was Sedley, that other gifted profligate, whose slim, graceful person and almost feminine beauty gave little indication of the roistering soul within. Young Rochester should have been of the party, but he was at that moment in the Tower, whither he had been sent as a consequence of his utterly foolish and unnecessary attempt to abduct Miss Mallet two nights ago. But Sir Harry Stanhope filled his vacant place — or, at least, half-filled it, for whilst Rochester was both wit and libertine, young Stanhope was a libertine only. And of course there was Sir Thomas Ogle, that boon companion of Sedley's, and two other gentlemen whose names have not survived. The ladies were of less distinguished lineage. There was the ravishingly fair little Anne Seymour from the Duke's House, her white shoulders displayed in a *décolletage* that outraged even the daring fashion of the day. Seated between Stanhope and Ogle, she was likely to become a bone of contention between them in a measure as they drowned restraint in wine. There was Moll Davis from the King's House seated on the Duke's left, with Etheredge immediately below her and entirely engrossing her, and there

was that dark, statuesque, insolent-eyed Jane Howden,
languidly spreading her nets for Sir Charles Sedley, who
showed himself willing and eager to be taken in them. A
fourth lady on Ogle's left was making desperate but futile
attempts to draw Sir Thomas's attention from Miss Seymour.

The feast was worthy of the exalted host, worthy of that
noble chamber with its richly carved wainscoting, its lofty
ceiling carried on graceful fluted pillars, lighted by a hundred
candles in colossal gilded girandoles. The wine flowed freely,
and the wit, flavoured with a salt that was not entirely Attic,
flowed with it. Laughter swelled increasing ever in a measure
as the wit diminished. Supper was done, and still they kept
the table, over their wine, waiting for that belated guest
whose seat continued vacant.

Above that empty place sat the Duke — a dazzling figure
in a suit of shimmering white satin with diamond buttons
that looked like drops of water. Enthroned in his great
gilded chair, he seemed to sit apart, absorbed, aloof, fretted
by the absence of the lady in whose honour he had spread
this feast, and annoyed with himself for being so fretted, as
if he were some callow schoolboy at his first assignation.

Alone of all that company he did not abuse the wine.
Again and again he waved away the velvet-footed lackeys
that approached to pour for him. Rarely he smiled as some
lively phrase leapt forth to excite the ready laughter of his
guests. His eyes observed them, noting the flushed faces and
abandoned attitudes as the orgy mounted to its climax.
He would have restrained them, but that for a host to do so
were in his view an offence against good manners. Gloomily,
abstractedly, his eyes wandered from the disorder of the
table, laden with costly plate of silver and of gold, with
sparkling crystal, with pyramids of fragrant fruits and
splendours of flowers that already were being used as missiles
by his hilarious guests.

From the chilly heights of his own unusual sobriety he found them gross and tiresome; their laughter jarred on him. He shifted his weary glance to the curtains masking the long windows. They draped the window-spaces almost from floor to ceiling, wedges of brilliant colour — between blue and green, upon which golden peacocks strutted — standing out sharply from the sombre richness of the dark wainscot. He strained his ears to catch some rumble of wheels in the courtyard under those windows, and he frowned as a fresh and prolonged burst of laughter from his guests beat upon his ears to shut out all other sounds.

Then Sedley in a maudlin voice began to sing a very questionable song of his own writing, whilst Miss Howden made a comedy of pretending to silence him. He was still singing it, when Stanhope sprang up and mounted his chair, holding aloft a dainty shoe of which he had stripped Miss Seymour, and calling loudly for wine. Pretty little Anne would have snatched back her footgear but that she was restrained by Ogle, who not only held her firmly, but had pulled her into his lap, where she writhed and screamed and giggled all in one.

Solemnly, as if it were the most ordinary and natural of things, a lackey poured wine into the shoe, as Stanhope bade him. And Stanhope, standing above them, gay and flushed, proposed a toast the terms of which I have no intention of repeating.

He was midway through when the twin doors behind the Duke were thrown open by a chamberlain, whose voice rang solemnly above the general din.

"Miss Sylvia Farquharson, may it please your grace."

There was a momentary pause as of surprise; then louder than ever rose their voices in hilarious acclamation of the announcement.

Buckingham sprang up and round, and several others rose

with him to give a proper welcome to the belated guest.
Stanhope, one foot on his chair, the other on the table,
bowed to her with a flourish of the slipper from which he
had just drunk.

She stood at gaze, breathless and suddenly pale, on the
summit of the three steps that led down to the level of the
chamber, her startled, dilating eyes pondering fearfully that
scene of abandonment. She saw little Anne Seymour, whom
she knew, struggling and laughing in the arms of Sir Thomas
Ogle. She saw Etheredge, whom she also knew, sitting with
flushed face and leering eyes, an arm about the statuesque
bare neck of Miss Howden, her lovely dark head upon his
shoulder; she saw Stanhope on high, capering absurdly, his
wig awry, his speech halting and indecorous; and she saw
some others in attitudes that even more boldly proclaimed
the licence presiding over this orgy to which she had been
bidden.

Lastly she saw the tall white figure of the Duke advancing
towards her, his eyes narrowed, a half-smile on his full lips,
both hands outheld in welcome. He moved correctly, with
that almost excessive grace that was his own, and he at
least showed no sign of the intoxication that marked the
guests at this Circean feast. But that afforded her no re-
assurance. From pale that they had been, her cheeks — her
whole body, it seemed to her — had flamed a vivid scarlet.
Now it was paling again, paling this time in terror and
disgust.

Fascinatedly she watched his grace's advance for a moment. Then incontinently she turned, and fled, with the
feelings of one who had looked down for a moment into the
pit of hell and drawn back in shuddering horror before being
engulfed.

Behind her fell a dead silence of astonishment. It endured
whilst you might have counted six. Then a great peal of

demoniac laughter came like an explosion to drive her fearfully onward.

Down the long panelled gallery she ran as we run in a nightmare, making for all her efforts but indifferent speed upon the polished, slippery floor, gasping for breath in her terror of a pursuit of which she fancied that already she heard the steps behind her. She reached the hall, darted across this, and across the vestibule, her light silk mantle streaming behind her, and so gained at last the open door, stared at by lackeys, who wondered, but made no attempt to stay her.

Too late came the shout from the pursuing Duke ordering them to bar her way. By then she was already in the courtyard, and running like a hare for the gateway that opened upon Whitehall. Out of this the hackney-coach that had brought her was at that moment slowly rumbling. Panting she overtook it, just as the driver brought it to a halt in obedience to her cry.

"To Salisbury Court," she gasped. "Drive quickly!"

She was in, and she had slammed the door as the Duke's lackeys — three of them — ran alongside the vehicle, bawling their commands to stop. She flung half her body through the window on the other side to countermand the order.

"Drive on! Drive quickly, in God's name!"

Had they still been in the courtyard, it is odds that the driver would not have dared proceed. But they were already through the gateway in Whitehall itself, and the coach swung round to the left in the direction of Charing Cross. Here in the open street the driver could defy the Duke's lackeys, and the latter dared not make any determined attempt to hinder him.

The coach rolled on, and Miss Farquharson sank back to breathe at last, to recover from her nameless terror and to regain her calm.

The Duke went back with dragging feet and scowling brow to be greeted by a storm of derision upon which in more sober mood his guests would hardly have ventured. He attempted to laugh with them, to dissemble the extent to which he had been galled. But he hardly made a success of it, and there was distinct ill-temper in the manner in which he flung himself down into his great chair. Mr. Etheredge, leaning across Miss Howden, laid a white jewelled hand on his friend's arm.

He alone of all the company, although he had probably drunk more deeply than any, showed no sign of intoxication beyond the faint flush about his eyes.

"I warned you," he said, "that the little prude is virtuous, and that she will require much patience. This is your chance to exercise it."

CHAPTER VIII

MR. ETHEREDGE ADVISES

TOWARDS midnight, when all the guests but Etheredge had departed, and the candles lighting the disordered room were guttering in their sconces, the Duke sat alone in council with the younger libertine. He had dismissed his servants; the doors were closed, and they were entirely private.

The Duke unburdened himself, bitterly and passionately. The patience which Etheredge counselled was altogether beyond him, he confessed. More than ever now, when, by the exercise of it, by moving circuitously to his ends, he had so scared the little prude that he was worse off than at the outset.

Etheredge smiled.

"You're a prodigiously ungrateful fellow. You go clumsily to work and then you blame me for the failure of your endeavours. Had you asked me, I could have told you what must happen with a parcel of fools and sluts who haven't learnt the art of carrying their wine in decent fashion. Had she arrived at the appointed time, whilst they were still sober, all might have been well. She might have come to share, in part, at least, their intoxication, and so she would have viewed their antics through eyes that wine had rendered tolerant and kindly. As it is, you merely offended her by a disgusting spectacle; and that is very far from anything that I advised."

"Be that as it may," said the ill-humoured Duke, "there is a laugh against me that is to be redeemed. I am for directer measures now."

"Directer measures?" Etheredge's brows went up. He

uttered a musical, scornful little laugh. "Is this your patience?"

"A pox on patience . . ."

"Then she is not for you. Wait a moment, my sweet Bucks. I have no illusions as to what you mean by direct measures. You are probably more sober than I am; but then I am more intelligent than you. Out of my intelligence let me inform your sobriety."

"Oh, come to the point."

"I am coming to it. If you mean to carry the girl off, I'll be reminding you that at law it's a hanging matter."

The Duke stared at him in disdainful amazement. Then he uttered a sharp laugh of derision.

"At law? Pray, my good George, what have I to do with the law?"

"By which you mean that you are above it."

"That is where usually I have found myself."

"Usually. The times are not usual. The times are monstrous unusual. Rochester, no doubt, thought as you do when he carried off Miss Mallet on Friday night. Yet Rochester is in the Tower in consequence."

"And you think they'll hang him?" Buckingham sneered.

"No. They won't hang him, because the abduction was an unnecessary piece of buffoonery — because he is ready to mend Miss Mallet's honour by marrying her."

"Let me perish, George, but you're more drunk than I thought. Miss Mallet is a person of importance in the world with powerful friends . . ."

"Miss Farquharson, too, has friends. Betterton is her friend, and he wields a deal of influence. You don't lack for enemies to stir things up against you . . ."

"Oh, but a baggage of the theatre!" Buckingham was incredulously scornful.

"These baggages of the theatre are beloved of the people,

and the mood of the people of London at present is not one I should care to ruffle were I Duke of Buckingham. There is a war to excite them, and the menace of the plague to scare them into making examinations of conscience. There are preachers, too, going up and down the Town, proclaiming that this is a visitation of God upon the new Sodom. The people are listening. They are beginning to point to Whitehall as the source of all the offences that have provoked the wrath of Heaven. And they don't love you, Bucks, any more than they love me. They don't understand us, and — to be plain — our names, yours and mine and several others, are beginning to stink in their nostrils. Give them such an argument as this against you, and they'll see the law fulfilled. Never doubt that. The English are an easy-going people on the surface, which has led some fools to their undoing by abusing them. The spot where His Majesty's father lost his head is within easy view of these windows.

"And so I tell you that the thing which you intend to do, which would be fraught with risks at any time, is certain destruction to you at this present. The very eminence upon which you count for safety would prove your undoing. The fierce light that beats upon a throne beats upon those who are about it. A more obscure man might do this thing with less risk to himself than you would run."

His grace discarded at last his incredulous scorn, and gave himself up to gloomy thought. Etheredge, leaning back in his chair, watched him, faintly, cynically amused. At length the Duke stirred and raised his handsome eyes to his friend's face.

"Don't sit there grinning — damn you! — advise me."

"To what end, since you won't follow my advice?"

"Still, let me hear it. What is it?"

"Forget the girl, and look for easier game. You are hardly young enough for such an arduous and tiring hunt as this."

His grace damned him roundly for a scoffer, and swore that he would not abandon the affair; that, at whatever cost, he would pursue it.

"Why, then, you must begin by effacing the bad impression you have made to-night. That will not be easy; indeed, it is the most difficult step of all. But there are certain things in your favour. For one, you were not, for a wonder, drunk, yourself, when you rose to welcome her. Let us hope that she observed it. Pay her a visit on Monday at the theatre to tender your most humble apologies for the disgraceful conduct of your guests. Had you known them capable of such abandoned behaviour, you would never have bidden her make one of such a company. You will profess yourself glad that she departed instantly; that is what you would, yourself, have advised."

"But I pursued her. My lackeys sought to stay her coach."

"Naturally — so that you might make her your apologies, and approve a departure which in the circumstances you must have urged. Damme, Bucks! You have no invention, and you desire to deem yourself a dramatist."

"You think she will believe me?" His grace was dubious.

"That will depend upon your acting, and you are reputed something of an actor. God knows you played the mountebank once to some purpose. Have you forgotten?"

"No, no. But will it serve, do you think?"

"As a beginning. But you must follow it up. You must reveal yourself in a new character. Hitherto she has known you, first by repute and to-night by experience, a rake. That in itself makes her wary of you. Let her behold you as a hero; say, as a rescuer of beauty in distress — herself in the distressful part. Deliver her from some deadly peril, and thereby earn her gratitude and her wonder at your prowess.

Women love a hero. So be heroical, and who knows what good fortune may attend your heroism."

"And the deadly peril?" quoth the Duke gloomily, almost suspecting that his friend was rallying him. "Where shall I find that?"

"If you wait to find it, you may have long to wait. You must, yourself, provide it. A little contriving, a little invention, will soon supply what you lack."

"Can you propose anything? Can you be more than superiorly vague?"

"I hope so. With a little thought . . . "

"Then, in God's name, think."

Etheredge laughed at his host's vehemence. He brimmed himself a cup of wine, surveyed the rich glow of it in the candlelight and drank it off.

"Inspiration flows. Invention stirs within me. Now listen." And sitting forward he propounded a plan of campaign with that rascally readiness of wit that was at once his glory and his ruin.

CHAPTER IX

ALBEMARLE PROPOSES

NED TUCKER did not long leave his proposal to Holles unconfirmed. He sought him in the matter again at the Paul's Head three days later, on the Sunday, and sat long in talk with him in the little parlour, to the profound disquieting of Mrs. Quinn, who had observed from the gentleman's bearing and apparel that he was a person of consequence.

He found the Colonel a little more malleable to-day, a little less insistent upon serving only governments *in esse.* The fact was that, as day followed day without word from Albemarle, Holles approached the conclusion that things were indeed as Tucker had represented them. His hopes sank, and his dread of that score of his which was daily mounting at the Paul's Head added to his despair.

Still, he did not altogether yield to Tucker's persuasions; but neither did he discourage him when the latter promised to visit him again on the morrow, bringing another old friend of their Parliament days. And on the Monday, true to his promise, Tucker came again, accompanied this time by a gentleman some years his senior, named Rathbone, with whom Colonel Holles recalled some slight acquaintance. This time they came with a very definite proposal, empowered, so they told him, by one whose name they would not yet utter, but which, if uttered, must remove his every doubt.

"For that, Randal, you will accept our word, I know," said the grave Tucker.

Holles nodded his agreement, and the proposal was disclosed. It offered him a position which in an established government would have been dazzling. It was dazzling even as things were, to one in his desperate case, driven to the need of making a gambler's throw. If on the one side he probably set his head, at least the stake they offered could hardly have been greater.

And they tempted him further by revelations of how far their preparations were advanced, and how thorough these were.

"Heaven," said Rathbone, "is on our side. It has sent this plague to stir men to bethink themselves of the rulers they have chosen. Our agents have discovered four cases in the City to-day: one in Wood Street, one in Fenchurch Street, and two in Crooked Lane. The authorities hoped to keep it from the knowledge of the people. But we are seeing to that. At this moment our preachers are proclaiming it, spreading terror that men may be driven by it to the paths of righteousness."

"When the devil was sick the devil a monk would be," said Holles. "I understand."

"Then you should see that all is ready, the mine is laid," Tucker admonished him. "This is your opportunity, Randal. If you delay now . . ."

A tap at the door interrupted him. Tucker bounded up, propelled by his uneasy conspirator's conscience. Rathbone, too, glanced round uneasily.

"Why, what's to startle you?" said the Colonel quietly, smiling to behold their fears. "It is but my good hostess."

She came in from the common room bearing a letter that had just been brought for Colonel Holles.

He took it, wondering; then, observing the great seal, a little colour crept into his cheeks. He spread the sheet, and read, under the observing eyes of his friends and his hostess, and they were all alike uneasy.

Twice he read that letter before he spoke. The unexpected

had happened, and it had happened at the eleventh hour, barely in time to arrest him on the brink of what might well prove a precipice. Thus he saw it now, his vision altering with his fortunes.

"Luck has stood your friend sooner than we could have hoped," wrote Albemarle. "A military post in the Indies has, as I learn from letters just received, fallen vacant. It is an important command full worthy of your abilities, and there, overseas, you will be safe from all inquisitions. If you will wait upon me here at the Cockpit this afternoon, you shall be further informed."

He begged his friends to excuse him a moment, took pen, ink, and paper from the sideboard and quickly wrote a few lines in answer.

When Mrs. Quinn had departed to convey that note to the messenger, and the door had closed again, the two uneasy conspirators started up. Questions broke simultaneously from both of them. For answer Holles placed Albemarle's letter on the table. Tucker snatched it up, and conned it, whilst over his shoulder Rathbone read it, too.

At last Tucker lowered the sheet, and his grave eyes fell again upon Holles.

"And you have answered — what?" he demanded.

"That I will wait upon his grace this afternoon as he requires of me."

"But to what end?" asked Rathbone. "You can't mean that you will accept employment from a government that is doomed."

The Colonel shrugged. "As I have told Tucker from the first, I serve governments; I do not make them."

"But just now . . ." Tucker was beginning.

"I wavered. It is true. But something else has been flung into the scales." And he held up Albemarle's letter.

They argued with him after that; but they argued vainly.

"If I am of value to your government when you shall have established it, you will know where to find me; and you will know from what has happened now that I am trustworthy."

"But your value to us is now, in the struggle that is coming. And it is for this that we are prepared to reward you richly."

He was not, however, to be moved. The letter from Albemarle had reached him an hour too soon.

At parting he assured them that their secret was safe with him, and that he would forget all that they had said. Since, still, they had disclosed no vital facts whose betrayal could frustrate their purpose, it was an almost unnecessary assurance.

They stalked out resentfully. But Tucker returned alone a moment later.

"Randal," he said, "it may be that upon reflection you will come to see the error of linking yourself to a government that cannot endure, to the service of a king against whom the hand of Heaven is already raised. You may come to prefer the greatness that we offer you in the future to this crust that Albemarle throws you at the moment. If you are wise, you will. If so, you know where to find me. Seek me there, and be sure of my welcome as of my friendship."

They shook hands and parted, and with a sigh and a smile Holles turned to load himself a pipe. He was not, he thought, likely to see Tucker again.

That afternoon he waited upon Albemarle, who gave him particulars of the appointment he had to offer. It was an office of importance, the pay was good, and so that Holles discharged his duties well, which the Duke had no occasion to doubt, there would be even better things in store for him before very long.

"The one thing to efface the past is a term of service now, wheresoever it may be. Hereafter when I commend you for some other place, here at home, perhaps, and I am asked what are your antecedents, I need but point to the stout service you will have done us in the Indies, and men will inquire no further. It is a temporary exile, but you may trust me to see that it endures no longer than is necessary."

No such advocacy was needed to induce Holles to accept an office that, after all, was of an importance far beyond anything for which he could reasonably have hoped. He said so frankly by way of expressing his deep gratitude.

"In that case, you will seek me again here to-morrow morning. Your commission shall be meanwhile made out."

The Colonel departed jubilant. At last — at long last — after infinite frowns, Fortune accorded him a smile. And she accorded it in the very nick of time, just as he was touching the very depths of his despair and ready to throw in his lot with a parcel of crazy fanatics who dreamed of another revolution.

So back to the Paul's Head he came with his soaring spirits, and called for a bottle of the best Canary. Mrs. Quinn read the omens shrewdly.

"Your affairs at Whitehall have prospered, then?" said she between question and assertion.

Holles reclined in an armchair, his legs, from which he had removed his boots, stretched luxuriously upon a stool, his head thrown back, a pipe between his lips.

"Aye. They've prospered. Beyond my deserts," said he, smiling at the ceiling.

"Never that, Colonel. For that's not possible." She beamed upon him, proffering the full stoup.

He sat up to take it, and looked at her, smiling.

"No doubt you're right. But I've gone without my deserts so long that I have lost all sense of them."

"There's others who haven't," said she; and timidly added a question upon the nature of his prosperity.

He paused to drink a quarter of the wine. Then, as he set down the vessel on the table at his elbow, he told her.

Her countenance grew overcast. He was touched to note it, inferring from this manifest regret at his departure that he had made a friend in Mrs. Quinn.

"And when do you go?" she asked him, oddly breathless.

"In a week's time."

She considered him, mournfully he thought; and he also thought that she lost some of her bright colour.

"And to the Indies!" she ejaculated slowly. "Lord! Among savages and heathen blacks! Why, you must be crazed to think of it."

"Beggars may not choose, ma'am. I go where I can find employment. Besides, it is not as bad as you imagine."

"But where's the need to go at all, when, as I've told you already, such a man as yourself should be thinking of settling down at home and taking a wife?"

She realized that the time had come to deliver battle. It was now or never. And thus she sent out a preliminary skirmishing party.

"Why, look at yourself," she ran on, before he could answer. "Look at the condition of you." And she pointed a denunciatory finger at the great hole in the heel of his right stocking. "You should be seeking a woman to take care of you, instead of letting your mind run on soldiering in foreign parts."

"Excellent advice," he laughed. "There is one difficulty only. Who takes a wife must keep a wife, and, if I stay in England, I shan't have enough to keep myself. So I think it'll be the Indies, after all."

She came to the table, and leaned upon it, facing him.

"You're forgetting something. There's many a woman well endowed, and there's many a man has taken a wife with a jointure who couldn't ha' taken a wife without."

"You said something of the kind before." Again he laughed. "You think I should be hunting an heiress. You think I have the figure for the part."

"I do," said she, to his astonishment. "You're a proper man, and you've a name and a position to offer. There's many a wealthy woman of modest birth would be glad of you, as you should be glad of her, since each would bring what the other lacks."

"Faith! You think of everything. Carry your good offices further than mere advice, Mrs. Quinn. Find me this wealthy and accommodating lady, and I'll consider the rejection of this Indian office. But you'll need to make haste, for there's only a week left."

It was a laughing challenge, made on the assumption that it would not be taken up, and, as she looked away uncomfortably under his glance, his laughter increased.

"That's not quite so easy as advising, is it?" he rallied her.

She commanded herself, and looked him squarely in the eyes.

"Oh, yes, it is," she assured him. "If you was serious I could soon produce the lady — a comely enough woman of about your own age, mistress of thirty thousand pounds and some property, besides."

That sobered him. He stared at her a moment; the pipe between his fingers.

"And she would marry a vagabond? Odds, my life! What ails her?"

"Naught ails her. If you was serious I'd present her."

"'Sblood! you make me serious. Thirty thousand pounds! Faith, that is serious enough. I could set up as a country squire on that."

"Then why don't you?"

Really, she was bewildering, he thought, with her calm assumptions that it was for him to say the word.

"Because there's no such woman."

"And if there was?"

"But there isn't."

"I tell you there is."

"Where is she, then?"

Mrs. Quinn moved away from the table, and round to his side of it.

"She is . . . here."

"Here?" he echoed.

She drew a step or two nearer, so that she was almost beside him.

"Here in this room," she insisted, softly.

He looked up at her, still uncomprehending. Then, as he observed the shy smile with which she sought to dissemble her agitation, the truth broke upon him at last.

The clay stem of his pipe snapped between his fingers, and he dived after the pieces, glad of any pretext to remove his eyes from her face and give him a moment in which to consider how he should conduct himself in this novel and surprising situation.

When he came up again, his face was flushed, which may have been from the lowering of his head. He wanted to laugh; but he realized that this would be utterly unpardonable. He rose, and set the pieces of the broken pipe on the table. Standing thus, his shoulder to her, he spoke gently, horribly embarrassed.

"I . . . I had no notion of . . . of your meaning . . ." And there he broke down.

But his embarrassment encouraged her. Again she came close.

"And now that you know it, Colonel?" she whispered.

"I . . . I don't know what to say."

His mind was beginning to recover its functions. He understood at last why a person of his shabby exterior and obvious neediness should have been given unlimited credit in this house.

"Then say nothing at all, Colonel dear," she was purring. "Save that you'll put from you all notion of sailing to the Indies."

"But . . . but my word is pledged already." It was a straw at which he clutched, desperately. And it was not a very fortunate one, for it suggested that his pledged word was the only obstacle.

The effect was to bring her closer still. She was almost touching him, as he stood there, still half averted, and she actually leaned against him, and set a hand upon his shoulder as she spoke, coaxingly, persuasively.

"But it was pledged before . . . before you knew of this. His grace will understand. He'll never hold you to it. You've but to explain."

"I . . . I couldn't. I couldn't," he cried weakly.

"Then I can."

"You?" He looked at her.

She was pale, but resolute. "Yes, me," she answered him. "If your pledge is all that holds you, I'll take coach at once and go to Whitehall. George Monk'll see me, or if he won't his Duchess will. I knew her well in the old days, when I was a young girl, and she was a sempstress glad to earn a groat where she could. Nan Clarges'll never deny herself to an old friend. So if you but say the word, I'll soon deliver you from this pledge of yours."

His face lengthened. He looked away again.

"That is not all, Mrs. Quinn," he said, very gently. "The truth is . . . I am not of a . . . a nature to make a woman happy."

This she deemed mere coyness, and swept it briskly aside. "I'd take the risk of that."

"But . . . but . . . you see I've lived this roving life of

mine so long, that I do not think I could ever settle. Besides, ma'am, what have I to offer?"

"If I am satisfied with my bargain, why take thought for that?"

"I must. The fact is, I am touched, deeply touched. I did not think I had it in me to arouse the affection, or even the regard, of any woman. Even so, ma'am, whilst it moves me, it does not change my purpose. I am not a marrying man."

"But . . ."

He raised a hand, dominantly, to check her. He had found the correct formula at last, and he meant to keep to it.

"Useless to argue, ma'am. I know my mind. My reasons are as I have said, and so is the fact. I am touched; I am prodigiously touched, and grateful. But there it is."

His firmness turned her white with mortification. To have offered herself, and to have been refused! To have this beggar turn his shoulder upon her, finding her so little to his taste that not even her thirty thousand pounds could gild her into attractiveness! It was a bitter draught, and it called up bitterness from the depths of her soul. As she considered him now with her vivid blue eyes, her face grew mottled. She was moved to sudden hatred of him. Nothing short of killing him could, she felt, extinguish that tormenting hate.

She felt impelled to break into violent recriminations, yet could find nothing upon which to recriminate. If only she could have thrown it in his face that he had afforded her encouragement, trifled with her affections, lured her on, to put this terrible affront upon her, she might have eased herself of some of the gall within her. But she could charge him with nothing that would bear the form of words.

And so she considered him in silence, her abundant bosom heaving, her eyes growing almost baleful in their glance, whilst he stood awkwardly before her, his gaze averted, staring through the open window, and making no attempt to add anything to what already he had said.

At last on a long indrawn breath she moved.

"I see," she said quietly. "I am sorry to have . . ."

"Please!" he exclaimed, throwing up his hand again to arrest her, an infinite pity stirring in him.

She walked to the door, moving a little heavily. She opened it, and then paused under the lintel. Over her shoulder she spoke to him again.

"Seeing that things is like this, perhaps you'll make it convenient to find another lodging not later than to-morrow."

He inclined his head a little in agreement.

"Naturally . . ." he was beginning, when the door closed after her with a bang and he was left alone.

"Phew!" he breathed, as he sank limply into his chair again. He passed a hand wearily across his brow, and found it moist.

CHAPTER X

BUCKINGHAM DISPOSES

COLONEL HOLLES hummed softly to himself as he dressed with care to keep his momentous appointment at the Cockpit, and when his toilet was completed you would scarcely have known him for the down-at-heel adventurer of yesterday, so fine did he appear.

Early that morning he had emptied the contents of his purse upon the bed, and counted up his fortune. It amounted to thirty-five pounds and some shillings. And Albemarle had promised him that, together with his commission, he should that morning receive an order on the Treasury for thirty pounds to meet his disbursements on equipment and the rest. He must, he considered, do credit to his patron. He argued that it was a duty. To present himself again at Whitehall in his rags were to disgrace the Duke of Albemarle; there might be introductions, and he would not have his grace blush for the man he was protecting.

Therefore, immediately after an early breakfast — at which, for once, he had been waited upon, not by Mrs. Quinn, but by Tim the drawer — he had sallied forth and made his way to Paternoster Row. There, yielding to the love of fine raiment inseparable from the adventurous temperament and to the improvident disposition that accompanies it, and also having regard to the officially military character he was about to assume, he purchased a fine coat of red camlet laced with gold, and small-clothes, stockings, and cravat in keeping. By the time he added a pair of boots of fine Spanish leather, a black silk sash, a new, gold-broidered baldric, and a black beaver with a trailing red plume, he found that fully three quarters of his slender

fortune was dissipated, and there remained in his purse not
above eight pounds. But that should not trouble a man
who within a couple of hours would have pocketed an order
upon the Treasury. He had merely anticipated the natural
course of events, and counted himself fortunate to be,
despite his reduced circumstances, still able to do so.

He had returned then with his bundle to the Paul's Head,
and, as he surveyed himself now in his mirror, freshly
shaven, his long thick gold-brown hair elegantly curled, and
a clump of its curls caught in a ribbon on his left, the long
pear-shaped ruby glowing in his ear, his throat encased in
a creaming froth of lace, and the fine red coat that sat so
admirably upon his shoulders, he smiled at the memory of
the scarecrow he had been as lately as yesterday, and assured himself that he did not look a day over thirty.

He created something of a sensation when he appeared
below in all this finery, and, since it was unthinkable that
he should tread the filth of the streets with his new Spanish
boots, Tim was dispatched for a hackney-coach to convey the
Colonel to Whitehall.

It still wanted an hour to noon, and this the Colonel
considered the earliest at which he could decently present
himself. But early as it was there was another who had been
abroad and at the Cockpit even earlier. This was His Grace
of Buckingham, who, accompanied by his friend Sir Harry
Stanhope, had sought the Duke of Albemarle a full hour
before Colonel Holles had been ready to leave his lodging.

A gentleman of the Duke's eminence was not to be kept
waiting. He had been instantly admitted to that pleasant
wainscoted room overlooking the Park in which His Grace
of Albemarle transacted business. Wide as the poles as were
the two dukes asunder, the exquisite libertine and the
dour soldier, yet cordial relations prevailed between them.
Whilst correct and circumspect in his own ways of life,

Monk was utterly without bigotry and as utterly without prejudices on the score of morals. Under his dour taciturnity, and for all that upon occasion he could be as brave as a lion, yet normally he was of the meekness of a lamb, combined with a courteous aloofness, which, if it earned him few devoted friends, earned him still fewer enemies. As a man gives, so he receives; and Monk, being very sparing both of his love and his hate, rarely excited either passion in others. He was careful not to make enemies, but never at pains to make friends.

"I desire your leave to present to your grace my very good friend Sir Harry Stanhope, a deserving young soldier for whom I solicit your grace's good offices."

Albemarle had heard of Sir Harry as one of the most dissolute young profligates about the Court, and, observing him now, his grace concluded that the gentleman's appearance did justice to his reputation. It was the first time that he had heard him described as a soldier, and the description awakened his surprise. But of this he betrayed nothing. Coldly he inclined his head in response to the diving bow with which Sir Harry honoured him.

"There is no need to solicit my good offices for any friend of your grace's," he answered, coldly courteous. "A chair, your grace. Sir Harry!" He waved the fop to the second and lesser of the two chairs that faced his writing-table, and when they were seated he resumed his own place, leaning forward and placing his elbows on the table. "Will your grace acquaint me how I may have the honour of being of service?"

"Sir Harry," said Buckingham, leaning back in his armchair, and throwing one faultlessly stockinged leg over the other, "desires, for certain reasons of his own, to see the world."

Albemarle had no illusions as to what those reasons were. It was notorious that Harry Stanhope had not only gamed away the inheritance upon which he had entered three years ago, but that he was colossally in debt, and that, unless some one came to his rescue soon, his creditors might render life exceedingly unpleasant for him. He would not be the first gay butterfly of the Court to make the acquaintance of a sponging house. But of that thought, as it flashed through the mind of the Commander-in-Chief, no indication showed on his swart, set face and expressionless dark eyes.

"But Sir Harry," Buckingham was resuming after the slightest of pauses, "is commendably moved by the wish to render his absence from England of profit to His Majesty."

"In short," said Albemarle, translating brusquely, for he could not repress a certain disdain, "Sir Harry desires an appointment overseas."

Buckingham dabbed his lips with a lace handkerchief. "That, in short," he admitted, "is the situation. Sir Harry will, I trust, deserve well in your grace's eyes."

His grace looked at Sir Harry, and found that he did nothing of the kind. From his soul, unprejudiced as he was, Albemarle despised the mincing fop whom he was desired to help to cheat his creditors.

"And the character of this appointment?" he inquired tonelessly.

"A military character would be best suited to Sir Harry's tastes and qualities. He has the advantage of some military experience. He held for a time a commission in the Guards."

"In the Guards!" thought Albemarle. "My God! What a recommendation!" But his expression said nothing. His owlish eyes were levelled calmly upon the young rake, who smiled ingratiatingly, and thereby, did he but know it, provoked Albemarle's disgust. Aloud, at length, he made answer: "Very well. I will bear in mind your grace's application on Sir Harry's behalf, and when a suitable position offers . . ."

"But it offers now," Buckingham interjected languidly.
"Indeed?" The black brows went up, wrinkling the
heavy forehead. "I am not aware of it."

"There is this command in Bombay, which has fallen
vacant through the death of poor Macartney. I heard of it
last night at Court. You are forgetting that, I think. It is
an office eminently suitable to Sir Harry here."

Albemarle was frowning. He pondered a moment; but
only because it was ever his way to move slowly. Then he
gently shook his head and pursed his heavy lips.

"I have also to consider, your grace, whether Sir Harry is
eminently suitable to the office, and, to be quite frank, and
with all submission, I must say that I cannot think so."

Buckingham was taken aback. He stared haughtily at
Albemarle. "I don't think I understand," he said.

Albemarle fetched a sigh, and proceeded to explain himself.

"For this office — one of considerable responsibility — we
require a soldier of tried experience and character. Sir
Harry is no doubt endowed with many commendable qualities, but at his age it is impossible that he should have gained
the experience without which he could not possibly discharge
to advantage the onerous duties which would await him.
Nor is that the only obstacle, your grace. I have not only
chosen my man — and such a man as I have described —
but I have already offered, and he has already accepted, the
commission. So that the post can no longer be considered
vacant."

"But the commission was signed only last night by His
Majesty — signed in blank, as I have reason to know."

"True. But I am none the less pledged. I am expecting
at any moment now, the gentleman upon whom the appointment is already conferred."

Buckingham did not dissemble his annoyance. "May one

inquire his name?" he asked, and the question was a demand.

Albemarle hesitated. He realized the danger to Holles in naming him at this unfortunate juncture. Buckingham might go to any lengths to have him removed, and there was that in Holles's past, in his very name, which would supply abundant grounds. "His name would not be known to your grace. He is a comparatively obscure soldier, whose merits, however, are fully known to me, and I am persuaded that a fitter man for the office could not be found. But something else will, no doubt, offer within a few days, and then . . ."

Buckingham interrupted him arrogantly.

"It is not a question of something else, your grace, but of this. I have already obtained His Majesty's sanction. It is at his suggestion that I am here. It is fortunate that the person you had designated for the command is obscure. He will have to give way, and you may console him with the next vacant post. If your grace requires more explicit instruction I shall be happy to obtain you His Majesty's commands in writing."

Albemarle was checkmated. He sat there grim and impassive as if he were carved of stone. But his mind was a seething cauldron of anger. It was always thus. The places of trust, the positions demanding experienced heads and able hands that England might be served to the best advantage by her most meritorious sons, were constantly being flung away upon the worthless parasites that flocked about Charles's lecherous Court. And he was the more angered here, because his hands were tied against resistance by the very identity of the man he was appointing. Had it been a question of any other man of Holles's soldierly merit, but of such antecedents as would permit the disclosure of his name, he would clap on his hat and step across to the palace to argue the matter with the King. And he would know how to

conduct the argument so as to prevail against the place-
seeking insolence of Buckingham. But, as it was, he was
forced to realize that he could do none of this without
perhaps dooming Holles and bringing heavy censure fruitlessly upon himself. "Oddsfish!" the King would cry. "Do
you tell me to my face that you prefer the son of a regicide
to the friend of my friend?" And what should he answer
then?

He lowered his eyes. The commission which was the subject of this discussion lay there on the table before him, the
space which the name of Randal Holles was intended to oc-
cupy still standing blank. He was defeated, and he had best,
for the sake of Holles as much as for his own, accept the situation without further argument.

He took up a pen, dipped it, and drew the document to
him.

"Since you have His Majesty's authority, there can be, of
course, no further question."

Rapidly, his quill scratching and spluttering across the
sheet, he filled in the name of Sir Harry Stanhope, bitterly
considering that he might as profitably have filled in Nell
Gwynn's. He dusted the thick writing with pounce, and
proffered it without another word. But his looks were heavy.

Buckingham rose, smiling, and Sir Harry bounced up
with him, smiling also. For the first and last time in the
course of that short interview Sir Harry spoke.

"Your grace's devoted servant," he professed himself,
bowing and smirking. "I shall study to discharge my office
creditably, and to allay any qualms my youth may leave in
your grace's mind."

"And youth," said Buckingham, smiling, to reassure
Albemarle, "is a fault that time invariably corrects."

Albemarle rose slowly to his feet, and the others bowed
themselves out of his presence.

Then he sat down again heavily, took his head in his hands, and softly loosed an oath.

Holles came an hour later, radiant with expectation, a gay, youthful-looking, commanding figure in his splendid red coat, to be crushed by the news that proved him Fortune's fool again, as ever.

But he bore it well on the face of him, however deeply the iron was thrust into his soul. It was Albemarle who for once showed excitement, Albemarle who inveighed in most unmeasured terms against the corrupt influence of the Court and the havoc it was working.

"It needed a man for this office and they have constrained me to give it to a fribble, a dolly in breeches, a painted daw-cock."

Holles remembered Tucker's denunciations of the present government and began to realize at last how right he was and how justified he and his associates might be of their conviction that the people were ready to rise and sweep this Augean stable clean.

Albemarle was seeking to comfort him with fresh hope. No doubt something else would offer soon.

"To be snatched up again by some debt-ridden pimp who wants to escape his creditors," said Holles, his tone betraying at last some of the bitterness fermenting in his soul.

Albemarle stood sorrowfully regarding him. "This hits you hard, Randal, I know."

The Colonel recovered and forced a laugh.

"Pooh! Hard hits have mostly been my portion."

"I know." Albemarle paced to the window and back, his head sunk between his shoulders. Then he came to a halt before the Colonel. "Keep me informed of where you are lodged, and look to hear from me again as soon as may be. Be sure that I will do my best."

The Colonel's glance kindled again. It was a flicker of the expiring flame of hope.

"You really think that something else will offer?"

His grace paused before answering, and, in the pause, the sorrowful gravity of his face increased.

"To be frank with you, Randal, I hardly dare to *think* it. Chances for such as you are, as you understand, not . . . frequent. But the unexpected may happen sooner than we dare to hope. If it does, be sure I'll not forget you. Be sure of that."

Holles thanked him steadily, and rose to depart, his radiance quenched, despondency in every line of him.

Albemarle watched from under furrowed brows. As he reached the door the Duke detained him.

"Randal! A moment."

The Colonel turned and waited whilst slowly Albemarle approached him. His grace was deep in thought, and he hesitated before speaking.

"You . . . you are not urgently in need of money, I trust?" he said at last.

The Colonel's gesture and laugh conveyed a shamefaced admission that he was.

Albemarle's eyes considered him a moment still. Then, slowly, he drew a purse from his pocket. It was apparently a light purse. He unfastened it.

"If a loan will help you until . . ."

"No, no!" cried Holles, his pride aroused against accepting what amounted almost to alms.

Even so the repudiation was no more than half-hearted. But there was no attempt from Albemarle to combat it. He did not press the offer. He drew the purse-strings tight again, and his expression was almost one of relief.

CHAPTER XI

A WOMAN SCORNED

Colonel Holles retraced his steps to the City on foot. A hackney-coach, such as that in which he had driven almost in triumph to the Cockpit, was no longer for him; nor yet could he submit to the expense of going by water now that the unexpected was all that stood between himself and destitution.

And yet the unexpected was not quite all. An alternative existed, though a very desperate one. There was the rebellion in which Tucker had sought fruitlessly hitherto to engage him. The thought of it began to stir in his dejected mind, as leaden-footed he dragged himself towards Temple Bar through the almost stifling heat which was making itself felt in London at the end of that month of May. Temptation urged him now, nourished not only by the circumstance that in rebellion lay his last hope of escaping starvation, but also by hot resentment against an inclement and unjust government that drove able soldiers such as himself into the kennels, whilst befriending the worthless minions who pandered to the profligacy of a worthless prince. Vice, he told himself, was the only passport to service in this England of the restored Stuarts. Tucker and Rathbone were right. At least what they did was justified and hallowed by the country's need of salvation from the moral leprosy that was fastening upon it, a disease more devastating and deadly than this plague upon which the republicans counted to arouse the nation to a sense of its position.

He counted the cost of failure; but he counted it derisively. His life would be claimed. That was the stake he set upon the board. But, considering that it was the only stake remaining him, why hesitate? What, after all, was this life of his worth that he should be tender of setting it upon a last throw with Fortune? Fortune favours boldness. Perhaps in the past he had not been bold enough.

Deep in his musings he had reached St. Clement Danes, when he was abruptly aroused by a voice, harsh and warningly commanding.

"Keep your distance, sir!"

Checking, he looked round to the right, whence the order came.

He beheld a man with a pike, who stood before a padlocked door that was smeared with a red cross a foot in length, above which also in red was heavily daubed the legend: LORD HAVE MERCY UPON US.

Taken thus by surprise, the Colonel shuddered as at the contact of something unclean and horrible. Hastily he stepped out into the middle of the unpaved street, and, pausing there a moment, glanced up at the closed shutters of the infected house. It was the first that he had seen; for although he had come this way a week ago, when the plague was already active in the neighbourhood, yet it was then confined to Butcher's Row on the north side of the church and to the mean streets that issued thence. To find it thus upon the main road between the City and Whitehall was to be rendered unpleasantly conscious of its spread. And, as he now pursued his way with instinctively quickened steps, he found his thoughts thrust more closely than ever upon the uses which the revolutionaries could make of this dread pestilence. Much brooding in his disturbed state of mind distorted his mental vision, so that he came presently to adopt the view that this plague was a visitation from Heaven upon a city abandoned to ungodliness. Heaven, it followed, must be on the side of those who laboured to effect a purifying change.

The end of it was that, as he toiled up Ludgate Hill towards Paul's, his resolve was taken. That evening he would seek Tucker and throw in his lot with the republicans.

Coming into Paul's Yard, he found a considerable crowd assembled before the western door of the Cathedral. It was composed of people of all degrees: merchants, shopkeepers, prentices, horseboys, scavengers, rogues from the alleys that lay behind the Old 'Change, idlers and sharpers from Paul's Walk, with a sprinkling of women, of town-gallants, and of soldiers. And there, upon the steps of the portico, stood the magnet that had drawn them in the shape of that black crow of a Jack Presbyter preaching the City's doom. And his text — recurring like the refrain of a song — was ever the same:

"Ye have defiled your sanctuaries by the multitude of your iniquities, by the iniquity of your traffic."

And yet, from between the Corinthian pillars which served him for his background, had been swept away the milliners' shops that had stood there during the Commonwealth.

Whether some thought of this in the minds of his audience rendered his words humorously inapt, or whether it was merely that a spirit of irresponsible ribaldry was infused into the crowd by a crowd of young apprentices, loud derision greeted the preacher's utterance. Unshaken by the laughter and mocking cries, the prophet of doom presented a fearless and angry front.

"Repent, ye scoffers!" His voice shrilled to dominate their mirthful turbulence. "Bethink you of where ye stand! Yet forty days and London shall be destroyed! The pestilence lays siege unto this city of the ungodly! Like a raging lion doth it stalk round, seeking where it may leap upon you. Yet forty days, and . . ."

An egg flung by the hand of a butcher's boy smashed full

in his face to crop his period short. He staggered and gasped
as the glutinous mass of yolk and white crept sluggishly
down his beard and dripped thence to spread upon the
rusty black of his coat.

"Deriders! Scoffers!" he screamed, and with arms that
thrashed the air in imprecation, he looked like a wind-tossed
scarecrow. "Your doom is at hand. Your . . . "

A roar of laughter provoked by the spectacle he presented
drowned his frenzied voice, and a shower of offensive missiles pelted him from every quarter. The last of these was a
living cat, which clawed itself against his breast spitting
furiously in its terror.

Overwhelmed, the prophet turned, and fled between the
pillars into the shelter of Paul's itself, pursued by laughter
and insult. But scarcely had he disappeared than with un-
canny suddenness that laughter sank from a roar to a splut-
ter. To this succeeded a moment of deadly silence. Then the
crowd broke, and parted, its members departing at speed in
every direction with cries in which horror had taken now the
place that was so lately held by mirth.

Colonel Holles, finding himself suddenly alone, and as yet
very far from understanding what had taken place to scatter
those men and women in such panic, advanced a step or two
into the suddenly emptied space before the cathedral steps.
There on the roughly cobbled ground he beheld a writhing
man, a well-made, vigorous fellow in the very prime of life,
whose dress was that of a tradesman of some prosperity.
His round hat lay beside him where he had fallen, and he
rolled his head from side to side spasmodically, moaning
faintly the while. Of his eyes nothing was visible but the
whites, showing under the line of his half-closed lids.

As Holles, perceiving here no more than a sick man, continued his advance, a voice from the retreating crowd shouted
a warning to him.

"Have a care, sir! Have a care! He may be stricken with the plague."

The Colonel checked, involuntarily arrested by the horror that the very word inspired. And then he beheld a stoutish, elderly man in a heavy wig, plainly but scrupulously dressed in black, whose round countenance gathered a singularly owlish expression from a pair of horn-rimmed spectacles, walk calmly forward to the stricken citizen. A moment he stood beside him looking down; then he turned to beckon a couple of burly fellows who had the appearance and carried the staves of billmen. From his pocket the sturdy gentleman in black produced a kerchief upon which he sprinkled something from a phial. Holding the former to his nostrils with his left hand, he knelt down beside the sufferer, and quietly set himself to unfasten the man's doublet.

Observing him, the Colonel admired his quiet courage, and thence took shame at his own fear for his utterly worthless life. Resolutely putting it from him, he went forward to join that little group.

The doctor looked round and up at his approach. But Holles had no eyes at the moment for any but the patient, whose breast the physician had laid bare. One of the bill·men was pointing out to the other a purplish tumid patch at the base of the sufferer's throat. His eyes were round, his face grave, and his voice came hushed and startled.

"See! The tokens!" he said to his companion.

And now the doctor spoke, addressing Holles.

"You would do well not to approach more closely, sir."

"Is it . . . the plague?" quoth Holles in a quiet voice.

The doctor nodded, pointing to the purple patch. "The tokens are very plain to see," he said. "I beg, sir, that you will go." And on that he once more held the handkerchief to his mouth and nostrils, and turned his shoulder upon the Colonel.

Holles withdrew as he was bidden, moving slowly and thoughtfully, stricken by the first sight of the plague at work upon a fellow-creature. As he approached the edges of the crowd, which, keeping its distance, yet stood at gaze as crowds will, he observed that men shrank back from him as if he were himself already tainted.

A single thing beheld impresses us more deeply than twenty such things described to us by others. Hitherto these London citizens had treated lightly this matter of the plague. Not ten minutes ago they had been deriding and pelting one who had preached repentance and warned them of the anger of Heaven launched upon them. And then suddenly, like a bolt from the blue, had come the stroke that laid one of them low, to freeze their derision and fill their hearts with terror by giving them a sight of this thing which hitherto they had but heard reported.

The Colonel stalked on, reflecting that this event in Paul's Yard had done more proselytizing for the cause of the Commonwealth than a score of advocates could have accomplished. It was very well, he thought. It was a sign. And if anything had been wanting to clinch his decision to throw in his lot with Tucker, this supplied it.

But first to quench the prodigious thirst engendered by his long walk through that sweltering heat, and then on to Cheapside and Tucker to offer his sword to the revolutionaries. Thus he would assure himself of the wherewithal to liquidate his score at the Paul's Head and take his leave of the amorous Mrs. Quinn, with whom he could not in any case have afforded now to continue to lodge.

As he entered the common room, she turned from a group of citizens with whom she was standing to talk to follow him with her eyes, her lips compressed, as he passed on into his own little parlour, at the back. A moment later she went after him.

He was flinging off his hat, and loosening his doublet to
cool himself, and he gave her good-morning airily as if yesterday there had not been an almost tragic scene between
them. She found his light-hearted and really tactful manner
highly offensive, and she bridled under it.

"What may be your pleasure, Colonel?" she demanded
forbiddingly.

"A draught of ale if I deserve your charity," quoth he.
"I am parched as an African desert. Phew! The heat!"
And he flung himself down on the window-seat to get what
air he could.

She went off in silence, and returned with a tankard,
which she placed upon the table before him. Thirstily he set
it to his lips, and as its cool refreshment began to soothe his
throat, he thanked Heaven that in a world of much evil
there was still so good a thing as ale.

Silently she watched him, frowning. As he paused at last
in the enjoyment of his draught, she spoke.

"Ye'll have made your plans to leave my house to-day as
we settled it last night?" said she between question and assertion.

He nodded, pursing his lips a little. "I'll remove myself to the Bird in Hand across the Yard this afternoon,"
said he.

"The Bird in Hand!" A slight upward inflection of her
voice marked her disdain of that hostelry, which, indeed,
was but a poor sort of tavern. "Faith, it will go well with
your brave coat. Ah, but that's no affair of mine. So that
ye go, I am content."

There was something portentous in her utterance. She
came forward to the table, and leaned heavily forward upon
it. Her expression and attitude were calculated to leave him
in no doubt that this woman, who had been so tender to him
hitherto, was now his declared enemy. "My house," she

said, "is a reputable house, and I mean to keep it so. I want no traitors here, no gallows' birds and the like."

He had been on the point of drinking again. But her words arrested him, the tankard midway to his lips.

"Traitor? Gallows' bird!" he ejaculated slowly. "I don't think I take your meaning, mistress. D'ye apply these terms to me? To me?"

"To you, sir." Her lips came firmly together.

He stared, frowning, a long moment. Then he shrugged and laughed.

"Ye're mad," he said with conviction, and finished his ale at a draught.

"No, I'm not mad, nor a fool neither, master rebel. A man's to be known by the company he keeps. Birds of a feather flock together, as the saying goes. And how should you be other than a traitor that was friends with traitors, that was close with traitors, here in this house of mine, as I have seen and can swear to at need, and would if I wanted to do you a mischief. I'll spare you that. But you leave my house to-day, or maybe I'll change my mind about it."

He crashed the tankard down upon the board, and came to his feet.

"'Sdeath, woman! Will you tell me what you mean?" he roared, his anger fanned by uneasiness. "What traitors have I been close with?"

"What traitors, do you say?" She sneered a little. "What of your friend Danvers, that's being sought at this moment by the men from Bow Street?"

He was instantly relieved. "Danvers?" he echoed. "My friend Danvers? Why, I have no such friend. I never even heard his name before."

"Indeed!" She was terribly derisive now. "And maybe you've never heard the names of his lieutenants neither — of Tucker and of Rathbone, that was in here with you no later than yesterday as I can swear. And what was they doing with you? What had you to do with them? That's what you can perhaps explain to the satisfaction of the Justices. They'll want to know how you came to be so close with they two traitors that was arrested this morning, along of a dozen others, for conspiring to bring back the Commonwealth. Oh, a scoundrelly plot — to murder the King, seize the Tower, and burn the City, no less."

It was like a blow between the eyes. "Arrested!" he gasped, his jaw fallen, his eyes startled. "Tucker and Rathbone arrested, do you say? Woman, you rave!" But in his heart already he knew that she did not. For unless her tale were true how could she have come by her knowledge of their conspiring.

"Do I?" She laughed again, evilly mocking. "Step out into Paul's Yard, and ask the first man you meet of the arrest made in Cheapside just afore noon, and of the hunt that is going on this minute for Danvers, their leader, and for others who was mixed up in this wicked plot. And I don't want them to come a-hunting here. I don't want my house named for a meeting-place of traitors, as you've made it, taking advantage of me that haven't a man to protect me, and all the while deceiving me with your smooth pleasantness. If it wasn't for that, I'd inform the Justices myself at once. You may be thankful that I want to keep the good name of my house, if I can. And that's the only reason for my silence. But you'll go to-day or maybe I'll think better of it yet."

She picked up the empty tankard, and reached the door before he could find words in his numbed brain to answer her. On the threshold she paused.

"I'll bring you your score presently," she said. "When you've settled that, you may pack and quit." She went out, slamming the door.

The score! It was a small thing compared with that terrible menace of gaol and gallows. It mattered little that — save in intent — he was still completely innocent of any complicity in the rash republican plot which had been discovered. Let him be denounced for association with Tucker and Rathbone, and there would be no mercy for the son of Randal Holles the Regicide. His parentage and antecedents would supply the crowning evidence against him. That was plain to him. And yet the score, whilst a comparatively negligible evil, was the more immediate, and therefore gave him at the moment the greater preoccupation.

He knew that it would be heavy, and he knew that the balance of his resources was utterly inadequate to meet it. Yet unless it were met he could be assured that Mrs. Quinn would show him no mercy; and this fresh trick of Fate's, in bringing him into association with Tucker on the very eve of that conspirator's arrest, placed him in the power of Mrs. Quinn to an extent that did not bear considering.

It was, of course, he reflected bitterly, the sort of thing that must be for ever happening to him. And then he addressed his exasperated mind to the discovery of means to pay his debt. Like many another in his case, it but remained for him to realize such effects as he possessed. Cursing his confident extravagance of the morning, he set about it.

And so you behold him presently, arrayed once more in the shabby garments that he had thought to have discarded for ever, emerging from the Paul's Head carrying a bundle that contained his finery, and making his way back to those shops in Paternoster Row where it had been so lately and so jubilantly acquired.

Here he discovered that there is a world of difference between the treatment offered to a seller and to a buyer. He further discovered that the main value of a suit of clothes would appear to be the mere bloom upon it. Once this has

been a little rubbed, the garments become, apparently, next¬
door to worthless. The fact is that he was a soldier who understood soldiering, and they were traders who understood
trade. And the whole art of successful trading, in whatsoever degree, lies in a quick perception of the necessities of
others and a bowelless readiness to take advantage of them.

Ten pounds was all that he could raise on gear for which a
few hours ago he had paid close upon thirty. Perforce, however ill-humoured, he must sell   He was abusive over the
negotiations; at one moment he was almost threatening. But
the merchant with whom he made his traffic was not at all
disturbed. Insults were nothing to him, so that he made his
profit.

Back to the Paul's Head went Colonel Holles to find his
hostess awaiting him with the score. And the sight of the
latter turned him almost sick. It was the culminating blow
of a day of evil fortune. He studied the items carefully, en-
deavouring to keep the dismay from his countenance, for
Mrs. Quinn was observing him with those hard blue eyes,
her lips compressed into a tight, ominous line.

He marvelled at the prodigious amount of Canary and
ale that he had consumed during those weeks. Irrelevantly
he fell to considering that this very costly thirst of his was
the result of a long sojourn in the Netherlands, where the
habit of copious drinking is a commonplace. Then he came
back to the main consideration, which was that the total
exceeded twenty pounds. It was a prodigious sum. He had
expected a heavy score; but hardly so heavy a score as this.
He conceived that perhaps Mrs. Quinn had included in it the
wound to her tender susceptibilities, and he almost wondered
whether marriage with her, after all, were not the only
remaining refuge, assuming that she would still consider
marriage. Short of that, he did not see how he was to pay.

He raised eyes that, despite him, were haggard and betraying from those terrifying figures, and met that baleful glance of the lady who, because she could not be his wife, was now his relentless enemy. Her glance scared him more than her total. He lowered his eyes again to the lesser evil and cleared his throat.

"This is a very heavy bill," he said.

"It is," she agreed. "You have drunk heavily and otherwise received good entertainment. I hope you'll fare as well at the Bird in Hand."

"Mrs. Quinn, I will be frank. My affairs have gone awry through no fault of my own. His Grace of Albemarle, upon whom I had every reason to depend, has failed me. At the moment I am a man . . . hard-pressed. I am almost without resources."

"That nowise troubled you whiles you ate and drank of the best my house could offer. Yours is a tale that has been told afore by many a pitiful rogue . . ."

"Mrs. Quinn!" he thundered.

But she went on, undaunted, joying to deal a wound to the pride of this man who had lacerated her own pride so terribly.

" . . . and there's a way to deal wi' rogues. You think that, perhaps because I am a woman, I am soft and tender; and so perhaps I am with them as deserves it. But I think I know your sort, Colonel Holles — if so be that you be a colonel. You're not new to a house like mine; but I've never yet been bested by any out-at-elbow ruffler, and I'll see to it as how you don't best me now. I'll say no more, though I could. I could say a deal. But I'll say only this: if you gives me trouble I'll ha' the constable to you, and maybe there'll be more than a matter of this score to settle then. You know what I mean, my man. You know what I could say an I would. So my advice to you is that you pay your bill without whimperings that won't move me no more than they'll move that wooden table."

Scorched with shame, he stood before her, curbing himself with difficulty, for he could be very violent when provoked, though thanks to an indolent disposition he did not permit himself to be provoked very easily. He suppressed his fury now, realizing that to loose it would be to have it recoil upon him and precipitate his ruin.

"Mrs. Quinn," he answered as steadily as he could, "I have sold my gear that I might pay my debt to you. Yet even so this debt exceeds the amount of my resources."

"Sold your gear, have you?" She uttered a laugh that was like a cough. "Sold the fine clothes you'd bought to impose upon them at Whitehall, you mean. But you've not sold everything. There's that jewel a-flaunting in your ear that alone would pay my score twice over."

He started, and put a hand to the ear-ring — that ruby given to him as a keepsake by the lovely, unknown royalist boy whose life he had saved on the night after Worcester fight some fifteen years ago. The old superstitions that his fancy had woven about it had placed it outside his realizable assets. Even now, in this desperate pass, when reminded of its value, the notion of selling it was repugnant to him. And yet perhaps it was against this very dreadful need, perhaps it was that he might save his neck — for she made it clear to him that nothing less was now at stake — that in all these years he had hugged that jewel against every blow of fortune.

His head drooped. "I had forgot," he said.

"Forgot?" she echoed in tones that plainly called him a liar and a cheat. "Ah, well, ye're reminded of it now."

"I thank you for the reminder. It . . . it shall be sold at once. Your score shall be paid to-day. I . . . I am sorry that, that . . . Oh, no matter."

He flung out upon the business of finding a Jew who practised the transmutation of jewels into gold.

CHAPTER XII

BUCKINGHAM'S HEROICS

MISS SYLVIA FARQUHARSON occupied very pleasant lodgings in Salisbury Court, procured for her upon her accession to fame and some measure of fortune by Betterton, who himself lived in a house opposite. And it was in the doorway of Betterton's house that she first beheld the lean and wolfish face of Bates.

This happened on that same morning of Colonel Holles's disappointment at the hands of Albemarle and subsequent tribulations at the hands of Mrs. Quinn.

Miss Farquharson was in need of certain dress materials which, she had been informed, were to be procured at a certain mercer's in Cheapside. On this errand she came forth in the early afternoon of that day, and entered the sedanchair that awaited her at her door. As the chairmen took up their burden it was that, looking from the unglazed window on her left across towards the house of her friend Betterton, she beheld that sly, evil face protruded from the shadows of the doorway as if to spy upon her. The sight of it instinctively chilled her a moment, and, again instinctively, she drew back quickly into the depths of the chair. A moment later she was laughing at her own foolish fancies, and upon that dismissed from her mind the memory of that evil-looking watcher.

It took her a full half-hour to reach her mercer's at the sign of the Silver Angel in Cheapside, for the chairmen moved slowly. It would have been uncharitable to have urged them to go faster in the sweltering heat, and uncharitableness was not in Miss Farquharson's nature. Also she was not pressed. And so she suffered herself to be borne in leisurely fashion along Paul's Yard, whilst the preacher of doom on the steps was still haranguing that crowd which, as we know, ended by rising in mockery against him.

When at last her chair was set down at the door of the Silver Angel, she stepped out and passed in upon a business over which no woman hurries.

It may be well that Master Bates — who had come slinking after that chair with three tough bullies following some distance behind him, and another three following at a still greater distance — was something of a judge of feminine nature, and so came to the conclusion that it would perhaps be best part of an hour before Miss Farquharson emerged again. He had dark, wicked little eyes that observed a deal, and very wicked wits that were keenly alert. He had noted the little crowd about the steps of Paul's, he had heard the burden of the preacher's message, and those wicked inventive wits of his had perceived here a stage very opportunely set for the nasty little comedy which he was to contrive on His Grace of Buckingham's behalf. It remained to bring the chief actor — the Duke, himself — at once within reasonable distance of the scene. Provided this could be contrived, all should now flow merrily as a peal of wedding-bells.

Master Bates slipped like a shadow into a porch, produced a pencil and tablets, and set himself laboriously to scrawl three or four lines. He folded his note, as one of the bullies, summoned by an unostentatious signal, joined him there in that doorway.

With the note Bates slipped a crown into the man's hand.

"This at speed to his grace," he snapped. "Take a coach, man, and make haste. Haste!"

The fellow was gone in a flash, and Bates, leaning back in the shadow, leisurely filled a pipe and settled down to his vigil. A little lantern-jawed fellow he was, with leathery, shaven cheeks, and long, wispy black hair that hung like sca-weed about his face and scraggy neck. He was dressed in rusty black, in almost clerkly fashion, which, together with his singular countenance and his round rather high-crowned hat, gave him an air of fanatical piety.

Miss Farquharson made no haste. An hour passed, and the half of a second, before she came forth at last, followed by the mercer, laden with parcels, which, together with herself, were packed into the chair. The chairmen took up, and, whilst the mercer bowed himself double in obsequious gratitude to the famous actress, they swung along westward by the way they had come.

Providence, it would almost seem, was on the Duke's side that morning to assist the subtle Bates in the stage-management of the affair. For it was not more than half an hour since the removal of that citizen who had been smitten with the pestilence at the very foot of Paul's steps when Miss Farquharson's chair came past the spot, making its way through a fear-ridden crowd fallen into voluble groups to discuss the event.

She became conscious of the sense of dread about her. The grave, stricken faces of the men and women standing there in talk, with occasional loudly uttered lamentations, drew her attention and set her uneasily wondering and speculating upon the reason.

Suddenly dominating all other sounds, a harsh, croaking voice arose somewhere behind but very close to the chair:

"There goes one of those who have drawn the judgment of the Lord upon this unfortunate city!"

She heard the cry repeated with little variation, again and yet again. She saw the groups she was passing cease from their talk, and those whose backs were towards her swing round and stand at gaze until it seemed that every eye of all that motley crowd of citizens was directed upon herself.

Thus it was borne in upon her that it was herself this

dreadful pursuing voice behind her was denouncing, and, intimidated for all her stout spirit under the dreadful stare of all those apparently hostile eyes, she shrank back into the depths of the chair, and even dared to draw one of its leather curtains the better to conceal herself.

Again the voice beat upwards, shrilly, fiercely.

"There sits a playhouse wanton in her silks and velvets, while the God-fearing go in rags, and the wrath of Heaven smites us with a sword of pestilence for the sin she brings among us!"

Her chair rocked a little, as if her bearers were being hustled, for in truth some three or four of the scurvier sort, those scourings of the streets who are ever on the watch for fruitful opportunities of turbulence, had joined that raving fanatic who followed her with his denunciations, and were pressing now upon the chair. Miss Farquharson's fear increased. It requires no great imagination — and she possessed imagination in abundance — to conceive what may happen to one at the hands of a crowd whose passions have been inflamed. With difficulty she commanded herself, repressing the heave of her bosom and the wild impulse to scream out her fear.

But her chairmen, stolid, massive fellows, who held her in the esteem she commanded in all who knew her closely, plodded steadily onward despite this jostling; and, what was more to their credit, they continued to keep their tempers and to affect unconcern. They could not believe that the people would turn upon a popular idol at the bidding of this rusty black crow of a fanatic who came howling at their heels.

But those few rogues who had joined him were being reinforced by others who supported with inarticulate growls of menace the rascal's denunciations; and these grew fiercer at every moment.

"It is Sylvia Farquharson of the Duke's Playhouse," he cried. " A daughter of Belial, a shameless queen. It is for the sins of her kind that the hand of the Lord is heavy upon us. It is for her and those like her that we are suffering and shall suffer until this city is cleansed of its iniquities."

He was alongside of the chair now, brandishing a short cudgel, and Miss Farquharson's scared eyes had a glimpse of his malevolent face. To her amazement she recognized it for the face that had peered at her two hours ago from the shadows of Betterton's house in Salisbury Square.

"You have seen one of yourselves smitten down with the plague under your very eyes," he was ranting. "And so shall others be smitten to pay for the sin of harlotry with which this city is corrupt."

Now, for all the fear that was besetting the naturally stout spirit in her frail white body, Miss Farquharson's wits were not at all impaired. This fanatic — to judge him by the language he used — represented himself as moved to wrath against her by something that had lately happened in Paul's Yard. His words implied that his denunciation was prompted by that latest sign of Heaven's indignation at the sins of the City. But since he had been on the watch in Salisbury Court to observe her going forth, and had followed her all the way thence, it was clear that the facts were quite otherwise, and that he acted upon a premeditated design.

And now the knaves who had joined him were hustling the chairmen with greater determination. The chair was tossed alarmingly, and Miss Farquharson flung this way and that within it. Others from amongst the spectators — from amongst those upon whom she had almost been depending for ultimate protection — began to press upon the heels of her more immediate assailants and insults were being flung at her by some of the women in the crowd.

Hemmed about by that hostile mob, the chair came at

last perforce to a standstill just opposite the Paul's Head, on the steps of which Colonel Holles was at that moment standing. He had been in the act of coming forth upon the errand of finding a purchaser for his jewel, when his attention was drawn by the hubbub, and he stood arrested, frowning and observant.

The scene nauseated him. The woman they were persecuting with their insults and menaces might be no better than that dirty fanatic was pronouncing her. But she was a woman and helpless. And apart from this there was in all the world no vice that Holles found more hideous than virtue driven to excess.

Over the heads of the crowd he saw the wildly rocking chair set down at last. Of its occupant he had but a confused glimpse, and in any case the distance at which he stood would hardly have permitted him to make out her face distinctly. But so much wasn't necessary to conceive her condition, her peril, and the torment of fear she was suffering at the hands of those ignoble persecutors.

Colonel Holles thought he might find pleasant distraction, and at the same time perform a meritorious deed, in slitting the ears of that black fanatic who was whipping up the passions of the mob.

But no sooner had he made up his mind to this, and before he could stir a foot to carry out his intention, assistance came suddenly and vigorously from another quarter. Precisely whence or how it came was not easily determinable. The tall, graceful man in the golden periwig with the long white ostrich plumes in his broad hat, seemed, together with those who followed him, to materialize suddenly upon the spot, so abrupt was his appearance. At a glance his dress proclaimed him some great gentleman. He wore the tiny coat and kilt-like petticoat above his breeches that marked him for a native of Whitehall. The sapphire velvet of their fabric was stiff with gold lace, and at waist and breast and from the cuffs which ended at the elbow bulged forth a marvel of dazzling linen, with a wealth of lace at the throat and a hundred ribbons fluttering at his shoulders and his knees. The flash of jewels rendered his figure still more dazzling: a great brooch of gems secured the clump of ostrich plumes to his broad beaver, and of gems were the buttons on his sleeves and in his priceless necktie.

He had drawn his sword, and with the menace of this and of his voice, combined with his imperiously commanding mien, he clove himself a way through the press to the chair itself. After him, in plain striped liveries with broad fawn hats, came four stalwart lads, obviously lackeys with whips which they appeared nowise timid of employing. Their lashes fell vigorously upon the heads and shoulders of that black fanatic and those rough-looking knaves who more immediately supported his attack upon the chair.

Like an archangel Michael scattering a legion of demons did that gay yet imposing rescuer scatter those unclean assailants of that helpless lady. The bright blade of his sword whirled hither and thither, beating ever a wider ring about the chair, and his voice accompanied it:

"You mangy tykes! You filthy vermin! Stand back there! Back, and give the lady air! Back, or by Heaven I'll send some of you where you belong."

They proved themselves as cowardly as they had lately been aggressive, and they skipped nimbly beyond the reach of that darting point of his. His followers fell upon them afterwards with their whips and drove them still farther back, relentlessly, until they were absorbed and lost in the ranks of the crowd of onlookers which in its turn fell back before the continued menace of those impetuous grooms.

The gentleman in blue swung to the chairmen.

"Take up," he bade them. And they, seeing themselves

now delivered from their assailants, and their main anxiety
being to remove themselves and their charge from so hostile
a neighbourhood whilst they might still enjoy the protection
of this demigod, made haste to obey him.

His Grace of Buckingham — for already the people had
recognized him, and his name had been uttered with awe in
their ranks — stepped ahead, and waved back those who
stood before him.

"Away!" he bade them, with the air of a prince speaking
to his grooms. "Give room!" He disdained even to use the
menace of his sword, which he now carried tucked under
his left arm. His voice and mien sufficed, and a lane was
opened in that living press through which he advanced with
calm assurance, the chairmen hurrying with their burden in
his wake.

The lackeys closed in behind the chair and followed to
form a rear-guard; but there was scarcely the need, for all
attempt to hinder or molest the chair was at an end. Indeed, none troubled to accompany it farther. The people
broke up into groups again, or moved away about their business, realizing that here the entertainment was at an end.
The fanatic who had led the attack and the knaves who had
joined him had vanished suddenly, mysteriously, and completely.

Of the very few spectators whom curiosity or interest
still attracted was Holles, and this perhaps chiefly because
Miss Farquharson was being carried in the direction in
which his own business was taking him.

He came down the steps of the inn, and followed leisurely
at some little distance.

They swung steadily along as far as Paternoster Row,
where the traffic was slight. Here the Duke halted at last,
and turned, and at a sign from him the men set down the
chair.

His grace advanced to the window, swept off his broad plumed hat, and bowed until the golden curls of his periwig almost met across his face.

Within the chair, still very pale, but quite composed again by now, sat Miss Farquharson, regarding his grace with a very odd expression, an expression best described as speculative.

"Child," he exclaimed, a hand upon his heart, a startled look on his handsome face, "I vow that you have taught me the meaning of fear. For I was never frightened in my life until to-day. What imprudence, my dear Sylvia, to show yourself here in the City, when men's minds are so distempered by war and pestilence that they must be seeking scapegoats wherever they can find them. None may call me devout, yet devout I feel at this moment. From my soul I return thanks to Heaven that by a miracle I chanced to be here to save you from this peril!"

She leaned forward, and her hooded cloak of light silk, having fallen back from head and shoulders, revealed the white lustre of her beauty. She was smiling slightly, a smile that curled her delicate lip and lent something hard and disdainful to eyes that naturally were soft and gentle — long-shaped, rather wistful eyes of a deep colour that was something between blue and green.

"It was a most fortunate chance, your grace," she said, almost tonelessly.

"Fortunate, indeed!" he fervently agreed with her, and, hat in hand, dabbed his brow with a fine handkerchief.

"Your grace was very opportunely at hand!"

And now there was a world of mocking meaning in her tone. She understood at last, she thought, upon whose behalf that fanatic had spied upon her going forth, afterwards to follow and assail her, thus providing occasion for this very romantic rescue. Having thus shrewdly appraised the situation, the actress in her awoke to play her part in it.

And so she had mocked him with that phrase: "Your grace was very opportunely at hand!"

"I thank God for 't, and so may you, child," was the quick answer, ignoring the mockery, which had not escaped him.

But Miss Farquharson was none so disposed, it seemed, to the devout thanksgiving he advised.

"Is your grace often east of Temple Bar?" was her next rallying question.

"Are you?" quoth he, possibly for lack of better answer.

"So seldom that the coincidence transcends all that yourself or Mr. Dryden could have invented for one of your plays."

"Life is marvellously coincident," the Duke reflected, conceiving obtuseness to be the proper wear for the innocence he pretended. "Coincidence is the salt that rescues existence from insipidity."

"So? And it was to rescue this that you rescued me; and so that you might have opportunity for rescuing me, no doubt yourself you contrived the danger."

"I contrived the danger?" He was aghast. He did not at first understand. "I contrived the danger! Child!" It was a cry of mingled pain and indignation, and the indignation at least was not pretended. The contempt of her tone had cut him like a whip. It made him see that he was ridiculous in her eyes, and His Grace of Buckingham liked to be ridiculous as little as another, perhaps less than most. "How can you think it of me?"

"Think it of you?" She was laughing. "Lord! I knew it, sir, the moment I saw you take the stage at the proper cue — at what you would call the dramatic moment. Enter hero, very gallant. Oh, sir, I am none so easily cozened. I was a fool to allow myself to be deceived into fear by those other

silly mummers, the first murderer and his myrmidons. It
was poorly contrived. Yet it carried the groundlings in
Paul's Yard quite off their feet, and they'll talk of your
brave carriage and mighty mien for a whole day, at least.
But you could scarce expect that it should move me as well;
since I am in the play, as it were."

It was said of him, and with truth, that he was the most
impudent fellow in England, this lovely, accomplished, foolish son of a man whose face had made his fortune. Yet her
raillery now put him out of countenance, and it was only
with difficulty that he could master the fury it awoke in
him. Yet master it he did, lest he should cut a still sorrier
figure.

"I vow . . . I vow you're monstrously unjust," he contrived at last to stammer. "You ever have thought the
worst of me. It all comes of that cursed supper party and
the behaviour of those drunken fools. Yet I have sworn to
you that it was through no fault of mine, that my only satisfaction lay in your prompt departure from a scene with
which I would not for all the world have offended you. Yet,
though I have sworn it, I doubt if you believe me."

"Does your grace wonder?" she asked him coolly.

He looked at her a moment with brooding, wicked eyes.
Then he loosed some little of his anger, but loosed it on a
pretence.

"I would to Heaven I had left you to those knaves that
persecuted you."

She laughed outright. "I wonder what turn the comedy
would have taken then, had you failed to answer to your
cue. Perhaps my persecutors would have been put to the
necessity of rescuing me, themselves, lest they should incur
your anger. That would have been diverting. Oh, but
enough!" She put aside her laughter. "I thank your grace
for the entertainment provided; and since it has proved un-

profitable I trust your grace will not go to the pains of providing yet another of the same kind. Oh, sir, if you can take
shame for anything, take shame for the dullness of your
invention."

She turned from him with almost contemptuous abrupt-
ness to command the chairman standing at her side.

"Take up, Nathaniel. Let us on, and quickly, or I shall be
late."

She was obeyed, and thus departed without so much as
another glance for the gay Duke of Bucks, who, too crestfallen to attempt to detain her, or to renew his protestations,
stood hat in hand, white with anger, gnawing his lip, conscious, above all, that she had plucked from him a mask that
left him an object of derision and showed his face to appear
the face of a fool.

In the background his lackeys sought with pains to preserve a proper stolidity of countenance, whilst a few pas-
sersby paused to stare at that splendid bareheaded figure of
a courtliness rarely seen on foot in the streets of the City.
Conscious of their regard, investing it with a greater pene-
tration than it could possibly possess, his grace conceived
them all to be the mocking witnesses of his discomfiture.

He ground his heel in a sudden spasm of rage, clapped on
his hat, and turned to depart, to regain his waiting coach.
But suddenly his right arm was seized in a firm grip, and a
voice, in which quivered wonder, and something besides,
assailed his ears.

"Sir! Sir!"

He swung round, and glared into the shaven, aquiline face
and wonder-laden eyes of Colonel Holles, who had come up
behind the chair whilst the Duke was in conversation with
its occupant, and had gradually crept nearer as if drawn by
some irresistible attraction.

Amazed, the Duke looked him over from head to toe.

Conceiving in this shabby stranger another witness of his humiliation, his anger, seeking a vent, flamed out.

"What's this?" he rasped. "Do you presume to touch me, sirrah?"

The Colonel, never flinching as another might have done under a tone that was harsh and arrogant as a blow, before eyes that blazed upon him out of that white face, made answer simply:

"I touched you once before, I think, and you suffered it with a better grace. For then it was to serve you that I touched you."

"Ha! And it will be to remind me of it that you touch me now," came our fine gentleman's quick, contemptuous answer.

Stricken by the brutality of the words, Holles crimsoned slowly under his tan, what time his steady glance returned the Duke's contempt with interest. Then, without answering, he swung on his heel to depart.

But there was in this something so odd and so deliberately offensive to one accustomed to be treated ever with the deepest courtesy that it was now the Duke who caught him by the arm in a grip of sudden anger, arresting his departure.

"Sir! A moment!"

They were face to face again, and now the arrogance was entirely on the side of Holles. The Duke's countenance reflected astonishment and some resentment.

"I think," he said at last, "that you are something wanting in respect."

"There, at least your discernment is not at fault," the Colonel answered him.

Deeper grew the Duke's wonder. "Do you know who I am?" he asked, after another pause.

"I learnt it five minutes since."

"But I thought you said that you did me a service once."

"That was many years ago. And I did not know then your name. Your grace has probably forgotten."

Because of the disdainful tone he took, he commanded the respect and attention of one who was a very master of disdain. Also the Duke's curiosity was deeply stirred.

"Will you not assist my memory?" he invited, almost gently.

The Colonel laughed a little grimly. Then shaking the Duke's still detaining grip without ceremony from his arm, he raised his hand, and holding back the light brown curls, revealed his left ear and the long ruby that adorned it.

Buckingham stared an instant, then leaned nearer to obtain a closer view, and he caught his breath in sudden surprise.

"How came you by that jewel?" he asked, his eyes scanning the soldier's face as he spoke.

And out of his abiding sense of injury the Colonel answered him:

"It was given me after Worcester as a keepsake by an empty fribble whose life I thought worth saving."

Oddly enough there was no answering resentment from his grace. Perhaps his wonder overwhelmed and stilled at the moment every other emotion.

"So! It was you!" His eyes continued to search that lean countenance. "Aye!" he added after a moment, and it sounded like a sigh. "The man had just such a nose and was of your inches. But in no other respect do you look like the Cromwellian who befriended me that night. You had no ringlets then. Your hair was cropped to a godly length, and ... But you're the man. How odd to meet you again thus! How passing odd!" His grace seemed suddenly bemused. "They cannot err!" he muttered, continuing to regard the Colonel from under knitted brows, and his eyes were almost the eyes of a visionary. "I have been expecting you," he said, and again he used that cryptic phrase: "They cannot err."

It was Holles's turn to be surprised, and out of his surprise he spoke: "Your grace has been expecting me?"

"These many years. It was foretold me that we should meet again — aye, and that for a time our lives should run intertwined in their courses."

"Foretold?" ejaculated Holles. Instantly he bethought him of the superstitions which had made him cling to that jewel through every stress of fortune. "How foretold? By whom?" he asked.

The question seemed to arouse the Duke from the brooding into which he had fallen.

"Sir," he said, "we cannot stand talking here. And we have not met thus, after all these years, to part again without more." His manner resumed its normal arrogance. "If you have business, sir, it must wait upon my pleasure. Come!"

He took the Colonel by the arm, whilst over his shoulder he addressed his waiting lackeys in French, commanding two of them to follow.

Holles, unresisting, curious, bewildered, a man walking in a dream, suffered himself to be led whither the other pleased, as a man lets himself drift upon the bosom of the stream of Destiny.

CHAPTER XIII

BUCKINGHAM'S GRATITUDE

In a room above-stairs which his grace had commanded in an inn at the corner of Paternoster Row, they sat alone, the Duke of Buckingham and the man to whom he owed his life. There was no doubt of the extent of the debt, as both well knew. For on that night, long years ago, when his grace lay faint and wounded on that stricken field of battle, he had fallen a prey to a pair of those human jackals who scour the battle-ground to strip the living and the dead. The young Duke had sought gallantly enough, considering his condition, to defend himself from their depredations, whereupon, whilst one of them held him down, the other had bared a knife to make an end of his rash resistance. And then out of the surrounding gloom had sprung young Holles, brought to that spot by merest chance. His heavy cut-and-thrust blade had opened the skull of the villain who wielded the knife, whereupon his fellow had incontinently fled. Thereafter, half supporting, half carrying the lovely wounded boy whom he had rescued, the young Cromwellian officer had assisted him to the safety and shelter of a royalist yeoman's cottage. All this they both remembered, and upon this they dwelt a moment now.

A table stood between them, and on that table a quart of Burgundy which the Duke had called for, that he might entertain his guest.

"In my heart," said Holles, "I always believed that we should meet again one day; which is why I have clung to this jewel. Had I known your name, I should have sought you out. As it was, I harboured the conviction that Chance would bring me across your path."

"Not Chance. Destiny," said his grace, with quiet conviction.

"Why, Destiny, if you prefer to call it so. This jewel now — it is very odd! I have clung to it through all these years, as I have said; I have clung to it through some odd shifts which the sale of it might have relieved: clung to it against the day when we should meet again, that it might serve as my credential." He did not add that to him the oddest thing of all was that to-day, at the very moment of this meeting, he was on his way to sell the jewel, compelled to it at last by direst need.

The Duke was nodding, his face thoughtful. "Destiny, you see. It was preordained. The meeting was foretold. Did I not say so?"

And again Holles asked him, as he had asked before: "Foretold by whom?"

This time the Duke answered him.

"By whom? By the stars. They are the only true prophets, and their messages are plain to him who can read them. I suppose you never sought that lore?"

Holles stared at him a moment. Then he shook his head, and smiled in a manner to imply his contempt of charlatanry.

"I am a soldier, sir," he said.

"Why, so am I — when the occasion serves. But that does not prevent me from being a reader of the heavens, a writer of verse, a law-giver in the north, a courtier here, and several other things besides. Man in his time plays many parts. Who plays one only may as well play none. To live, my friend, you must sip at many wells of life."

He developed that thesis, discoursing easily, wittily, and with the indefinable charm he could command, a charm which was fastening upon our adventurer now even as it had fastened upon him years ago in that hour of their brief but fateful meeting.

"When just now you chanced upon me," he concluded, "I was playing hero and lover, author and mummer all in one, and playing them all so unsuccessfully that I never found myself in a more vexatious part. On my soul, if there lay no debt between us already, you must have rendered me your debtor now that you can rescue my mind for an hour or so from the tormenting thought of that sweet baggage who keeps me on the rack. You saw, perhaps, how the little wanton used me." He laughed, and yet through his laughter ran a note of bitterness. "But I contrived the mummery clumsily, as she reproached me. And no doubt I deserved to be laughed off the stage, which is what happened. But she shall pay me, and with interest, one of these fine days, for all the trouble she has given me. She shall . . . Oh, but a plague on the creature! It is of yourself, sir, that I would hear. What are you now, that were once a Commonwealth man?"

"Nobody's man at present. I have seen a deal of service since those days, both at home and abroad, yet it has brought me small gear, as you can see for yourself."

"Faith, yes." Buckingham regarded him more critically. "I should not judge your condition to be prosperous."

"You may judge it to be desperate and never fear to exaggerate."

"So?" The Duke raised his eyebrows. "Is it so bad? I vow I am grieved." His face settled into lines of courteous regret. "But it is possible I may be of service to you. There is a debt between us. I should welcome the opportunity to discharge it. What is your name, sir? You have not told me."

"Holles — Randal Holles, lately a colonel of horse in the Stadtholder's service."

The Duke frowned reflectively. The name had touched a chord of memory and set it faintly vibrating in his brain. Awhile the note eluded him. Then he had it.

"Randal Holles?" he echoed slowly, questioningly. "That was the name of a regicide who . . . But you cannot be he. You are too young by thirty years . . ."

"He was my father," said the Colonel.

"Oh!" The Duke considered him blankly. "I do not wonder that you lack employment here in England. My friend, with the best intentions to repay you the great service that you did me, this makes it very difficult."

The new-risen hope perished again in the Colonel's face.

"It is as I feared . . ." he was beginning gloomily, when the Duke leaned forward, and set a hand upon his arm.

"I said difficult, my friend. I did not say impossible. I admit the impossibility of nothing that I desire, and I swear that I desire nothing at present more ardently than your better fortune. Meanwhile, Colonel Holles, that I may serve you, I must know more of you. You have not told me yet how Colonel Holles, sometime of the Army of the Commonwealth, and more lately in the service of the Stadtholder, happens to be endangering his neck in the London of Old Rowley — this King whose memory for injuries is as endless as a lawsuit."

Colonel Holles told him. Saving the matter of how he had been tempted to join the ill-starred Danvers conspiracy under persuasion of Tucker and Rathbone, he used the utmost candour, frankly avowing the mistakes he had made by following impulses that were never right. He spoke of the ill-luck that had dogged him, to snatch away each prize in the moment that he put forth his hand to seize it, down to the command in Bombay which Albemarle had already practically conferred upon him.

The debonair Duke was airily sympathetic. He condoled and jested in a breath, his jests being in themselves a promise that all this should now be mended. But when Holles came to the matter of the Bombay command, his grace's laughter sounded a melancholy note.

"And it was I who robbed you of this," he cried. "Why, see how mysteriously Destiny has been at work! But this multiplies my debt. It adds something for which I must make amends. Rest assured that I shall do so. I shall find a way to set you on the road to fortune. But we must move cautiously, as you realize. Depend upon me to move surely, none the less."

Holles flushed this time in sheer delight. Often though Fortune had fooled him, yet she had not utterly quenched his faith in men. Thus, miraculously, in the eleventh hour had salvation come to him, and it had come through that precious ruby which a wise intuition had made him treasure so tenaciously.

The Duke produced a purse of green silk netting, through the meshes of which glowed the mellow warmth of gold.

"Meanwhile, my friend — as an earnest of my good intent . . ."

"Not that, your grace." For the second time that day Holles waved back a proffered purse, his foolish pride in arms. Throughout his career he had come by money in many questionable ways, but never by accepting it as a gift from one whose respect he desired to preserve. "I am in no such immediate want. I . . . I can contrive awhile."

But His Grace of Buckingham was of a different temper from His Grace of Albemarle. He was as prodigal and lavish as the other was parsimonious, and he was not of those who will take a refusal.

He smiled a little at the Colonel's protestations, and passed to a tactful, ingratiating insistence with all the charm of which he could be master.

"I honour you for your refusal, but . . ." He continued to hold out the purse. "See. It is not a gift I offer you, but

an advance, a trifling loan, which you shall repay me presently when I shall have made it easy for you to so do.
Come, sir, there is that between us which is not to be repaid
in gold. Your refusal would offend me."

And Holles, be it confessed, was glad enough to have the
path thus smoothed for his self-respect.

"As a loan, then, since you are so graciously insistent . . ."

"Why, what else do you conceive I had in mind?" His
grace dropped the heavy purse into the hand that was at
last held out to receive it, and rose. "You shall hear from
me again, Colonel, and as soon as may be. Let me but know
where you are lodged."

Holles considered a second. He was leaving the Paul's
Head, and it had been his announced intention to remove
himself to the Bird in Hand, a humble hostelry where lodgings were cheap. But he loved good food and wine as he
loved good raiment, and he would never lodge in so vile a
house save under the harsh compulsion of necessity. Now,
with this sudden accession of fortune, master of this heavy
purse and assured of more to follow soon, that obnoxious
necessity was removed. He bethought him of, and decided
upon, another house famous for its good cheer.

"Your grace will find me at The Harp in Wood Street,"
he announced.

"There look to hear from me, and very soon."

They left the tavern together, and the Duke went off to
his coach, which had been brought thither for him, his
French lackeys trotting beside it, whilst Colonel Holles, with
his head in the clouds and a greater swagger than ever in
his port to emphasize the shabby condition of his person,
rolled along towards Paul's Yard, fingering the jewel in his
ear, which there no longer was the need to sell, although
there was no longer the need to retain it, since it had fulfilled, at last, after long years, Destiny's purpose with himself.

Thus in high good-humour he strutted into the Paul's Head, to plunge into a deplorable scene with Mrs. Quinn. It was the jewel — this fateful jewel — that precipitated the catastrophe. The sight of it inflamed her anger, driving her incontinently to unwarranted conclusions.

"You haven't sold it!" she shrilled as he stepped into the back parlour where she was at the moment stirring, and she pointed to the ear-ring, which glowed like an ember under a veil of his brown hair. "You've changed your mind. You think to come whimpering here again, that you may save the trinket at my cost." And then the devil whispered an unfortunate thought, and so begat in her a sudden furious jealousy. Before he could answer her, before he could recover from the gaping amazement in which he stood to receive the onslaught of her wrath, she was sweeping on: "I understand!" She leered an instant evilly. "It's a love-token, eh? The gift of some fat Flemish burgomaster's dame, belike, whom ye no doubt cozened as ye would have cozened me. That's why ye can't part with it — not even to pay me the money you owe for bed and board, for the food ye've guzzled and the wine ye swilled, ye good-for-nothing out-at-elbow jackanapes. But ye've had your warning, and since ye don't heed it ye'll take the . . ."

"Hold your peace, woman," he interrupted, thundering, and silenced her by his sudden show of passion. He advanced upon her, so that she recoiled in some alarm, yet bridling even then. Then as suddenly he checked, curbed himself, and laughed. Forth from his pocket he lugged the heavy ducal purse, slid back the gold rings that bound it and brought the broad yellow pieces into view at its gaping mouth.

"What is the total of this score of yours?" he asked contemptuously, in the remnants of his anger. "Name it, take your money, and give me peace."

But she was no longer thinking of her score. She was stricken with amazement at the sight of the purse he held, and the gold with which it bulged. Round-eyed she stared at it, and then at him. And then, because she could not conjecture the source of this sudden wealth, she must assume the worst, with the readiness to which such minds as hers are prone. The suspicion narrowed her blue eyes; it settled into conviction, and fetched an unpleasant curl to the lips of her broad mouth.

"And how come you by this gold?" she asked him, sinisterly quiet.

"Is that your affair, ma'am?"

"I thought you was above purse-cutting," she said, mightily disdainful. "But it seems I was as deceived in you there as in other ways."

"Why, you impudent bawd!" he roared in his rage, and turned her livid by the epithet.

"You vagrant muck-rake, is that a word for an honest woman?"

"Honest, you thieving drab! Do you boast yourself honest? Your cheating score gives the lie to that. Give me the total of it, that I may pay the swindling sum, and shake the dust of your tavern from my heels."

That, as you realize, was but the beginning of a scene of which I have no mind to give you all the details. Some of them are utterly unprintable. Her voice shrilled up like an oyster-woman's, drawing the attention of the few who occupied the common room, and fetching Tim the drawer in alarm to the door of the little parlour.

And for all his anger, Colonel Holles began to be vaguely alarmed, for his conscience, as you know, was not altogether easy, and appearances might easily be construed against him.

"You thieving, brazen traitor," she was bawling. "Do

you think to come roaring it in here at me, you that have turned my reputable house into a den of treason! I'll learn you manners, you impudent gallow's-bird." And she then caught sight of Tim's scared face looking round the opening door. "Tim, fetch the constable," she bawled. "The gentleman shall shift his lodgings to Newgate, which is better suited to his kind. Fetch the constable, I tell you. Run, lad."

Tim departed. So did the Colonel, realizing suddenly that there would be no profit in remaining. He emptied the half of the contents of the ducal purse into his palm, and, as Jupiter wooed Danaë, but without any of Jupiter's amorous intention, he scattered it upon and about her in a golden shower.

"There's to stop your noisy, scolding mouth!" he cried. "Pay yourself with that, you hag. And the devil take you!"

He flung out in a towering rage, almost on the very heels of Tim; and of the half-dozen men in the common room not one dared to dispute his passage. He gained the street, and was gone, leaving behind him some odds and ends of gear as a memento of his eventful passage, and a hostess reduced to tears of angry exhaustion.

CHAPTER XIV

DESPAIR

FOR three weeks Colonel Holles waited in vain at The Harp in Wood Street for the promised message from His Grace of Buckingham, and his anxieties began to grow at last in a measure as he saw his resources dwindling. For he had practised no husbanding of his comparatively slender funds. He was well-lodged, ate and drank of the best, ruffled it in one or the other of two handsome suits which he had purchased from the second-hand clothiers in Birchin Lane, — considering this more prudent and economical than a return to the shops of Paternoster Row, — and he had even indulged with indifferent fortune a passion for gaming, which was one of his besetting sins.

Hence in the end he found himself fretted by the continued silence of the Duke who had led him into so confident a state of hope. And he had anxieties on another score. There was, he knew, a hue-and-cry set afoot by the vindictive fury of Mrs. Quinn, and it was solely due to the fact that his real whereabouts were unknown to her that he had escaped arrest. He was aware that search for him had been made at the Bird in Hand, whither he had announced to her his intention of removing himself. That the search had been abandoned he dared not assume. At any moment it might result in his discovery and seizure. If it had not hitherto been more vigorously prosecuted, it was, he supposed, because there were other momentous matters to engage the public attention. For these were excited, uneasy days in London.

On the third of the month the people had been startled in the City by the distant boom of guns, which had endured throughout the day to intimate that the Dutch and English fleets were engaged and rather alarmingly close at hand. The engagement, as you know, was somewhere off the coast in the neighbourhood of Harwich, and it ended in heavy loss to the Dutch, who drew off back to the Texel. There were, of course, the usual exaggerations on both sides, and both English and Dutch claimed a complete victory and lighted bonfires. Our affair, however, is not with what was happening in Holland. In London from the 8th June, when first the news came of the complete rout of the Dutch and the destruction of half their ships, until the 20th, which was appointed as a thanksgiving day for that great victory, there were high junketings over the business, junketings which reached their climax at Whitehall on the 16th to welcome back the victorious Duke of York, returning from sea — as Mr. Pepys tells us — all fat and lusty and ruddy from being in the sun.

And well it was — or perhaps not — that there should have been such excitements to keep the mind of the people diverted from the thing happening in their midst, to blind them to the spread of the plague, which, if slow, was nevertheless relentlessly steady, a foe likely to prove less easily engaged and beaten than the Dutch.

After the wild public rejoicings of the 20th, people seemed suddenly to awaken to their peril. It may be that the sense of danger and dismay had its source in Whitehall, which was emptying itself rapidly now. The Court removed itself to the more salubrious air of Salisbury, and throughout the day on the 21st and again on the 22d there was a constant westward stream of coaches and wagons by Charing Cross, laden with people departing from the infected town to seek safety in the country

That flight struck dismay into the City, whose inhabitants felt themselves in the position of mariners abandoned

aboard a ship that is doomed. Something approaching
panic ensued as a consequence of the orders promulgated by
the Lord Mayor and the measures taken to combat the
dread disease. Sir John Lawrence had been constrained to
issue stringent regulations, to appoint examiners and
searchers, and to take measures for shutting up and isolating
infected houses — measures so rigorous that they finally
dispelled any remains of the fond illusion that there was
immunity within the walls of the City itself.

A wholesale flight followed. Never were horses in such
request in London, and never did their hire command such
prices, and daily now at Ludgate, Aldgate, over London
Bridge, and by every other exit from the City was there that
same congestion of departing horsemen, pedestrians, coaches,
and carts that had earlier been seen at Charing Cross. A
sort of paralysis settled upon London life and the transac-
tion of its business by the rapidly thinning population. In
the suburbs it was reported that men were dying like flies at
the approach of winter.

Preachers of doom multiplied, and they were no longer
mocked or pelted with offal, but listened to in awe. And so
reduced in ribaldry were the prentices of London that they
even suffered a madman to run naked through the streets
about Paul's with a cresset of live coals upon his head,
screaming that the Lord would purge with fire the City of
its sins.

But Colonel Holles was much too obsessed by his own
affairs to be deeply concerned with the general panic. When
at last he heard of the exodus from Whitehall, he bestirred
himself to action, from fear lest His Grace of Buckingham
— in whom his last hope now rested — should depart with
the others. Therefore he ventured to recall himself in a
letter to the Duke. For two days he waited in vain for a
reply, and then, as despondency was settling upon him,

came an added blow to quicken this into utter and absolute despair.

He returned after dusk one evening from an expedition in the course of which he had sold at last that jewel which had now served whatever purpose he had fondly imagined that Fate intended by it, so that its conversion into money was the last use to which it could be put. He had made an atrociously bad bargain, for these were not times — the buyer assured him — in which folk were thinking of adornments. As he reëntered the inn, Banks, the landlord, approached him, and drew him on one side out of sight and earshot of the few who lingered in the common room.

"There's been two men here seeking you, sir."

Holles started in eagerness, his mind leaping instantly to the Duke of Buckingham. Observing this, the landlord, grave-faced, shook his head. He was a corpulent, swarthy man of a kindly disposition, and it may be that this wistful guest of his had commanded instinctively his sympathy. He leaned closer, lowering his voice, although there was hardly the need.

"They was messengers from Bow Street," he said. "They didn't say so. But I know them. They asked a mort o' questions. How long you had been in my house, and whence you came and what you did. And they ordered me at parting to say nothing about this to you. But ..." The landlord shrugged his great shoulders, and curled his lip in contempt of that injunction. His dark eyes were on the Colonel, and he observed the latter's sudden gravity. Holles was not exercised by any speculations on the score of the business that had brought those minions of justice. His association with Tucker and Rathbone had been disclosed, possibly at the trial of the former, who had just been convicted and sentenced to be hanged and quartered. And he had no single doubt that, if he once came within the talons of the law, his own conviction would follow, despite his innocence.

"I thought, sir," the landlord was saying, "that I'd warn you. So that if so be you've done aught to place yourself outside the law, ye shouldn't stay for them to take you. I don't want to see you come to no harm."

Holles collected himself. "Mister Banks," he said, "ye're a good friend, and I thank you. I have done nothing. Of that I can assure you. But appearances may be made to damn me. The unfortunate Mr. Tucker was an old friend of mine . . ."

The landlord's sigh interrupted him. "Aye, sir, I thought it might be that, from something they let fall. That's why I take the risk of telling you. In God's name, sir, be off whiles ye may."

It took the Colonel a little by surprise. Here for once Fortune was his friend in that the landlord of The Harp was a secret sympathizer with the republicans.

He took the man's advice, paid his score — which absorbed most of the proceeds of the jewel — and, without so much as waiting to collect what gear he possessed, he set out at once from quarters grown suddenly so very dangerous.

He was not a moment too soon. Even as he stepped into the gloom of the street, two shadowy forms loomed abruptly before him to bar his way, a lantern was suddenly uncovered, and thrust into his face.

"Stand, sir, in the King's name!" a gruff voice commanded him.

He could not see whether they had weapons in their hands or not, nor did he wait to ascertain. At a blow he sent the lantern flying, at another he felled the man who had advanced it. The arms of the second messenger wound themselves about his body, and the fellow steadied himself to throw him. But before that could happen Holles had

knocked the breath out of the man's body by a jolt of his elbow, and, as the catchpoll's arms slackened in their grip, he
was flung off and violently hurled against the wall. As you
conceive, Holles did not stay to verify what damage he had
done. He was off like a hare, down the dark street, whilst
behind him came shouts and the patter of running feet.
The pursuit was not long maintained, and presently the
Colonel was able with safety to resume a more leisurely and
dignified progress. But fear went with him, driving him
ever farther into the depths of the City, and it kept him
company throughout the night. He lay in a tavern in the
neighbourhood of Aldgate, and reflected grimly upon the
choice position in which he found himself. Before dawn he
had reached the conclusion that there was but one thing for
a sane man in his position to do, and that was to quit this
England where he found nothing but bitterness and disappointment. He cursed the ill-conceived patriotism that had
brought him home, pronounced love of country a delusion,
and fools all those who yielded to it. He would depart at
once, and never trouble this evil land of his birth again.
Now that the Dutch were back in the Texel and the seas
open once more, there need be no difficulty; not even his
lack of funds should prove an obstacle. He would ship as one
of the hands aboard some vessel bound for France. With
this intention he made his way to Wapping betimes next
morning.

Vessels there were, and hands were needed, but no master
would ship him until he had procured himself a certificate of
health. The plague had rendered this precaution necessary,
not only for those going abroad, but even for such as desired
to go into the country, where no town or village now would
receive any man who came from London unless he came
provided with a certificate that pronounced him clean.

It was a vexatious complication. But it must be accepted.

So the Colonel trudged wearily to the Guildhall, going by sparsely tenanted, darksome city streets, where he saw more than one door marked with a cross and guarded by a watchman who warned all wayfarers to keep their distance. And the wayfarers, of whom he met by no means many, showed themselves eager enough to keep to the middle of the street, giving as wide a berth as possible, not only to those infected dwellings, but also to all persons whom they might chance to meet. Not a few of those whom Holles found abroad were officials whose appointment the pestilence had rendered necessary — examiners, searchers, keepers, and chirurgeons — each and all of them distinguishable at a glance by a red wand borne well displayed as the law prescribed, and all of them shunned as if they were themselves plague-stricken.

It made the Colonel realize the extent of the spread of this infection which was now counting its victims by thousands. The extent of the panic he realized when he came at last to the Guildhall, and found it besieged by coaches, sedan-chairs, and a vast mob on foot. All here were come upon the same errand as himself; to procure the Lord Mayor's certificate of health that should enable them to escape from this stricken city.

Most of the day he waited in that throng, enduring the stifling heat and the pangs of hunger and of thirst. For the only hawkers moving in the crowd were vendors of preventive medicines and amulets against the plague. Instead of the cry of "Sweet oranges," which in normal times would have been heard in such a gathering, and which he would now have welcomed, here the only cries were: "Infallible Preservative Against Infection," "The Royal Antidote," "Sovereign Cordial Against the Corruption of the Air," and the like.

He could ill afford to purchase the favour of the ushers and bribe them into according him some precedence. He must wait and take his turn with the humblest there, and, as he had arrived late, his turn did not seem likely to come that day at all.

Towards evening — unlike the more prudent, who determined to remain in their ranks all night, that they might be among the first served next day — he departed empty-handed and disgruntled. Yet within the hour he was to realize that perhaps he had been better served by Fate than he suspected.

In a sparsely tenanted eating-house in Cheapside, where he sought to stay the pangs of thirst and hunger — for he had neither eaten nor drunk since early morning — he overheard some scraps of conversation between two citizens at a neighbouring table. They were discussing an arrest that had been made that day, and in the course of this they let fall the words which gave pause to Colonel Holles.

"But how was he taken? How discovered?" one of them asked.

"Why, at the Guildhall, when he sought a certifiçate of health that should enable him to leave Town. I tell you it's none so easy to leave London nowadays, as evil-doers are finding when they attempt it. Sooner or later they'll get Danvers this way. They're on the watch for him, aye, and for others too."

Colonel Holles pushed away his platter, his appetite suddenly dead. He was in a trap, it seemed, and it had needed those words overheard by chance to make him realize it. To attempt flight was but to court discovery. True, it might be possible to obtain a certificate of health in a false name. But, on the other hand, it might not. There must be inquisition into a person's immediate antecedents if only to verify that he was clean of infection, and this inquisition must speedily bring to light any prevarication or assumption of false identity.

And so he was on the horns of a dilemma. If he remained in London, sooner or later he would be run to earth by those who sought him, who would be seeking him more relentlessly than ever now, after his manhandling of those messengers of the law last night. If he attempted to go, he delivered himself up to justice by the very act.

He determined, after much gloomy cogitation, to seek the protection of Albemarle in this desperate pass, and with that intent went forth. He persisted in it until he reached Charing Cross, when a doubt assailed him. He remembered Albemarle's selfish caution. What if Albemarle should refuse to take the risk of believing his innocence, considering the nature of the alleged offence? He hardly thought that Albemarle would push caution quite so far, especially with the son of his old friend — though it was a friend the Duke must disown in these days. But because he perceived the risk he hesitated, and finally determined that first he would make one last attempt to move the Duke of Buckingham.

Acting upon that impulse, he turned into the courtyard of Wallingford House.

CHAPTER XV

THE SHADOW OF THE GALLOWS

HIS GRACE OF BUCKINGHAM had not accompanied the Court in its flight to Salisbury. His duties, indeed, recalled him to his lord-lieutenancy in York. But he was as deaf to the voice of duty as to that of caution. He was held fast in London, in the thraldom of his passion for Miss Farquharson, and enraged because that passion prospered not at all. It had prospered less than ever since his attempt to play the hero and rescuer of beauty in distress had ended in making him ridiculous in the lady's eyes.

It was his obsession on the score of Miss Farquharson that was responsible for his neglect of the letter that Holles had written to him. That appeal had reached him at a moment when he was plunged into dismay by the news that Sir John Lawrence's orders had gone forth that all theatres and other places of assembly should close upon the following Saturday, as a very necessary measure in the Lord Mayor's campaign against the plague. The Court was no longer present to oppose the order, and it is doubtful if it would have dared still to oppose it in any case. Now the closing of the theatres meant the withdrawal of the players from Town, and with that the end of his grace's opportunities. Either he must acknowledge defeat, or else act promptly.

One course, one simple and direct course, there was, which he would long ago have taken but for the pusillanimous attention he had paid to Mr. Etheredge's warning. In a manner the closing of the theatre favoured this course, and removed some of the dangers attending it, dangers which in no case would long have weighed with His Grace of

Buckingham, accustomed as he was to flout all laws but those of his own desires.

He took his resolve at last and sent for the subtle Bates, who was the Chaffinch of Wallingford House. He gave him certain commands — whose full purport Master Bates did not completely apprehend — in the matter of a house. That was on the Monday of the week whose Saturday was to see the closing of the theatres. It was the very day on which Holles made his precipitate departure from The Harp.

On Tuesday morning the excellent and resourceful Bates was able to report to his master that he had found precisely such a domicile as his grace required — though why his grace should require it Bates could not even begin to surmise. It was a fairly spacious and excellently equipped dwelling in Knight Ryder Street, lately vacated by a tenant who had removed himself into the country out of dread of the pestilence. The owner was a certain merchant in Fenchurch Street, who would be glad enough to let the place on easy terms, considering how impossible it was just at present to find tenants for houses in the City or its liberties.

Bates had pursued his inquiries with characteristic discretion, as he now assured his grace, without allowing it to transpire on whose behalf he was acting.

His grace laughed outright at the assurance and all that it implied that Bates had taken for granted.

"Ye're growing a very competent scoundrel in my service."

Bates bowed, not without a tinge of mockery. "I am glad to merit your grace's approval," said he dryly. There was a strain of humorous insolence in the fellow, of which the Duke was disposed to be tolerant; perhaps because nothing else was possible with one so intimately acquainted with his conscience.

"Aye. Ye're a trustworthy rogue. The house will do

admirably, though I should have preferred a less populous district."

"If things continue as at present, your grace should have no cause for complaint on that score. Soon the City will be the most depopulated spot in England. Already more than half the houses in Knight Ryder Street are empty. I trust your grace is not thinking of residing there."

"Not . . . not exactly." His grace was frowning, thoughtfully. "There's no infection in the street, I hope?"

"Not yet. But there's an abundant fear of it, as everywhere else in the City. This merchant in Fenchurch Street didn't trouble to conceal the opinion that I was crazy to be seeking a house in London at such a time."

"Pooh, pooh!" His grace dismissed the matter of fear contemptuously. "These cits frighten themselves into the plague. It's opportune enough. It will serve to keep men's minds off the concerns of their neighbours. I want no spying on me in Knight Ryder Street. To-morrow, Bates, you'll seek this merchant and engage the house — and ye're to acquire the tenancy of it in your own name. Ye understand? My name is not to be mentioned. To avoid questions you'll pay him six months' rent at once."

Bates bowed. "Perfectly, your grace."

His grace leaned back in his great chair, and considered his servant through half-closed, slyly smiling eyes.

"You'll have guessed, of course, the purpose for which I am acquiring this house."

"I should never presume to guess any purpose of your grace's."

"By which you mean that my purpose baffles you. That is an admission of dullness. You recall the little comedy we played a month ago for the benefit of Miss Farquharson?"

"I have occasion to. My bones are still sore from the

cudgelling I got. It was a very realistic piece of acting, on the part of your grace's cursed French grooms."

"The lady didn't think so. At least, it did not convince her. We must do better this time."

"Yes, your grace." There was the least dubiety in the rascal's tone.

"We'll introduce a more serious note into the comedy. We'll carry the lady off. That is the purpose for which I require this house."

"Carry her off?" said Bates, his face grown suddenly very serious.

"That is what I require of you, my good Bates."

"Of me?" Bates gasped. His face lengthened, and his wolfish mouth fell open. "Of me, your grace?" He made it plain that the prospect scared him.

"To be sure. What's to gape at?"

"But, your grace. This . . . this is . . .very serious."

"Bah!" said his grace.

"It . . . it's a hanging matter."

"Oh, damn your silliness. A hanging matter! When I'm behind you?"

"That's what makes it so. They'll never venture to hang your grace. But they'll need a scapegoat, if there's trouble, and they'll hang your instruments to pacify the rabble's clamour for justice."

"Are ye quite mad?"

"I'm not only sane, your grace; I'm shrewd. And if I may presume to advise your grace . . ."

"That would, indeed, be a presumption, you impudent rogue!" The Duke's voice rose sharply, a heavy frown rumpled his brow. "You forget yourself, I think."

"I beg your grace's pardon." But he went on, none the less. "Your grace, perhaps, is not aware of the extent of the panic in the City over this pestilence. The cry everywhere is that it is a visitation provoked by the sins of the Court. That's what the canting Nonconformist preachers have put about. And if this thing that your grace contemplates . . ."

"My God!" thundered Buckingham. "But it seems you presume to advise me in spite of all."

Bates fell silent; but there was obstinacy in every line of him as he stood there facing his master now. More calmly Buckingham continued:

"Listen, Bates. If we are ill served on the one hand by the pestilence, we are very well served on the other. To carry Miss Farquharson off while she is playing at the theatre would be to have a hue-and-cry set up at once that might lead to discovery and unpleasant consequences. But the Lord Mayor has ordered the closing of all theatres on Saturday, and it is on Saturday after the theatre, therefore, that this thing must be done, when Miss Farquharson will no longer be missed and her disappearance give rise to no excitement — particularly at a time when this very fear of the plague is giving people enough to think about."

"And afterwards, your grace?"

"Afterwards?"

"When the lady makes complaint."

Buckingham smiled in his knowledge of the world. "Do ladies ever make complaints of this kind — afterwards? Besides, who will believe her tale that she went to this house of mine against her will? She is an actress, remember; not a princess. And I still command some measure of authority in this country."

But Bates solemnly shook his head. "I doubt if your grace commands enough to save my neck should there be trouble, and trouble there will be. Be sure of that, your grace. There's too many malcontents abroad, spying the opportunity to make it."

"But who's to accuse you?" cried the Duke impatiently.

"The lady herself, if I carry her off for you. Besides, has not your grace said that the house is to be taken in my name? If more were wanted, that would supply it. I am your grace's very dutiful servant, and God knows I'm not overscrupulous on the score of my service. But . . . not this, your grace. I durstn't."

Amazement and scorn were blent on Buckingham's countenance. He wanted to explode in anger and he wanted to laugh at the same time at the absurdity of finding an obstacle in Bates. His fingers drummed the table what time he reflected. Then he determined to cut the game short by playing trumps.

"How long have you been in my service, Bates?"

"Five years this month, your grace."

"And you are tired of it, eh?"

"Your grace knows that I am not. I have served you faithfully in all things . . ."

"But you think the time has come when you may pick and choose the things in which you will serve me still. Bates, I think you have been in my service too long."

"Your grace!"

"I may be mistaken. But I shall require proof before believing it. Fortunately for you, it lies within your power to afford me that proof. I advise you to do so."

He looked at Bates coldly, and Bates looked back at him in dread. The little rascal fidgeted with his neckcloth, and his lean knuckly hand for a moment caressed his throat. The gesture almost suggested that his thoughts were on the rope which he might be putting about that scraggy neck of his.

"Your grace," he cried on a note of appeal, "there is no service I will not perform to prove my devotion. Command me to do anything, your grace — anything. But not . . . not this."

"I am touched, Bates, by your protestations." His grace

was coldly supercilious. "Unfortunately, this is the only service I desire of you at the moment."

Bates was reduced to despair.

"I can't, your grace! I can't!" he cried. "It is a hanging matter, as your grace well knows."

"For me, Bates, at law — at strict law — I believe it might be," said the Duke indifferently.

"And since your grace is too high for hanging, it's me that would have to be your deputy."

"How you repeat yourself! A tiresome habit. And you but confirm me in my opinions. Yet there might be a hundred pounds or so for you as a douceur . . ."

"It isn't money, your grace. I wouldn't do it for a thousand."

"Then there is no more to be said." Inwardly Buckingham was very angry. Outwardly he remained icily cold. "You have leave to go, Bates, and I shall not further require your services. If you will apply to Mr. Grove he will pay you what moneys may be due to you."

A wave of the white jewelled hand dismissed the crestfallen little scoundrel. A moment Bates wavered, hesitating, swayed by his reluctance to accept dismissal. But not even that reluctance could conquer his dread of the consequences, a dread based upon conviction that they could not fail to overtake him. Had it been anything less than a hanging matter he might have risked it. But this was too much. So, realizing that further pleadings or protestations would be wasted upon the cold arrogance of the Duke, he bowed in silence, and in silence removed himself.

If he withdrew in discomfiture, at least he left discomfiture behind him. The Duke's trump card had failed to win him the game, and he knew not where to find another agent for the enterprise which now obsessed him.

Mr. Etheredge, coming later that day to visit him, found

his grace still in a bedgown, pacing the handsome library, restless as a caged beast.

Mr. Etheredge, who well knew the attraction that held the Duke fast in Town, and who had, himself, just completed his preparations for departure, came to make the last of several recent attempts to recall his friend to his senses, and persuade him to leave London for healthier surroundings.

Buckingham laughed at him without mirth.

"You alarm yourself without occasion, George. This pestilence is born of uncleanliness and confines itself to the unclean. Look into the cases that are reported. The outbreaks are all in mean houses in mean streets. The plague practises a nice discrimination, and does not venture to intrude upon persons of quality."

"Nevertheless, I take my precautions," said Mr. Etheredge, producing a handkerchief from which a strong perfume of camphor and vinegar diffused itself through the room. "And I am one of those who believe that flight is the best physic. Besides, what is there to do here? The Court is gone; the Town is hot and reeking as an anteroom of hell. In Heaven's name let us seek a breath of clean, cool, country air."

"Pish! Ye're bucolic. Like Dryden ye've a pastoral mind. Well, well, be off to your sheep. We shall not miss you here."

Mr. Etheredge sat down and studied his friend, pursing his lips.

"And all this for a prude who has no notion of being kind! Let me perish, Bucks, but I don't know you!"

The Duke fetched a sigh. "Sometimes I think I don't know myself. Gad, George, I believe I am going mad!" He strode away to the window.

"Comfort yourself with the reflection that you won't have far to go," said the unsympathetic Mr. Etheredge.

"How a man of your years and experience can take the risks and the trouble over a pursuit that . . ."

The Duke swung round to interrupt him sharply.

"Pursuit! That is the cursed word. A pursuit that maddens because it never overtakes."

"Not a bad line, that — for you," said Mr. Etheredge. "But in love, remember, 'they fly that wound, and they pursue that die.'"

But Buckingham raved on without heeding the gibe, his voice suddenly thick with passion. "I have the hunter's instinct, I suppose. The prey that eludes me is the prey that at all costs must be reduced into possession. Can't you understand?"

"No, thank God! I happen to retain my sanity. Come into the country, man, and recover yours. It's waiting for you there amid the buttercups."

"Pshaw!" Buckingham turned from him again with an ill-humoured shrug.

"Is that your answer?"

"It is. Don't let me detain you."

Etheredge got up, and went to set a hand upon his arm.

"If you stay, and at such a time, you must have some definite purpose in your mind. What is it?"

"What was in my mind before you came to trouble it, George. To end the matter where I should have begun it." And he adapted three lines of Suckling's:

> "If of herself she will not love,
>   Myself shall make her,
>   The devil take her!"

Etheredge shrugged in despair and disgust.

"Ye're not only mad, Bucks," said he. "Ye're coarse. I warned you once of the dangers of this thing. I've no mind to repeat myself. But you'll give me leave to marvel that you can take satisfaction in . . ."

"Marvel all you please," the other interrupted him with a touch of anger. "Perhaps, indeed, I am a matter for marvel. I am a man racked, consumed, burnt up by my feelings for this woman who has scorned and spurned and made a mock of me. If I could believe in her virtue, I would go my ways, bending to her stubborn will. But virtue in an actress! It is as likely as snow in hell. She indulges a cruel and perverse zest to torture a man whom she sees perishing of love for her." He paused a moment, to pursue with even greater fierceness, his face livid with the working of the emotion that possessed him — that curious and fearful merging of love and hatred that is so often born of baffled passion. "I could tear the jade limb from limb with these two hands, and take joy in it. I could so. Or with the same joy I could give my body to the rack for her sweet sake! To such an abject state have her wiles reduced me."

He swung away, and went to fling himself petulantly into a chair, taking his blond head in his fine jewelled hands.

After that explosion Mr. Etheredge decided that there was nothing to be done with such a man but abandon him to his fate. He said so with engaging candour and took his leave.

His grace made no attempt to detain him, and for some time after his departure sat there alone in that sombre book-lined room, a fool enshrined in wisdom and learning. Gloomily he brooded the matter, more than ever exasperated by the defection of Bates, and the consideration that he was left thereby without a minister to assist him in the execution of his wishes.

He was disturbed at last by the appearance of a footman, who brought the announcement that a Colonel Holles was demanding insistently to see his grace.

Irritated, Buckingham was about to pronounce dismissal.

"Say that . . ." He checked. He remembered the letter received three days ago, and its urgent appeal. That awoke

an idea, and set his grace speculating. "Wait!" He moistened his lips and his eyes narrowed in thought. Slowly they
lighted from their gloom. Abruptly he rose. "Bring him in,"
he said.

Holles came, erect and soldierly of figure, still tolerably
dressed, but very haggard now of countenance at the end of
that weary day spent between Wapping and the Guildhall
with the sense that he was being hunted.

"Your grace will forgive, I trust, my importunities," he
excused himself, faltering a little. "But the truth is that my
need, which was very urgent when I wrote, has since grown
desperate."

Buckingham considered him thoughtfully from under his
bent brows without directly replying. He dismissed the
waiting footman, and offered his visitor a chair. Holles sat
down wearily.

His grace remained standing, his thumbs hooked into the
girdle of his bedgown.

"I received your letter," he said in his slow, pleasant
voice. "From my silence you may have supposed that you
had passed from my mind. That is not so. But you realize,
I think, that you are not an easy man to help."

"Less than ever now," said Holles grimly.

"What's that?" There was a sudden unmistakable quickening of the Duke's glance, almost as if he welcomed the
news.

Holles told him without preamble.

"And so your grace perceives," he ended, "that I am now
not only in danger of starving, but of hanging."

His grace had not moved throughout the rendering of that
account. Now at last he stirred. He turned from his visitor,
and sauntered slowly away in thought.

"But what an imprudence," he said at last, "for a man in
your position to have had relations, however slight with

these wretched fifth-monarchy dogs! It is to put a halter about your neck."

"Yet there was no wrong in those relations. Tucker was an old brother-in-arms. Your grace has been a soldier and knows what that means. It is true that he tempted me with proposals. I admit it, since that can no longer hurt him. But those proposals I incontinently refused."

His grace smiled a little. "Do you imagine that the Justices will believe you when you come to tell them that?"

"Seeing that my name is Randal Holles, and that a vindictive government would be glad of any pretext to stretch the neck of my father's son, I do not. That is why I describe my state as desperate. I am a man moving in the shadow of the gallows."

"Sh! Sh!" the Duke reproved him gently. "You must not express yourself in such terms, Colonel. Your very tone savours of disloyalty. And you are unreasonable. If you were really loyal, there was a clear duty which you would not have neglected. When first this proposal was made to you, whatever your friendship for Tucker, you should have gone straight to the Justices and laid information of this plot."

"Your grace advises something that in my own case you would not have performed. But even had I acted so, how should I have compelled belief? I knew no details of this plot. I was not in a position to prove anything. It would have been my bare word against Tucker's, and my name alone would have discredited me. My action might have been regarded as an impudent attempt to earn the favour of the powers in being. It might even, in some tortuous legal manner, have been construed against me. Therefore I held my peace."

"Your assurance is enough for me," said his grace amiably. "And God knows I perceive your difficulty, and how

you have been brought into your present danger. Our first
care must be to deliver you from this. You must do at last
what should have been done long since. You must go before
the Justices, and frankly state the case as you have stated
it to me."

"But your grace yourself has just said that they will not
believe me."

His grace paused in his pacing, and smiled a little slyly.

"They will not believe your unsupported word. But if
some person of eminence and authority were to answer for
your good faith, they would hardly dare to doubt; the matter
would be at an end, and there would be no further question
of any impeachment."

Holles stared, suddenly hopeful, and yet not daring to
yield entirely to his hope.

"Your grace does not mean that you . . . that you would
do this for me?"

His grace's smile grew broader, kindlier. "But, of course,
my friend. If I am to employ you, as I hope I shall, so much
would be a necessary preliminary."

"Your grace!" Holles bounded to his feet. "How to
thank you?"

His grace waved him back again to his chair. "I will show
you presently, my friend. There are certain conditions I
must impose. There is a certain task I shall require of you."

"Your grace should know that you have but to name it."

"Ah!" The Duke paused, and again considered him intently. "You said in your letter that you were ready for
any work, for *any* service."

"I said so. Yes. I say so again."

"Ah!" Again that soft, relieved exclamation. Then the
Duke paced away to the book-lined wall and back again
before continuing. "My friend, your despair comes opportunely to my own. We are desperate both, though in

different ways, and it lies within the power of each to serve the other."

"If I could believe that!"

"You may. The rest depends upon yourself." He paused a moment, then on a half-humorous note proceeded: "I do not know how much of squeamishness, of what men call honesty, your travels and misfortune may have left you."

"None that your grace need consider," said Holles, with some self-derision.

"That is . . . very well. Yet, you may find the task distasteful."

"I doubt it. God knows I'm not fastidious nowadays. But if I do, I will tell you so."

"Just so." The Duke nodded, and then — perhaps because of the hesitation that still beset him to make to Holles the proposal that he had in mind — his manner suddenly hardened. It was almost that of the great gentleman speaking to his lackey. "That is why I warn you. For should you wish to tell me so, you will please to tell me without any unnecessary roaring, without the airs of a Bobadil or a Pistol, or any other of your fire-eating, down-at-heel fraternity. You have but to say 'No,' and spare me the vapourings of outraged virtue."

Holles stared at the man in silence for a moment, utterly dumbfounded by his tone. Then he laughed a little.

"It would surprise me to discover that I've any virtue left to outrage."

"All the better," snapped the Duke. He drew up a chair, and sat down, facing Holles. He leaned forward. "In your time, no doubt, you will have played many parts, Colonel Holles?"

"Aye — a mort of parts."

"Have you ever played . . . Sir Pandarus of Troy?"

The Duke keenly watched his visitor's face for some sign

of understanding. But the Colonel's classical education had
been neglected.

"I've never heard of him. What manner of part may that
be?"

His grace did not directly answer. He took another way
to his ends.

"Have you ever heard of Sylvia Farquharson?"

Surprised anew, it was a moment before the Colonel answered him.

"Sylvia Farquharson?" he echoed, musing. "I've heard
the name. Oh! I have it. That was the lady in the sedan-
chair your grace rescued yonder in Paul's Yard on the day
we met. Aye, aye. I heard her named at the time. A baggage of a play actress from the Duke's House, I think. But
what has she to do with us?"

"Something I think — unless the stars are wrong. And
the stars are never wrong. They stand immutable and true
in a false and fickle world. It is written in them — as I have
already told you — that we were to meet again, you and I,
and be jointly concerned in a fateful matter with one other.
That other, my friend, is this same Sylvia Farquharson."

He rose, casting off all reserve at last, and his pleasant
voice was thickened by the stress of his emotions.

"You behold in me a man exerting vast power for good
and ill. There are in life few things, however great, that I
desire without being able to command them. Sylvia Farquharson is one of these few things. With affectations of
prudery this wanton keeps me on the rack. That is where
I require your help."

He paused. The Colonel stared at him round-eyed. A
faint colour stirred in his haggard cheeks. At last he spoke,
in a voice that was cold and level.

"Your grace has hardly said enough."

"Dullard! What more is to be said? Don't you understand that I mean to make an end of this situation? — to conquer the prudish airs with which this wanton jade repels me?"

"Faith! I think I understand that well enough." Holles laughed a little. "What I don't understand is my part in this — a doxy business of this kind. Will not your grace be plain?"

"Plain? Why, man, I want her carried off for me."

They sat conning each other in silence now, the Colonel's face utterly blank, so that the Duke looked in vain for some sign of how he might be taking this proposal. At last his lips curled in a rather scornful smile, and his voice drawled with a mildly humorous inflection.

"But in such a matter your grace's own vast experience should surely serve you better than could I."

In his eagerness, the Duke took him literally, never heeding the sarcasm.

"My experience will be there to guide you."

"I see," said Holles.

"I'll tell you more precisely how I need you — where you can serve me."

And Buckingham proceeded to inform him of the well-equipped house in Knight Ryder Street, which he now desired Holles to take in his own name. Having taken it, he was to make the necessary arrangements to carry the girl thither on the evening of Saturday next, after the last performance at the Duke's House.

"Taking what men you need," the Duke concluded, "it should be easy to waylay and capture her chair as it is being borne home. We will consider that more closely if the service is one that you are disposed to accept."

The Colonel's face was flushed. He felt his gorge rising. At last his anger mastered him, and he heaved himself up to confront the handsome profligate who dared in cold blood to make him this proposal.

"My God!" he growled. "Are you led by your vices like a blind man by his dog?"

The Duke stepped back before the sudden menace of that tone and mien. At once he wrapt himself in a mantle of arrogance.

"I warned you, sir, that I will suffer no heroics; that I will have no man play Bobadil to me. You asked service of me. I have shown you how I can employ you."

"Service?" echoed Holles, his voice almost choked with anger. "Is this service for a gentleman?"

"Perhaps not. But a man standing in the shadow of the gallows should not be over-fastidious."

The flush perished in the Colonel's face; the haunting fear returned to his eyes. The Duke, seeing him thus suddenly stricken by that grim reminder, was moved to sudden laughter.

"It seems you have to realize, Colonel Holles, that there is no music without frets. You resent that I should ask a trifling service of you when in return I am offering to make your fortune. For that is what I am offering. You come as opportunely to my need as to your own. Serve me as I require, and I pledge you my word that I shall not neglect you."

"But this ... this ... " faltered Holles, protesting. "It is a task for bullies, for jackals."

The Duke shrugged. "Damme! Why trouble to define it?" Then he changed his tone again. "The choice is yours. Fortune makes the offer: gold on the one hand; hemp on the other. I do not press either upon you."

Holles was torn between fear and honour. In imagination he felt already the rope about his neck; he beheld that wasted life of his finding a fitting consummation on Tyburn at the hands of Derrick. Thus fear impelled him to accept. But the old early notions that had inspired his ambition and had made him strive to keep his honour clean rose up to hold him back. His tortured thoughts evoked an image of Nancy Sylvester, as he had last seen her set in the frame of her casement, and he conceived the shame and horror in that face could she behold him engaged upon so loathly an enterprise — he who had gone forth so proudly to conquer the world for her. Many a time in the past had that image delivered him from the evil to which he was tempted.

"I'll go my ways, I think," he said heavily, and half turned as if to depart.

"You know whither it leads?" came the Duke's warning voice.

"I care not an apple-paring."

"As you please."

In silence Holles bowed, and made his way to the door with dragging feet, hope's last bubble pricked.

And then the Duke's voice arrested him again.

"Holles, you are a fool."

"I have long known it. I was a fool when I saved your life, and you pay me as a fool should be paid."

"You pay yourself. And of your own choice you do so in fool's coin."

Seeing him standing arrested there, still hesitating, the Duke approached him. His grace's need, as you know, was very urgent. It was no overstatement that Holles's coming had been opportune. Unless he could make of Holles the tool that he required so sorely, where should he find another? It was because of this he decided to use yet some persuasion to conquer a frame of mind that was obviously still balancing. He set a friendly hand upon the Colonel's shoulder. And Holles, shrinking almost under that touch, could not guess that this Duke, who sought to make a tool of him, was himself the blind tool of Destiny hewing a way to her inscrutable ends.

And whilst the Duke now talked persuasively, tempting him with promises on the one hand and intimidating him with a picture of what must otherwise happen on the other, the Colonel's own tormented mind was reconsidering.

Were his hands really so clean, his life so blameless, his honour so untarnished, that he must boggle at this vileness, and boggle at it to the extent of allowing them to stretch his neck and disembowel him sooner than perform it? And what was this vileness when all was said? A baggage of the theatre, a trull of an actress, had played upon the Duke that she might make the greater profit out of him in the end. The Duke, wearied of her tricks and wiles, desired to cut the game short. Thus the Duke represented the situation. And what cause had Holles to assume that it was other than a true representation? The girl was an actress and therefore, it followed, wanton. The puritanical contempt of the play-house and its denizens — heritage of his Commonwealth days — left him no doubt upon that score. If she were a lady of quality, a woman of virtue, the thing would be different. Then, indeed, to be a party to such an act were a wickedness unthinkable, a thing sooner than which he would, indeed, suffer death. But where was the vileness here, since the object itself was vile? Against what, then, really, did this thing offend? Against himself; against his soldier's dignity. The act required of him was one proper to a hired bully. It was ignoble. But was hanging less ignoble? Was he to let them put a rope about his neck and the brand of the gallows on his name out of tenderness for a baggage of the theatre whom he did not even know?

Buckingham was right. He was a fool. All his life he had been a fool, scrupulous in trifles, negligent in the greater things. And now upon the most trifling scruple of all he would fitly sacrifice his life.

Abruptly he swung round and squarely faced the Duke.

"Your grace," he said hoarsely, "I am your man."

CHAPTER XVI

THE SEDAN-CHAIR

HIS GRACE behaved generously, and at the same time with a prudence which reveals the alert and calculating mind of this gifted man, who might have been great had he been less of a voluptuary.

He attended with Holles before the Justices early on the morrow, announcing himself able to confirm out of his own knowledge the truth of the account which the Colonel gave of his relations with the attainted Tucker. To that his grace added the assertion that he was ready — if more were needed — to stand surety for the loyalty of this suspected man whom he now pronounced his friend. More was not needed. The sycophantic court bent the knee before this great gentleman who enjoyed the close friendship of his King, and even professed regret that certain reckless and malicious statements should have deceived it into troubling the peace of Colonel Holles, and putting His Grace of Buckingham to the present inconvenience. The Colonel's antecedents, which, without Buckingham's protection, might have been the gravest source of trouble, were not so much as touched upon.

There was in all this nothing in the least unreasonable. Had the offence of which Colonel Holles was suspected been anything less than treason, it is not to be supposed that the Duke would have been able to carry matters with quite so high a hand. But it was utterly unthinkable that His Grace of Buckingham, whose loyalty stood so high, whose whole life bore witness to his deep attachment to the House of Stuart, and who was notoriously one of His Majesty's closest and most intimate companions, should offer to stand surety for a man against whom the merest suspicion of disloyalty would be justified.

Thus at the outset was Holles delivered from his worst peril. Next he was informed that, since service of any distinction in England was almost out of the question for his father's son, Buckingham would supply him with letters to several high-placed friends of his own in France, where a capable soldier well recommended need never lack employment. If Colonel Holles made the most of the opportunity thus afforded him, his future should be assured and his days of adversity at an end. This Holles clearly preceived for himself, and the reflection served to stifle any lingering qualms of conscience over the unworthy nature of the immediate service to which he was committed and to assure him that he would, indeed, have been a fool had he permitted any mawkish sentimentality to deprive him of this the greatest opportunity of all his life.

In this resolve to send Holles out of England the moment the service required of him should be accomplished, Buckingham again reveals his astuteness. Further, he reveals it in the fact that to assist the Colonel he placed at his disposal four of the French lackeys in his pay. It was his intention to repatriate them, packing them off to France together with Holles, as soon as the thing were done.

Thus, in the event of any trouble afterwards with the law, he would have removed the only possible witnesses. The unsupported word of Miss Farquharson — even in the extreme, and in his grace's view unlikely, event of her not accepting the situation — would be the only thing against him; and in that case he did not think that he need gravely apprehend the accusations of an actress, which he would have no great difficulty in answering.

From attendance before the Justices, Colonel Holles repaired straight to Fenchurch Street to conclude arrangements with the owner of the house in Knight Ryder Street. Of this he now acquired the tenancy in his own name for the term of one year. The merchant did not trouble to conceal the fact that he regarded Colonel Holles as crazy to desire to take up his residence in an infected city from which all who were able were making haste to remove themselves. Had the Colonel needed a reminder of it, he had it in the fact that he was constrained to go on foot, not only because hackney-coaches were now rare, but because the use of them was considered highly imprudent, since so many had been used by infected persons. Doors smeared with the red cross and guarded by watchmen were becoming commonplaces, and the comparatively few people met in the streets who still sought to maintain the normal tenor and business of their lives moved with the listlessness of despondency or else with the watchfulness of hunted creatures. The pungent smell of electuaries, and particularly of camphor, was wafted to the Colonel's nostrils from the person of almost every man he met.

He may have thought again that — as he had already admirably expressed it — Buckingham was led by his passion like a blind man by his dog, to come thrusting himself at such a time into the City, and he may have taken satisfaction in the thought that he, himself, so soon as this business should be accomplished, was to shake the poisonous dust of London from his feet.

Matters concluded with the merchant, the Colonel went to take possession of the house, and he installed there two of the four French lackeys the Duke had lent him for myrmidons.

After that there was little to do but wait until Saturday, since, for reasons which the Duke had given him, the attempt should not be made before. That evening, however, and the next, the Colonel repaired to Lincoln's Inn to watch from a safe distance Miss Farquharson's departure from the theatre, and so inform himself precisely of her habits in the matter. On both occasions she came forth at the same time — a few minutes after seven, and entered her waiting sedan-chair, in which she was borne away.

On Friday evening Holles went again, at six o'clock, and he had been waiting half an hour before the chair that was to convey her home made its appearance. It was the same chair as before and borne by the same men.

Holles lounged forward to engage them in talk. Of set purpose and despite the warm weather, he had donned a well-worn leather jerkin to cover and conceal his fairly pre-sentable coat. He had removed the feather from his hat, and all minor ornaments, replacing his embroidered baldric by one of plain leather. A pair of old boots completed the stud-ied shabbiness of his appearance, and gave him the air of a down-at-heel ruffler, ready to make a friend of any man.

He slouched towards the chairmen, pulling at a clay pipe, a man with time on his hands. And they, sitting on the shafts of the chair — one on each side, so as to balance each other — were nothing loath to have the tedium of their wait-ing beguiled by the thrasonical garrulousness his appearance led them to expect.

He did not disappoint them. He talked of the pestilence and of the war, and of the favouritism practised at Court, which bestowed commands upon all manner of incompetent fops and kept a hardened and stout old soldier like himself cooling his heels in London's plague-ridden streets. In this last respect he made them find him ridiculous, so that they rallied and covertly mocked him and hugely enjoyed them-selves at his expense, to all of which it appeared to them that his monstrous ruffler's vanity made him blind. Finally he invited them to come and drink with him, and they were nothing reluctant to permit him thus to add physical to the mental entertainment he had already afforded them. In their spirit of raillery, and to involve this foolish fellow in the utmost expense, they would have conducted him to The Grange. But the foolish fellow had more reasons than one for preferring an obscure little alehouse at the corner of Portugal Row, and it was thither that he now conducted his newly made friends and guests.

When at last they parted, the chairmen compelled to it by the necessity to be back at their post by seven o'clock, it was with voluble protestations of friendship on the part of Holles. He must come and see them soon again, he vowed. They were fellows after his own heart, he assured them. Eagerly they returned the compliment, and, as they made their way back to the theatre, they laughed not a little over the empty vanity of that silly pigeon, and their own wit and cleverness in having fooled him to the top of his ridiculous bent.

It might have given their hilarity pause could they have seen the grimly cunning smile that curled the lips of that same silly pigeon as he trudged away from the scene of their blithe encounter.

On the following evening — which was that of Saturday — you behold him there again, at about the same hour, joyously hailed by Miss Farquharson's chairmen in a manner impudently blending greeting with derision.

"Good-evening, Sir John," cried one, and, "Good-evening, my lord," the other.

The Colonel, whose swaggering carriage was suggestive of a mild intoxication, planted his feet wide, and regarded the twain owlishly.

"I am not Sir John, and I am not my lord," he reproved them, whereupon they laughed. "Though, mark you," he added, more ponderously, "mark you, I might be both if I had my dues. There's many a Whitehall pimp is my lord with less claim to the dignity than I have. Aye, a deal less."

"Any fool can see that to look at you," said Jake.

"Aye — any fool," said Nathaniel, sardonic and ambiguous.

The Colonel evidently chose the meaning that was flattering to himself.

"You're good fellows," he commended them. "Very good fellows." And abruptly he added: "What should you say, now, to a cup of sack?"

Their eyes gleamed. Had it been ale they would have assented gladly enough. But sack! That was a nobleman's drink that did not often come their lowly way. They looked at each other.

"Eh, Jake?" questioned one.

"A skew o' bouze'll never hurt, Nat," said the other.

"That it won't," Nat agreed. "And there's time to spare this evening. Her ladyship'll be packing a while."

They took the Colonel between them, and with arms linked the three set a course for the little alehouse at the corner of Portugal Row. The Colonel was more garrulous than ever, and very confidential. He had met a friend, he insisted upon informing them — an old brother-in-arms who had come upon fortunate days, from whom he had succeeded in borrowing a good round sum. Extending his confidence, he told them that probably it would be many days before he would be perfectly sober again. To this he added renewed assurances that he found them both very good fellows, lively companions these plaguy days, when the Town was as dull as a nunnery, and he swore that he would not be separated from them without a struggle.

Into the alehouse they rolled, to be skilfully piloted by the Colonel into a quiet corner well away from the windows and the light. He called noisily, tipsily, for the landlady, banging the table with the hilt of his sword. And when she made her appearance, he silenced her protests by his order.

"Three pints of Canary stiffly laced with brandy."

As she departed, he pulled up a three-legged stool, and sat down facing the chairmen, who were licking their chops in anticipatory delight.

"'S norrevery day we meet a brother-in-arms whose norr-only fortunate, but willing . . . share 'sfortune. The wine, madam! And of your best."

"Well said, old dog of war!" Nat approved him, where-upon the twain abandoned themselves to uproarious laughter.

The wine was brought, and the facetious pair swilled it greedily, whereafter they praised it, with rolling of eyes and resounding lip-smackings; they even subdued their raillery of the provider of this nectar. When he proposed a second pint, they actually grew solemn; and when after that he called for a third, they were almost prepared to treat him with respect.

There was a vacuousness in the eyes with which he pondered them, swaying never so slightly on his three-legged stool.

"Why . . . you stare at me like tha'?" he challenged them.

They looked up from the replenished but as yet untasted measures. His manner became suddenly stern. "P'raps you think I haven't . . . money . . . pay for all this swill?"

An awful dread assailed them both. He seemed to read it in their glances.

"Why, you rogues, d'ye dare . . . doubt . . . gen'l'man? D'ye think gen'l'man calls for wine, and can't pay? Here's to put your lousy minds at rest."

Violently he pulled a hand from his pocket, and violently he flung it forward under their noses, opening it as he did so. Gold leapt from it, a half-dozen pieces that rolled and rang upon greasy table and greasier floor.

In a flash, instinctively, the pair dived after them, and grovelled there on hands and knees about the table's legs, hunting the scattered coins. When at length they came up again, each obsequiously placed two pieces before the Colonel.

"Your honour should be more careful handling gold," said Jake.

"Ye might ha' lost a piece or two," added Nat.

"In some companies I might," said the Colonel, looking very wise. "But I know hones' fellows; I know how to choose my friends. Trust a cap'n o' fortune for that." He picked up the coins with clumsy, blundering fingers. "I thank you," he said, and restored them to his pocket.

Jake winked at Nat, and Nat hid his face in his tankard lest the grin which he could not suppress should be perceived by the Colonel.

The pair were spending a very pleasant and profitable evening with this stray and thirsty rodomont.

They drank noisily. And noisily and repeatedly Jake smacked his lips thereafter, frowning a little as he savoured the draught.

"I don't think it's as good as the last," he complained.

The Colonel picked up his own tankard with solicitude and took a pull at it.

"I have drunk better," he boasted. "But 'sgood enough, and just the same as last. Just the same."

"May be my fancy," said Jake, at which his companion nodded.

Then the Colonel fell to talking volubly, boastfully.

The landlady, who began to mislike their looks, drew near. The Colonel beckoned her nearer still, and thrust a piece of gold into her hand.

"Let that pay the reckoning," said he, very magnificent.

She gaped at such prodigality, dropped him a curtsy, and withdrew again at once, reflecting that appearances can be very deceptive.

The Colonel resumed his talk. Whether from the soporific

dreariness of this or from the potency of the libations, Jake's eyelids were growing so heavy that he appeared to have a difficulty in keeping them from closing, whilst Nat was hardly in better case. Presently, surrendering to the luxurious torpor that pervaded him, Jake folded his arms upon the table, and laid his sleepy head upon them.

At this, his fellow took alarm, and leaned across in an attempt to rouse him.

"Hi! Jake! We gotter carry . . . ladyship home."

"Dammer ladyship," grunted Jake in the very act of falling asleep.

With dazed eyes Nat looked helplessly at the Colonel and shaped his lips to utterance by a visible effort.

"Too much . . . drink," he said thickly. "Not used . . . wine."

He made a feeble attempt to rise, failed, and then suddenly resigned himself. Like Jake, who was already snoring, he made on the table a pillow of his arms, and lowered his head to it.

In a moment both the chairmen were soundly asleep.

Colonel Holles softly pushed back his stool, and rose. A moment he stood considering whether he should recover the two or three gold pieces which he was perfectly aware the rogues had filched from him. In the end he concluded that this would be an unnecessary additional cruelty.

He lurched out of the corner, and the hostess hearing him move came forward. He took her by the arm with one hand, whilst with the other, to her amazement, he pressed a second gold piece into her palm. He closed one eye solemnly, and pointed to the sleeping twain.

"Very good fellows . . . friends o' mine," he informed her. "Very drunk. Not used . . . wine. Lerrem sleep in peace."

She smirked, clutching that second precious piece. "Indeed, your honour, they may sleep and welcome. Ye've paid for their lodgings."

Holles considered her critically.. "Goo' woman. Ye're a goo' woman." He considered her further. "Handsome woman! Lerrem sleep in peace. Gobbless you."

She thought a kiss was coming. But he disappointed her. He loosed her arm, reeled away a little, swung round, and lurched out of the place and off down the street. Having gone some little way, he halted unsteadily and looked back. He was not observed. Having assured himself of this, he resumed his way, and it is noteworthy that he no longer staggered. His step was now brisk and certain. He flung something from him as he went, and there was a faint tinkle of shivering glass. It was the phial that had contained the powerful narcotic which he had added to his guests' wine whilst they were grovelling for the money he had spilled.

"Animals!" he said contemptuously, and upon that dismissed them from his mind.

The hour of seven was striking from St. Clement's Danes as he passed the back door of the playhouse and,the untended chair that waited there for Miss Farquharson. Farther down the narrow street a couple of men were lounging who at a little distance might have been mistaken for the very chairmen he had left slumbering in the alehouse. Their plain liveries at least were very similar, and they were covered with broad round hats identical with those of Miss Farquharson's bearers, worn at an angle that left their faces scarcely visible.

Sauntering casually, Colonel Holles came up with them. The street thereabouts was practically untenanted.

"Is all well?" he asked them.

"The people have quitted the theatre some ten minutes since," one of them answered him in indifferent English.

"To your places, then. You know your tale if there are any questions."

They nodded, and lounged along, eventually to lean against the theatre wall in the neighbourhood of the chair, obviously its bearers. The tale they were to tell at need was that Jake had been taken ill; it was feared that he was seized with the plague. Nat, who was remaining with him, had begged these two to take their places with the chair.

Holles took cover in a doorway, whence he could watch the scene of action, and there disposed himself to wait. The vigil proved a long one. As Jake had remarked to his companion, Miss Farquharson was likely to be late in leaving. On this the final evening at the Duke's Theatre she would have packing to do, and there would perhaps be protracted farewells among the players. Of the latter several had already emerged from that little doorway and had departed on foot. Still Miss Farquharson did not come, and already the evening shadows began to deepen in the street.

If Colonel Holles was exercised by a certain impatience on the one hand, on the other he was comforted by the reflection that there was gain to his enterprise in delay. The thing he had to do would be better accomplished in the dusk; best, indeed, in the dark. So he waited, and Buckingham's two French lackeys, disguised as chairmen, waited also. They had the advantage of knowing Miss Farquharson by sight, having twice seen her at close quarters, once on the occasion of her visit to Wallingford House and again on the day of her mock-rescue in Paul's Yard.

At last, at a little after half-past eight, when already objects were become indistinctly visible at a little distance, she made her appearance in the doorway. She came accompanied by Mr. Betterton, and was followed by the theatre doorkeeper. She paused to deliver to the latter certain instructions in the matter of her packages, then Mr. Betterton escorted her gallantly to her chair. The chairmen were already at their places to which they had sprung immediately upon her coming forth. One, standing behind the chair, by raising its hinged roof made of this a screen for himself. The other, by the foreshafts endeavoured to find cover beside the body of the chair itself.

Gathering her hooded cloak about her, she stepped into the sedan. Betterton bowed low over her hand in valediction. As he stood back, the chairman in front closed the apron, whilst the one behind lowered the roof. Then, taking their places between the shafts, they raised the chair and began to move away with it. From within Miss Farquharson waved a delicate hand to Mr. Betterton, who stood bowing, bareheaded.

CHAPTER XVII

THE ABDUCTION

THE chair swung past the grotesque wooden structure of Temple Bar and along Fleet Street in the deepening dusk of that summer evening, and this being the normal way it should have taken there was so far nothing to alarm its occupant. But as its bearers were about to turn to the right, to plunge into the narrow alley leading down to Salisbury Court, a man suddenly emerged from that black gulf to check their progress. The man was Holles, who had gained the place ahead of them.

"Back!" he called to them, as he advanced. "You cannot pass. There is a riot down there about a plague-stricken house which has been broken open, and the pestilence is being scattered to the four winds. You cannot go this way."

The bearers halted. "What way, then?" the foremost inquired.

"Whither would you go?" the man asked him.

"To Salisbury Court."

"Why, that is my way. You must go round by the Fleet Ditch, as I must. Come, follow me." And he went ahead briskly down Fleet Street.

The chair resumed its way in the altered direction. Miss Farquharson had leaned forward when it halted to hear what was said. She had observed no closed house in the alley upon coming that way some hours ago in daylight. But she saw no reason to doubt the warning on that account. Infected houses were, after all, growing common enough by now in London streets, and she was relieved that the closing of the theatre was to permit her own withdrawal into the country, away from that pestilential atmosphere.

She sat back again with a little sigh of weariness, and in silence suffered herself to be borne along.

But when they came to the Fleet Ditch, instead of turning to the right her bearers kept straight on, following ever in the wake of that tall cloaked man who had offered to conduct them. They were halfway over the bridge before Miss Farquharson became aware of what was happening. She leaned forward and called to them that they were mistaking the way. They took no more heed of her than if they had been stone-deaf, and trudged stolidly onward. She cried out to them more loudly and insistently. Still they took no notice. They were across the bridge, and swinging away now to the right towards the river. Miss Farquharson came to the conclusion that there must be some way back of which she was not aware, and that some good reason inspired their guide. So, for all that she still accounted it strange that the chairmen should have been so deaf to her commands, she allowed them now to proceed without further interference. But when far from finding any way to recross the ditch, the chair suddenly turned to the left in the direction of Baynard's Castle, her bewilderment suddenly redoubled. .

"Stop!" she called to them. "You are going the wrong way. Set down the chair at once. Set down, I say!" .

They heeded her as little as before. Not only did they press steadily onward, but they even quickened their pace, stumbling over the rough cobbles of the street in the darkness that pervaded it. Alarm awoke in her.

"Nathaniel," she called shrilly, leaning forward, and vainly seeking to grasp the shoulder just beyond her reach. "Nathaniel!" .

Her alarm increased. Was this really Nathaniel or was it some one else? There was something sinisterly purposeful in the stolid manner in which the fellow plodded on unheeding. The tall man ahead who led them, little more than a dark outline now, had slackened his step, so that the chair was rapidly overtaking him.

She attempted to rise, to force up the roof of the chair, to thrust open the apron in front of her. But neither yielded to her exertions. And in the end she realized that both had been fastened. That made an end of any doubt with which she may still have been deluding herself. She yielded to terror and her screams for help awoke the silent echoes of the street. The tall man halted, turned, rapped out an oath, and authoritatively commanded the men to set down. But even as he issued the order the flare of a link suddenly made its appearance at the corner of Paul's Chains, and in the ring of yellow light it cast they could discern the black outlines of three or four moving figures. Light and figures paused a moment there, checked by the girl's cries. Then abruptly they flung forward at clattering speed.

"On! On!" Holles bade the chairmen curtly, and himself went forward again, the chair now following with Miss Farquharson steadily shrieking for help and beating frenziedly upon roof and apron.

She, too, had seen those Heaven-sent rescuers rushing swiftly to meet them, and she may have caught in the torch-light the livid gleam of swords drawn for her deliverance.

They were a party of three gentlemen lighted by a link-boy, on their homeward way. They were young and adventurous, as it chanced, and very ready to bare their blades in defence of a lady in distress.

But it happened that this was a contingency for which Holles was fully prepared, one, indeed, which he could not have left out of his calculations.

The foremost of those hastening gallants was suddenly upon him, his point at the level of the Colonel's breast, and bawling dramatically:

"Stand, villain!"

"Stand yourself, fool," Holles answered him in tones of impatient scorn, making no shift to draw in self-defence. "Back — all of you — on your lives! We are conveying this poor lady home. She has the plague."

That checked their swift advance. It even flung them back a little, treading on one another's toes in their sudden intimidation. Brave enough against ordinary men and ordinary lethal weapons, they were stricken with instant panic before the horrible, impalpable foe whose presence was thus announced to them.

Miss Farquharson, who had overheard the Colonel's warning and perceived its paralyzing effect upon those rescuers whom she had been regarding as Heaven-sent, leaned forward, in frenzied fear that the trap was about to close upon her.

"He lies! He lies!" she shrieked in her terror. "It is false! I have not the plague! I have not the plague! I swear it! Do not heed him, sirs! Do not heed him! Deliver me from these villains. Oh, of your charity, sirs . . . in God's name . . . do not abandon me, or I am a lost woman else!"

They stood at gaze, moved by her piteous cries, yet hesitating what to believe. Holles addressed them, speaking sadly:

"She is distraught, poor soul. Demented. I am her husband, sirs, and she fancies me an enemy. I am told it is a common enough state in those upon whom this terrible disease has fastened." It was a truth of which all London was aware by now that the onslaught of the plague was commonly attended by derangement of the mind and odd delusions. "And for your governance, sirs, I should tell you that I greatly fear I am, myself, already infected. I beg you, then, not to detain me, but to stand aside so that we may regain our home before my strength is spent."

Behind him Miss Farquharson continued to scream her

furious denials and her piteous entreaties that they should deliver her.

If they still doubted, yet they dared not put their doubts to the test. Moreover, her very accents by now in their frenzy seemed to confirm this man's assertion that she was mad. A moment yet those rescuers hung there, hesitating. Then suddenly one of them surrendered to his mounting fear and horror.

"Away! Away!" he cried, and, swinging round, dashed off down the street. His panic communicated itself instantly to his fellows, and they went clattering after him, the link-boy bringing up the rear, his streaming torch held high.

Aghast, spent by her effort, Miss Farquharson sank back with a moan, feeling herself exhausted and abandoned. But when one of the chairmen, in obedience to an order from the Colonel, pulled the apron open, she at once leapt up and out, and would have gone speeding thence but that the other bearer caught her about her slender body, and held her firmly whilst his fellow wound now about her head a long scarf which Holles had tossed him for the purpose. That done, they made fast her hands behind her with a handkerchief, thrust her back into the chair, and shut her in.

She sat now helpless, half-choked by the scarf, which not only served to muffle her cries, but also blindfolded her, so that she no longer knew whither she was being conveyed. All that she knew was that the chair was moving.

On it went, then away to the left, and up the steep gradient of Paul's Chains, and lastly to the right into Knight Ryder Street. Before a substantial house on the north side of this, between Paul's Chains and Sermon Lane, the chair came to a final standstill and was set down. The roof was raised and the apron pulled open, and hands seized upon her to draw her forth. She hung back, a dead weight, in a last futile

attempt at resistance. Then she felt herself bodily lifted in
strong arms, and swung to a man's shoulder.

Thus Holles bore her into the house, wherein the chair, the
poles having been removed, was also presently bestowed.
The Colonel turned to the right of the roomy hall in which
two silent figures stood at attention — Buckingham's other
two French lackeys — and entered a moderate-sized square
chamber, sombrely furnished and sombrely wainscoted
from bare floor to whitened ceiling. In the middle of the
room a table with massive corkscrew legs was laid for supper, and on its polished surface gleamed crystal and silver
in the light from the great candle-branch that occupied its
middle. The long window overlooking the street was close-
shuttered, the shutters barred. Under this stood a daybed
of cane and carved oak, furnished with velvet cushions of
a dull wine colour. To this daybed Holles conveyed his
burden. Having set her down, he stooped to remove the
handkerchief that bound her wrists.

It was a compassionate act, for he knew that the pinioning
must be causing pain by now to her arms. Under the broad
brim of his hat, his face, moist from his exertions, gleamed
white, his lips were tightly compressed. Hitherto intent
upon the accomplishment of the business as he had planned
it, he had given little thought to its ugly nature. Now suddenly as he bent over this figure, at once so graceful, so
delicate and frail, as a faint sweet perfume that she used
assailed his nostrils conveying to his senses a suggestion of
her daintiness and femininity, disgust of the thing he did
overwhelmed him, like physical nausea.

He turned away, to close the door, tossing aside his hat
and cloak, and mopping his brow as he went, for the sweat
was running down him like basting on a capon. Whilst he
was crossing the room she struggled to her feet, and her
hands being now at liberty she tugged and tore at the scarf

until she loosed it so that it slipped down from her face and hung in folds about her neck and shoulders above the line of her low-cut, modish bodice.

Erect there, breathing hard, her eyes flaming, she flung her words angrily at the tall loose-limbed figure of her captor.

"Sir," she said, "you will let me depart at once, or you shall pay dearly for this villainy."

He closed the door and turned again, to face her. He attempted to smother in a smile the hangdog expression of his countenance.

"Unless you suffer me to depart at once, you shall . . ."

There she paused. Abruptly she broke off, to lean forward a little, staring at him, her parted lips and dilating eyes bearing witness to an amazement so overwhelming that it overrode both her anger and her fear. Hoarse and tense came her voice at last:

"Who are you? What . . . what is your name?"

He stared in his turn, checking in the very act of mopping his brow, wondering what it was she saw in him to be moving her so oddly. Where she stood, her face was more than half in shadow, whilst the light of that cluster of candles on the table was beating fully upon his own. He was still considering how he should answer her, what name assume, when she startled him by sparing his invention further trouble in the matter.

"You are Randal Holles!" she cried on a wild, strained note.

He advanced a step in a sort of consternation, breathless, some sudden ghastly emotion tearing at his heart, eyeing her wildly, his jaw fallen, his whole face livid as a dead man's.

"Randal Holles!" she repeated in that curiously tortured voice. "You! You of all men — and to do this thing!"

Where there had been only wild amazement in her eyes, he beheld now a growing horror, until mercifully she covered her face with her hands.

For a moment he copied her action. He, too, acting spasmodically, covered his face. The years rolled back; the room with its table laid for that infamous supper melted away to be replaced in his vision by a cherry orchard in bloom, and in that orchard a girl on a swing, teasing yet adorable, singing a song that brought him, young and clean and honourable, hastening to her side. He saw himself a lad of twenty going out into the world with a lady's glove in his hat — a glove that to this day he cherished — bent upon knight-errantry for that sweet lady's sake, to conquer the world, no less, that he might cast it in her lap. And he saw her — this Sylvia Farquharson of the Duke's Theatre — as she had been in those long-dead days when her name was Nancy Sylvester.

The years had wrought in her appearance a change that utterly disguised her. Where in this resplendently beautiful woman could he discover the little child he had loved so desperately? How could he have dreamt of his little Nancy Sylvester transformed into the magnificent Sylvia Farquharson, whose name he had heard used as a byword for gallantry, lavishness, and prodigality, whose fame was as widespread and questionably lustrous as that of Moll Davies or Eleanor Gwynn?

He reeled back until his shoulders came to rest against the closed door, and stared and stared in dazed amazement, his soul revolted by the horror of the situation in which they found themselves.

"God!" he groaned aloud. "My Nan! My little Nan!"

CHAPTER XVIII

THE PARLEY

AT any other time and in any other place this meeting must have filled him with horror of a different kind. His soul might have been swept by pain and anger to find Nancy Sylvester, whom his imagination had placed high and inaccessible as the very stars, whose memory had acted as a beacon to him, casting a pure white light to guide him through the quagmire of many a vile temptation, reduced to this state of — as he judged it — evil splendour.

Just now, however, the consciousness of his own infamous position blotted out all other thought.

He staggered forward, and fell on his knees before her.

"Nan! Nan!" he cried in a strangled voice, "I did not know. I did not dream. . ."

It was enough to confirm the very worst of the fears that were assailing her, to afford her that explanation of his presence against which she had been desperately struggling in defiance of the overwhelming evidences.

She stood before him, a woman of little more than average height and of an almost sapling grace, yet invested with something proud and regal and aloof that did not desert her even now in this terrible situation at once of peril and of cruellest disillusion.

She was dressed, as it chanced, entirely in white, and all white she stood before him save where the folds of the blue scarf with which she had been muffled still hung about her neck and bosom. No whiter than her oval face was her gown of shimmering ivory satin. About her long-shaped eyes, that could by turns be provocative, mocking, and caressing

in their glances, dark stains of suffering were growing manifest, whilst in their blue-green depths there was nothing but
stark horror.

She put a delicate, tapering hand to her brow, brushing
thence the modish tendrils of her chestnut hair, and twice
she attempted to speak before words would come from her
stiff lips.

"You did not know!" Pain rendered harsh and rasping
the voice whose natural music had seduced whole multitudes,
and the sound of it was a sword of sharpness to that kneeling,
distracted man. "It is, then, as I thought. You have done
this thing at the hiring of another. You are so fallen that
you play the hired bully. And you are Randal Holles!"

A groan, a wild gesture of despair were the outward signs
of his torment. On his knees he dragged himself nearer, to
her very feet.

"Nan, Nan, don't judge until you have heard, until . . ."

But she interrupted him. His very abjectness was in
itself an eloquent admission of the worst.

"Heard? Have you not told me all? You did not know.
You did not know that it was I whom you were carrying off.
Do you think I cannot guess who is the master-villain that
employs you for his jackal? And you did not know it was
I — that it was one who loved you once, when you were
clean and honest . . ."

"Nan! Nan! O God!"

"But I never loved you as I loathe you now for the foul
thing you are become, you that were to conquer the world
for me. You did not know that it was I whom you were
paid to carry off! And you are so shameless, so lost to honour,
that you dare to urge that ignorance as your excuse. Well,
you know it now, and I hope you are punished in the knowledge. I hope that, if any lingering sense of shame abides
in you, it will scorch your miserable soul to ashes. Get

up, man," she bade him, regally contemptuous, splendidly tragic. "Shall grovelling there mend any of your vileness?"

He came instantly to his feet. Yet it was not, as she supposed, in obedience to her command, so much as out of a sudden awakening to the need for instant action. All the agony that was threatening to burst his soul must be repressed, all that he had to say in expression and perhaps relieving of that agony, must wait.

"What I have done, I can undo," he said, and, commanding himself under the stress of that urgent necessity, he assumed a sudden firmness. "Shall we stand talking here instead of acting, when every moment of delay increases your danger? Come! As I carried you hither, in defiance of all, so will I carry you hence again at once while yet there is time."

She recoiled before the hand that he flung out as if to seize her and compel her. There was a sudden fury of anger in her eyes, a fury of scorn on her lips.

"You will carry me hence! You! I am to trust myself to you!"

He never winced under the lash of her contempt, so intent was he upon that one urgent thing.

"Will you stay, then, and trust yourself to Buckingham?" he flung fiercely back at her. "Come, I say," he commanded, oddly masterful in his overwhelming concern for her.

"With you? Oh, not that! Never with you! Never!"

He beat his hands together in his frenzy of impatience.

"Will you not realize that there is no time to lose? That if you stay here you are lost? Go alone, if you will. Return home at once. But since you must go afoot, and you may presently be pursued, suffer me at least to follow after you, to do what I can to make you safe. Trust me in this . . . for your own sake trust me . . . In God's name!"

"Trust you?" she echoed, and almost she seemed to laugh. "You? After this?"

"Aye, after this. Because of this. I may be as vile as you are deeming me; not a doubt I am. But I never could have been vile to you. It may not excuse me to protest that I did not know it was against you that I was acting. But it should make you believe that I am ready to defend you now — now that I know. You must believe me! Can you doubt me in such a matter? Unless I meant honestly by you, why should I be urging you to depart? Come!"

This time he caught her by the wrist, and maintained his hold against her faint attempt to liberate herself. He attempted to draw her after him across the room. A moment she hung back, resisting still.

"For God's sake!" he implored her madly. "At any moment Buckingham may arrive!"

This time she yielded to a spur that earlier her passion had made her disregard. Between such evils there could be no choice. She looked into his livid, gleaming face, distorted by his anguish and anxiety.

"I . . . I can trust you in this? If I trust you . . . you will bear me safely home? You swear it?"

"As God's my witness!" he sobbed in his impatience.

There was an end to her resistance now. More: she displayed a sudden urgency that matched his own.

"Quick! Quick, then!" she panted.

"Ah!" He drew a deep breath of thankfulness, snatched up hat and cloak from the chair where he tossed them, and drew her across the room by the wrist, of which he still retained his grip.

And then, just as they reached the door, it was thrust open from without, and the tall, graceful figure of the Duke of Buckingham, his curled fair head almost touching the lintel, stood before them, a flush of fevered expectancy on his handsome face. In his right hand he held his heavily feathered hat: his left rested on the pummel of the light dress rapier he was wearing.

The pair recoiled before him, and Holles loosed her wrist upon the swift, instinctive apprehension that here he was like to need his hands for other things.

His grace was all in glittering satin, black and white like a magpie, with jewels in the lace at his throat and a bald-ric of garter blue across his breast.

A moment he stood there at gaze, with narrowing eyes, puzzled by something odd in their attitudes, and looking from Miss Farquharson's pale, startled loveliness to the stiff, grim figure of her companion. Then he came slowly forward, leaving the door wide behind him. He bowed low to the lady without speaking; as he came erect again it was to the Colonel that he addressed himself.

"All should be here, I think," he said, waving a hand towards table and sideboard.

Holles half-turned to follow the gesture, and he stood a moment as if pondering the supper equipment, glad of that moment in which to weigh the situation. Out there, in the hall, somewhere just beyond that open door, would be waiting, he knew, Buckingham's four French lackeys, who at their master's bidding would think no more of slitting his throat than of slicing the glazed capon on the sideboard yonder. He had been in many a tighter corner than this in his adventurous life, but never before had there been a woman on his hands to hamper him and at the same time to agonize and numb his wits with anxiety. He thanked Heaven for the prudence which had silenced his impulse to bid Buckingham stand aside when he had first made his appearance. Had he acted upon that, there would very likely have been an end of him by now. And once there was an end of him, Nan would lie entirely at the Duke's mercy.

His life had come suddenly to matter very much. He must go very warily.

The Duke's voice, sharp with impatience, roused him:

"Well, booby? Will you stand there all night considering?"

Holles turned.

"All is here, under your grace's hand, I think," he said quietly.

"Then you may take yourself off."

Holles bowed submissively. He dared not look at Nan; but he caught the sudden gasp of her breath, and without looking beheld her start, and imagined the renewed horror and wide-eyed scorn in which she regarded this fresh display of cowardice and vileness.

He stalked to the door, the Duke's eyes following him with odd suspicion, puzzled ever by that something here which he perceived, but whose significance eluded him. Holding the edge of the open door in his hand, Holles half-turned again. He was still playing for time in which to decide upon his course of action.

"Your grace, I take it, will not require me further to-night?"

His grace considered. Beyond the Duke Holles had a glimpse of Nan, standing wide-eyed, livid as death, leaning against the table, her right hand pressed upon her heaving breast as if to control its tumult.

"No," said his grace slowly, at last, "Yet you had best remain at hand with François and the others."

"Very well," said Holles, and turned to go. The key was, he observed, on the outside of the door. He stooped and withdrew it from the lock. "Your grace would perhaps prefer the key on the inside," he said, with an odious smirk, and, whilst his grace impatiently shrugged his indifference, Holles made the transference.

Having made it, he closed the door swiftly, and he had quietly turned the key in the lock, withdrawn and pocketed it before his grace recovered from his surprise at the eccentricity of his behaviour.

"What's this?" he demanded sharply, taking a step towards the Colonel, and from Nan there came a faint cry — a sob scarcely more than to announce the reaction caused by sudden understanding and the revival of her hopes from the despair into which she had fallen.

Holles, his shoulders to the door, showed a face that was now grim and set. He cast from him again the hat and cloak which he had been holding.

"It is, your grace, that I desire a word in private with you, safe from the inconvenient intrusion of your lackeys."

The Duke drew himself up, very stiff and stern, not a little intrigued as you conceive by all this; but quite master of himself. Fear, as I think I have said, was an emotion utterly unknown to him. Had he but been capable of the same self-mastery in other directions he might have been the greatest man in England. He made now no outcry, put no idle questions that must derogate from the dignity with which he felt it incumbent to invest himself.

"Proceed, sir," he said coldly. "Let us have the explanation of this insolence, that so we may make an end of it."

"That is soon afforded." Holles, too, spoke quietly. "This lady, your grace, is a friend of mine, an ... an old friend. I did not know it until ... until I had conveyed her hither. Upon discovering it, I would have escorted her hence again, and I was about to do so when your grace arrived. I have now to ask you to pledge me your word of honour that you will do nothing to prevent our peaceful departure — that you will offer no hindrance either in your own person or in that of your servants."

For a long moment, Buckingham stood considering him

without moving from the spot where he stood, midway between Holles and the girl, his shoulder to the latter. Beyond a heightening of the colour about his eyes and cheekbones, he gave no sign of emotion. He even smiled, though not quite pleasantly.

"But how simple," he said, with a little laugh. "Nothing, indeed, could be of a more engaging simplicity. And how touching is the situation, how romantic. An old friend of yours, you say. And, of course, because of that, the world is to stand still." Then his voice hardened. "And should I refuse to pledge my word, what does Colonel Holles propose?"

"It will be very bad for your grace," said Holles.

"Almost, I think, you threaten me!" Buckingham betrayed a faint amazement.

"You may call it that."

The Duke's whole manner changed. He plucked off his mask of arrogant languor.

"By God!" he ejaculated, and his voice was rasping as a file. "That is enough of this insolence, my man. You'll unlock that door at once, and go your ways, or I'll call my men to beat you to a jelly."

"It was lest your grace should be tempted to such ungentle measures that I took the precaution to lock the door." Holles was smooth as velvet. "I will ask your grace to observe that it is a very stout door and that the lock is a very sound one. You may summon your lackeys. But before they can reach you, it is very probable that your grace will be in hell."

Buckingham laughed, and, even as he laughed he whipped the light rapier from its scabbard, and flung forward in a lunge across the distance which he had measured with his very practised swordsman's eye.

It was an action swift as lightning and of a deadly precision, shrewdly calculated to take the other by surprise and transfix him before he could make a move to guard himself. But swift as it was, and practised as was the Duke's skill, he was opposed to one as swift and practised, one who had too often kept his life with his hands not to be schooled in every trick of rough-and-tumble. Holles had seen that calculating look in the Duke's eyes as they measured the distance between them, and, because he had more than once before seen just such a calculating look in the eyes of other men and knew what followed, he had guessed the Duke's purpose, and he had been prepared. Even as the duke drew and lunged in one movement, so, in one movement, too, Holles drew and fell on guard to deflect that treacherous lightning-stroke.

Nan's sudden scream of fear and the clash of the two blades rang out at the same moment. The Colonel's parry followed on into the enveloping movement of a *riposte* that whirled his point straight at the Duke's face on the low level to which this had been brought by the lunge. To avoid it, Buckingham was forced to make a recovery, a retreat as precipitate as the advance had been swift. Erect once more, his grace fell back, his breathing quickened a little, and for a moment the two men stood in silence, their points lowered, measuring each other with their eyes. Then Holles spoke.

"Your grace, this is a game in which the dice are heavily cogged against you," he said gravely. "Better take the course I first proposed."

Buckingham uttered a sneering laugh. He had entirely mistaken the other's meaning.

"Why, you roaring captain, you pitiful Bobadil, do you think to affright me with swords and antics? It is against yourself the dice are loaded. Unlock that door, and get you hence or I'll carve you into ribbons."

"Oho! And who's the roaring captain now? Who the

Bobadil? Who the very butcher of a silk button?" cried Holles, stung to anger. He would have added more, perhaps, but the Duke stemmed him.

"Enough talk!" he snapped. "The key, you rogue, or I'll skewer you where you stand."

Holles grinned at him. "I little thought when I saved your life that night at Worcester that I should be faced with the need to take it thus."

"You think to move me with that reminder, do you?" said the Duke, and drove at him.

"Hardly. I'll move you in another way, you lovelorn ninnyhammer," Holles snarled back.

And then the blades ground together again, and they were engaged in deadly earnest.

CHAPTER XIX

THE BATTLE

I DO not suppose that any two men ever engaged with greater confidence than those. Doubt of the issue was in the mind of neither. Each regarded the other half contemptuously, as a fool rushing upon his doom.

Holles was a man of his hands, trained in the hardest school of all, and although for some months now swordpractice had been a thing neglected by him, yet it never occurred to him that he should find serious opposition in a creature whose proper environment was the Court rather than the camp. The Duke of Buckingham, whilst making no parade of the fact, was possibly the best blade of his day in England. He, too, after all, had known his years of adversity and adventurous vagrancy, years in which he had devoted a deal of study to the sword, for which he was gifted with a natural aptitude. Of great coolness in danger, vigorous and agile of frame, he had a length of reach which would still give him an advantage on those rare occasions where all else was equal. He regarded the present affair merely as a tiresome interruption to be brushed aside as speedily as possible.

Therefore he attacked with vigour, and his very contempt of his opponent made him careless. It was well for him in the first few seconds of that combat that Holles had reflected that to kill the Duke would be much too serious a matter in its ultimate consequences and possibly in its immediate ones. For Buckingham's lackeys were at hand, and, after disposing of their master, he must still run the gauntlet of those fellows before he could win to freedom with Nancy. His aim, therefore, must be to disarm or disable the Duke, and then,

holding him at his mercy, compel from him the pledge to
suffer their unmolested departure which the Duke at present
refused. Thus it happened that in the first moments of the
engagement he neglected the openings which the Duke's
recklessness afforded him, intent instead upon reaching and
crippling the Duke's sword-arm.

Two such attempts, however, each made over the Duke's
guard on a *riposte*, disclosed to Buckingham not only the
intention, but also something of the quality of the swordsman to whom he was opposed, whilst the ease with which the
Duke foiled those attempts caused Holles also to correct the
assumption upon which he had engaged. The next few seconds fully revealed to each of them the rashness of under-
rating an antagonist, and as their mutual respect increased
they settled down now to fight more closely and cautiously.

In the background in a tall armchair to which she had
sunk and in which she now reclined bereft of strength, white
with terror, her pulses drumming, her breathing so shortened
that she felt as if she must suffocate, sat Nancy Sylvester,
the only agonized witness of that encounter of which she
was herself the subject. At first the Duke's back was towards her, whilst, beyond him, Holles faced her, so that
she had a full view of his countenance. It was very calm
and set, and there was a fixed, unblinking intentness about
the grey eyes that never seemed to waver in their steady
regard of his opponent's. She observed the elastic, half-
crouching poise of his body, and, in the ease with which his
sword was whirled this way and that, she realized the
trained skill and vigorous suppleness of his wrist. She began
to take courage. She gathered as she watched him some
sense of the calm confidence in which he fought, a confidence
which gradually communicated itself to her and came to
soothe the terror that had been numbing her wits.

Suddenly there was a change of tactics. Buckingham

moved swiftly aside, away to his left; it was almost a leap; and as he moved he lunged in the new line he now confronted, a lunge calculated to take Holles in the flank. But Holles shifted his feet with the easy speed of a dancer, and veered to face his opponent in this new line, ready to meet the hard-driven point when it was delivered.

As a result of that breaking of ground, she now had them both in profile, and it was only now, when too late, that she perceived what an opportunity she had missed to strike a blow in her own defence. The thing might have been done, should have been done whilst the Duke was squarely offering her his undefended back. Had she been anything, she told herself, but the numbed, dazed, witless creature that she was, she would have snatched a knife from the table to plant it between his shoulder-blades.

It may have been the sense of some such peril, the fighter's instinctive dread of an unguarded back, that had driven the Duke to break ground as he had done. He repeated the action again, and yet again, compelling Holles each time to circle so that he might meet the ever-altered line of attack, until in the end the Duke had the door behind him and both Holles and the girl in front.

Meanwhile, the sounds of combat in that locked room — the stamp of shifting feet and the ringing of blades — had drawn the attention of the men in the hall outside. There came a vigorous knocking on the door accompanied by voices. The sound was an enheartening relief to Buckingham, who was finding his opponent much more difficult to dispatch than he had expected. Not only this, but, fearless though he might be, he was growing conscious that the engagement was not without danger to himself. This rascal Holles was of an unusual strength. He raised his voice suddenly:

"À moi! François, Antoine! À moi!"

"Monseigneur!" wailed the voice of François, laden with alarm, from beyond the oak.

"Enfoncez la porte!" Buckingham shouted back.

Came heavy blows upon the door in answer to that command; then silence and a shifting of feet, as the grooms set their straining shoulders to the oak. But the stout timbers withstood such easy methods. The men's footsteps retreated, and there followed a spell of silence, whose meaning was quite obvious to both combatants. The grooms were gone for implements to break down the door.

That made an end of the Colonel's hopes of rendering the Duke defenceless, a task whose difficulty he began to perceive that he must find almost insuperable. He settled down, therefore, to fight with grimmer purpose. There was no choice for him now but to kill Buckingham before the grooms won through that door, or all would be lost, indeed. The act would no doubt be followed by his own destruction at the hands either of Buckingham's followers or of the law; but Nancy, at least, would be delivered from her persecutor. Full now of that purpose, he changed his tactics, and from a defensive which had aimed at wearing down the Duke's vigour, he suddenly passed to the offensive. Disengage now followed disengage with lightning swiftness, and for some seconds the Duke found the other's point to be everywhere at once. Hard-pressed, his grace was compelled to give ground. But as he fell back he side-stepped upon reaching the door, not daring now to set his shoulders to it lest, by thus cutting off his own retreat, he should find himself pinned there by the irresistible blade of his opponent. It was the first wavering of his confidence, this instinctive craving for space behind him in which to retreat.

So far Holles had fought on almost academic lines, no more, indeed, being necessary for the purpose he had been setting himself. But now that this purpose was changed, and finding that mere speed and vigour could not drive his point beyond the Duke's iron guard, he had recourse to more liberal methods. There was a trick — a deadly, never-failing trick — that he had learned years ago from an Italian master, a soldier of fortune who, like himself, had drifted into mercenary service with the Dutch. He would essay it now.

He side-stepped to the left, and lunged on a high line of tierce, his point aimed at the throat of his opponent. The object of this was no more than to make the Duke swing round to parry. The lunge was not intended to go home. It was no more than a feint. Without meeting the opposing blade as it shifted to the threatened line, Holles dropped his point and his body at the same time, until he was supported, at fullest stretch, by his left hand upon the ground. Upward under the Duke's guard he whirled his point, and the Duke, who had been carried — as Holles had calculated that he would be — a little too far round in the speed required, thus unduly exposing his left flank, found that point coming straight for his heart. He was no more than in time to beat it aside with his left hand, and even so it ripped through the sleeve of his doublet and tore his flesh just above the elbow.

But for that wound there might well have been an end of Holles. For this trick of his was such that it must succeed or else leave him that essays it momentarily at the mercy of his antagonist. That moment presented itself now; but it was gone again before the Duke had mastered the twitch occasioned him by the tearing of his arm. His recovery and downward-driven *riposte* were swift, but too late by half a heart-beat. Holles was no longer there to be impaled.

They smiled grimly at each other as erect they stood, pausing a second after that mutually near escape of death. Then, as a succession of resounding blows fell upon the door, Holles drove at him again with redoubled fury. From the sound of the blows it would seem that the grooms had got an axe to work, and were bent upon hacking out the lock.

Holles realized that there was no time to lose; Buckingham, that his safety lay in playing for time, and allowing the other's furious attacks to spend themselves against his defence. Twice again, despite his wound, he used his left hand, from which the blood was dripping freely, to dash aside the other's blade. Once he did it with impunity. But when he repeated the action, Holles took advantage of it to fling himself suddenly forward inside the Duke's guard, until they were breast to breast, and with his own left he seized the Duke's sword-wrist in a grip that paralyzed it. Before, however, he could carry out his intention of shortening his sword, his own wrist was captive in the Duke's blood-smeared left hand. He sought to force himself free of that grip. But the Duke maintained it with the tenacity born of the desperate knowledge that his life depended on it, that if he loosed his hold there would be an instant end of him.

Thus now in this fierce *corps-à-corps* they writhed and swayed hither and thither, snarling and panting and tugging, whilst the sound of the blows upon the door announced the splintering of a panel, and Nancy, half-swooning in her chair, followed the nightmare struggles of the two men in wide-eyed but only half-seeing terror.

They crashed across the room to the daybed under the window, and the Duke went down upon it backwards in a sitting posture. But still he retained his grip of the Colonel's sword-wrist. Holles thrust his knee into the Duke's stomach to gain greater leverage.

Now at last, with the increased strain that Holles brought to bear, Buckingham's fingers were beginning to slip. And then under a final blow the door all splintered about, the lock flew open and the grooms flowed into the room to their master's rescue.

Holles tore his wrist free at the same moment by a last wrench. But it was too late. Casting the Duke's sword hand from him, he sprang away and round with a tearing sob to face the lackeys. For a second his glittering point held them at bay. Then the blow of a club shivered the blade, and they rushed in upon him. He felled one of them with a blow of the hilt which he still retained, before a club took him across the skull. Under that blow he reeled back against the table, his limbs sagged, and he sank down in a heap, unconscious.

As he lay there one of the grooms, standing over him, swung his club again with the clear intention of beating out his brains. But the Duke arrested the descending blow.

"It is not necessary," he said. He was white and breathing hard from his exertions and there was a fevered glitter in his eyes. But these signs apart he was master of himself.

"Your arm, monseigneur!" cried François, pointing to the blood that filled his sleeve.

"Bah! A scratch! Presently." Then he pointed to the prone limp figure of Holles, from whose head the blood was slowly trickling. "Get a rope, François, and truss him up." François departed on his errand. "You others, carry Antoine out. Then return for Bobadil. I may have a use for him yet."

They moved to obey him, and picked up their fellow whom Holles had felled before he, himself, went down.

The Duke was not pleased with them at all. A little more and they might have been too late. But to reproach them with it entailed an admission which this proud, vain man was reluctant to make.

They trooped out obediently, and Buckingham, still very pale, but breathing now more composedly, turned to Nancy with a queer little smile on lips that looked less red than usual.

CHAPTER XX

THE CONQUEROR

SHE had reached that point of endurance at which sensibility becomes mercifully dulled. She sat there, her head resting against the tall back of the chair, her eyes closed, a sense of physical nausea pervading her.

Yet, at the sound of the Duke's voice gently addressing her, she opened her long blue eyes, set now in deep stains of suffering, and looked at this handsome satyr who stood before her in an attitude of deference that was in itself a mockery.

"Dear Sylvia," he was saying, "I am beyond measure pained that you should have been subjected to this . . . this unseemly spectacle; I need not protest that it was no part of my intention."

She answered him almost mechanically, yet the ironical answer she delivered was true to her proud nature and the histrionic art which would not be denied expression even in the extremity to which she was reduced.

"That, sir, I can well believe."

He considered her, wondering a little at that flash of spirit, from one in her condition. If anything it but served to increase his admiration. He sighed.

"Ah, my Sylvia, you shall forgive me the shifts to which my love has driven me, and this last shift of all with that roaring fool's heroics and what they have led to. Endeavour not to think too harshly of me, child. Don't blame me altogether. Blame that *cos amoris*, that very whetstone of love — your own incomparable loveliness and grace."

She sat now stiffly upright, dissembling her fear behind a mask of indignant scorn that was sincere enough.

"Love!" she answered him in a sudden gust of that same scorn. "You call this violence love?"

He answered her with a throbbing vehemence of sincerity, a man pleading his own defence.

"Not the violence, but that which has moved me to it, that which would move me to tear down a world if it stood between you and me. I want you, Sylvia, more than I have ever wanted anything in life. It is because of the very fervency and sincerity of my passion that I have gone so clumsily to work, that in every attempt to lay my homage and devotion at your feet, I have but provoked your resentment. Yet, child, I swear to you that, if it lay in my power, if I were free to make you my Duchess, that is the place I should be offering to you now. I swear it by everything I hold sacred."

She looked at him. There had been a humility in his bearing which, together with that vibrant sincerity in his voice, must surely have moved her at any other time. It moved her now, but only to a still greater scorn.

"Is anything sacred to such a man as you?" She rose by an effort, and stood before him, swaying, slightly conscious of dizziness and of shivers, and marvelling a little that she should be unable better to command herself. But she commanded herself at least sufficiently to give him his answer. "Sir, your persecution of me has rendered you loathly and abhorrent in my sight, and nothing that you may now do can alter that. I tell you this in the hope that some spirit of manliness, some sense of dignity, will cry a halt to you; so that you may disabuse your mind of any notion that you can prevail by continuing to pursue and plague me with your hateful attentions. And now, sir, I beg you to bid your creatures fetch the chair in which I was brought hither and carry me hence again. Detain me further, and I promise you, sir, that you shall be called to give a strict account of this night's work."

The whiplash of her contempt, which she was at pains to render manifest in every word she uttered, the loathing that scorched him from her lovely eyes, served but to stir a dull resentment and to arouse the beast in him. The change was instantly apparent in the sneer that flickered over his white face, in the ugly little soft laugh with which he greeted her demand.

"Let you depart so soon? How can you think it, Sylvia? To have been at such infinite pains to cage you, you lovely bird, merely to let you fly away again!"

"Either you let me depart at once, sir," she told him almost fiercely, her weakness conquered now in her own indignation, "or the Town shall ring with your infamy. You have practised abduction, sir, and you know the penalty. I shall know how to make you pay it. I swear that you shall hang, though you be Duke of twenty Buckinghams. You do not want for enemies, who will be glad enough to help me, and I am not entirely without friends, your grace."

He shrugged. "Enemies!" he sneered. "Friends!" He waved a disdainful hand toward the unconscious Holles. "There lies one of your friends, if what the rascal said was true. The others will not be more difficult to dispose of."

"Your grooms will not suffice to save you from the others."

That stung him. The blood leapt to his face at that covert taunt that it was only the intervention of his men had saved him now.

But he made answer with a deadly smoothness. "So much even will not be needed. Come, child, be sensible. See precisely where you stand."

"I see it clearly enough," she answered.

"I will take leave to doubt it. You do as little justice to my wits, it seems, as ever you have done to my poor person. Who is to charge me, and with what? You will charge me.

You will accuse me of bringing you here by force, against your will, and here retaining you. Abduction, in short, you say; and you remind me that it is a grave offence at law."

"A hanging matter, even for dukes," said she.

"Maybe; maybe. But first the charge must be made good. Where are your witnesses? Until you produce them, it will be your word against mine. And the word of an actress, however exalted, is . . . in such matters . . . the word of an actress." He smiled upon her. "Then this house. It is not mine. It is tenanted by a ruffian named Holles; it was taken by him a few days ago in his own name. It was he who brought you here by force. Well, well, if there must be a scapegoat, perhaps he will do as well as another. And, anyhow, he is overdue for the gallows on quite other crimes. He brought you here by force. So far we shall not contradict each other. What follows? How came I here into that man's house? Why, to rescue you, of course, and I stayed to comfort you in your natural distress. The facts will prove my story. My grooms will swear to it. It will then be seen that in charging me you are a scheming adventuress, returning evil for good, seeking to profit by my unwary generosity. You smile? You think the reputation bestowed upon me by a scandalmongering populace will suffice to give that tale the lie. I am not of your opinion; and, anyway, I am prepared to take the risk. Oh, I would take greater risks for you, my dear."

She made a little gesture of contempt. "You may be a very master of the art of lying, as of all other evil arts. But lies shall not avail you if you dare to detain me now."

"If I dare to detain you?" He leaned nearer to her, devouring her with his smouldering eyes. "If I dare, child? Dare?"

She shrank before him in sheer terror. Then, conquering

herself, stiffening in every limb, she drew herself erect. Ma-
jestically, a very queen of tragedy, she flung out an arm in
a gesture of command.

"Stand back, sir! Stand back, and let me pass, let me
go."

He fell back, indeed, a pace or two, but only that he might
the better contemplate her. He found her magnificent, in
the poise of her graceful body, the ivory pallor of her face,
the eyes that glowed and burned and looked the larger for
the deep, dark shadows in which they were now set. Suddenly, with an almost inarticulate cry, he sprang forward to
seize her. He would make an end of this maddening resistance, he would melt this icy disdain until it should run like
water.

She slipped aside and away in panic before his furious onslaught, oversetting the high-backed chair in which she had
lately been sitting.

The crash of its fall seemed to penetrate to the slumbering
mind of Holles, and disturb his unconsciousness. For he
stirred a little, uttering a faint moan.

Beyond that, however, her flight accomplished nothing.
Two yards away the wainscot faced her. She would have
run round the table, but, before she could turn to do so, the
Duke had seized her. She faced him, savagely at bay, raising
her hands to protect herself. But his arms went round her
arms, forcing her hands down to her sides, and crushing her
hurtfully against him, heedless, himself, in his frenzy of the
hot pain in his own lacerated shoulder in which the bleeding
was redoubled by this effort.

Helpless in his arms she lay.

"You coward, you beast, you vileness!" she gasped. And
then he stopped her mouth with kisses.

"Call me what you will, I hold you, I have you, and not
all the power of England shall tear you from me now.

Realize it, child," — he fell to pleading. "Realize and accept, and you will find that I have but mastered you only so that I may become your slave."

She answered him nothing; again that dizziness, that physical sickness was assailing her. She moaned a little, lying helpless there in that grip of his that to her was as loathly and deadly as the coiling embrace of some great snake of which it brought the image to her mind. Again he was kissing her, her eyes, her mouth, her throat, about which still hung the folds of the blue scarf that had served to muffle her. Because this offended him and was in some sense an obstacle, a barrier, he seized one end of it, and, tearing it roughly away, laid bare the lovely throat and breast it had so inconveniently veiled.

Over that white throat he now bent his head like some evil vampire. But his fevered lips never reached it. In the very act of bending, he paused, and stiffened.

Behind him he could hear the footsteps of his grooms re-entering the chamber. But it was not their coming that imposed this restraint upon him, that dilated and bulged his eyes with horror, that fetched the ashen pallor to his cheeks, and set him suddenly trembling and shuddering from head to foot.

For a moment he was as a man paralyzed. His limbs refused their office; they seemed turned to lead. Slowly, where he would have had them swift, his arms relaxed their grip of that sweet body. Slowly they uncoiled themselves, and slowly he fell back before her, crouching forward the while, staring ever, his jaw fallen, his face the face of a man in the last extremity of terror.

Suddenly he raised his right hand to point with a shaking finger at her throat. Hoarsely, in a cracked voice, he spoke. "The tokens! The tokens!"

The three grooms, entering at that moment, checked and

stood there just within the threshold as if suddenly turned to stone.

The awakening Holles, on the ground, raising himself a little, and thrusting back the tumbled hair which was being matted to his brow by blood from his cracked head, looked dazedly round and up to see the Duke's shaking, pointing hand, to hear the Duke's quavering voice, this time, saying yet again:

"The tokens!"

His grace fell back step by step, gasping with dread, until suddenly he swung about to face his men.

"Back," he bade them, his voice shrill. "Back! Away! Out of this! She is infected! My God! She has the plague! The tokens are upon her!"

A moment still they stood at gaze in this horror which they fully shared with him. They craned forward, to look at Miss Farquharson, leaning faint and limp against the wainscot, her white neck and shoulders thrown into dazzling relief against the dark brown of the background, and from where they stood they could make out quite plainly stamped upon the white loveliness of that throat the purple blotch that was the brand and token of the pestilence.

As the Duke reached them, they turned, in sudden dread of him. Might he not, himself, already carry upon him the terrible infection? With wild cries of terror they fled before him out of the room, and out of the house, never heeding the commands which, as he precipitately followed, he flung after them.

CHAPTER XXI
UNDER THE RED CROSS

THE main door slammed upon those precipitately departing men. Their running steps clattered over the cobbles of the street, and receded quickly out of earshot.

Colonel Holles and the woman he had sought so passionately long years ago, until despair had turned him from the quest, were alone together at last in that house, brought thither by that ironic destiny of his, in circumstances of horror piled on horror. The very act by which at last he had found her irrevocably lost her to him again. The very chance that had brought them together, after all these years, flung them at the same time farther apart than they had ever been; and this, without taking into account the fact that she was a woman now with the seal of death upon her. Was he not Fortune's fool indeed?

The violent slamming of that door appeared to rouse him to a further degree of consciousness. Painfully he got to his knees, and with dazed eyes looked round the room. Again he brushed back the tangle of hair from his brow, and thereafter dully considered his hand which was wet and smeared with blood. The mists that enveloped his brain, obscuring and confusing his mental view of the events that had occurred before he was stricken down and since consciousness had begun to return to him, were now gradually dispersing. Understanding of where he was and how he had come there grew clear at last. He rose to his feet, and stood swaying a moment, looking round, dull-eyed as a drunkard.

He beheld Nancy, her shoulders turned to him, contemplating herself in an oblong Venetian mirror that adorned the wall beyond the table, and in the mirror itself he beheld the reflection of her face. It was ashen, and there was a staring, ghastly horror in her eyes. It was then that he began to remember and piece together the incidents of the confused scene upon which his gaze had fallen when first his mind was dimly rousing itself. Again he saw Buckingham, crouching and shuddering as he backed away from Nancy, pointing to her the while with a palsied hand, and again he heard the Duke's quavering voice, and the dread words it uttered.

He understood. Nancy was safe from Buckingham. She had been snatched from the Duke at the eleventh hour by a ravisher even more merciless and infinitely more foul.

This she was herself realizing as she contemplated her image in that little mirror and beheld the brand of the pestilence on her white breast. Although she had never before seen that betraying purple blotch, yet she had heard it described, and she could have had no doubt of its significance even without the terrified explanation that Buckingham had supplied. Whether it was from horror of what she beheld, or whether from the workings of the fell disease — which may also have been responsible for those moments of dizziness by which she had been earlier assailed, but which she had assigned to emotion — she found her image contracting and expanding now before her eyes; then she felt the room rocking about her, the ground heaving under her feet as if it had been the unstable deck of a ship. She reeled back, and knew, without power to help herself, that she was falling, when suddenly she felt herself caught, and supported.

She looked up, and beheld the ghastly, blood-smeared face of Randal Holles, who had sprung instinctively to her assistance. For a long moment she stared at him, dull-eyed, a little frown of effort drawing her brows together. Dully then she spoke:

"Do not touch me. Did you not hear? I have the plague."

"Aye . . . I heard," he answered.

"You will take the infection," she warned him.

"It is very likely," said he, "but no great matter."

On that he lifted her in his arms, as he had lifted her once before that night. Despite his shaken condition, the act cost him but little effort, for she was very slim and light. Unresisting — for she was too dazed and weak for any physical resistance now — she suffered him to bear her to the daybed. There he set her down at full length, carefully adjusting the wine-coloured cushions, so as to give ease to her head and limbs.

Then he passed round the couch to the shuttered windows, unbarred them, and set the casement wide to let a draught of the clean, cool night air into the stifling room. That done, he turned, and remained standing there beside the couch, looking down upon her with eyes that were as the eyes of some poor dumb beast in pain.

The cool air revived her a little, set her pulses beating more steadily, and cleared her mind of some of the numbness that had been settling upon it. For a spell she lay there, panting a little, remembering and realizing the situation and her own condition. Then she raised her eyes to look at the ghastly, haggard face above her, and to meet that anguished glance. For a little while she stared at him, her own countenance expressionless.

"Why do you stay?" she asked him at length in a dull voice. "Go . . . go your ways, sir, and leave me to die. It is, I think, all that remains to do. And . . . and I think that I shall die the easier without your company."

He stepped back as if she had struck him. He made as if to answer her; then his parted lips came together again, his chin sank until it touched his breast. He turned, and with dragging feet walked slowly out of the room, softly closing the door.

She lay there invaded suddenly by a great fear. She strained her ears to catch the sounds of his footsteps in the passage, until finally the slamming of the door leading to the street announced to her that, taking her at her word, he was gone, indeed. She sat up in alarm, holding her breath, listening to his steps moving quickly now, almost at a run, up the street. At last she could hear them no longer. Her fears mounted. For all her brave talk, the thought of dying alone, abandoned, in this empty house filled her with terror; so that it seemed to her now that even the company of that dastard would have been better than this horror of loneliness in the hour of death.

She attempted to rise, to follow, to seek the companionship of human beings who might yet afford her some assistance and ease her sufferings. But her limbs refused their office. She got to her feet merely to collapse again, exhausted. And now she flung herself prone upon the daybed, and sobbed aloud until the searing pain in her breast conquered even her self-pity, and stretched her writhing in agony as if upon a rack. At last a merciful unconsciousness supervened.

And meanwhile Holles was moving mechanically and instinctively at speed up Sermon Lane in the direction of Paul's. Why he should have chosen to go that way sooner than another he could not have told you. The streets were utterly deserted even at that early hour, for this was not a time in which folk chose to roam abroad at nights, and, moreover, the Lord Mayor's enactments now compelled all taverns and houses of entertainment to close at nine o'clock.

Without hat or cloak, his empty scabbard dangling like a limp tail about his legs, he sped onward, a man half-distracted, with but a vague notion of his object and none of the direction in which its fulfilment would be likeliest. As he was approaching Carter Lane, a lantern came dancing like a will-o'-the-wisp round the corner to meet him, and presently the dark outline of the man who carried it grew visible. This man walked with the assistance of a staff which at closer quarters the lantern's rays revealed to be red in colour. With a gasp of relief, Holles flung forward towards him.

"Keep your distance, sir! Keep your distance!" a voice warned him out of the gloom. "'Ware infection."

But Holles went recklessly on until the long red wand was raised and pointed towards him to arrest his advance.

"Are you mad, sir?" the man cried sharply. Holles could make out now the pallid outline of his face, which the broad brim of his steeple-hat had hitherto kept almost entirely in shadow. "I am an examiner of infected houses."

"It is as I hoped," panted Holles . . . "that yours might be some such office. I need a doctor, man, quickly, for one who is taken with the plague."

The examiner's manner became brisk at once.

"Where?" he demanded.

"Close at hand here, in Knight Ryder Street."

"Why, then, Dr. Beamish, there at the corner, is your man. Come."

And thus it happened that, from the sleep which had succeeded the swoon that so mercifully whelmed her senses, Nancy was aroused by a sound of steps and voices. Where she lay she faced the door of the room. And, as through billows of mist that now rolled before her eyes, she saw the tall figure of Colonel Holles enter followed by two strangers. One of these was a little birdlike man of middle age; the other was young and of a broad frame and a full countenance. Both were dressed in black, and each carried the red wand which the law prescribed.

The younger man, who was the examiner met by Holles in Sermon Lane, came no farther than the threshold. He was holding close to his nostrils a cloth that gave out a pungent, vinegary smell, and his jaws worked vigorously the while, for he was chewing a stick of snake-root as a further measure of prevention. Meanwhile, his companion, who was that same Dr. Beamish he had recommended, approached the patient and made a swift, practised, and silent examination.

She suffered it in silence, too utterly trammelled by lethargy to give much thought or care to what might now betide her.

The physician held her wrist for a moment in his bony fingers, the middle one upon her pulse. Next he carefully examined the blotch upon her throat. Finally he raised first one of her arms and then the other, whilst Holles at his bidding held the candle-branch so as to cast the light into the armpit. A grunt escaped him upon the discovery of a swelling in the right one.

"This is unusually soon," he said. "It is seldom before the third day that there is such a manifestation."

With the forefinger he tested the consistency of that swelling, sending sharp, fiery streams of pain through all her body as it seemed to her.

He lowered the arm again, and straightened himself, considering her a moment with pursed lips and thoughtful eyes.

At his elbow Holles spoke in a toneless voice:

"Does it . . . does it mean that her case is beyond hope?"

The physician looked at him.

"*Dum vivimus, speremus,*" said he. "Her case need not be hopeless any more than another's. Much depends upon the energy with which the disease is fought."

He saw the flash of Holles's eyes at that, as through the Colonel's mind sped the vow that if it was a matter of a fight he was there to wage it. He would fight the plague for her as fiercely as he had fought Buckingham. Beholding his sudden transfiguration, the physician, in charity — lest the man should delude himself with false hopes — thought well to add:

"Much depends upon that. But more — indeed all — upon God, my friend." He spoke to Holles as to a husband, for that, indeed, was the relationship in which he conceived him to stand to the afflicted lady. "If suppuration of that swelling can be induced, recovery is possible. More I cannot say. To induce that suppuration infinite pains and tireless labour may be necessary."

"She may depend on that," said Holles.

The physician nodded. "Nurses," he added slowly, "are scarce and difficult to procure. I will do my best to find you one as soon as possible. Until then you will have to depend entirely upon yourself."

"I am ready."

"And in any case the law does not allow you to leave this house until you can receive a certificate of health — which cannot be until one month after her recovery or . . ." He broke off, leaving the alternative unnamed, and added hurriedly: "That is Sir John Lawrence's wise provision for checking the spread of the infection."

"I am aware of it and of my position," said Holles.

"So much the better, then. And now, my friend, there is no time to lose. Speed in applying remedies is often all. She must be brought as quickly as may be into a free and full perspiration and for that she must be got to bed without delay. If her life is to be saved, you must get to work at once."

"Tell me but what to do, sir."

"Not only that; I come prepared to leave you all that you will require."

He produced a bulky package from his pocket, and, beckoning Holles to the table, there opened it, and enumerated the lesser packages it contained and the purposes of each.

"Here is a stimulating ointment with which you will rub

the swelling in the armpit every two hours. Thereafter you
will apply to it a poultice of mallows, linseed, and palm oil.
Here is mithridate, of which you will administer a dose as an
alexipharmic, and two hours later you will give her a posset
drink of Canary and spirits of sulphur. The spirits of sulphur
are here. Make a fire of sea-coal in her bedroom, and heap
all available blankets upon her, that she may throw out as
much as may be of the poison in perspiring.

"For to-night, if you do that, you will have done all that
can be done. I shall return very early in the morning, and
we will then consider further measures."

He turned to the examiner: "You have heard, sir?"

The man nodded. "I've already bidden the constable
send a watchman. He will be here by now and I'll see the
house closed when we go forth."

"It but remains, then," said the doctor, "to have the
lady put to bed. Then I will take my leave of you until to-
morrow."

This, however, was a service the lady was still able to perform for herself. When Holles, disregarding the physician's
aid, had, single-handed, carried her to the room above, she
recovered sufficiently to demand that she should be left to
herself; and, despite her obvious weakness, Dr. Beamish
concurred that to permit her to have her own way in the
matter would be to make the more speed in the end.

The effort of undressing, however, so exhausted her and
awoke such torturing pains that, when at last she got to bed,
she lay there, panting, reduced to a state of utter prostration.

Thus Holles and the physician found her on their return.
Dr. Beamish placed upon a table at the foot of the bed all the
things that Holles would require, and, repeating his injunc-
tions, took his leave at last. The Colonel went with him to
the door of the house. This was standing open, and by the
light of a lantern held by the watchman the examiner was

completing the rudely wrought inscription, *Lord have mercy upon us*, under the ominous red cross which he had daubed above.

Bidding Holles a good-night and a stout courage, the physician and the examiner departed together. The watchman, who remained to hinder any unauthorized person from passing in or out, then closed the door. Holles heard the key being turned on the outside, and knew himself a prisoner in that infected house for weeks to come, unless death should chance to set him free meanwhile.

Quickly now, urged by the thought of his task, utterly disregarding the dull aching of his bruised head, he mounted the stairs again. A memory flashed through his mind of those three gallants whom her cries had attracted to her rescue, and who would have delivered her from his clutches, but that he had scared them away with the lie — as he supposed it then — that she was infected with the plague. Had their rescue succeeded, in what case would she be now? Would there be one at hand to fight such a fight as that for which he was braced and ready; to give his life at need, freely and without a pang, that he might save her own? Out of the anguish of his soul, out of the depths into which he was plunged, he thanked God for this fight that lay before him, for this disposition which made good come out of evil.

He found her in a state of lethargy which, whilst leaving her a full consciousness of all that had occurred and was occurring about her, yet robbed her of all power of speech or movement. Lying there, her head supported by the pillows, which it had been the doctor's last service to adjust, her wide, fevered eyes followed every movement of the Colonel's as, stripped now of his doublet, he went briskly about the business of preparation. Anon under the pain which his ministrations caused her, she sank into unconsciousness, and thence into a raving delirium which for days thereafter was to alternate with periods of lethargic, exhausted slumber.

CHAPTER XXII

THE CRISIS

For five days, which to Randal Holles were as five years of mortal anguish, she lay suspended between this world and the next. The lightest straw of chance would suffice to tip against her the fearful balance of the scales, the slightest lack of care and watchfulness might result in the snapping of the slender thread by which life was still tethered to her exhausted, fever-wasting frame.

The doctor had succeeded beyond all his hopes in his quest of a nurse-keeper, and he brought her with him to the house in Knight Ryder Street, on the morrow of Nancy's taking ill — a lean, capable, good-natured, henlike woman of forty. But for all her competency and willingness, had this Mrs. Dallows been alone in charge of the patient, it is long odds that Nancy would quickly have succumbed. For no hired attendant could ever have ministered to her with the self-sacrificing, remorseful devotion of the broken adventurer who loved her. No hired attendant could have brought to the task the strength of will and singleness of purpose that drove the weary, faltering flesh relentlessly along the path of this self-imposed duty.

Not for a moment did Holles suffer himself to relax his vigilance, to pause for a breathing in that grim fight with death. Of sleeping he never so much as thought, whilst the snatches of food and drink that constituted his meals, forced upon him by the nurse-keeper, were taken there at Nancy's bedside.

Mrs. Dallows remonstrated with him, urging him to take some rest in the hours during which she was herself on duty. It was in vain. Equally vain were the same remonstrances when more authoritatively urged by Dr. Beamish. Holles left them unheeded as he did the physician's recommendations that he should take some of the ordinary precautions to keep himself immune. The balsam of sulphur which the little doctor left with him to be used as a disinfectant was never touched; the wormwood, masterwort, and zedoary pressed upon him as prophylactics were equally neglected.

"My friend," the doctor had said to him as early as the second day of her illness, "if you continue thus you will end by killing yourself."

Holles had smiled as he replied: "If she lives, her life will have been cheaply purchased at the price. If she dies, it will not signify."

The doctor, ignorant of her true identity, and persuaded ever that the twain were husband and wife, was touched by what he conceived to be an expression of exemplary conjugal devotion. That, however, did not turn him from his endeavours to reason Holles out of this obstinacy.

"But if she should survive and you should perish?" he asked him, whereupon Holles had amazed him by a sudden flash of anger.

"Plague me no more!"

After that Dr. Beamish had left him to follow his own inclinations, reflecting — in accordance with the popular belief, which the doctor fully shared — that after all the man carried in himself the most potent of all prophylactics in the fact that he was without fear of the infection.

But, although Holles neglected all the preventive measures which the doctor had so urgently prescribed for him, he nevertheless smoked a deal, sitting by the window of her chamber, which was kept open day and night to the suffocating heat of that terrible July. And the great fire constantly maintained by the doctor's orders, this heat notwithstanding, did much to cleanse and purify the air. These things

may have helped to keep him safe despite himself, procuring
for him a measure of disinfection.

It was entirely as a result of that tireless vigilance of his
and of the constant poulticings which he applied, that on the
fourth day the swelling in the patient's armpit, having been
brought to a head, began to vent the deadly poison with
which her veins were laden.

Beamish was as amazed as he was delighted.

"Sir, sir," he commended the Colonel on the evening of
that fourth day, "your pains are being rewarded. They have
wrought a miracle already."

"You mean that she will live?" cried Holles in fearful
hope.

The doctor paused, moderating his satisfaction, afraid of
his own optimism.

"So much I cannot promise yet. But the worst is over.
With proper care and God's help I trust that we may save
her."

"Never doubt that the care will be forthcoming. Tell me
but what is to do."

The doctor told him, and the exhausted yet unyielding
Holles listened greedily to his instructions, flung off his
deadly lassitude, and applied himself diligently to the execution of all exactly as he was bidden.

And meanwhile, as if incubated by that terrific heat, the
plague was spreading now through London at a rate that
seemed to threaten the City with the utter extermination
which the preachers of doom had presaged. It was from
Beamish that Holles learnt of that sudden, upward, devastating leap of the pestilential conflagration, of the alarming
bill of mortality, and of the fact that the number of victims
within the walls amounted in that week alone to nearly a
thousand. And, apart from what the doctor told him, there
were abundant evidences of the havoc even within the nar-

row survey possible to him from his prison. From that first-floor window, at which he spent long hours of day and night, he beheld Knight Ryder Street — that once busy thoroughfare — become daily less and less frequented, whilst daily, too, the hum of London's activity, which might be likened to the very heart-beat of that great city, growing feebler and ever feebler, bore witness to its ebbing life.

There in Knight Ryder Street he could see the closed houses — and there were already three of them within the radius of his view on the opposite side of the street — each with its red cross and an armed watchman day and night before its padlocked door.

Victuals and what else was needed from outside reached them through the agency of their own watchman. Holles, who was still plentifully supplied with funds from what Buckingham had furnished him for this adventure, would lower the necessary money from the window in a basket. By the same means the watchman would send up the purchases he made on behalf of those within, absenting himself when necessary for the purpose, but always leaving the door locked and taking the key with him.

On the comparative and ever ominously increasing stillness of the air came intermittently, to increase the general melancholy, the tolling of bells, ringing out the knell of the departed, and nightly, just after dark and again before peep of day, there came now the clang of another bell infinitely more hideous because of the hideous ideas with which it had become associated, and the stillness of the street would be disturbed by a creak and rumble of wheels, a slow clatter of hooves, and a raucous voice uttering a dreadful summons:

"Bring out your dead!"

Peering down, as he ever did, he could make out the ghastly outline of the dead-cart loom into view as it came slowly rumbling by, attracted thither by those sealed

houses, like some carrion-bird in expectation of its prey.
Invariably it paused before Holles's own door, arrested by
the sight of the watchman and the red cross dimly revealed
by the light of his lantern; and that raucous voice would
ring out again, more direct in its summons, sounding now
like a demand, revoltingly insolent and cynical.

"Bring out your dead!"

Then, at a word from the watchman, the horrible vehicle
would toil slowly on, and Holles with a shudder would fling
a glance over his shoulder at the sufferer where she lay
fevered and tossing, wondering fearfully whether duty and
pitiless necessity would compel him to answer that summons when next it came, and surrender that lovely body to
join the abominable load in that hideous cart.

Thus, until the morning of the sixth day, when from day-
break until past eight o'clock he waited in a sudden frenzy
of impatience for the coming of Beamish. When at last he
arrived, Holles met him at the stair-head.

The Colonel's face was ghastly, his eyes fevered, and he
was trembling with fearful excitement.

"She sleeps — quietly and peacefully," he informed the
doctor, in a whisper, a finger to his lips.

Very softly they entered the chamber now and tiptoed
to the bedside, Holles in an agony of hope taking up his
position at the foot between the carved bedposts. A glance
confirmed the news with which Holles had met the physician. Not only was she in an easy, tranquil slumber, such
as she had not known since taking to this bed, but the
fever had entirely left her. This the doctor's practised
eye judged at once, even before he moved to take her
pulse.

At that touch of his hand upon her wrist, she stirred,
sighed, and opened her eyes, sanely and calmly awake at
last. She looked up into the wizened, kindly little spectacled

face of the doctor, blankly at first, then with a little frown of bewilderment. But he was speaking at the moment, and the words he used helped her groping wits to piece together the puzzle of her surroundings and condition.

"The danger is overpast," he was saying. "She will recover now, thanks be to God and to your own tireless care of her. It is yourself gives me more concern than she does. Leave her now to the care of Mrs. Dallows, and do you go rest yourself, or I tell you I will not answer for your life." He had been looking at Holles whilst he spoke. Now he turned to consider her again, and found her conscious glance upon him. "See! She is awake," he cried.

"The danger is overpast?" Holles echoed, his voice thick and unnatural. "You say the danger is overpast? I am awake, good doctor? I have not by chance fallen asleep at my post and come to dream this thing?"

"You are awake, man, and I repeat the danger is at an end. Now go and rest."

Wondering to whom it was the doctor spoke, whose was that raucous, weary voice that questioned him, she slowly turned her head, and beheld a gaunt, hollow-eyed ghost of a man, whose pallid, sunken cheeks were overgrown with a course stubble of unshaven beard, standing between the bedposts, clutching at one of them as if for support. Meeting her gaze, he recoiled a step and loosed his hold. Then he swung half-round, a hand to his brow.

"Naught ails me, doctor," he mumbled, and now she knew who he was and remembered. "I would sooner . . ."

His voice abruptly ceased in mid-period; he reeled, steadied himself for an instant, and then toppled slowly forward and crashed at full length upon the floor. Instantly Mrs. Dallows, with a little outcry of alarm, was on her knees beside him; she turned him over, raised his head, by an effort, and pillowed it in her lap as Dr. Beamish came hastening up. The same thought was in the mind of both nurse and physician.

Nancy sought painfully — for she was very weak — to raise herself, that she might see what was taking place there on the floor, beyond the foot of the bed.

Swiftly the doctor tore open the breast of the Colonel's doublet; but not even so much was necessary. At once he perceived what had happened. It was as if the assurance that she was out of danger, and so no longer in need of his ministrations, had snapped the reins of will by which Holles had held his lassitude in subjection. Instantly Nature had claimed from him the dues which he had so long withheld.

"He is asleep," said Dr. Beamish; and he almost chuckled. "That is all. Help me to lift him to that couch, Mrs. Dallows. No need to carry him farther or to do more for him at present. Never fear, you'll not rouse him — not until the clock has gone round once, at least."

They laid him there, a pillow under his head, and Beamish returned to his patient's side. She had sunk back again, but her eyes, looking enormous now in her wasted cheeks, were still upon the figure of Holles where he lay inert as stone, just within the orbit of her vision.

"Sleep?" she questioned the doctor, wonderingly. "Is that sleep?"

Never had she — nor, indeed, have many — seen slumber fell a man as if he had been shot.

"Nothing worse, ma'am. The Colonel has never so much as closed his eyes for a whole week. Nature compassionately has closed them for him. No need to afflict yourself on his behalf. Sleep is all he now requires. So give yourself peace, and beware of making demands upon the little strength that's left you."

She looked at him intently. "I have the plague, have I not?"

"Say rather that you had it, ma'am. You have it no longer. It has been cast out of you. It has left you feeble; but that is all that ails you at present. And you are a safe woman now. When you shall have recovered your strength, you may go whither you will without further fear of the infection. The plague will not touch you again. For the great mercy thus vouchsafed you, you may render thanks to God, and, next to God, to your husband."

She frowned, perplexed.

"My husband?"

"Your husband, ma'am. And a husband in a thousand — nay, in ten thousand. I have seen many a husband lately, and I speak with knowledge — alas! The terror of the pestilence can blot out every other feeling. I have seen it happen time and again. But Colonel Holles is not of those. His is a devotion that makes a hero of him; and, because he has been fearless, he has been spared. Fortune favours the brave, ma'am."

"But . . . but he is not my husband."

"Not your husband?" said the doctor, confounded. And he repeated, "Not your husband!" Then, with an affectation of cynicism very alien in reality to the genial, kindly little man, "Gadso!" he ejaculated, "perhaps that explains it. But what is he, then, who has all but given his life for you?"

She hesitated, at a loss how to define their relationship. At last:

"Once he was my friend," she answered.

"Once?" The physician raised his bushy brows. "And when, pray, did he cease to be your friend — this man who stayed with you in this infected house when he might have fled; this man who has denied himself sleep or rest of any kind in all these days, that he might be ever at hand against your need of him; this man who has wrestled with death for you, and rescued you at the risk of taking the pestilence a thousand times for your sake?"

"Did he do all this?" she asked.

Dr. Beamish entertained her with the details of the heroism and self-sacrifice that Holles had displayed.

When the tale was done, and she lay silent and very thoughtful, the doctor permitted himself a slyly humorous smile.

"He may once have been your friend, as you say," he concluded, smiling. "But I cannot think that he was ever more your friend than now. God send me such a friend in my own need!"

She made no response, but continued very still and thoughtful for a while, staring up at the carved canopy of this great strange bed, her face a blank mask in which the little doctor sought in vain for a clue to the riddle of the relations of those two. Had he yielded to his inquisitiveness, he would have questioned her. But, other considerations apart, he was restrained by thought for her condition. Nourishment and rest were to be prescribed, and it was not for him, by probing questions, to prove himself perhaps a disturber of the latter.

CHAPTER XXIII
THE WALLS OF PRIDE

THAT evening Dr. Beamish returned, bringing with him, as on the occasion of his first visit, a public examiner. This official came to assure himself formally of the doctor's assertion that a cure had been effected, so that he might make his report thereupon, to the end that after the lapse of twenty-eight days — provided that in the meanwhile there were no fresh outbreak of pestilence in either of the other inmates — the reopening of the house should be permitted.

Holles, awakening from eleven hours of uninterrupted lethargic sleep, but still heavy with lassitude, stood dully at hand whilst the examiner held his formal inquisition into the conditions of the patient, of Mrs. Dallows, and of Holles himself. As the Colonel stood there, gaunt, pale, unshaven, and dishevelled, Nancy's eyes considered him very gravely, whilst he himself dared to turn never so much as a single glance in her direction.

When the examiner and the doctor passed at last from the room, Holles dragged himself wearily after them. He followed them below-stairs, and remained there alone after they had taken their departure.

For twenty-eight days he was doomed to imprisonment in this house, and he made his dispositions. That night he slept in a back bedroom on the ground floor. In the morning, having prepared himself breakfast in the kitchen, a matter in which Mrs. Dallows came to his assistance, he went to straighten out the dining-room so that it might serve him for a lodging during the period of incarceration that lay ahead.

He found the room in utter darkness. It had not been entered since the night of Nancy's coming thither. He groped his way across to the shutters, which he remembered to have closed by request of the examiner after carrying Nancy from the room on that terrible night a week ago. He pulled them open and let in a flood of daylight upon a scene each detail of which reminded him poignantly of the happenings of that night. There lay the chair overturned by Nancy as she retreated before Buckingham. He imagined the circumstances in which it had fallen. There on the polished blocks of the floor, under the table — where it had escaped the eyes of Dr. Beamish — gleamed the blade of his own broken sword, and yonder in a corner, whither it had rolled, the hilt which his nerveless fingers had relinquished when he was struck down. On the floor by the table there was a dull brown patch which he knew to have been made by his own blood, and there were similar stains on the daybed and on the napery of the table, which he guessed to have been made by the blood of Buckingham.

Fallen between the daybed and the window, he found the slender dress rapier which Buckingham had used. The Duke had dropped it there when he rose at the end of their grim struggle, and he had not paused to recover it in his precipitate flight.

For the rest, guttered candles, withered flowers, and rotting fruits encumbered the table, and the lustre of glass and silver was dulled by a film of dust. On the sideboard stood the array of dainty dishes that had been prepared for that infamous intimate supper which had never been consumed, rotting there, and loading the atmosphere of the room with the evil odour of decay, which to Holles was like an exhalation of the ugly memories they held for him.

He flung the windows wide, and spent some time in setting the room to rights, and ridding it of all that refuse.

Thereafter he lay on the daybed smoking and thinking, and very listless. And it was thus, in the days that followed, that most of his hours were spent. If he did not regard himself as actually dead already, at least he regarded himself as one whose life was ended, one to whom death would bring a welcome relieving rest. Vaguely he hoped — he would have prayed, but that he had long since lost the habit of prayer — that the infection which he supposed present in this house might claim him for her victim. Morning and evening, and ever and anon throughout the day, he would open his doublet to finger his breast and explore his armpits in expectancy, eager to discover upon himself the tokens of the plague.

But the irony that had ever pursued him thwarted now his desire of death as it had thwarted his every desire concerned with life. Living and moving in that house of pestilence, breathing its mephitic atmosphere, he yet remained as immune as if he had been a "safe man."

For the first three days his existence was one of completest, listless idleness. There were books in the house; but he had no desire to read. He was content to lie there smoking and moping. Each morning Mrs. Dallows reported to him the condition of the patient, which was one of steady improvement, and this was confirmed by the doctor, who paid two visits in the course of those three days. On the second of those occasions he remained some time in talk with Holles, giving him news of the dreadful state of things outside.

Whitehall was empty now of all its courtly tenants with the single exception of the Duke of Albemarle. Honest George Monk had elected to remain undaunted at his post as the representative of his King, to perform in the King's name — and whilst His Majesty was busy at Salisbury with the amorous pursuit of Miss Frances Stewart — all that which a king himself should be at hand to perform in time of national stress, to mitigate the tribulations of his subjects.

Hopefully Holles inquired of Beamish if he knew aught of Buckingham. Hopefully, that is, because he was expecting to hear that the Duke was laid low by the infection.

"Gone with the rest," the doctor informed him. "He left Town for the North a week ago, aroused to a sudden sense of his duty as Lord Lieutenant of York by the fact that a French lackey in his household was stricken with the plague. He'll be safe enough in York, no doubt."

"A French lackey, eh? Only a lackey!" The Colonel's face was overspread with disappointment. "The devil watches over his own," he grumbled. "A wretched lackey pays for the sins of his master. Well, well, I suppose there is a God — somewhere."

"Have you no cause to know it, sir, and to give thanks?" Beamish reproved him. And Holles turned away without answering, beyond a sigh and a shrug, which but served to increase the doctor's perplexity over the behaviour of the members of this odd household. That all was very far from well there was abundantly clear.

Acting upon a sudden impulse, Dr. Beamish left the room, and mounted the stairs again — for all that his time was short and his patients many. Dismissing Mrs. Dallows upon some trivial errand to the kitchen, he remained closeted for five minutes with Miss Sylvester. That was the name by which he knew her, the name by which she had chosen to make herself known to both doctor and nurse.

Whether it was as a result of what he said to her in those five minutes, or whether other influences were at work, within an hour of the doctor's departure, Holles was sought by Mrs. Dallows with a message that Miss Sylvester was risen, and desired to speak with him.

The eyes of that kindly nurse, sharpened by solicitude, saw him turn pale and tremble at the summons. His first impulse was to disregard it. But, before making any reply, he took a turn in that wainscoted sombre room. Then, with a sigh of resignation, he announced that he would go. Mrs. Dallows opened the door, and held it for him to pass out, tactfully refraining from following him.

He was washed and shaven, tolerably dressed, and his long, well-combed, golden-brown hair hung in long, smooth ringlets to the snowy collar which Mrs. Dallows had found time to wash and iron for him. Thus he no longer presented the wild, unkempt appearance that had been his when last Miss Sylvester had seen him. But there was a haggard dejection about the lines of his mouth, a haunting sadness about his eyes that nothing could relieve.

He found Miss Sylvester seated by the open window, where he himself had sat throughout the greater part of those five days and six nights when he had so unceasingly watched over her to beat back hungry death from her pillow. She occupied a great chair set for her there by Mrs. Dallows, a rug about her knees. She was very pale and weak, yet her loveliness seemed to draw added charms from her condition. She wore that gown of ivory white in which she had been carried to this evil house, and her chestnut hair had been dressed with care and was intertwined with a thread of pearls. Her long eyes seemed of a darker, deeper blue than usual, perhaps because of the hollows her illness had left about them. And there were other changes in her that in their sum appeared almost to spiritualize her, so that to Holles she seemed to have recovered something of her lost childhood, of her early youth, and looked less like Sylvia Farquharson, the idolized player, and more like the Nancy Sylvester whom he had known and loved so dearly.

Wistfully she looked up at him as he entered, then away

through the open window into the hot sunlight that scorched the almost empty street.

He closed the door, advanced a pace or two, and halted.

"You sent for me," he said, "else I should not have ventured to intrude." And he stood now like a groom awaiting orders.

A tinge of colour crept into her cheeks. One of her slender, tapering hands, that in these days had grown almost transparent, plucked nervously at the rug about her knees. Ill at ease as she was, her speech assumed, despite her, a stilted, formal shape.

"I sent for you, sir, that I might acknowledge the great debt in which you have placed me; to thank you for your care of me, for your disregard of your own peril in tending me; in short, sir, for my life, which had been lost without you."

She looked at him suddenly as she ceased, whereupon he shifted his glance to the sunlight in the open so as to avoid the unbearable gaze of her eyes that were gleaming like wet sapphires.

"You owe me no thanks — no thanks at all," he said, and his voice was almost gruff. "I but sought to undo the evil I had done."

"That . . . that was before the plague came to my rescue. In what you did then, you sought at the risk of your life to make me the only possible amend, and to deliver me from the evil man into whose power you had brought me. But the plague, now. It was no fault of yours that I took that. It was already upon me when you brought me hither."

"No matter for that," said he. "Reparation was due. I owed it to myself."

"You did not owe it to yourself to risk your life for me."

"My life, madam, is no great matter. A life misused,

misspent, has no great value. It was the least that I could offer."

"Perhaps," she answered gently. "But also it was the most, and, as I have said, far more than you owed."

"I do not think so. But the matter is not wcrth contending."

He did not help her. Persuaded of the scorn that must underline her utterances, however smooth — because conscious that scorn was his only desert — he accepted her words as expressions of a pitying gratitude that offended. He stood before her, overwhelmed by the consciousness of his unworthiness, in a mood of the most abject humility. But unconsciously, without suspecting it, he had empanoplied this humility in pride. His desire, above all, was to withdraw from an interview that could be nothing but a source of pain.

But she detained him, persisting in what he accounted her cruel charity.

"At least the reparation you have made is a very full one."

"It would comfort me to hear you say it, could I believe you," he answered grimly, and would have taken his leave of her on that but that she stayed him by her interjection.

"Why should you not believe me? Why should I be other than sincere in my desire to thank you?"

He looked at her at last, and in his eyes she saw some reflection of the pain he was suffering.

"Oh, I believe you sincere in that. You wish to thank me. It is natural, I suppose. You thank me; but you despise me. Your gratitude cannot temper your contempt. It is not possible."

"Are you so sure?" she asked him gently, and her eyes were very piteous.

"Sure? What else can I be? What else is possible? Do I

not loathe and despise myself? Am I so unconscious of my own infamy that I should befool myself into the thought that any part of it can escape you?"

"Don't!" she said. "Ah, don't!" But in the sorrow in her face he read no more than the confirmation of the very thing she was feebly attempting to deny.

"Is it worth while to close our eyes to a truth so self-evident?" he cried. "For years I sought you, Nan, a man without a stain upon his name, to find you at last in an hour in which I was so besmirched that I could not bear your eyes upon me. The very act that by a cruel irony of chance brought us together here at last was an act by which I touched the very bottom of the pit of infamy. Then — that dreadful night — you regarded me rightly with loathing. Now you regard me with pity because I am loathsome. Out of that pity, out of your charity, you fling me thanks that are not due, since what I have done was done in mitigation of my offence. What more is there to say? If this house were not locked, and I a prisoner here, I should have gone by now. I should have departed in that blessed moment that Beamish announced your danger at an end, taking care that our paths should never cross again, that I might never again offend you with the sight of my loathsomeness or the necessity to render thanks for benefits received from unclean hands, that you properly despise."

"You think that sums all up?" she asked him, sadly incredulous. "It does not. It leaves still something to be said — indeed, a deal."

"Spare it me," he begged her passionately. "Out of that same charity that bids you thank me, spare me." Then, more briskly, with a certain finality, he added: "If you have commands for me, madam, I shall be below until this house is reopened, and we can go our separate ways again."

He bowed formally, and turned away.

"Randal!" she called to him as he reached the door. He paused, his firm resolve beaten down by that pleading utterance of his name. "Randal, won't you tell me how . . . how you came into . . . into the position in which I found you here? Won't you tell me that? Won't you let me know all — all — so that I may judge for myself?"

A moment he stood there, white to the lips and trembling, fighting his pride — that pride which was masquerading in the garment of humility, and so deceived him that he suffered it to prevail.

"Judge me, madam, upon the evidence you possess. It is sufficient to enable you to do me justice. Nothing that went before, no vicissitudes of my vagrant life, can extenuate the thing you know of me. I am a scoundrel, a loathsomeness, an offence, and you know me to be this — you in whose eyes I would ever have appeared as a man of shining honour. Oh, God pity me! Don't you see? Don't you see?"

Her eyes were suddenly aswim in tears.

"I see that perhaps you judge yourself too hardly. Let me judge for myself, Randal. Don't you see that I am aching to forgive? Is my forgiveness nothing to you?"

"It would be all," he answered her. "But I could never believe in it. Never. You are aching to forgive, you say. Oh, blessed, healing words! But why is this? Because you are grateful to me for the life I have helped to save. That is the true source of your pity for my soul's deformity, which is urging you to utter this forgiveness. But behind that gratitude and that forgiveness there must ever remain the contempt, the loathing of this deformity of mine. It must be so. I know it, or I know nothing. Because of that . . ." He broke off, leaving the sentence there, completing it with a wry smile and a despairing shrug. But she saw neither. She had averted her eyes again, and she was looking straight before her into the sunlight, across to the black-timbered, yellow houses opposite which were blurred in her sight by tears.

Softly he went out, and closed the door. She heard him go, and suffered him to do so, making no further attempt to stay him, knowing not what to say to combat his desperate convictions.

Heavy-footed he went down the stairs, back to that room where he had his being. And as he went his thoughts confirmed him. They had met at last, those two, only that they might part again. Their ways could never lie together. Overshadowing their joint lives there must ever be the loathly memory of that irrevocable thing he had done. Even if he were not the broken vagrant that he was, even if he had anything to offer in life to the woman of his dreams, his action when he played the jackal for Buckingham must render impossible between them any tenderness that should be sincere and unalloyed.

He was in a mood from which there was no escape. Pride hemmed his soul about with walls of humility and shame, and there was no issue thence save by the door that the plague might open. Yet even the plague refused to stand his friend.

CHAPTER XXIV

EVASION

THE weeks crept on, and August was approaching. Soon now the period of quarantine would be at an end, and the house in Knight Ryder Street reopened to liberate its inmates. Yet the passing of time wrought no change in the mood of Holles. Not once again did he seek to approach Nancy, and not again did she bid him to her presence.

He informed himself constantly of her progress, and learnt with satisfaction that she was fast recovering her strength. But Mrs. Dallows who brought him this daily information was also at pains to let him know at the same time that there was no recovery in spirits to be observed in her charge.

"She is very sad and lonely, poor, sweet lady. It would melt your heart to see her, sir."

"Aye, aye," Holles would gloomily make answer to that oft-reiterated report. And that was all.

Mrs. Dallows was not a little afflicted. And affliction in Mrs. Dallows had the effect of heightening her resemblance to a hen. She perceived, of course, that a mystery enshrouded the relations of these two, saw that some obstacle stood between them, holding them apart — to their mutual torment, since obviously they were designed to be lovers; and more than once she sought to force the confidence now of one, now of the other. Her motives, no doubt, were entirely charitable. She was eager to help them, if it were possible, to a better understanding. But her efforts to probe their secret remained unavailing, and she could but sorrow in their sorrow. It was the more grievous and vexatious to her because the deep concern of each for the other was manifest in the questions each set her daily.

Holles kept to his quarters below-stairs, smoking contin-
uously and drinking deeply, too, until he had consumed the
little store of wine the house contained. Then not even the
nepenthe of the cup remained to assuage his grim despondency, his repeated assertions to himself that his life was
lived, that he was a dead man without further business
above-ground.

Thus August found them, and from the watchman he
heard incredible stories of London's deepening plight,
whilst from the window he nightly beheld the comet in the
heavens, that latest portent of menace, the flaming sword of
wrath — as the watchman termed it — that was hung above
the accursed city, stretching, as it seemed, from Whitehall
to the Tower.

They were within three days of the reopening of the house
when at last one evening Mrs. Dallows came to him trembling with excitement, and a little out of breath.

"Miss Sylvester, sir, bids me say that she will be obliged
if you will step upstairs to see her."

The message startled him.

"No, no!" he cried out like a man in panic. Then, con-
trolling himself, he took refuge in postponement that would
give him time to think: "Say . . . say that if Miss Sylvester
will excuse me . . . not this evening. I am tired . . . the
heat . . ." he vaguely explained.

The nurse cocked her head on one side and her bright little
birdlike eyes considered him wistfully. "If not this evening,
when? To-morrow morning?"

"Yes, yes," he answered eagerly, thinking only of averting
the immediate menace. "In the morning. Tell her that I . . .
I shall wait upon her then."

Mrs. Dallows withdrew, leaving him oddly shaken and
afraid. It was himself he feared, himself he mistrusted.
Where once the boy had worshipped, the man now loved

with a love that heaped up and fed the fires of shame in his
soul until they threatened to consume him. At his single
interview with Nancy he had exposed his mind. He had
been strong; but he might not be strong again. The gentleness of purpose of which she had allowed him a glimpse, a
gentleness born of her cursed gratitude, might lead him yet
to play the coward, to give her the full confidence that she
invited, and so move her pity and through pity her full forgiveness. And then if — as might well betide — he should
prove so weak as to fling himself at her feet, and pour out
the tale of his longings and his love, out of her sense of debt,
out of her pity and her gratitude she might take him, this
broken derelict of humanity, and so doom herself to be
dragged down with him into the kennels where his future
lay.

There stood a peril of a wrong far worse than that which
already he had done her, and for which in some measure he
had perhaps atoned. And because he could not trust himself
to come again into her presence preserving the silence that
his honour demanded, he suffered tortures now at the
thought that to-morrow, willy-nilly, he must see her, since it
was her wish, and she was strong enough herself to seek him
should he still refuse to go.

He sat, and smoked, and thought, resolved that at all costs
that interview must not take place. One way there was to
avoid it and definitely to set a term to the menace of it.
That was to break out of the sealed house at once without
awaiting the expiry of the legal term. It was a desperate
way, and it might be attended by gravest consequences to
himself. But no other course presented itself, and the consequences mattered nothing, after all.

The thought became a resolve and, having reached it, he
gave his mind peace. This, indeed — and not the pains and
risks he had taken to save her from the plague — was repar-

ation. Anon, when she came to consider and weigh his action, she would perceive its true significance and purpose,
and the perception might at last blot out the contempt of
him which perforce must be abiding in her soul however she
might seek to overlay it with charity.

A thought seized him, and, growing to purpose, exalted
him. He sought pen, ink, and paper, drew a chair to the
table, and sat down to act upon his inspiration.

"You have asked," he wrote, opening abruptly thus, "to
know by what steps I descended to the hell of infamy in
which you discovered me. And I refrained from answering
you lest I should arouse in you a further measure of your
blessed, self-deceiving compassion. But now that I am on
the point of passing out of your life, now that there is no
chance that we should ever meet again, I am moved to tell
you all, that thus I may bear away with me the fortifying
hope that hereafter you will hold my memory in a pity that
shall be free of execration.

"The tale of the ill-fortune that has pursued me begins on
a May morning, many years ago, when I rode full of hope
and eagerness into Charmouth, a youth of some substance
and more pride, whose feet were firmly planted upon an
honourable road of life. I went to claim you for my own, to
lay my little achievement and the assured promise of my
greater ones at your dear feet."

He wrote on into the fading daylight. He lighted candles,
and wrote on with that swift fluency of the man who has a
clear tale to tell and the eloquence that comes naturally
from a bursting heart.

The candles, faintly stirred by the night breeze that came
through the open window, burnt down, and great stalactites
of wax were hanging from the sconces; still he wrote without
pause. He heard, but did not heed, the changing of the
watchman at the door below. Later he heard, but did not

heed, the passing of the dead-cart with its accompaniment of clanging bell and raucous summons.

Once only he paused, to procure and light fresh candles, and then wrote on. Not until long after midnight, not until the approach of dawn, did he cease, his task accomplished.

He sat back then in his tall chair, and stared straight before him, a man bemused, considering. Thus awhile. Then from an inner pocket of his doublet he drew a tasselled yellow glove that was slim and long and sorely rubbed and stained with age. He considered it as it lay there across his palm, and bethought him of that dawn many years ago when it had dropped to him from his lady's casement, and he had set it in his hat, to be worn as a favour. He sighed, and a tear, wrung by the anguish of this renunciation from his hardened, adventurer's heart, fell on his hand.

Abruptly then he sat forward, and, snatching up the quill again, he scrawled at fierce speed on the foot of the last of the written sheets:

"Here is a glove that you bestowed on me in the long ago. I wore it, as your knight wearing his lady's favour in the lists of life, proudly by the right of your gift and my unsullied honour. For years it was an amulet to maintain that honour still unsullied against all trials and temptations. Now that it has failed of this purpose through my own cowardice and unworthiness, you may not wish me to retain it longer."

That manuscript — for it is hardly to be termed a letter — still survives. Its faded characters cover some thirty pages of paper that the centuries have tinted yellow. It has been — as you will surmise — in my possession. It has supplied me with more than the mere elements of this history, which without it could never have been written.

He did not read it through when it was done. There was no time for that. As he had poured it from his heart, so he left it. He folded the sheets together, enclosing the glove within them, wrapped a thread of silk about the package, and on the knot of this he made a disc of wax which he sealed with his thumb. He superscribed the package, quite simply, "To Miss Nancy Sylvester," and stood it there on the table against the stem of the candle-branch within view of the first person who should enter that room.

Next he drew forth his still well-filled purse, and emptied its contents on to the table. One half he replaced; of the other he made two packets, addressing one to Dr. Beamish and the other to Mrs. Dallows.

Softly then he pushed back his chair, and rose. He tip-toed to the window, and peered down into the shadows where the watchman kept his post, propped in a corner of the pad-locked doorway. A sound of snoring came to inform Holles that, as he had reckoned, the fellow slept. Why should he have troubled to weary himself with a strict and wakeful vigilance? Who could be so mad as to wish to incur all the penalties of evasion from a house that was to be opened now in three days' time?

Holles went back. He took up his hat and cloak. Then, acting upon a sudden thought, he sought his baldric, and to the empty scabbard that was attached to it he fitted the slender dress-rapier that Buckingham had left behind him. The blade was rather loose in that sheath, but he contrived to jam the hilt.

Having passed the baldric over his head and settled it on his shoulder, he blew out the candles, and a moment later he was at the window again.

He scarcely made a sound as he straddled the window-sill; then very gently he let himself down, until he hung at full length, his toes not more than three feet above the kidney stones of the dark, empty, silent street. A moment he hung there, steadying himself, then loosed his hold. He dropped very lightly, and, as he was wearing no spurs, he made practically no noise at all. At once he set off in the direction of Sermon Lane.

The watchman, momentarily disturbed by the movements so near at hand, caught a sound of footsteps retreating quickly up the street, but never dreamed of connecting them with any one from the house he guarded. He settled himself more comfortably in his restful angle, and sank back peacefully into his slumbers.

Nevertheless, the evasion of Holles had not gone as entirely unperceived as he imagined. Slight as had been the noise he made, yet it had reached the window of the room immediately above, and by that window — which was the window of Nancy's room — sat Nancy driven to that vigil by thoughts that rendered sleep impossible.

Her attention aroused by those furtive sounds below, she had leaned far out from the casement and peered down into the darkness. She had heard the soft thud of feet as Holles dropped to the street, and immediately thereafter the patter of his retreating footsteps. Very faintly she thought she made out at the same time the receding figure of a man, a deeper shadow amid shadows. But however little she may have seen with the eyes of the flesh, she saw all with the eyes of her imagination. She was on the point of crying out, but suddenly checked herself, fearful of rousing the watchman and setting afoot a pursuit which, if successful, might be attended by direst consequences for Holles. And it was only that same dread that lent her strength to repress the instinctive impulse to call him back and arrest that flight of his.

Then she steadied herself. After all, it was possible that she was at fault, that she was the victim of her own imaginings, that her overwrought senses had played a trick upon her. But the doubt was unbearable. She must make sure at once. With trembling, fumbling fingers she kindled a light. Then with a rug wrapped about her over her night-rail, she made her way below. Thus she descended the stairs for the first time, and as she went she blamed herself bitterly — in her conviction that she would find things as she feared — for not having earlier taken this step and gone to seek him who remained so obdurately absent.

When on the following morning an anxious Mrs. Dallows entered the dining-room in fearful quest of her charge, she found her there, at once to her infinite relief and infinite distress. In her night-rail, the rug fallen from her bare shoulders, Nancy sat on the daybed under the open window. She was pale and dry-eyed, but with such pain and misery stamped upon her face that the sight of tears would have been comforting by contrast. Beside her was a candlestick in which the single candle had been burnt to the socket, about her the floor was strewn with the sheets of Holles's letter, which had slipped from her nerveless fingers.

That letter had accomplished all that Holles could have hoped from it. It had quenched completely and finally any lingering embers of her scorn. It had aroused compassion, and the old love, and finally despair. For by his own act he was deliberately lost to her again. He was gone, irrevocably, as he announced, and by the very manner of his going had made himself an outlaw.

CHAPTER XXV
HOME

OUT of concern for her charge, Mrs. Dallows at once dispatched the watchman for Dr. Beamish, and, when the physician arrived some little while later, she acquainted him with the Colonel's evasion and the consequent partially stunned condition in which Miss Sylvester appeared to move.

The good doctor, who had come to conceive some measure of affection for those two, rooted, perhaps, in a certain pity which their mysterious, but obviously unhappy, relations aroused in him, went at once in deepest distress to seek Miss Sylvester, who had meanwhile returned to her own room above-stairs. He found her affliction the more distressing to observe by virtue of her unnatural composure.

"This is terrible, my dear," he said, as he took her hands. "What can have driven that unhappy man to so . . . so unfortunate a course?"

"He must be sought. You will order search to be made for him?" she cried.

He sighed and sorrowfully shook his head: "There is no need for me to order that. My duty compels me to make his evasion known. Search for him will follow; but, should he be found, it may go very hard with him; there are rigorous penalties."

Thus, unavoidably, Dr. Beamish but added a fresh burden to her already surcharged heart. It reduced her to a state of mind bordering upon distraction. She knew not what to desire. Unless he were sought and found, it followed that she would never see him again, whilst if he were found he would have to reckon with the severity of the law, and she could have no assurance that she would see him even then.

Out of his anxiety to help her, Dr. Beamish invited her
confidence. He conceived here a case of stupid, headstrong,
human pride against which two hearts were likely to be
broken, and, because of that affection which they had come
to inspire in him, he would have done all in his power to assist them could he but have obtained an indication of the
way. But Miss Sylvester, greatly as it would have eased her
sorrow to have confided in him, greatly as she desired to do
so, found that no confidence was possible without divulging
the thing that Holles had done, the hideous act by which she
came to find herself in this house. A sudden sense of loyalty
to him made it impossible for her to publish his infamy.

So, rejecting the chance to ease by confidence the burden
that she carried, she continued to move, white-faced and
listless, under the load of it during the two remaining days of
her detention. Nor did the doctor come to her again until
that third morning, when he was once more accompanied by
the examiner, who presented her and her nurse-keeper each
with a certificate of health that permitted their free departure. Holles, she was then informed, had not yet been found;
but she knew not whether to rejoice or sorrow in that fact.

Bearers were procured for her, the watchman himself vol-
unteering to act as one of them, and the chair in which she
had been carried thither, which had been bestowed in the
house itself, was brought forth again at her request, to carry
her away.

"But whither are you going?" the doctor questioned her
in solicitude.

They were standing in the doorway of the house, she with
her light hooded mantle of blue taffetas drawn over her
white gown, the chair standing in the sunlight, waiting to
receive her.

"Why, home. Back to my own lodging," she answered
simply.

"Home?" he echoed, in amazement. "But . . . but, then . . . this house?"

She looked at him as if puzzled by his astonishment. Then she smiled wanly. "This house is not mine. I was here by . . . by chance when I was taken ill."

The belated revelation of that unsuspected circumstance filled him with a sudden dread on her behalf. Knowing the changes that had come upon that unfortunate City in the month that was overpast, knowing how many were the abandoned houses that stood open now to the winds of heaven, he feared with reason that hers might be one of these, or, at least, that the odds were all against her finding her home, as she imagined, in the condition in which she had left it.

"Where is your lodging?" he asked her.

She told him, adding that upon arrival there she would determine her future movements. She thought, she ended, that she would seek awhile the peace and quiet of the country. Perhaps she would return to London when this visitation was at an end; perhaps she would not. That was what she said. What she meant was really something very different.

The announcement served to increase his dismay on her behalf. It was easier now-a-days to project withdrawal into the country than to accomplish it unless one commanded unusual power and wealth — and all those who commanded these things had long since gone. The wholesale flight from London that had taken place since she was stricken down had been checked at last by two factors. There was no country town or village for many and many a mile that would receive fugitives from London, out of dread of the infection which these might carry. To repel them the inhabitants of rural districts had even had recourse to arms, until, partly because of this and to avoid disturbances and

bloodshed, partly as an heroic measure against the spread
of the plague throughout England, the Lord Mayor had
been constrained to suspend the issue of certificates of
health, without which no man could depart from London.
Those who still remained in the infected area — where the
plague was taking now a weekly toll of thousands of lives —
must abandon all hope of quitting it until the pestilence
should have subsided.

Considering now her case and weighing what she had told
him, Dr. Beamish perceived that her need of him was far
from being at an end. Practical and spiritual assistance
might be as necessary to her presently as had lately been
his physician's ministrations.

"Come," he said abruptly, "I will go with you to your
lodging, and see you safely bestowed there — that is, if you
permit it."

"Permit it? Oh, my friend!" She held out her hand to
him. "Shall I permit you to do me this last kindness? I
shall be more grateful than ever I could hope to tell you."

He smiled through his owlish spectacles, and in silence
patted the little hand he held; then he made shift to lead her
forward to her chair.

But a duty yet remained her. In the shadows of the hall
behind lingered still the kindly Mrs. Dallows, almost
tearful at this parting from the sweet charge for whom she
had conceived so great a kindness. Miss Sylvester ran back
to her.

"Keep this in memory of one who will never forget her
debt to you and never cease to think of you fondly." Into
her hand she pressed a clasp of brilliants that she had taken
from her bodice — a thing of price far beyond the gold that
Holles had left behind in payment for the nurse's services.
Then, as Mrs. Dallows began at one and the same time to
thank her and to protest against this excessive munificence,

Nancy took the kindly woman in her arms and kissed her. Both were in tears when Nancy turned away and ran out to the waiting sedan.

The bearers — the watchman, and the fellow he had fetched to assist him — took up the chair and swung away towards Paul's Chains. The little black figure of the doctor strutted beside it, swinging the long red wand that did him the office of a cane, whilst Mrs. Dallows, standing at the door of the house in Knight Ryder Street, watched it out of sight through a blur of tears.

And within the chair Miss Sylvester, too, was giving way at last to tears. They were the first she had shed since she had received the Colonel's letter, which letter was the only thing she carried away with her from that ill-starred house. Lost thus to consciousness of her surroundings, she took no heed of the emptiness and silence of the streets, and of the general air of furtiveness and desolation that hung about the few wayfarers upon whom they chanced and that marked the very houses they were passing.

Thus at last they came to Salisbury Court and to the house that Nancy had indicated. And here at once Dr. Beamish saw that his worst fears were realized.

Its door hung wide, and the dust lay thick upon the window-panes, two of which were broken. Miss Sylvester, having alighted from her chair, stood looking up, arrested by the unusual aspect of the place, and chilled by a nameless dismay. In awe-stricken wonder, she looked round the court, utterly untenanted, and presenting everywhere the same forsaken aspect. From behind a dusty window of a house across the way, whose door was marked and locked and guarded, an aged yellow face revealed itself, and a pair of eyes that seemed malignant in their furtiveness were watching her. Beyond that ill-omened visage there was in all the court no single sign of life.

"What does it mean?" she asked the doctor.

Sadly he shook his head. "Can you not guess? Here as elsewhere the plague and the fear of the plague have been busy in your absence." He sighed, and added abruptly: "Let us go in."

They entered the gloomy vestibule, where dried leaves swept thither by the winds crackled under their feet, and thence they began the ascent of a narrow staircase on the baluster of which there was a mantle of dust. Miss Sylvester called out once or twice as they advanced. But there was no answer to those calls other than the hollow echoes they awoke in that untenanted house.

The three rooms that had composed her home were situated on the first floor, and as they ascended to the landing they saw the three doors standing open. Two of the chambers were shuttered, and, therefore, in darkness; but the drawing-room, which directly faced the stair-head, was all in sunlight, and even before they entered it they had a picture of the devastation wrought there. The furniture was not merely disarranged; it was rudely tumbled, some of it broken, and some was missing altogether. Drawers hung open, as they had been pulled by thieving hands, and that part of their contents which had not been considered worth removing now strewed the floor. A glass cabinet which had stood in one angle lay tumbled forward and shattered into fragments. The *secrétaire* stood open, its lock broken, its contents rifled, a litter of papers tossed upon and about it. The curtains, torn from their poles — one of which hung broken across a window — had disappeared, as had an Eastern rug that had covered a portion of the floor.

Dr. Beamish and the lady stood in silence just within the doorway for a long moment, contemplating that dreadful havoc. Then Miss Sylvester moved swiftly forward to the *secrétaire,* in an inner drawer of which she had left a considerable sum of money — representing most of her immediate resources. That inner drawer had been wrenched open; the money was gone.

She turned and looked at Dr. Beamish, her face piteous in its white dismay. She tried to speak, but her lip trembled, and her eyes filled again with tears. To have endured so much, and to come home to this!

The doctor started forward in answer to the pitiful appeal of that glance. He advanced a chair that happened to be whole, and urged her to sit down and rest, as if the rest she needed were merely physical. She obeyed him, and with hands folded in her lap she sat there looking helplessly around upon the wreckage of her home.

"What am I to do? Where am I to turn?" she asked, and almost at once supplied the answer: "I had better go from this accursed place at once. I have an old aunt living in Charmouth. I will return to her."

She had also, she added, certain moneys in the hands of a banker near Charing Cross. Once she should have withdrawn these there would be nothing to keep her in London. She rose on the announcement as if there and then to act upon it. But the doctor gently restrained her, gently revealed to her the full helplessness of her position which was more overwhelming even than she supposed.

It must be almost certain that the banker she named would temporarily have suspended business and withdrawn himself from a place in which panic and confusion had made an end of commerce for the present. But even if he should still be at his counting-house and able at once to supply her demands, such a journey into the country as she contemplated was almost utterly impossible. True, the accident of her having had the plague had supplied her with a certificate of health, and in view of this no one could hinder her departure. But, considering whence she came, it would be with difficulty that out of London she would find any one to give her shelter; most likely, indeed, that she would be driven back by sheer necessity if not by force before she had gone farther than a day's journey.

The realization of this unsuspected thing, that she was doomed to imprisonment in this dreadful city which seemed abandoned alike by God and man, inhabited only by the unfortunate and the unclean, a city of dead and dying, drove her almost to the uttermost limits of despair.

For a while she was half stunned and silent. Then speech came from her wild and frantic.

"What then? What then remains? What am I to do? How live? O God, if only I had perished of the plague! I see now . . . I see that the worst wrong Randal Holles ever did me was when he saved my miserable life."

"Hush, hush! What are you saying, child?" The doctor set a comforting arm about her shoulders. "You are not utterly alone," he assured her gently. "I am still here, to serve you, my dear, and I am your friend."

"Forgive me," she begged him.

He patted her shoulder. "I understand. I understand. It is very hard for you, I know. But you must have courage. While we have health and strength, no ill of life is beyond repair. I am old, my dear; and I know. Let us consider now your case."

"My friend, it is beyond considerations. Who can help me now?"

"I can, for one; that is my intention."

"But in what way?"

"Why, in several ways at need. But first I can show you how you may help yourself."

"Help myself?" She looked up at him, frowning a little in her mystification.

"It is in helping others that we best help ourselves," he explained. "Who labours but for himself achieves a barren life, is like the unfaithful steward with his talents. Happiness lies in labouring for your neighbour. It is a twofold happiness. For it brings its own reward in the satisfaction of achievement, in the joy of accomplishment; and it brings another in that, bending our thoughts to the needs and afflictions of our fellows, it removes them from the comtemplation of the afflictions that are our own."

"Yes, yes. But how does it lie in my power now to do this?"

"In several ways, my dear. I will tell you of one. By God's mercy and the loving heroism of a fellow-creature you have been cured of the plague, and by that cure you have been rendered what is commonly known as a 'safe woman' — a person immune from infection who may move without fear among those who suffer from the pestilence. Nurse-keepers are very difficult to find, and daily their diminishing numbers grow less equal to the ever-increasing work that this sad visitation provides. Many of them are noble, self-sacrificing women who, without even such guarantees of immunity as you now possess, go heroically among the sufferers, and some of these — alas! — are constantly succumbing." He paused, peering at her shortsightedly through his spectacles.

She looked up at him in round-eyed amusement.

"And you are suggesting that I . . ." She broke off, a little appalled by the prospect opened out to her.

"You might do it because you conceive it to be a debt you owe to God and your fellow-creatures for your own preservation. Or you might do it so that, in seeking to heal the afflictions of others, you may succeed in healing your ɒwn. But, however you did it, it would be a noble act, and would surely not go unrewarded."

She rose slowly, her brows bent in thought. Then she uttered a little laugh of self-pity. "And unless I do that, what else, indeed, am I to do?" she asked.

"Nay, nay," he made haste to reassure her. "I do not wish to force you into any course against your will. If the task is repugnant to you — and I can well understand that it might be — do not imagine that I shall on that account forsake you. I will not leave you helpless and alone. Be sure of that."

She looked at him, and smiled a little.

"It is repugnant, of course," she confessed frankly. "How should it be otherwise? I have lived soft and self-indulgently from childhood. Therefore, if I do this thing, perhaps it will on that account be more acceptable in the eyes of Heaven. As you say, it is a debt I owe." She put out a hand and took his arm. "I am ready, my friend, to set about discharging it."

CHAPTER XXVI

THE DEAD-CART

HAD you asked Colonel Holles in after-life how he had spent the week that followed immediately upon his escape from the house in Knight Ryder Street, he could have supplied you with only the vaguest and most incomplete of accounts. His memories were a confused jumble, from which only certain facts detached themselves with any degree of sharpness. The ugly truth, which must be told, is that in all that week he was hardly ever entirely sober. The thing began on the very night — or, rather, morning — of his evasion.

Without definite destination, or even aim beyond that of putting as great a distance as possible between himself and Knight Ryder Street, Holles came by way of Carter Lane into Paul's Yard. There he hung a moment hesitating — for a man may well hesitate when all directions are as one to him; then he struck eastward, down Watling Street, finally plunging into the labyrinth of narrow alleys to the north of it. Here he might have wandered until broad daylight, but that, lost in the heart of that dædal, he was drawn by sounds of revelry to a narrow door, from under which a blade of light was stretched across the cobbles of the street.

It was the oddness of those sounds, as incongruous in this plague-stricken London as if they had issued from the bowels of a sepulchre, that gave him pause. On that mean threshold he stood hesitating, peering up at the sign, which he could just discern to be in the shape of a flagon, whence he must have concluded, had other evidences been lacking, that the place was a tavern. Further he concluded, from his knowledge of the enactment by which all such resorts were to close to custom at nine o'clock, that here a breach of the law was being flagrantly committed.

Attracted, on the one hand, by the thought of the oblivion that might be purchased within, repelled, on the other, by the obviously disreputable character of the place and by a curious sense of the increased scorn he must evoke in Nancy's mind could she witness his weak surrender to so foul a temptation, he ended by deciding to pass on. But, even as he turned to do so, the door was suddenly pulled open, and across the street was flung a great shaft of yellow light in which he stood revealed. Two drunken roisterers, lurching forth, paused a moment, surprised, at the sight of him, arrested there. Then, with drunken inconsequence, they fell upon him, took him each by an arm, and dragged him, weakly resisting, over the threshold of that unclean den, amid shouts of insensate, hilarious welcome from its inhabitants.

Holles stood there in the glare and stench of a half-dozen fish-oil lamps suspended from the beams of the low, grimy ceiling, blinking like an owl, whilst the taverner, vehemently cursing the fools who had left his door agape, made haste to close it again, shutting out as far as possible sight and sound of this transgression of the recent rigorous laws.

When presently the Colonel's eyes had grown accustomed to the light, he took stock of his surroundings. He found himself in a motley gathering of evil-looking, raffish men, and no less evil-looking women. In all there may have been some thirty of them huddled there together in that comparatively restricted space. The men were rufflers and foists and worse; the women were trulls of various degrees, with raddled cheeks and glittering eyes. Some were maudlin, some hilarious, and some lay helpless and inert as logs. All of them had been drinking to excess, save, perhaps, some four or five who were gathered about a table apart, snarling over a pack of greasy cards. They were men and women of the underworld, whom circumstances, and the fact that no further certificates of health were being issued, confined to the plague-ridden city; and, in an excess of the habits of debauch that were usual to them, they took this means of cheating for a brief while the terror in which normally they lived and moved in that stronghold of death. It was a gathering typical of many that Asmodeus might have discovered had he troubled on any of those August nights to lift the roofs of London's houses.

Holles surveyed them with cold disgust, whilst they stared questioningly back at him. They had fallen silent now, all save one who, maudlin, in a corner, persisted in continuing an obscene song with which he had been regaling the company when the Colonel entered.

"Gads my life!" said Holles, at length. "But that I am told the Court has gone to Salisbury, I might suppose myself in Whitehall."

The double-edged gibe shook them into an explosion of laughter. They acclaimed him for a wit, and proceeded to pronounce him free of their disreputable company, whilst the two topers who had lugged him in from the open dragged him now to one of the tables where room was readily made for him. He yielded to the inevitable. He had a few pieces in his pocket, and he spent one of these on burnt sack before that wild company broke up, and its members crept to their homes, like rats to their burrows, in the pale light of dawn.

Thereafter he hired a bed from the vintner, and slept until close upon noon. Having broken his fast upon a dish of salt herrings, he wandered forth again, errant and aimless. He won through a succession of narrow, unclean alleys into the eastern end of Cheapside, and stood there, aghast to survey the change that the month had wrought. In that

thoroughfare, usually the busiest in London, he found emptiness and silence. Where all had been life and bustle, a continual stream of coaches and chairs of wayfarers on foot and
on horseback, of merchants and prentices at the shop doors
with their incessant cries of "What d'ye lack?" and clamor-
ous invitations to view the wares and bargains that they offered, the street from end to end was now empty of all but
some half-dozen stragglers like himself, and one who with
averted head was pushing a wheelbarrow whose grim load
was covered by a cloak.

Not a coach, not a chair, not a horse in sight, and not a
merchant's voice to be heard; not even a beggar's whine.
Here and there a shop stood open, but where there were no
buyers there was no eagerness to sell. Some few houses he
beheld close-shuttered and padlocked, each marked with
the red cross and guarded by its armed watchman; one or
two others he observed to stand open and derelict. Last of
all, but perhaps most awe-inspiring, as being the most eloquent witness to the general desolation, he saw that blades of
grass were sprouting between the kidney stones with which
the street was paved, so that, but for those lines of houses
standing so grim and silent on either side, he could never
have supposed himself to be standing in a city thoroughfare.

He turned up towards St. Paul's, his steps echoing in the
noontide through the empty street as echo at midnight the
steps of some belated reveller.

It were unprofitable further to follow him in those aimless
wanderings, in which he spent that day and the days that
followed. Once he made an excursion as far as Whitehall, to
assure himself that His Grace of Buckingham was, indeed,
gone from Town, as Dr. Beamish had informed him. He
went spurred by the desire to vent a sense of wrong that
came to the surface of his sodden wits like oil to the surface
of water. But he found the gates of Wallingford House

closed and its windows tight-shuttered, as were by then practically all the windows that overlooked that forsaken courtly thoroughfare.

Albemarle, he learnt from a stray sailor with whom he talked, was still at the Cockpit. True to his character, Honest George Monk remained grimly at his post unmoved by danger; indeed, going freely abroad in utter contempt of it, engrossed in the charitable task of doing whatever a man in his position could do to mitigate the general suffering.

Holles was tempted to seek him. But the temptation was not very strong upon him, and he withstood it. Such a visit would but waste the time of a man who had no time to waste; therefore, Albemarle was hardly likely to give him a welcome.

His nights were invariably spent at the sign of the Flagon in that dismal alley off Watling Street into which merest chance had led him in the first instance. What attraction the place could have held for him he would afterwards have found it difficult to define. There is little doubt that it was just his loneliness that impelled thither his desire for the only society that he knew to be available, a company of human beings in similar case to himself, who sought in the nepenthes of the wine-cup and in riotous debauch a temporary oblivion of their misery and desolation. Low though he might previously have come, neither was this the resort nor were the thieves and harlots by whom it was frequented the associates that he would ordinarily have chosen. Fortune, whose sport he had ever been, had flung him among these human derelicts; and there he continued, since the place afforded him the only thing he craved until death should — as he hoped — bring him final peace.

The end came abruptly. One night — the seventh that he spent in that lewd haunt of recklessness — he drank more deeply even than his deep habit. As a consequence, when,

at the host's bidding, he lurched out into the dark alley, the
last of all those roisterers to depart, his wits were drugged to
the point of insensibility. He moved like an automaton, on
legs that mechanically performed their function. Staggering
under him, they bore his swaying body in long lurches down
the lane, until he must have looked like some flimsy sim-
ulacrum of a man with which the wind made sport.

Without apprehension or care of the direction in which
he was moving, he came into Watling Street, crossed it,
plunged into a narrow alley on the southern side, and reeled
blindly onward until his feet struck an obstacle in their unconscious path. He pitched over it, and fell forward heavily
upon his face. Lacking the will and the strength to rise
again, he lay where he had fallen, and sank there into a
lethargic sleep.

A half-hour passed. It was the half-hour immediately before the dawn. Came a bell tinkling in the distance. Slowly
it drew nearer, and a cry repeated at intervals might have
been audible and intelligible to Holles had he been conscious. Soon to these were added other sounds: the melancholy creak of an axle that required greasing, and the slow
clank and thud of hooves upon the cobbles. Nearer rang the
cry upon the silent night:

"Bring out your dead!"

The vehicle halted at the mouth of the alley in which the
Colonel lay, and a man advanced, holding a flaming link
above his head so as to cast its ruddy glare hither and
thither to search the dark corners of that by-way.

This man beheld two bodies stretched upon the ground:
the Colonel's and the one over which the Colonel had
stumbled. He shouted something over his shoulder and advanced again. He was followed a moment later by the cart,
conducted by his fellow, who walked at the horse's head,
pulling at a short pipe.

Whilst he who held the torch stood there to light the other in his work, his companion stooped and rolled over the first body, then stepped forward, and did the same by Colonel Holles. The Colonel's countenance was as livid as that of the corpse that had tripped him up, and he scarcely seemed to breathe. They bestowed no more than a glance upon him with the terrible callous indifference that constant habit will bring to almost any task, and then returned to the other.

The man with the link thrust this into a holder attached to the front of the dead-cart. Then the two of them on their knees made an examination of the body, or rather of such garments as were upon it.

"Not much to trouble over here, Larry," said one.

"Aye," growled Larry. "They're sorry enough duds. Come on, Nick. Let's heave her aboard."

They rose, took down their hooks, and seizing the body by them they swung it up into the vehicle.

"Fetch the prancer nearer," said Nick, as he turned and stepped towards Holles. The horse was led forward some few paces, so that the light from the cart now fell more fully upon the Colonel's long supine figure.

Nick went down on one knee beside him, and uttered a grunt of satisfaction. "This is better."

His fellow came to peer over his shoulder.

"A gentry-cove, damme!" he swore with horrible satisfaction. Their practised ghoulish fingers went swiftly over Holles, and they chuckled obscenely at sight of the half-dozen gold pieces displayed in Larry's filthy paw.

"Not much else," grumbled one after a further inspection.

"There's his sword — a rich hilt; look, Larry."

"And there's a fine pair o' stampers," said Larry, who was already busy about the Colonel's feet. "Lend a hand, Nick."

They pulled the boots off and made a bundle of them,

together with the Colonel's hat and cloak. This bundle
Larry dropped into a basket that hung behind the cart,
whilst Nick remained to strip Holles of his doublet. Suddenly he paused.

"He'll still warm, Larry," he said querulously.

Larry approached, pulling at his pipe. He growled a lewd
oath, expressive of contempt and indifference.

"What odds?" he added cynically. "He'll be cold enough
or ever we comes to Aldgate." And he laughed as he took the
doublet Nick flung to him.

The next moment their filthy hooks were in the garments
they had left upon Holles, and they had added him to the
terrible load that already half-filled their cart.

They backed the vehicle out of the alley, and then
trundled on, going eastward, their destination being the pit
at Aldgate. Ever and anon in their slow progress they would
halt either at the summons of a watchman or at what they
found for themselves. At every halt they made an addition
to their load which they bore away for peremptory burial
in that Aldgate plague-pit, above which on these hot nights
the corpse-candles flickered almost constantly to increase the
tale of portents and to scare the credulous into the belief that
the place was haunted by the souls of those unfortunates
whose bodies lay irreverently tumbled there under the
loosely shovelled clay.

They were already approaching their destination, and the
first light of dawn, pallid, cold, and colourless as a moonstone, was beginning to dispel the darkness, when, be it
from the jolting of the cart, or from the flow of blood where
one of those foul hooks had scraped his thigh, or yet from
preserving Nature, quickening his wits that he might save
himself from suffocation, the Colonel was aroused from his
drunken trance.

He awakened, thrusting fiercely for air, and seeking to

dislodge a heavy mass that lay across his face. The efforts that at first he made were but feeble, as was to be expected from one in his condition; so that he gained no more than brief respites, in each of which, like a drowning man struggling repeatedly to the surface, he gasped a breath of that foul contamination about him. But finding each effort succeeded by a suffocation that became ever more painful, a sort of terror seized upon him, and pulled his senses out of their drunken torpor. He braced himself and heaved more strenuously, until at length he won clear, so far, at least, as his head was concerned.

He saw the paling stars above and was able at last to breathe freely and without effort. But the burden which he had succeeded in thrusting from his head, now lay across his breast, and the weight of it was troublesome and painful. He put forth a hand, and realizing by the sense of touch that what he grasped was a human arm, he shook it vigorously. Eliciting no response, he began to grow angry.

"Afoot there, ye drunken lob," he growled in a thick voice. "Get up, I say. Get up! O's my life! D'ye take me for a bed that you put yourself to sleep across me? Gerrup!" he roared, his anger increasing before that continued lack of response. "Gerrup, or I'll . . . "

He ceased abruptly, blinking in the glare of light that suddenly struck across his eyes from the flaming head of the torch which had been thrust upwards. The cart had come to a standstill, and above the tall sides of it, rising into his field of vision, came the two horrible figures of the carters, whom the sound of his voice had brought to mount the wheels of the vehicle.

There was something so foul and infernal in those faces, as seen there in the ruddy glare of the torch, that the sight of them brought the Colonel a stage nearer to sobriety. He struggled up into a sitting position, and looked about him, bewildered, uneasy, furiously endeavoring to conjecture where he might be.

In plaintive impatience came the nasal voice of one of those ghouls.

"I told ye the gentry-cove was warm, Larry."

"Aye! Well? And what now?" quoth the other querulously.

"Why, fling him out, o' course."

"Bah! Let him ride. If he's not stiff yet, he soon will be. What's the odds?"

"And what o' the plague examiner, you fool? Won't he see that it's just a drunken cove who was sleeping off his booze? And what'll he say to us? Here! Lend a hand! Let's get him out."

But Holles was no longer in need of their assistance. Their words and what he saw of that grim load of which he was a part had made him realize at last his ghastly situation. The sheer horror of it not only sobered him completely; it lent him a more than ordinary strength. He heaved himself clear, and struggled, gasping, to his knees. Thence he gripped the side of the cart, pulled himself to his feet, flung a leg over and leapt down, stumbling as he did so, and sprawling full length upon the ground.

By the time he had gathered himself up, the cart was already trundling on again, and the peals of hoarse, obscene laughter from the carters were ringing hideously through the silent street.

Holles fled from the sound, back by the way that he had been carried, and it was not until he had gone some distance, not until the foul hilarity of the carters and the clatter of the accursed cart itself had faded out of earshot, that he began to grow conscious of his condition. He was without cloak or hat or doublet or boots. The fact that his sword was gone, as well as the little money that still remained him, seemed to him just then to matter rather less. What chiefly troubled him was that he was cold and dizzy. He shivered every now and then as with an ague; his head was a globe of pain and his senses reeled. Yet he was sober, he assured himself. He could think coherently, and he was able to piece together, not only the thing that had happened to him, but the very manner of its happening.

Mechanically he trudged on and on, aimlessly now, a man walking in a nightmare. The light grew. The moonstone light of early dawn took on colour and began to glow as with the fires of the opal; the sky was invaded and suffused by the saffron heralds of the sun.

At last he paused, without knowledge or care of where he was; utterly bereft of strength, he sank presently into the shelter of the doorway of a deserted house, and there fell asleep.

When next he awakened, he was lying in the full glare of a sun that was already high in the heavens. He looked about him, and found himself in surroundings that were utterly strange to him, so that he could form no notion of whither he had strayed.

In mid-street stood a man in a steeple hat dressed in black, leaning upon a red wand and regarding him attentively.

"What ails you?" the man asked him, seeing him awake and conscious.

Disgruntled, Holles glared at him. "The sight of you," he snapped, and struggled stiffly up. "Naught else."

Yet, even as he gained his feet, a giddiness assailed him. He steadied himself a moment against the door-post: then reeled and sank down again upon the step that had been his couch. For some few seconds he sat there bemused, marvelling at his condition. Then, acting on a sudden thought, he tore open the breast of his shirt.

"I lied!" he shouted wildly. When next he looked up, he was laughing, a ringing, exultant laugh. "I lied! There is something else. Look!" And he pulled his shirt wider apart, so that the man might see what he had found. And that was the last thing that he remembered.

On his breast the flower of the plague had blossomed while he slept.

CHAPTER XXVII

THE PEST–HOUSE

THERE ensued for Colonel Holles on some plane other than that of mundane life a period of fevered activity, of dread encounters and terrible combats, of continual strife with a relentless opponent dressed in black and white satin who wore the countenance of His Grace of Buckingham and who was ever on the point of slaying him, yet, being unmerciful, never slayed. These combats usually took place in a sombre panelled room by the light of a cluster of candles in a silver branch, and they had for witness a white-clad, white-faced woman with long blue-green eyes and heavy chestnut hair, who laughed in glee and clapped her hands at each fresh turn of the encounter. Sometimes, however, the battle-ground was a cherry orchard, sometimes the humble interior of a yeoman's cottage in the neighbourhood of Worcester. But the actors were ever the same three.

The fact is that Holles lived in a world of delirium, whence at last he awakened one day to sanity — awakened to die, as he thought, when he had taken stock of his surroundings and realized them by the aid of the memories he assembled of his last waking conscious hours.

He found himself lying on a pallet, near a window, through which he had a glimpse of foliage and of a strip of indigo sky. Directly overhead were the bare rafters of a roof that knew no ceiling. He turned his head on his pillow and looked away to his left, down a long barnlike room in which stood a half-dozen such pallets as his own, and upon each a sufferer like himself. One or two of them lay inert, as if in death; the others tossed and moaned, whilst one, still more violent, was struggling fiercely with his keepers.

It was not a pleasant sight for a man in his condition, so he rolled his head back to its first position, and thus returned to the contemplation of that strip of sky. A great calm settled upon the soul that clung to his fever-wasted body. He understood his situation perfectly. He was stricken with the plague, and he was vouchsafed this interval of consciousness — the consciousness, perhaps, that is the herald of dissolution — in order that he might return thanks to God that at last the sands of his miserable life were run and peace awaited him. The very contemplation of this sufficed to blot out at last the shame that could never in life have left him, the haunting spectre of the loathing he must have inspired in her against whom he had so grossly sinned. He remembered that full confession he had left for her. And it was sweet to reflect, before passing out into the cold shadows, that its perusal, revealing all that had gone to make an utter villain of him, showing how Fate had placed him between the hammer and the anvil, might mitigate the contempt in which inevitably she must have held him.

Tears gathered in his eyes, and rolled down his wasted cheeks. They were tears at once of physical weakness and of thanksgiving, rather than of self-pity.

Steps were softly approaching his bedside. Some one was leaning over him. He turned his head once more and looked up. And then a great fear took possession of him, so that for a moment his heart seemed to contract. Aloud, he explained to himself that apparition.

"I am at my dreams again!" he complained in a whisper.

At his bedside stood a woman, young and comely in the grey homespun, with the white bands and bib and coif that made up the garb of Puritans. Her face was small and pale and oval, her eyes were long, of a colour between blue and green, very wistful now in their expression, and from under the wings of her coif escaped one or two heavy chestnut curls, to lie upon her white neck. A fine cool hand sought his own where it lay upon the coverlet, a voice that was full of soft, sad music answered him.

"Nay, Randal. You are awake at last — thank God!"

And now he saw that those long wistful eyes were aswim in tears.

"Where am I, then?" he asked, in his first real bewilderment since awakening. Almost he began to imagine that he must have dreamt all those things which he had deemed actual memories of a time that had preceded his delirium.

"In the pest-house in Bunhill Fields," she told him, which only served to increase the confusion in his mind.

"That is . . . I can understand that. I have the plague, I know. I remember being stricken with it. But you? How come you here . . . in a pest-house?"

"There was nowhere else for me to go, after . . . after I left that house in Knight Ryder Street." And very briefly she explained the circumstances. "So Dr. Beamish brought me here. And here I have been by the blessing of Providence," she ended, "tending the poor victims of the plague."

"And you tended me? You?" Incredulous amazement lent strength to his enfeebled voice.

"Did not you tend me?" she answered him.

He made a gesture of repudiation with one of his hands, grown so pale and thin. Then he sighed and smiled contentedly.

"God is very good to me a sinner. As I lay here now all that I craved was that you, knowing the full truth of my villainy, of the temptation by which I fell, should speak a little word of pity and forgiveness to me to . . . to make my dying easier."

"Your dying? Why do you talk of death?"

"Because it comes, by the mercy of God. To die of the plague is what I most deserve. I sought it and it fled before me. Yet in the end I stumbled upon it by chance. All my life is it thus that things have come to me. That which I desire and pursue eludes me. When I cease the pursuit, it turns and takes me unawares. In all things have I been the sport of Fortune; even in my dying, as it seems."

She would have interrupted, but he hurried on, deceived by his own weakness.

"Listen a moment yet, lest I go before I have said what is yet to add to the letter that I left for you. I swear, by my last feeble hope of heaven, that I did not know it was you I was to carry off, else I had gone to the hangman before ever I had lent myself to the Duke's business. You believe me?"

"There is no need for your assurances, Randal. I never doubted that. How could I?"

"How could you? Aye, that is true. You could not. So much, at least, would not have been possible, however I might have fallen." Then he looked at her with piteous eyes. "I scarce dare hope that you'll forgive me all . . ."

"But I do, Randal. I do. I have long since forgiven you. I gave you my forgiveness and my gratitude when I knew what you had done for me, how you risked your life in reparation. If I could forgive you then, can I harbour resentment now that I know all? I do forgive — freely, utterly, completely, Randal dear."

"Say it again," he implored her.

She said it, weeping quietly.

"Then I am content. What matter all my unrealized dreams of crowned knight-errantry, all my high-flown ambitions? To this must I have come in the end. I was a fool not to have taken the quiet good to which I was born. Then might we have been happy, Nan, and neither of us would have felt the need to seek the hollow triumphs of the world."

"You talk as if you were to die," she reproved him through her tears. "But you shall get well again."

"That surely were a crowning folly when I may die so happily."

And then the doctor supervened to interrupt them, and to confirm circumstantially her assertion that Holles was now out of danger.

The truth is that, what he had done for her when she was plague-stricken, she had now done for him. By unremitting care of him in the endless hours of his delirium, reckless of how she exhausted herself in the effort, she had brought him safely through the Valley of the Shadow, and already, even as he spoke of dying, deluded by his weakness and the great lassitude that attends exhaustion into believing that already he stood upon the threshold, his recovery was assured.

Within less than a week he was afoot, regaining strength, and pronounced clear of the infection. Yet, before they would suffer him to depart into the world again, he must undergo the period of sequestration that the law prescribed, so as to ensure against his conveying the infection to others. For this he was to be removed from the pest-house to a neighbouring abode of rest and convalescence.

When the hour of departure came, he went to take his leave of Nancy. She awaited him on the lawn under the tall old cedars of Lebanon that graced the garden of this farm which had been converted to the purposes of a hospital. Slimly graceful she stood before him, whilst in a voice, which he laboured to keep steady, he uttered words of an irrevocable farewell.

It was very far from what she had been expecting, as he might have read in the pale dismay that overspread her countenance.

There was a stone seat near at hand there in the shade, and she sank limply down upon this whilst he stood beside her awaiting her dismissal. He was very plainly clad, in garments which she had secretly caused to be procured for him, but which he supposed to be the parting gift of the charitable pest-house authorities.

She controlled herself to ask him steadily:

"What are you going to do? Where shall you go when . . . when the month is past?"

He smiled and shrugged a little. "I have not yet considered fully," he answered her in actual words, whilst his tone conveyed that he had neither thought nor care of what might follow. Fortune, it might be said, had been kind to him; for Fortune had given him back his life when it was all but lost. But it was the way of Fortune to fool him with gifts when he could no longer profitably use them. "It may be," he added, answering the round stare of her eyes, "that I shall go to France. There is usually work for a soldier there."

She lowered her glance, and for a long moment there was silence. Then she spoke again, calmly, almost formally, marshalling the points of an argument that she had well considered.

"You remember that day when we talked, you and I, in that house in Knight Ryder Street, just after my recovery? When I would have thanked you for my life, you rejected my thanks as you rejected the forgiveness that I offered. You rejected it, persuaded that I was moved only by gratitude for the life you had saved; that I sought by that forgiveness to discharge the debt in which you had placed me."

"It was so," he said, "and it is so. It cannot be otherwise."

"Can it not? Are you so very sure?" One upward appealing glance she flashed him as she asked the question.

"As I am sure that out of your sweet charity you deceive yourself," he answered.

"Do I? Let us say that I did. But if you say that I still do, then you are overlooking something. I am no longer in your debt. I have paid it in another and a fuller way. As you saved my life, so have I since saved yours. I thanked God for the merciful chance to do this, since by doing it I could wipe out this debt that seemed to stand between us. We are quits now, Randal. I no longer owe you anything. I have repaid you; therefore I am no longer under any necessity to be grateful. You cannot deny that."

"I would not if I could."

"Then, don't you see? Without indebtedness between us, no longer under any obligation to you, I have given you my forgiveness freely, frankly, and fully. Your offence, after all, was not really against me . . ."

"It was, it was," he interrupted fiercely. "It was against you inasmuch as it was against my own honour. It made me unworthy."

"Even so, you had my complete forgiveness from the moment that I came to know how cruelly you had been driven. Indeed, I think that I forgave you earlier, much earlier. My heart told me — my senses told me when you attempted to rescue me from the Duke of Buckingham — that some such tale of misfortune must lie behind your deed."

A little flush came to stain the pallor which his illness had left upon his cheeks. He bowed his head.

"I bless you for those words. They will give me courage to face . . . whatever may await me. I shall treasure the memory of them, and of your sweetness always."

"But still you do not believe me!" she cried out. "Still you think that behind it all there are some dregs of . . . of . . . resentment in my heart!"

"No, no, Nan. I believe you."

"And yet you will persist in going?"

"What else? You who know all now must see that there is no place for me in England."

There was a ready answer leaping to her lips. But she could not utter it. At least, not yet. So again she hung her head, and again there fell a pause, in which she was desperately seeking for another line of attack upon his obstinately proud humility. Arguments to reason failing her, she availed herself of an argument to sentiment. She drew from the bodice of her gown a rubbed and faded tasselled glove. She held it out to him, looking up at him, and he saw that her eyes were wet.

"Here is something that belongs to you, at least. Take it, Randal. Take it, since it is all that you will have of me."

Almost in hesitancy he took that little glove, still warm and fragrant from sweet contact with her, and retained also the hand that proffered it.

"It . . . it shall again be a talisman," he said softly, "to keep me worthy as . . . as it did not keep me once." Then he bowed over the hand he held, and pressed it to his lips. "Good-bye, and God guard you ever, Nan."

He would have disengaged his hand, but she clutched it firmly now.

"Randal!" she cried sharply, desperately driven to woo this man who would not woo her despite her clear invitation. In gentle, sorrowing rebuke she added: "Can you, then, really think of leaving me again?"

His face assumed the pallor of death, and his limbs trembled under him.

"What else is possible?" he asked her miserably.

"That is a question you had best answer for yourself."

"What answer can I supply?" He looked at her, almost fearfully, with those grey eyes that were normally so steady and could be so hard and arrogant. He moistened his lips before resuming. "Should I allow you to gather up these poor shards of my broken life with the hands of pity?"

"Pity?" she cried in repudiation. Then, shaking her

head a little; "And what if it were so?" she asked. "What then? Oh, Randal, if I have pity for you, have you then none for me?"

"Pity for you! I thank God you do not stand in need of pity."

"Do I not? What else but pitiful can you account my state? I have waited years, with what patience and forti-tude I could command, for one to whom I deemed myself to belong, and when at last he arrived, it is only to reject me."

He laughed at that, but without any trace of mirth.

"Nay, nay," he said. "I am not so easily deceived by your charitable pretence. Confess that out of your pity you but act a part."

"I see. You think that, having been an actress once, I must be acting ever. Will you believe me, I wonder, when I swear to you that, in all those years of weary waiting, I withstood every temptation that besets my kind, keeping myself spotless against your coming? Will you believe that? And if you believe it, will you cheat me now?"

"Believe it! O God! If I did not, perhaps I could now yield more easily. The gulf between us would be less wide."

"There is no gulf between us, Randal. It has been bridged and bridged again."

He disengaged his hand from her clasp at last. "Oh, why do you try me, Nan?" he cried out, like a man in pain. "God knows you cannot need me. What have I to offer — I that am as bankrupt of fortune as of honour?"

"Do women love men for what they bring?" she asked him. "Is that the lesson a mercenary's life has taught you? Oh, Randal, you spoke of Chance and how it had directed all your life, and yet it seems you have not learnt to read its signs. A world lay between us in which we were lost to each other. Yet Chance brought us together again, and if the way of it was evil, yet it was the way of Chance. Again we

strayed apart. You went from me driven by shame and
wounded pride — yes, pride, Randal — intending the sep-
aration to be irrevocable. And again we have come together.
Will you weary Chance by demanding that it perform this
miracle for a third time?"

He looked at her steadily now, a man redeemed, driven
back into the hard ways of honour by the scourge of all that
had befallen him.

"If I have been Chance's victim all my life, that is no
reason why I should help you to be no better. For you there
is the great world, there is your art, there is life and joy when
this pestilence shall have spent itself. I have nothing to offer
you in exchange for all that. Nothing, Nan. My whole es-
tate is just these poor clothes I stand in. If it were otherwise
. . . Oh, but why waste words and torturing thought on
what might be. We have to face what is. Good-bye!"

Abruptly he swung on his heel, and left her, so abruptly,
indeed, that his departure took her by surprise, found her
without a word in which to stay him. As in a dream she
watched the tall, spare, soldierly figure swinging away
through the trees towards the avenue. Then at last she
half rose and a little fluttering cry escaped her.

"Randal! Randal!"

But already he was too far to hear her even if, had he
heard, he would have heeded.

CHAPTER XXVIII
JESTING FORTUNE

JESTING Fortune had not yet done with Colonel Holles.

A month later, towards the middle of September, without having seen Nancy again — since that, of course, would have been denied him, as it would have nullified his sequestration from infected persons and surroundings — he found himself at liberty to return to the ordinary haunts of man, supplied with a certificate of health.

He had been considering, in the few days preceding his discharge, whither he should direct his steps once he were made free of the world again, and he had returned to that earlier resolve of his to embark as a hand aboard some vessel bound for France. But a vessel must be found quickly, for Holles was utterly penniless. He possessed, as he had reminded Nancy, nothing but the comparatively cheap garments in which he stood. He might have obtained a few shillings from the pest-house authorities, but his gorge rose at the thought of seeking charity, particularly where it would better become him to bestow it, out of considera-tion for the benefits received.

So within an hour of his discharge he found himself tramping along the empty streets of the City, bound for distant Wapping. He must go afoot, not only because he lacked the means to go otherwise, but because there were no longer any boats plying for hire at any of the steps along the river, nor any hackney-coaches remaining in the streets. More than ever was London become a city of the dead.

He trudged on, and everywhere now he beheld great fires of sea-coal burning in the streets, a sight that puzzled him at first, until a chance wayfarer informed him that it was done by order of the Lord Mayor and with the approval of His Grace of Albemarle as a means of purifying the tainted air. Yet, although these fires had been burning now for a week, there was no sign yet that they had any such effect as was desired. Indeed, the bill of mortality in that week had been higher than ever before, having risen — as that same wayfarer informed him — to the colossal figure of eight thousand. The marvel was, thought Holles, that any should still be left to die in London.

On through that desolate emptiness he tramped in the noontide heat, which still continued as intense as through the months that were past of that exceptional summer, until he came to the Fleet Ditch. Here it was that he bethought him of The Harp in Wood Street where he had lodged, and of its landlord, the friendly Banks, who at some risk to himself had warned him that the messengers of the law were on his heels. It was his utter destitution that now shaped his destiny. But for that, he might not have remembered that in his precipitate departure from that hostelry he had left some gear behind including a fine suit of clothes. He could have no personal use for such brave raiment now. The homespun in which he stood was better suited far to one who sought work as a hand aboard a ship. But, if he could recover that abandoned gear, it was possible that he might be able to convert it into a modest sum of money to relieve his present necessities. He laughed a little over the notion of Fortune being so kind to him as to permit him to find The Harp still open or Banks alive.

Still, forlorn hope though it might be, forlorn hopes were the only hopes that remained him. So in the direction of Wood Street he now turned his steps.

He found it much as other streets. Not more than one shop in four was standing open, and trade in these was idle and stagnant. Proctor's famous ordinary at the sign of

The Mitre — the most reputed eating-house in London —
was closed and shuttered. He regarded this as an evil omen.
But he passed on, and came presently to stand before the
more modest Harp. He could scarcely believe his eyes
when he saw its windows clean and open, its door flung
wide.

He crossed the threshold, and turned into the common
room on his left. The room was clean-swept, its long deal
tables were well scoured; but trade was slack, for the place
contained a single occupant, a man in an apron who started
up from a wooden armchair in which he had been dozing,
with an ejaculation of:

"As God's my life, a customer!"

Holles stared at him and the man stared back at Holles.
It was Banks, the vintner himself. But a Banks whose
paunch had shrunk, whose erstwhile ruddy cheeks had lost
their glow and fullness.

"Colonel Holles!" he cried. "Or is it your ghost, sir?
There's more ghosts than living men in this stricken city."

"We are both ghosts, I think, Banks," the Colonel answered him.

"Maybe, but our gullets ain't ghostly, praise the Lord!
And there's still some sack left at The Harp. It's the
greatest of all electuaries is sack, as Dr. Hodges has it.
Sack with plenty of nutmeg, says he, and avoid sweating.
And that's how I've kept myself alive. Shall we have a
bottle of the medicine, Colonel?"

"I'd say yes, with all my heart. But — lackaday! — I've
not the means to pay for the sack."

"Pay?" The vintner made a lip. "Sit ye down, Colonel."

Banks fetched the wine, and poured it.

"A plague on the plague, is the toast," said he, and they
drank it. " 'Slife, Colonel, but I am glad to see you alive.
I feared the worst for you. Yet you've contrived to keep

yourself safe, avoiding not only the plague, but them
pestilential fellows that was after you." Without waiting
for a reply, he dropped his voice to add: "Ye'll have heard
how Danvers was took, and how he broke away and won
free — good luck to him! But all that is a dream by now,
that conspiracy business, and no one bothers much about it.
Not even the government. There's other things to engage
them, and not much government left neither. But of yourself now, Colonel?"

"My tale's soon told. I've not fared quite as well as you
suppose. I've had the plague."

"The devil you have. And ye've won through!" Banks
regarded him with a new respect. "Well, ye were born
lucky, sir."

"You give me news," said the Colonel.

"There isn't many escapes," the vintner assured him rue-
fully. "And you having had the pestilence makes you a safe
man. Ye can come and go as ye please without uneasiness."

"And your sack as an electuary is wasted on me. But if
I'm safe I'm also penniless, which is what has brought me
here: to see if some gear of mine is still in your possession
that I may melt it into shillings."

"Aye, aye, I have it all safe," Banks assured him. "A
brave suit, with boots and a hat, a baldric, and some other
odds and ends. They're above-stairs, waiting for you when
you please. But what may you be thinking of doing, Colonel,
if I may make so bold as to ask?"

Holles told him of his notion of sailing as a hand aboard
a vessel bound for France.

The vintner pursed his lips and sadly shook his head,
regarding his guest the while from under bent brows.

"Why, sir," he said, "there's no French shipping and no
ships bound for France at Wapping, and mighty few ships
of any kind. The plague has put an end to all that. The

port of London is as empty as Proctor's yonder. There's not a foreign ship'll put into it, nor an English one go out of it, for she wouldn't be given harbour anywhere for fear of the infection."

The Colonel's face lengthened in dismay. This, he thought, was the last blow of his malignant Fortune.

"I shall have to go to Portsmouth, then," he announced gloomily. "God knows how I shall get there."

"Ye never will. For Portsmouth won't have ye, nor any other town in England neither, coming as ye do from London. I tell you, sir, the country's all crazed with fear of the plague."

"But I've a certificate of health."

"Ye'd need to have it backed by a minister of state or ever Portsmouth would let you inside her gates."

Holles looked at him blankly for a moment, then expressed his bitterness in a laugh.

"In that case I don't know what remains. Ye don't need a drawer these days, I suppose?"

The vintner was frowning thoughtfully, considering the first of those two questions.

"Why, ye say ye're a safe man. Ye'll not have seen His Grace of Albemarle's proclamation asking for safe men?"

"Asking for safe men? To what end?"

"Nay, the proclamation don't say. Ye'll find that out in Whitehall, maybe. But there's a service of some kind his grace has to offer to them as is safe. Things being like this with you, now, ye might think it worth while to ask. It might be something for ye, for the present at least."

"It might," said Holles. "And, apparently, it's that or nothing. He'll be needing scavengers, likely, or drivers for the dead-cart."

"Nay, nay, it'll be something better than that," said Banks, taking him literally.

Holles rose. "Whatever it may be, when a man is faced
with starvation he had best realize that pride won't fill an
empty belly."

"No more it will," Banks agreed, eyeing the Colonel's
uncouth garments. "But if ye're thinking of paying a visit
to Whitehall ye'd be wise to put on that other suit that's
above-stairs. Ye'll never get past the lackeys in that livery."

So you see issuing presently from the sign of The Harp a
Colonel Holles very different from the Colonel Holles who
had entered it an hour earlier. In a dark blue suit of camlet
enlivened by a little gold lace, black Spanish boots, and a
black beaver set off by a heavy plume of royal blue, without
a sword, it is true, but swinging a long cane, he presented a
figure rarely seen just then in London streets. Perhaps
because of that his appearance at the Cockpit made the
few remaining and more or less idle ushers bestir themselves
to announce him.

He waited but a moment in the empty anteroom where
three months ago he had overheard Mr. Pepys of the Navy
Office proclaiming England's need of practised soldiers.
The usher who went to announce him returned almost at
once to conduct him into that pleasant chamber overlooking
the park where His Grace of Albemarle acted to-day as
deputy for the pleasure-loving libertine prince who had
forsaken his stricken capital.

The Duke heaved himself up as the Colonel entered.

"So you're come at last, Randal!" was his astounding
greeting. "On my life, you've taken your own time in answering my letter. I concluded long since that the plague
had carried you off."

"Your letter?" said Holles. And he stared blankly at the
Duke, as he clasped the proffered hand.

"My letter, yes. You had it? The letter that I sent you
nigh upon a month ago to the Paul's Head?"

"Nay," said Holles. "I had no letter."

"But . . ." Albemarle looked almost as if he did not believe him. "The landlady there kept it for you. She said, I think, that you were absent at the time, but would be back in a day or two, and that you should have the letter at once on your return."

"A month ago, do you say? But it is two months and more since I left the Paul's Head!"

"What do you tell me? Ah, wait. My messenger shall speak for himself on this." And he strode away to the bell-rope.

But Holles checked him.

"Nay, nay," he cried with a wry smile. "There's not the need. I think I understand. Mrs. Quinn has been riding her malice on a loose rein. Your messenger would, no doubt, announce whence he came, and Mrs. Quinn, fearing that the news might be to my advantage, acted so as to prevent his making further search for me. Evidently the plague has spared that plaguy woman."

"What's this?" The Duke's heavy face empurpled. "Do you charge her with suppressing a communication from an office of state? By Heaven, if she's still alive I'll have her gaoled for it."

"Let be," said Holles, seizing him by the arm. "Devil take the woman! Tell me of the letter. Ye'll never mean that you had found employment for me, after all?"

"You seem incredulous, Randal? Did you doubt my zeal for you?"

"Oh, not your zeal. But the possibility of your helping one who was in my case."

"Aye, aye. But as to that, why, Buckingham improved it when he stood surety for your loyalty before the Justices. I heard of that. And when the chance came, the chance of this Bombay command that already I had earlier intended for you . . ."

"The Bombay command?" Holles began to wonder did he dream. "But I thought that it had been required by Buckingham for a friend of his own."

"Sir Henry Stanhope, yes. So it had, and Stanhope sailed for the Indies with the commission. But it seems that when he did so he already carried the seeds of the plague within him. For he died of it on the voyage. It was a Providence that he did, poor devil; for he was no more fitted for the command than to be Archbishop of Canterbury. I wrote to you at once asking you to seek me here, and I waited a fortnight to hear from you. As you made no sign, I concluded that either you were stricken with the plague, or no longer desired the office, and I proceeded to appoint another gentleman of promise."

Holles folded the pinions of his soaring hopes and let himself fall back into his despondency. He uttered a groan.

"But that's not the end," Albemarle checked him. "No sooner had I appointed this other than he, too, fell sick of the plague, and died a week ago. I have already found another suitable man — no easy matter in these days — and I had resolved to appoint him to-morrow to the vacant office. But, if ye're not afraid that the plague is bound up with this commission, it's at your disposal, and it shall be made out to you at once."

Holles was gasping for breath. "You . . . you mean that . . . that I am to have the command, after all!" It was incredible. He dared not believe it.

"That is what I have said. The commission is . . ." Albemarle broke off suddenly, and fell back before him. "What ails you man? You're white as a ghost. Ye're not ill?" And he lugged out a handkerchief that flung a reek of myrrh and ginger on the air, leaving Holles no single doubt of the thing his grace was fearing. Albemarle imagined that the plague which, as he had said, seemed bound up with this commission, was already besetting the man upon whom he now proposed to bestow it. The humour of it took Holles sharply, and his laugh rang out further to startle the Duke.

"There's no need for electuaries against me," he assured his grace. "I am certified in health and carry no infection. I left Bunhill Fields this morning."

"What?" Albemarle was astounded. "D'ye mean ye've had the plague?"

"That is the whole reason of my being here. I am a safe man now. And I came in answer to your proclamation asking for safe men."

Albemarle continued to stare at him in deepening amazement.

"So that is what brought you?" he said at last, when full understanding came to him.

"But for that I certainly should never have come."

"Gad!" said Albemarle, and he repeated the ejaculation with a laugh, for he found the situation curious enough to be amusing. "Gad! The ways of Chance!"

"Chance!" echoed Holles, suddenly very sober, realizing how this sudden, unexpected turn of Fortune's wheel had changed the whole complexion of his life. "Almost it seems that Chance has stood my friend at last, though it has waited until I had touched the very bottom of misfortune. But for your proclamation, and but for Mrs. Quinn, too, I should have been Fortune's fool again over the matter of this commission. It would have been here waiting for me, and I should never have known. The very malice by which Mrs. Quinn sought to do me disservice has turned to my benefit. For had she told your messenger the truth — that I had vanished and that she had no knowledge of my whereabouts — you would never have traced me just then, and you would never have waited that fortnight. Thus all might have been changed." He paused, lost in a wonder that Albemarle did not share.

"Maybe, maybe," said his grace briskly. "But what matters now is that you are here, and that the command is yours if you still wish it. There is not even the fear of the plague to deter you, since you are a safe man now. It is an important office, as I told you, and so that you discharge its duties, as I know you will, it may prove but a stepping-stone to greater things. What do you say?"

"Say?" cried Holles, his cheeks flushed, his grey eyes gleaming. "Why, I give you thanks with all my heart."

"Then you accept it. Good! For I believe you to be the very man for the office." Albemarle stepped to his writing-table, selected from among some documents a parchment bearing a heavy seal, sat down, took up a pen, and wrote briskly for a few seconds. He dusted the writing with pounce, and proffered the document. "Here, then, is your commission. How soon can you sail?"

"In a month," said Holles promptly.

"A month!" Albemarle was taken aback. He frowned. "Why, man, you should be ready in a week."

"Myself, I could be ready in a day. But I mean to take this new-found tide of fortune at the flood, and ... "

But Albemarle interrupted him impatiently.

"Don't you realize, man, the time that has been already lost? For four months now this office has stood vacant."

"Which means that there's a very competent lieutenant in charge. Let him continue yet awhile. Once I am there, I'll speedily make up for lost time. That I can promise you. You see, it may be that I shall have a companion, who cannot possibly be ready in less than a month."

With an odd, reckless trust in the continuance of Fortune's favour now, he boldly added: "You have said that I am the very man for the office. The government can wait a month, or you can appoint some one less likely to serve it as efficiently."

Albemarle smiled at him grimly across the table. "Ye're very full of surprises to-day, Master Randal. And this one baffles me."

"Shall I explain it?"

"It would be a condescension."

Holles poured out his tale, and Albemarle gave him a sympathetic hearing. When he had done, the Duke sighed and turned aside before replying, to examine the pages of a notebook at his elbow.

"Well, well," he said at length, having consulted an entry. "The *English Lass* is fitting at Portsmouth for the voyage, and should be ready, I am informed, in two weeks from now. But there are ever delays at present, and it is odds that in no case would she be ready in less than three weeks. I'll see to it that she is not ready under a month."

Impetuously the Colonel held out both hands to the Duke.

"What a friend you are!" he cried.

Albemarle wrung them hard. "You're damnably like your father, God rest him!" said he. Then, almost brusquely: "Away with you, now, and good-luck to you. I'll not ask you to stay to see her grace at present, since you're pressed. You shall kiss her hands before you sail. Be off!"

Holles took his leave. At the door he suddenly checked, and, turning, displayed a rueful countenance.

"Although I have the King's commission in my pocket and hold an important office in his service, I haven't a shilling in the world," he said. "Not a shilling."

Albemarle responded instantly by producing a purse from which he counted twenty pounds. There was no sign of parsimonious reluctance about his offer now.

"As a loan, of course," said Holles, gathering up the yellow coins.

"No, no," Albemarle corrected him. "An advance. Take no further thought for it. The Treasury shall refund me the money at once."

CHAPTER XXIX

THE MIRACLE

Away from Whitehall, where the ground was green with thriving grass, went Colonel Holles at speed. He set his face towards Islington once more, and swung along with great strides, carrying in his breast a heart more blithe than he had known for many a year. Blind and deaf to all about him, his mind sped ahead of his limbs to the goal for which he made.

Thus, until a sudden awful dread assailed him. Fortune had fooled and cheated him so often that it was impossible he should long continue in this new-born trust in her favour. It was, after all, four weeks since he had seen Nancy, and those in that house of rest where he had spent the period of his sequestration could tell him nothing of her since they held no direct intercourse with those who had their being in the pest-houses. In a month much may betide. Evil might have befallen her, or she might have departed thence. To soothe the latter dread came the recollection that any such departure would have been impossible until she, too, had undergone the prescribed period of disinfection. But the former dread was not so easily to be allayed. It would be so entirely of a piece with all his history that, now that apparently he held the earnest of Fortune in his hands, he should make the discovery that this had reached him too late; that, even as she bestowed with the one hand, so with the other did Fortune rob him.

You conceive, then, the dread anxiety in which he came, breathless, hot, and weary from the speed he had made, to the open fields and at last to the stout, spiked gates of that pleasant homestead that had been put to the uses of a lazaret. Here a stern and surly guardian denied him passage.

"You cannot enter, sir. What do you seek?"

"Happiness, my friend," said the Colonel, completing the other's conviction that he was mad. But mad or sane there was a masterful air about him now. He bristled with the old amiable arrogance that of late had been overlaid by despondency and lassitude of soul. And his demand that the gate should be unbarred for him held an authority that was not lightly to be denied.

"You understand, sir," the gatekeeper asked him, "that, once you enter here, you may not go back whence you come for twenty-eight days, at least?"

"I understand," said Holles, "and I come prepared to pay the price. So, in God's name, open, friend."

The gatekeeper shrugged. "Ye're warned," he said, and raised the bar, thus removing, as he thought, all obstacles that kept a fool from his folly.

Colonel Holles entered. The gates clashed behind him, and he took his way briskly, almost at a run, down the long avenue in the dappled shade of the beech trees and elms that bordered it, making straight for the nearest of the red-brick outhouses, which was the one which he himself had occupied during his sickness.

A broadly built, elderly woman perceived his approach from the doorway, and, after staring at him a moment in surprise and consternation, started forward to meet him, calling to him to stand. But he came on heedless and breathless until they were face to face.

"How came you in, you foolish man?" she cried.

"You don't know me, Mrs. Barlow?" he asked her.

Startled anew by that pleasant, familiar address, she stared at him again. And then, under the finery and vigour investing him and rendering him almost unrecognizable to eyes that remembered only the haggard, meanly clad fellow of a month ago, she discovered him.

"Save us! It's Colonel Holles!" And almost without pause she went on in a voice of distress: "But you were to have left the house of rest to-day. Whatever can have brought you back here to undo all again."

"Nay, not to undo. To do, Mrs. Barlow, by God's help. But ye've a singular good memory, to remember that I should be leaving to-day!"

She shook her head, and smiled with a touch of sadness. " 'Twasn't me that remembered, sir. It was Miss Sylvester." And again she shook her head.

"She's here, then! Ha! She is well?"

"Well enough, poor dear. But oh, so mortal sad. She's yonder, resting, under the cedars — a place she's haunted this past month."

He swung aside, and, without more than a hurriedly flung word of thanks or excuse, he was gone swiftly across the lawn, towards that cluster of cedars, amid whose gnarled old trunks he could discern the flutter of a grey gown.

She had haunted the spot this month past, Mrs. Barlow had said. And it was the spot where they had spoken their farewells. Ah, surely Fortune would not trick him this time! Not again, surely, would she dash away the cup from his very lips, as so often she had done!

As he drew nearer over the soft, yielding turf that deadened all sound of his steps, he saw her sitting on that stone seat where a month ago he had left her in the conviction that he was never to behold her again with the eyes of the flesh. Her shoulders were turned towards him, but even so he perceived in her attitude something of the listlessness by which she was possessed. He paused, his pulses throbbing, paused instinctively, fearing now to startle her, as startle her he must, however he approached.

He stood arrested there, breathless, at a loss. And then as if she sensed his presence, she slowly turned and looked behind her. A long while she stared, startled, white-faced.

"Randal!" She was on her feet, confronting him.

He plunged forward.

"Oh, Randal, why have you come here? You should have gone to-day . . ."

"I went, and I have returned, Nan," he told her, standing there beside her now.

"You have returned!" She looked him over more attentively now, and observed the brave suit of dark blue camlet that so well became his tall, spare frame, and the fine Spanish boots that were now overlaid with dust. "You have returned!" she said again.

"Nan," he said, "a miracle has happened." And from his breast he pulled that parchment with its great seal. "A month ago I was a beggar. To-day I am Colonel Holles in something more than name, commanding something more than a mere regiment. I have come back, Nan, because at last I can offer you something in exchange for all that you will sacrifice in taking me."

She sank down slowly, weakly, to the seat, he standing over her, until they were in the same attitude of a month ago. But how different now was all else! She leaned her elbows on her knees a moment, pressing her hands to her throbbing temples.

"It is real, this? It . . . it is true? True?" she asked aloud, though clearly not of him. And then she sat back again, and looked up into his face.

"It is not very much, perhaps, when all is said, though it seems much to me to-day, and with you beside me I shall know how to make it more. Still, such as it is, I offer it." And he tossed the parchment down into her lap.

She looked at the white cylinder without touching it, and then at him again, and a little smile crept about the corners of her sweet mouth, and trembled there. Into her mind there leapt the memory of the big boast of conquest for her sake with which he had set out in the long ago.

"Is this the world you promised me, Randal?" she asked him. And his heart bounded at the old rallying note, which laid his last doubt to rest.

"As much of it as I can contrive to get," said he.

"Then it will be enough for me," she answered. And there was no raillery in her voice now, only an infinite tenderness. She rose, and, standing there close before him, held out the parchment still unfolded.

"But you haven't looked," he protested.

"What need to look? It is your kingdom, you have told me. And I'll share your kingdom whatever it may be."

"It is situate in the Indies . . . in Bombay," said he, with a certain diffidence.

She considered.

"I always had a thirst for travel," she said deliberately.

He felt that it was due to her that he should explain the nature of this appointment and how he came by it. To that explanation he proceeded. Before he had reached the end she was in tears.

"Why? Why? What now?" he cried in dismay. "Does your heart misgive you?"

"Misgive me? Oh, Randal! How can you think that? I weep for thankfulness. I have spent a month of such hopeless anguish, and now . . ."

He put an arm about her shoulder, and drew her head down on to his breast. "My dear," he murmured. He sighed, and held her thus in a silence that was like a prayer, until, at length, she raised her face.

"Do you know, Randal, that it is more years than I care to think of since last you kissed me, and then you vexed me by stealing what is now yours to take."

He was a little awed. But, after all, with all his faults, he was never one to yield to fear.

They were married on the morrow, and their honeymoon was spent in that sequestration that the law exacted. Certified clear of infection at last, they were permitted to go forth to garner the honours that Fortune had stored up for Randal Holles to make amends for all that he had earlier suffered at her hands.

THE END

9 781596 056091